"I want to be with you...
forever."

"You're a stubborn little baggage, and will take strong handlin'. I don't know if I'm up to it." Cooper leaned against the tree, his long legs spread wide, and pressed her against him intimately. "You'd better get back to the house," he murmured, but his arms tightened around her even as he said the words. He kissed her throat just behind her ear. His lips moved to her face, his hands to her hips.

Under his stroking hands, Lorna's body went slack with sensuousness and moved wantonly against him, pressing into every crook and curve of his body. Hungrily, blindly, she sought his mouth, and her kiss conveyed the deep heat inside her which was a new and delicious feeling. Whatever the future held, she thought, tonight is mine. Tonight I'll know the joy of coupling with my mate.

"Sweetheart? We've got to stop—" His voice was ragged with emotion.

"No! I don't want to! I ache for you—"

"If we don't stop now—I'll not be able to!"

"I'm yours. I'm your woman."

"DOROTHY GARLOCK IS ONE OF THOSE GIFTED STORYTELLERS WHO IS ABLE TO BLEND BEAUTIFUL LOVE STORIES WHILE AT THE SAME TIME RECREATING THE DOWN-TO-EARTH REALITY OF OUR PIONEERING ANCESTORS."
—*Affaire de Coeur*

Also by Dorothy Garlock

ANNIE LASH

RESTLESS WIND

WILD SWEET WILDERNESS

WIND OF PROMISE

LONESOME RIVER

DREAM RIVER

Published by
POPULAR LIBRARY

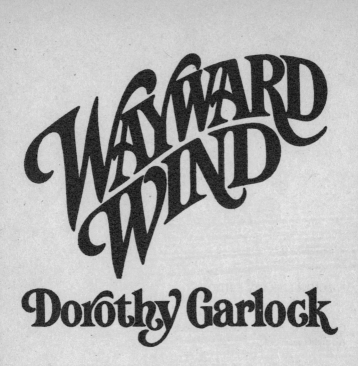

WAYWARD WIND

Dorothy Garlock

POPULAR LIBRARY

An Imprint of Warner Books, Inc.

A Warner Communications Company

i

POPULAR LIBRARY EDITION

Copyright © 1986 by Dorothy Garlock
All rights reserved.

Popular Library® and the fanciful P design are registered trademarks of
Warner Books, Inc.

Cover art by Sharon Spiak

Popular Library books are published by
Warner Books, Inc.
666 Fifth Avenue
New York, N.Y. 10103

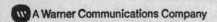 A Warner Communications Company

Printed in the United States of America

First Printing: September, 1986

10 9 8 7 6 5

This book is lovingly dedicated to the memory of my mother, Nan Carroll Phillips, who loved poetry, music and all things romantic.

She may have written the poem I used in this book, "Will You Love Me When I'm Old." I don't know—I found it among her papers.

Come live with me, and be my love;
And we will all the pleasures prove
That valleys, groves, hills and fields,
Woods or steepy mountains yields.

—*Christopher Marlowe,*
"The Passionate Shepherd to His Love"

Chapter
One

With a breathy hiss, the whip sliced through the air. It burned the man's bare buttocks like a firebrand and beads of blood popped out on his white skin.

"Yeeow!" he yelled as the thin leather of the whip struck him again. He reared up from the girl who was kicking and thrashing beneath him, and the leather wrapped itself around his thighs like a serpent.

"Get off her, you . . . ruttin' stud!" The whip descended again, this time striking him with even greater force as rage gave strength to the arm of the girl wielding it. "Get off her or I'll take your filthy hide off in strips and feed it to the buzzards!"

The man flung himself toward the gunbelt he had discarded when lust had been all that was on his mind, but the leather lashed out again and the gun spun out of his reach. The girl in the britches and long shirt, tightly belted at her waist, sprang from her horse and landed lightly on her feet without missing a stroke with the whip. It swished as it leaped to its target.

"Goddamn you, Lorna!" the man yelled. "What the hell's the matter with you? Brice said I could—" He pulled up his britches and dived for the underbrush to escape the lash. "You goddamn she-wolf—"

"Yellow-backed, belly-crawlin' buzzard bait! All the brains you got is *there*!" She grabbed up his gun and fired into the brush. "Damn you," she yelled. "I hope I shot *it* off!"

"Someday I'll haul you off that horse and slap the shit outta you—" His shouted threat was drowned out by the sound of the second shot fired from his gun.

"You're not man enough to haul a sick pup off a horse, Billy Tyrrell! Hear me?" Lorna grasped the gun by the barrel and flung it far out into a tangle of briar bushes. She heard the man's strangled bellow of fury and glimpsed him darting behind a curtain of cedars.

"Did he hurt you, Bonnie?" She turned to the girl who sat unanswering on the ground with her arm over her face, the bulge of her pregnancy obvious beneath her thin dress. Lorna knelt down beside her. "Does Brice know that polecat's after you?" she asked gently, her voice belying the fury that almost choked her.

Bonnie lowered her arm and looked at her. Her eyes were dry, dull, and reflected a hopelessness that tore at Lorna's heart. "Brice sent me down here knowin' that Billy'd be here." Her voice sank to the thinnest thread of sound.

"Oh, Bonnie." Dark, violet-blue eyes glittered with a cold light. "That low-down, miserable excuse for a man!"

Bonnie got shakily to her feet and pulled the twigs from her hair. She was a half-head taller than Lorna and thin to the point of gauntness, except for her ballooned abdomen. She wasn't pretty; her mouth was too wide, her nose slightly crooked, and her cheekbones too prominent. But her brown eyes had a gentle, doelike quality and her dark red hair curled tightly.

"He says I'm a crippled . . . slut, and this is all I'm good for." She pulled the sleeve of her dress down over the stub at the end of her left arm. "He says the sight of it makes him sick."

"Aah!" Lorna snorted angrily. She had a long mane of blue-black hair, and now she whipped it back over her shoulder with a quick toss of her head. "*He* makes me sick!" Her expression hardened. "You're coming home with me," she said firmly.

"I can't. He'd come for me." There was a fearful tremor in her voice.

"Pa won't let him take you if he knows how he's using you."

Bonnie shook her head. "He knows—"

"Godamighty!" The word exploded from Lorna. "You mean—"

"Not your pa," Bonnie said quickly. "But . . . he knows Brice told Billy Tyrrell he could have his way with me, if I was willin'. But I ain't, Lorna! I ain't no whore!"

"I know that. When is the baby due?"

"I don't rightly know, but I think in two or three months." She looked away from Lorna's angry stare. "There ain't nothin' I can do. Brice wed me. The preacher said the words."

"That addle-brained fool who spoke words over you was no more a preacher than I am. Brice is a low-down schemer. He knew just what would make you beholden to him."

The ring of iron on a stone caused both women to turn toward the man approaching on a big buckskin horse. He was hatless, and his anger was evident in the redness of his face. Lorna could feel the fear that radiated from the girl beside her.

"I heard shootin'," he said and pulled his horse to a halt. He laid his angry glance on Bonnie. "What in hell's goin' on?"

"*I* was shooting," Lorna said, her voice icy cold. "I was shooting at that no-good piece of trash you sent down here to pleasure himself on Bonnie."

"Is that what *she* said?"

"It's what *he* said, you cold-blooded . . . lout!"

The man drew in a deep quivering breath. His nostrils

flared angrily. "Have you ever tried mindin' your own god-damned business?" he snarled.

Lorna was fully aware that Bonnie would suffer from her interference, but it was too late to do anything except try to get her away from him.

"Come home with me, Bonnie." She caught the girl's arm and tried to turn her to face her.

"I can't . . . Lorna—"

"Get on back up to the house," Brice ordered.

"You don't have to," Lorna said urgently.

Bonnie hesitated, then moved away, her shoulders slumped dejectedly. Suddenly she paused and looked over her shoulder at the man on the horse.

"Mind me, goddammit!" Brice shouted.

Bonnie's terror burst from her in a choked sob as she ran, stumbling, up the path.

"You're going to kill her and the babe she's carrying!" Lorna accused. She stood with her hands on her hips, the whip curled around her wrist. "Not even an animal treats its mate the way you treat Bonnie."

"You keep your blasted nose out of my business, hear? And keep away from my wife."

"She's no more your *wife* than I am, Brice Fulton. You had some fake preacher say the words so she'd be docile. A man who'd sell a woman out as a whore is as low as a snake's belly. What's Billy paying, Brice? A jug of whiskey? Or are you getting him to steal a few steers for you?"

Brice Fulton was a large man with a ruddy coloring and pale green eyes that had a way of sliding away from a direct confrontation. But now he fixed his hard gaze on Lorna, and the anger in him came out and struck at her brutally.

"You little twat. You think you're so goddamn high, lordin' it over everybody. You're nothin' but a backwoods slut that's never been outta these mountains. You don't know the first thing 'bout actin' like a lady. Just look at ya—in those britches and your pa's old shirt and actin' so hoity-toity. I've been to places that'd make your eyes bug out—"

"Well, la-de-da!" Lorna threw back her head and loosed a shout of laughter that bounced back and forth between the walls of the narrow canyon. She looked up at the man's unshaven, unkempt, thoroughly disreputable face and her lips curled in a sneer. "Are you saying you're . . . quality?" Lorna could use her voice unkindly when crossed, and her tone made the word a profound insult. She laughed again and moved around him to go to her horse.

Brice jumped his mount in front of her and his hand reached for her hair. As swiftly as a deer she sprang out of his reach. He sidestepped his mount to pin her against a tree.

"What you need is a strap on your butt 'n a week on your back in my bed. That'd take the strut outta ya!"

"You make me want to puke!"

"I'm tellin' ya to stay away from Bonnie," he snarled and crowded his horse still closer to her.

"If you hurt her—"

"It ain't no business a yours what I do with the cripple."

"You dumb . . . jackass!" Lorna sneered. "You're the cripple. You've got nothing between your ears but hot air!"

"Someday I'll wring that blasted neck of yours!" He lifted his hand as if to strike her. At that instant an arrow cut through the air and passed inches from his head. The tip buried itself in the trunk of the tree so close to him that the flapping shaft almost touched him. Brice flung himself back and gigged his horse roughly. "What the hell."

"The next one will land right under your stupid ear and come out the other." Lorna leaned nonchalantly against the tree, her small, tight figure wholly relaxed now, amusement in her violet-blue eyes. "C'mon, Brice. Reach for me again," she taunted. "I want to see if White Bull can put a hole in your ugly head."

"You . . . bitch!" Only his fear of the Indian kept his hands off her. "Someday I'll get you off by yourself 'n take that smirk off your face!" He almost strangled on his anger. He jerked his horse roughly and sent it scurrying out of the clearing.

"If you hurt Bonnie I'll hear about it—then watch your back," she called after him. She picked up her battered flat-crowned hat, jammed it down on her head, and mounted her horse. "The varmint," she muttered. "The weasel, the stinking polecat, slimy snake, filthy hog—"

Volney Burbank sat his small dun horse on the brush-clogged shoulder of the hill overlooking the ravine. He watched with sharp, interested eyes as Lorna mounted her horse and turned him in the direction of the hill. He wiped the snuff stains from his lips with the back of his hand, grinned, and shook his head. If there were anyone in the world the old mountain man loved, it was this girl. Volney had been there when her grandmother had first spanked her bottom. He'd heard her squall just as he'd heard her mother squall when she'd first seen the light of day.

Since he first came to these mountains back in the thirties, more than forty years ago, Volney Burbank had known every generation of Lightbodys. Back in 1810, Baptiste Lightbody, known simply as Light, had brought his bride out from the Missouri Territory. They had crossed land never seen by the white man and had settled in these mountains. They made friends with the Cheyenne, the Dakota and the Sioux. Now they were a legend. Their story had been passed down from generation to generation among both Indian and the Wasicun. Light had been a fearless, deadly foe to his enemies, but true and faithful to his friends. It was said that Maggie, his child-like wife, was beautiful beyond belief, and that the Indians believed her to be of the spirit world. According to the stories passed down, she could run through the woods as fleet as a deer with her feet scarcely touching the ground. She could calm a wild beast with a soothing hand and could sing like a bird. Light loved her more than life. The Indians believed

that even the manner in which they died was magical. Light
and his beloved were struck by lightning during a thunder-
storm. They died and were buried together deep in the forest
they loved.

Two of their sons had had itchy feet and wandered on
West. The third stayed, wed an immigrant's daughter, Marthy,
and raised his family on the homestead in the tradition of his
mother and father. Volney had known Lorna's grandparents
when they were very young. He had celebrated the birth of
each of their six children. Only two girls had lived; one
married a teamster and went to Oregon to homestead; the
other daughter, pretty as a mountain flower, forever seeking
laughter and sunshine, stayed, wed, and had borne Lorna.
Marthy had said that Lorna was very much like Maggie.
Maggie's hair had been as black as midnight to the day she
died, and Lorna's was black and shiny as a crow's wing. The
girl had been raised wild and free by her mother and her
grandmother.

Volney frowned and his large, gnarled hands gripped the
saddle horn as he pondered what had caused a pretty young
woman like Lorna's mother to wed up with a sorry man like
Frank Douglas. Frank had come West during the gold rush
and completely dazzled the young mountain girl.

"Horseshit!" the old man muttered and spat in the grass.
"There's no explainin' women or their ways." The only good
thing to come from it, he mused, was Lorna. After her mother
died trying to have another child, there was nothing to hold
what little good there was in Frank. Old Marthy had kept a
fair hold on things until she keeled over a couple years back.
Now, all that was standing between Lorna and the riff-raff
that was filling the mountains was himself and White Bull,
Volney thought sadly.

Lorna's horse climbed to the shelf where Volney waited.
Her eyes searched for her Indian friend. She spied Volney
sitting in the shadows on his little dun and tried to hide the
pleasure she felt at seeing her old friend.

"You hiding, Volney?"

Volney's whispery laugh sounded as part of the wind. "Yo're aslippin', gal. Ya 'bout got yoreself cornered by that sidewinder."

"Ha!" Lorna snorted. "He couldn't catch me if I was walking on my hands. Besides, all I had to do was whistle and Gray Wolf would have kicked the stuffing out of him." She patted the big gray on the neck. "Where's White Bull?"

"Rode out when he saw ya was outta the fix ya got yoreself in."

"I wasn't in a fix," Lorna protested. "Why'd he ride out?"

"He don't tell me nothin', no more'n you do." Volney slipped his skinning knife out of its sheath, and tipped his head to the north. "He just said, 'tell Singing Woman my ears are sad.'"

"I've not felt much like singing lately. Besides, he's been up north. He'd not know if I sang or not," Lorna said, her face inscrutable, with a look of inner concentration. She watched her oldest and dearest friend dig a plug from the depths of one of the cavernous pockets of his tunic and busy himself trimming off a substantial chaw. He was waiting. He knew her so well.

Lorna had been singing in these mountains since she was a small child. A traveling man had told Volney he'd not heard a voice such as hers in New York or in the great opera houses of Europe, and that her voice could make her rich and famous. But, of course, Lorna didn't know that she possessed such a wondrous talent. She sang because the feelings inside her had to have an outlet.

She dismounted, walked to the edge of the shelf and stood with her back to Volney. She looked down the vast green mountainside to the river below, drew several deep breaths, and began to sing. The song she sang was a ballad, one Maggie had sung when she was young. Lorna felt strangely exultant when she was singing. Her soprano voice was high and sweet, wild and haunting. It had the carrying quality of a bell but with a suggestion of power held in reserve. The unearthly sound seemed to fill every crevice of the mountains and spill into the canyon below. It sent a shiver down Volney's spine.

> "Flesh of my flesh, heart of my heart,
> forever, hand in hand with wond'ring steps
> through the wide forests we go . . ."

On the side of the mountain, White Bull heard her. He stopped his spotted pony and listened, as did others. Billy Tyrrell, whose back and buttocks burned from the sting of her whip; Brice Fulton, dragging the saddle from his horse in the corral behind his cabin; Bonnie, dreading the moment Brice came to the house; all heard the glorious sound.

The high sweet notes seemed to dance along the valley from end to end. A Mexican drifter paused, lifted his head, listened, and crossed himself.

Three men driving a dozen head of stolen cattle looked at one another with superstitious fear in their eyes.

"Is that *her*?" one asked.

"It's *her*. The Indians call her Singing Woman," the younger man said in a subdued voice. "She's sacred to them. They'd die for 'er. She roams these mountains, day or night, 'n nobody dares lay a hand on 'er."

When Lorna finished her song, White Bull lifted his arm in silent tribute. He knew she had sung for him and it made his heart glad. He put his heels to his pony. It was time to return to the Wind River encampment and prepare his people for the trek south. They would break their journey here on Light's Mountain, and he would see Singing Woman again.

Lorna sat with her back to a mountain spruce, her hat on the ground beside her.

"I'm afraid Brice will kill Bonnie." She handed the sack of dried fruit back to Volney and met his eyes with her dark, violet-blue ones. Under strangely smoky lids and level black brows, they gave her an intense look of concentration.

"Ain't nothin' ya can do if'n she won't leave him."

"He's letting the men use her, and her carrying his babe." There was both worry and scorn in her voice. "Sometimes I think men are the lowest things on this earth. All they've got on their minds is fornicating. They don't care if a woman wants to do it or not. It's just like she's not human. Back in the olden days, Light *loved* Maggie and my grandpa *loved* my grandma. What's happened to people, Volney?"

"You bein' bothered by them no-goods?" he asked tartly.

"They know better than to bother me. I'd kill them."

"Brice's fondness for other folk's cows could get *him* killed."

"I can't wait for that, I've got to get Bonnie away from here." Lorna chewed the fruit slowly and spat out a seed. "When Brice came here four or five years ago, he wasn't so bad. He'd been discharged from the army and said he wanted to start a little ranch. But the longer he's here the worse he gets."

"He showed his good side at first. Your granny was alive then. She saw him fer what he was 'n told him to steer clear a you, or she'd clean his plow. Guess he feared she'd sic White Bull on 'em. Brice is the kind a man what's got to have a woman, 'n he went out 'n got hisself one."

"Bonnie's had it hard. Her folks made her feel like she was dirt because she was born with one hand. Godamighty! It wasn't her fault. Her own folks sold her for a keg of whiskey and a broken down horse and wagon." Lorna pounded the dust from her hat by slapping it against her leg, her dark lashes hiding the worry in her eyes. "She's only sixteen, Volney. At least that's how old she thinks she is."

"What're you now? Eighteen? Nineteen? My, how the years go. It ain't been no time a'tall since ya was wearin' rags on yore hind end."

"Don't change the subject, you old coot. Can't you see I'm worried about Bonnie?"

"I see it, youngun, but there ain't nothin' I can do. Talk to Frank. Maybe he can get Brice to let up on 'er."

"Fiddle-faddle! Pa won't do anything. I think he's scared of Brice. That's another thing, Volney. It's crossed my mind that Pa's up to something. He's throwing out a lot of big talk about maybe setting up a hauling business and going to California or Oregon."

This was news to Volney. He shook his unkempt mane from side to side. "What a ya think of it?"

"I'm thinking there's plenty to do here, if he'd just knuckle down and do it. He's never taken an interest in Light's Mountain. It's like he was here visiting. But if he's set to leave, he'll go alone. There have been Lightbodys on this mountain for more than sixty years. I'm the only one left. Here I stay, here I die."

Volney looked at the girl's set face. She always had a look of preoccupation about her, an air of listening to some distant music that no one else could hear. To him, she was the prettiest thing in the world. A shiny mass of hair was drawn back from her face and tied at the nape of her neck, accentuating her high cheekbones and the pure creamy pallor of her skin. The contrast of pale white skin and dark hair was still startling to Volney, who had known her all her life. She had a lovely mouth, full lipped and red, with a curious deep cleft in the low lip. Her slim young body moved with vibrancy, yet with the grace of the wind on the grass of the plains.

She needed a man by her side, Volney thought, just as Maggie had needed Light to stand between her and the varmints who would use and dishonor her. She was far too sightly to be left alone. A man had only to look at her to start a fever in his veins. White Bull loved her like a daughter, just as he did, but they wouldn't always be there to protect her.

"I've got to be getting on home." Lorna got to her feet.

"Ain't you got no better footgear'n that?"

"Of course I have, but what's wrong with these?" Lorna held out her foot. Her moccasins were well worn and her toe was coming through the end.

Volney's bony shoulders jiggled with his dry chuckling. "If ya ain't the damndest! I'd give a prime beaver pelt to see ya all gussied up in that white deerskin dress Little Owl made fer ya a few years back."

"For goodness sake, Volney! You've seen me in it," she sputtered. "Are you getting so old you've forgotten we spent a week at White Bull's Little Snake camp?"

He laughed. "I ain't forgot how White Bull yanked ya off'n that pony when ya thought to sneak off with a party huntin' a killer b'ar."

"You told him, or he wouldn't have seen me," she accused.

Volney ejected a stream of amber juice. "'Pears like even White Bull's got sense enuff to know his warriors don't have no bumps on their chest."

"Oh, shut up about it," Lorna said crossly. She swung into the saddle with her lips pressed together to keep from smiling. It was funny now, but it hadn't been at the time. She'd dressed in Gray Owl's clothes and had even put black river mud on her face. Just as the party was about to ride out—whish! White Bull had grabbed her by the back of the tunic and yanked her off the pony. He'd threatened to switch her legs with a willow switch if she tried to deceive him again.

"Are you going to be around long, Volney?"

"I'm athinkin' on it."

"Keep an eye on Brice's cabin, will you?"

"You knowed I was agoin' to anyhow."

"Come up to the house for supper."

"Nope. I got me things to see 'bout."

"All right then, you old goat, don't come!"

Lorna rode along the edge of the shelf until she found a break in the wall's sheer face and sent her horse downward in a dangerous descent that laid her almost flat over its croup. She grinned wickedly, knowing that Volney was watching and that she'd get the sharp edge of the old man's tongue when next they met. She struck the level ground with a jolt that rocked her forward and ran her horse in under the trees screening the canyon's lower end.

Half an hour later, coming out into the open, she saw, a hundred yards away, three riders driving a small herd. They were facing her and she saw alarm evident in their attitudes. There was a brief run of time in which she walked her horse toward them. No one spoke, but one man lifted his hand in greeting. Lorna dragged her horse to a halt and faced the men. She knew them all. They were cronies of her father.

"What are you doing with old man Prichard's cows? Are you taking them somewhere for him?" She looked at each of them with a level, searching gaze.

"It ain't no business of yores what we're adoin', missy," Eli, the older man, growled. "Ride on."

"Seems you're short handed. Looks like mighty hard work if it takes three men to drive a dozen steers. I'll be glad to give you a hand." Lorna leaned on the saddle horn and smiled sweetly. She stared at each man in turn. Luke, Eli's young son, looked away and didn't meet her eyes, but his cousin, Hollis, grinned and edged his horse close to hers so that his knee rubbed against her leg. Lorna sat her mount, holding a tight rein on her fidgeting horse, and eyed him with open distaste.

"Howdy, little purty gal."

"Move back. The smell of you is enough to make me puke."

He continued to grin at her, reaching out his hand and placing it on her thigh. His eyes were small and watery and his face dried and wrinkled beneath a stubble of whiskers. He made her skin crawl.

"If'n it's work yore awantin', I got me a itch ya can work on."

Lorna lifted her brows so that her eyes were wide and innocent. "Take your hands off me or I'll poke my knife in you." To give emphasis to her words she knicked his skin with the sharp tip of the knife she palmed. The sudden pain startled him and he jerked his hand, cutting his wrist even more. The knife that had slid down her sleeve was evident now, so she held it in front of her.

"Why'n hell did ya pull a stunt like that for?" Hollis looked at the blood dripping on his thigh and jerked the handkerchief from around his neck to wrap his wrist.

"The next time you lay a hand on me I'll cut the damn thing off!" She spoke quietly, with deadly intent.

"Yore pa needs to take a strap to yore butt!"

"Is that right?" Lorna looked past him and saw her father coming toward them. "Why don't you tell him?"

When Frank rode up Lorna knew every suspicion she'd had about his recent activities was true. His face was flushed and his eyes were fastened on her.

"What ye be doin' here, lass?" he growled.

"I came to help you steal old man Prichard's cows," she said lightly, her never still brain following another thought. Her father was weak, easily led. "It makes no never mind to me that the old man is barely scratching out a living for a houseful of kids, or that he's depending on these cows to see him through the winter. They were easy pickings, weren't they, Frank? What we ought to do is take these lazy, worthless friends of yours and go steal us a really big herd."

"Ye dinna know what ye're asayin'."

"The hell I don't!" Lorna shouted to keep from crying. Disappointment in her father caused her temper to explode suddenly and violently. "Do you think I don't know about these little cattle stealing trips of yours? Didn't you think I'd wonder where you were going to get the cash money to get into the hauling business? Did you have anything to do with that nester who was shot between the eyes a few weeks back? He left five children and no wife to take care of them. I know a hell of a lot more about what goes on in these mountains than you think I do, Frank."

"Shut yer mouth!"

"I won't shut my mouth! You and these men are thieves, rustlers. Stealing a dozen steers is just as bad as stealing a hundred. It's the truth, and if the truth hurts, you live with it, or have you sunk so low you've not got any conscience left at all?"

Frank's eyes widened and for a moment he was speechless in the face of his daughter's blazing defiance. Her contempt washed over him in a chilling torrent. He went red with rage and the need to salvage his pride.

"Damn ye fer a sassy split-tail!" His words came out in a hoarse shout. "I dinna mean to hae ye treat me like dirt!" His Scottish accent was never more pronounced than when he was angry. His arm swung out in a looping blow that would have knocked her out of the saddle, had it landed. Lorna swung back, her reaction purely instinctive despite her surprise. Frank had never lifted a hand to her before.

The momentum of the swing had pulled Frank half out of the saddle. He was off balance and striving to right himself when Lorna dug her heels into the sides of her mount and the big gray's powerful haunches propelled it forward, straight into Frank's floundering mount, knocking it to its knees.

"I'll get 'er, Frank!" Hollis yelled. "Head 'er off, dammit!"

Lying flat along the neck of her plunging horse, she passed Eli and Luke sitting their horses and knew she had only Hollis to contend with. She heard Frank's strangled bellow and then she was into the trees. She gave all her attention to the trail which was boulder strewn and at times half blocked by brush and deadfalls. But she'd had a lifetime of riding such trails—taught by the best, White Bull's people. Over the years she had developed a faultless sense of timing and a judgment of distances that made her handling of her wildly running mount wholly automatic. In a race on open ground, she was a formidable opponent, but over terrain such as this she had no match.

Within a short time she knew she had outdistanced her

pursuer. Knowing herself safe she eased the stallion down
from its straining run and shortly drew up to let the horse
regain its wind. After a while she made her way leisurely
along a route that would bring her out to the place she called
home.

Now that she had time to think, her mind digested what
she had learned. Her heart was heavy with disappointment
and grief. Frank didn't have the love for the mountains that
she did. For as long as she could remember his dream had
been to leave them. *And to get money to do that he would
steal!*

Now that she thought about it, her father had never been
a companion, or teacher, or friend, but she loved him and
knew he loved her. Since she had grown up their entire relationship had been one of mutual avoidance. They lived in
the same house, but each went his own way. She cooked for
him and washed his clothes, but days passed without their
saying more than a few words to each other. It had been that
way while her grandmother lived and continued after she was
gone. But until lately she'd never thought of him as being
. . . dishonorable.

It was strange, she mused, but she knew Volney, Moose
and Woody better than she knew her own father. They fit in
these mountains, like she did. Her father just never . . . fit.

She passed the boarded-up shack where Moose and Woody
lived during the winter. The two old prospectors had been in
the mountains for as long as she could remember. In the
spring they loaded their burros and trekked off over the mountain panning a little gold from the mountain streams, always
looking for their gold strike. In the fall they came back to
winter on Light's Mountain. Lorna wished they were here
now. It would be a comfort to sit and visit with her old friends.

The homestead and the mountains were Lorna's entire life.
It was unbearable to think of living any other place. Her roots
were here in the place where Light and Maggie had built their
home. She was a Lightbody. Not for one minute did she think

of herself as a Douglas. The homestead was hers by the right of her birth, and here she'd stay.

But what to do now that she had seen the evidence of her own father's thievery? Somehow she wished she hadn't ridden into that valley and had the truth thrown in her face. *A person's got to face whatever comes.* This thought came forward out of the chaos of her mind, and she took a deep, quivering breath and turned her attention toward getting home.

Lorna rode slowly down the path to the house. She felt a spurt of pleasure, as she did on each homecoming. The trail led off the mesa and into the coolness of a pine forest. A rocky stream, edged with cottonwoods, willows, and sycamore trees cut through the clearing beside the house that was built strong and true, blending perfectly with the mountains and trees from which it had sprung. The logs were thick and heavy, and fitted snugly together. The timbers were weathered and the stonework of the massive chimneys was smoke stained. The house seemed not only to belong there but as if it could be depended upon to be there forever. Lorna blinked back the sudden moisture that filled her eyes. This was all she had ever known or wanted.

She rode into the house yard and was greeted by her dogs, Ruth and Naomi, with yips and whines of pleasure. Why did some men spend a lifetime grabbing for things that weren't really important, she thought, when all they needed was right there?

Evening came and with it the dread of the confrontation with Frank that she knew was coming. Not that she was afraid of him. She was well able to protect herself and he knew it. They were at a crossroads, she and her father, and it was unsettling to her to not know what the future held.

Lorna lit a lamp. She found herself wandering about the house, touching familiar things. Her hand rested on the back of the rocker Grandpa had made for Grandma Marthy. Granny had sat in the chair on cold winter nights and told her about the trek Light and Maggie had made from the Missouri Territory to the Colorado mountains. Her fingers trailed across the humpbacked trunk that held the small, patched moccasins Maggie had worn and the hair necklace she had woven from her shiny black hair. She'd made a wristband out of her hair for Light, and he had worn it, protected by a soft doeskin band, every day of his life. Thinking about it now, Lorna decided that someday she would make a wristband out of her hair for her man. He would love and cherish it every bit as much as Grandpa Light had loved and cherished the one his beloved had made for him.

The quilt Granny had pieced was on her bed; the rag carpet her mother had helped to make was on the floor of her room. She slept in the bed Light had made from an oak tree he had felled when he built the small one-room cabin that had sheltered him and Maggie the first winter. Her grandfather had been born in that room, as had her mother. Three more rooms had been added as the years went by, and now the house was large and comfortable.

An hour passed and then another while Lorna kept her dark thoughts at bay by remembering the tales her grandmother had told her about Light and Maggie: how Light had killed a crazed mountain man to keep him from blowing up a cabin and killing an entire family, and how he had killed his best friend's brother who had forced himself on Maggie.

Darkness came and still Frank hadn't returned. Lorna blew out the lamp and went to bed to lie staring into the darkness, her mind filled with troubled thoughts about Frank, about Bonnie, and about the sudden loneliness of her life.

The dogs hadn't made a sound so she knew the instant she heard the rapping on her window that it was Volney. The insistent rapping also told her that the old mountain man knew Frank hadn't returned and that she was alone. *What was Volney doing there in the middle of the night?* A spasm of alarm shot through her.

"Don't break the window, Volney," she called. "I'll meet

you out front." She jumped out of bed, and holding up her long white nightdress, went quickly through the house to the porch. Volney came around the corner of the house. "What is it? What's happened? How'd you know Pa wasn't here?"

"Whoa, now. I knowed Frank wasn't here 'cause he's down at Brice's. I got Bonnie hid up in the hills. They all been out ahuntin' 'er."

Lorna emitted a groan. "What did he do? Did he hurt her?"

"He done a fair job. She dragged 'erself down to the creek 'n keeled over. If'n he gets 'er, the bastard'll kill 'er shore as shootin'. He's mad as hops at you 'n her 'cause Billy backed down on some deal they was in."

"Damn, damn him! Damn the trash that's come in to ruin these mountains! What'll we do, Volney?"

"He's got ever'thin' on two legs out alookin' fer Bonnie. I seed varmints like him afore. They got to have 'em somethin' to kick 'round. They ain't been here yet, 'cause Frank says she ain't here. Yore pa ain't wantin' to bring no trouble down on ya."

"I wish Moose and Woody were here. They'd know where to hide her."

"Wal, they ain't," Volney snorted. "If'n somethin's done we got to do it. 'Sides, what's them ole farts know of anythin' but lookin' fer a pot a gold?"

"You just don't like them, Volney."

"Like 'em?" Volney echoed disgustedly. "Why, hell no! I ain't got no use fer clabberheads lollygaggin' 'round alookin' fer somethin' they'd not know what to do with if'n they found it!"

"We don't have time to argue about Moose and Woody. We've got to think of Bonnie. Bring her here. Brice won't dare try and take her from me. I'll send a message to White Bull and—"

"No, missy. Ya ain't gonna be no cause a no Injun trouble. I got me a place to take her to, a place I found while ahuntin' some cats. It's north and west a here . . . t'other side of the mountain." He paused. "It's a far piece."

"I'll help you. Wait till I get dressed." She turned to dart into the house.

"Hold on, missy," Volney called impatiently. "Pack up salve, some fixin's 'n a grub bag. The little gal's ahurtin' right smart. I'll fix us up a travois to drag 'er on. Looks like it'll rain afore mornin'. If'n it does, it'll wash out the tracks." He stepped off the porch, then turned back. "Ya know, missy, ya could a gone tail-over-teakettle agoin' down the side a that steep ridge like ya done today. Ya tryin' to kill that horse?"

"Oh, don't fuss at me now, Volney. You say Bonnie's hurt bad? Do you think the baby will come?"

"That's up to the good Lord, youngun." His voice gentled. "It purdee is. Now get a move on. We got us a far piece to go."

Lorna turned and hurried into the house wishing her father had half the grit of old Volney Burbank.

Chapter Two

Several weeks later, fifty miles southwest of Light's Mountain, a man lying in his bedroll carefully lifted himself up to lean on one elbow, his ears reaching for the sound that had awakened him. His eyes flared wide and he stared into the darkness. He heard the muffled thud of hooves on the trail below the grassed bench where he had spread his blankets for the night. The sound was not made by one horse alone, but several. He felt for the gun in his holster and the knife in his boot to reassure himself that they were there, and reached for the rifle that leaned against his saddle. A short snort came from his own horse tied nearby, and he jumped to his feet, hissed a command for silence and placed his hand over the stallion's quivering nostrils.

"Quiet, boy. Quiet."

The riders coming down the trail were too noisy to be Indians and too quiet to be cowhands going home after a rowdy night of drinking. Their very stillness heightened his suspicion that there was a sinister reason for them to be on the trail at midnight. He maneuvered himself silently and cautiously through the dry grass to the edge of the overhang. He was a big, lean, wide-shouldered man who knew careful scrutiny and patience were essential in this country if you wanted to live. He eased his long length to the ground and flattened himself. His narrowed eyes focused on the trail below. Lying perfectly still, he listened and watched the shadowy figures approach.

"This here's all right." The riders stopped and bunched around a horse that danced nervously. A man swore softly and yanked on the reins. Another man lifted a coiled rope from his saddle.

The listener judged the riders to be not more than thirty yards away.

"Throw the rope up over that thar limb above yore head." The riders shifted so the command could be obeyed. They crowded the nervous horse beneath the limb, their positions close beneath the tree, the hooves of their horses clicking on the stones. "Get 'em under that 'n be quick about it. We been atrailin' this bastard three days, 'n I got a thirst."

The deep voice had a familiar ring of gloating to it that pierced the memory of the man lying in the grass. He cursed silently. What the hell were Clayhill riders doing over on the other side of the Blue? They must be a hundred miles from Clayhill land.

"The old man said hang 'em as a warnin' to anybody athinkin' they'll squat on that range." Saddle leather creaked as a rider stood in the stirrups to toss the rope over the limb.

On the shelf above the trail the man's mind worked furiously to sort out the information he'd just heard. The slimy old bastard was spreading out west. It was the only direction he could go now that Logan Horn had bought the south range.

"We ain't ort to be adoin' this so secret like. It ain't no crime to hang a horse thief. And that's what ya said he done." The voice held obvious distaste for the job they were doing.

"Nobody's askin' you. We're adoin' it like the ole man said to do it. If'n yore so womanish, ya can hightail it back to the ranch 'n draw yore pay. Then, by God, you'd better hot-foot it out of the country if'n ya ain't got shit for brains."

The voice of Clayhill's foreman was heavy with sarcasm,

and anger stiffened the man lying in the grass. He remembered the time several years ago when that same voice had urged the crowd to hang his half brother. Dunbar hadn't been fore- man then—just a paid gunman hired to do the old man's dirty work. The hatred the listener felt for Adam Clayhill choked him. With an effort he swallowed it down, lest it goad him into being careless and doing something foolish.

"Quit yore jawin', Dunbar, and get on with it."

"Goddammit! Don't be givin' me no orders. I'm aram- roddin' this here outfit."

The concealed man was sweating, and he wiped his face on the sleeve of his shirt. Once he'd witnessed a legal hanging and felt the murderer got what he had coming, but this was a lynching. This was a dark and ugly bunch carrying out the orders of a rich, powerful, old sonofabitch who was too rotten to live. Goddamn that old cuss! he fumed. He should have killed him a couple of years ago when— He held himself still, blocking that time from his mind as he took stock of the odds. Against three, even four, he might have a chance, but with six . . . If he drew down on them, they'd be sure to shoot the luckless homesteader they were going to hang. Poor bastard would probably rather be shot than hanged anyway, he decided, and pulled his rifle up beside him. He strained his eyes to sort out the shadowy figures of the Clayhill riders. He'd have to be careful to not shoot the horse out from under the nester.

"Pull that horse out easy 'n let 'em down! I want the sonofabitch to hang thar 'n think 'bout that slash he put in my leg."

"That ain't no way to hang a man, Dunbar! Do it quick, if'n yore agoin' to, 'n get it over."

"Shut yore mouth! I'm arunnin' this show." There was a snarl in the deep voice.

The listener heard the creak of a rope taking strain, then the jerking of it as the hanged man kicked and struggled.

Hell! The only chance now was if they'd leave and he could cut him down.

A horse took off on the run back up the trail and Dunbar laughed. "Goddamn yellow belly!" he yelled, his voice thick with irritation.

There was a sudden pounding of hooves as if the other riders were anxious to leave the grisly scene, too. Dunbar looked over his shoulder at the man kicking at the end of the rope. "Choke, goddamn ya!" He spurred his horse cruelly; the animal sank back on its haunches and leaped to follow the others.

The listener moved out of the grass and shimmied down the bank like a shadow. He held no liking for lynching a man, and there was a slight chance he could reach him before he choked to death. He ran soundlessly on the leaves and grass, keeping back from the rocky trail until he reached the tree. He went up it with swift agility, crawled out on the limb, and with a quick slash of his knife cut the rope. The body tumbled to the ground. He grasped the branch and swung himself down. He bent swiftly, loosened the noose, and pulled it up over the man's head. His knife slit the cloth that held the gag in his mouth. Almost at once he heard a hoarse gasp.

He turned his ear and leaned into the breeze, listening for a sound. He heard nothing, but that was no guarantee Dunbar wouldn't come back. Grasping the man by the arms, he yanked him to his feet. Bending so he could get his shoulder beneath the victim's armpit, he started propelling him toward the upper bench.

"Move your feet," he hissed. "I can't carry you up that bank."

Grasping painfully, the man stiffened his legs and with all his strength forced them to move. They staggered up the steep embankment. By the time they'd reached the top, the tall man was also straining for breath. Roscoe nickered softly when they reached the campsite and his owner whispered for him to keep quiet as he let the suffering man sink down onto his blankets. He reached for his canteen, uncapped it and put it in the man's hands.

"Can you drink?" He sank down on his haunches beside him.

"Gawd! Oh, Gawd . . . I th-thought it was the end."

"It almost was. It was a good thing Dunbar wanted you to choke slow or you'd be dead."

"I'll ki-kill 'em. I'll kill 'em—"

"What's this all about?"

"'Bout an ol' sonofabitch named Clay-Clayhill who wants the whole fuckin' territory for hisself . . ."

"I heard them say you're a horsethief. I've got no use for a horsethief, but if you're to be hung the law should do it."

"If stealin' back my own horses makes me one, I am." The man drank slowly, his muscles jumping nervously, his trembling fingers feeling his neck gingerly.

"Are you all right, now? We'd better move out of here. If they come back and find you gone they'll know you had help. I pick my own time and place when I buck those odds."

"Did they take my horse? He'd a put up a fight to stay with me."

"I don't know. I was too busy cutting you down to notice, but there was some commotion with a horse."

"I'm obliged to ya. Name's Griffin."

"Cooper Parnell."

"How'd ya happen to be here?"

"I'm tracking a mare that was stolen from me a couple days ago."

"I never thought I'd be obliged to a horsethief. I'm shore glad ya was here."

"So am I. That Dunbar's a sonofabitch."

The man slapped his empty holster. "Bastards took my gun and my knife, but if my horse is loose, I can whistle for him and he'll come. My throat feels like a hunk a raw meat." He got to his feet and held out his hand. He was almost as tall as Cooper and just as thin. It was too dark to see the man clearly, but Cooper was almost sure that he was much younger than his own twenty-six years. "I thank ya, mister."

Cooper shook his hand. "I'll saddle up. If you've got a pucker left, you'd better try for your horse and we'll get back up in the hills and get some sleep. Come morning I'm going after my mare."

After the second whistle the horse came down the rocky trail, dragging his reins and nickering softly. Griffin called to him and the horse scrambled up the incline.

"Damn, I'm glad to see ya, boy." The horse nudged him. He rubbed the side of its face affectionately and felt blood where the bit had torn the side of its mouth. "You fought 'em when they tried to lead ya away from me, didn't ya, old friend?" There was a huskiness in the whispered voice. "They caught us with our britches down, Firebird. It'll not happen again. Are ya all right? Ya took a tumble when they lassoed us." He ran his hands over the horse's sides, rump, and down over his haunches. "Ya've got a few cuts, but nothin' too bad for what we had done to us. An angel was sure asittin' on our shoulder tonight. We owe this here gent aplenty."

Cooper watched. Watchfulness was no new thing for him, and he was still somewhat leery of the stranger; but he was of the opinion that you could measure a man's worth by the way he treated his horse or his dog. The horse was a sorrel with a light mane and tail. It was deep chested, had strong legs and powerful haunches. Cooper prided himself on being knowledgeable about horse flesh, and he realized that this was a damn good horse. But what would a squatter be doing with such a valuable animal? They usually rode broken-down old cayuses.

With his bedroll tied on behind his saddle, Cooper mounted and rode out without a backward glance. Ordinarily he didn't turn his back on a stranger, but he was sure the man was without a weapon. He heard the creak of saddle leather and the soft thud of hooves on the dry grass and knew Griffin was following.

Cooper rode cautiously along the dim trail at the edge of the timber. It was rugged, lonely country where the spruce and pine clung to the hillside that sloped to the river. He'd been across the mountains into Utah Territory, bought a few horses, and sold all of them, except for a beautiful little mare, to a Mormon heading for the Salt Lake. He'd gotten a damn good price and was satisfied with the profit he'd made, which was as much or more than he'd have made if he'd driven them to Junction City. The mare, whom he'd put to his stallion, Roscoe, would produce fine colts.

He still couldn't understand how he could have been so careless as to let the mare be taken right out from under his nose. He'd staked her out in a small meadow to graze while he and Roscoe went down to the riverbank to catch a fish. He'd been on the trail two weeks. The mare, who was in foal, was growing gaunt, and he was getting mighty tired of rabbit and deer meat. When he went to look for her after he had eaten his fill of river trout and had had a leisurely nap, she was gone. The rope and the halter lay where he'd left her.

When he couldn't find a print other than that of the mare, he was sure she had been stolen by a lone Indian. It had taken him the rest of the day and part of the next to pick up the mare's trail after he lost it in the river. Whoever had taken her had been cagey. The riders had left marks on the rocks when they left the river, traveled up into the hills, then doubled back and jumped the horse back into the water. Of course it had taken Cooper several hours to figure this out. By the time he'd discovered where they had emerged from the river again, it was almost dark and he was forced to stop for the night.

Cooper didn't stop until after he had worked his way upward among the pines for several miles. He had come out from under the trees and now he turned to survey the area. He was backed to several large craggy boulders set among the trees, and there was an open space in front of him. It was unlikely anyone could sneak up on them, especially if Roscoe was close by. Mountain bred, with strong survival instincts, the horse would let him know if as much as a rabbit came near. Cooper dismounted and began to remove Roscoe's saddle.

Griffin pulled up a dozen yards away, sat his mount and waited. He made no move to get off his horse and Cooper's lips quirked in a grin. The man was trail wise. He was waiting for an invitation to share the camp, observing the strict etiquette of the trail that proclaimed a man's camp was his home.

"Get down, Griffin. We should be able to catch a few winks of sleep here without anybody slipping up on us. I doubt Dunbar and his bunch will come back before morning. He'll not want to make the trip down that trail alone. And I don't think his men had much of a stomach for the hanging."

Holding his shoulders and neck stiffly erect, Griffin slid from the saddle, removed it and threw it on the ground. "A man feels naked out here without a gun," he commented uneasily.

"I understand the feeling. You're welcome to trail along with me. As soon as I get my mare I'll be heading for Junction City."

"I'm obliged. I've got me some unfinished business with the Clayhill men."

"You're jumping back into it, huh?" Cooper sat down with his back to the boulder. "Did you file on your place, or were you just squatting on it?"

"I was afixin' to file. I was breakin' in some horses to sell to raise money for winter supplies. Clayhill moved that bunch up to hold the range 'n when I didn't scare off they stole my horses. I got 'em back with the help of a friend a mine. They come alookin' for me and jumped me last night. You know the rest."

"Did they get the horses?"

"No, by Gawd!" He paused and when Cooper didn't comment, he said, "They'll not find 'em." There was a long silence. "That land grabbin' old buzzard's not arunnin' me off that land. I've had me all the hunger, thirst 'n cold of hard winters, dry range 'n long dusty drives to last a lifetime. I'm ahavin' my own hearth fire, grass with cattle on it, 'n horses alookin' over my gate bars. I got me a place picked out to light on 'n I'm astayin', by Gawd!"

"They might bury you there."

"I'll take some of 'em with me."

"When the old man sinks his teeth, he doesn't let go."

"I heared tell of one time he did. The talk is he had a son by a Injun woman 'n run out on 'em. The kid was raised back East by some of the old man's folks 'n when he come into some money he come back 'n bought up everything to the south of ole Clayhill, closin' him in. That's why he's spreadin' west. It's said he hates that Injun like a polecat 'cause he bested him, and tried to get him hung on a trumped-up charge. That ole man must be meaner than a rattler."

There was another long silence, then Cooper said dryly, "Compared to that old man a rattler's a . . . fishing worm." He pulled down his hat, folded his arms, and lowered his chin to his chest.

Cooper woke at first light. He glanced over to see Griffin leaning against his saddle, his teeth worrying a strip of dry meat.

"How ya feel 'bout jerky for breakfast?"

"I'd rather have a mess of eggs."

"So would I."

Cooper grinned and held out his hand. Griffin tossed him a leather pouch and he was able to see the face of the man he had rescued for the first time in the light of day. He was younger than Cooper judged him to be from the way he talked last night. He estimated his age as not far from the top side of twenty. Griffin's hair was brown and curly, his whiskers a shade lighter. There was a tough, confident look in his face that was boyish, yet old—and something about the long slender fingers reminded Cooper of a gunfighter. There was vigilance in his alert eyes that looked straight into Cooper's and refused to let him stare him down. His tied-down holster, the loop in his belt for a knife, the good leather boots and saddle, all told Cooper the boy had been "up the trail and over the mountain."

"You a wanted man?" Cooper's blunt question didn't seem to faze his companion.

"Why do ya ask?"

"I'll keep Clayhill's men off your back till you can fend for yourself, but I'll not stand against a marshal or a ranger."

"No worry 'bout that. I was wanted once, but not now. I served my time in Yuma."

"Been out long?"

"Three years."

Cooper looked him straight in the eye. He felt he had the right to know something about a man who was going to share his camp for a week or more. He stuck a strip of the dried meat in his mouth and tossed the pouch back to Griffin.

"What were you in for?"

"Killin' a man," he said without hesitation, and a look of intense hatred came over the boyish features. "He beat my ma to death with a shovel 'n I killed the no-good sonofabitch. I was thirteen 'n spent five years for it, but I'd a done it again. Anythin' else ya awantin' to know?" His voice grated coldly, tensely. He seemed to draw back into himself, got to his feet, and picked up his saddle.

"No. I was trying to find out if it'd be foolhardy to turn my back on you. I slept with one eye open last night."

"Both a mine was—ya got the guns."

Cooper threw back his head and laughed. "I never thought of it from your side of the fence." He got to his feet, pounded the dust from his hat by slapping it against his thigh before he put it on his head. "We've got to backtrack to pick up the mare's trail. I hope to hell whoever's got her won't ride her to death." He stood, swatted Roscoe on the rump, and threw the saddle up onto his back.

At the riverbank they picked up the mare's trail and followed it south. It crossed a grassy meadow and climbed to circle a hill, and then veered downward and turned back northeast. This puzzled Cooper. They were doubling back to the west side of the large high bluff that rose above the meadow where he had hobbled the mare.

Griffin had a sharp eye and they were able to travel at a faster rate of speed than Cooper had traveled while tracking the previous day. They stopped one time to examine a track and it was Griffin's opinion that it had been made the night before. This told them the rider knew the territory and was anxious to reach a destination.

In the middle of the afternoon they came down onto a bench and found a dim two-wheel track going through the aspens and cottonwoods. They followed it to a narrow stream of rushing water where it turned and ran parallel with the creek. In the distance they saw a long narrow meadow and an old corral overgrown with grass. As they approached they saw that it was empty, the bars down. However, beyond the corral, not fifty or sixty yards from the creek, was a cabin, and behind that a pole corral and a lean-to shed backed up to the bluff. There was no sign of the mare or of any livestock. The place looked deserted except for a thin plume of smoke coming from the chimney.

Cooper and Griffin withdrew to the cover of the trees, dismounted and tied their horses to a tree stump so they could crop the grass.

"This seems to be the end of the line," Cooper said, and adjusted his gunbelt. "If my horse is here, I'm getting her and kicking the shit out of whoever took her." He studied the scene. It behooved a man to understand what he was getting into. The cabin was old and patched with cut boards, more than likely taken from a wagon bed. The grass around it

hadn't been tramped down, which meant it hadn't been occupied for long. There were no horses in the corral, and that
had to mean they were hidden somewhere nearby.

"We can get pretty close without 'em spottin' us if'n we
stay in the trees till we reach that high grass, then belly it up
as far as the woodpile," Griffin said after he'd studied the
layout carefully.

"You don't have to stick your neck out. Stay with the
horses, I'll go in by myself."

"I wouldn't miss it. I always did wanna see the shit kicked
outta somebody. 'Sides that, I want his hat."

Cooper grinned back over his shoulder and led off through
the trees. They came out closer to the house than the shed,
and ran in a crouched position to reach the high grass and
prickly bushes that extended to the downed dead limbs that
made up the woodpile. When they reached it, Cooper sat
back on his heels, took off his hat, and wiped the sweat from
his face with the sleeve of his shirt.

"Damn quiet," he said when Griffin squatted down beside
him.

"Yeah. I think there's a woman in there."

Cooper lifted an eyebrow in query. "What makes you think
that?"

"Two things. Whoever chopped on that limb took a lot of
light swings at it, and that ax ain't sunk in that stump more'n
a inch or two. 'Sides that, all the light stuff's been taken and
the heavy's stuff's still here."

"Could be somebody's been laid up a spell."

"Could be, but if'n it is he's wearin' women's drawers.
There's a pair adryin' on a bush on the other side of the cabin.
I saw 'em when we come through the grass." There was a
quirk of humor at the corners of the young nester's mouth
when he spoke, and Cooper looked at him with new appre-
ciation.

"Goddamn! You don't miss much."

"I didn't stay alive for five years in Yuma by shuttin' my eyes and sittin' on my hands."

"Well even if a woman's in there, she sure as hell isn't out here by herself. What worries me is that I don't see my mare."

"They might a hid 'er up in the hills."

"The tracks lead here. They brought her here first. I figure he must have climbed the bluff, walked over the mountain and saw her grazing below. He couldn't bring her back down the bluff and had to take the long way around."

Cooper's eyes were fastened on the cabin. Sunlight gleamed on water being thrown out the door from a pan. There was the ring of a tin bucket hitting stone and the murmur of voices. The sounds were too far away for them to catch the words, but from the tone, it seemed the woman was pleading.

Griffin heard it too, and his eyes questioned Cooper's.

At that instant a scream of agony tore through the silence. It was so startling that it drew the two men to their feet.

"He's killin' 'er!" Griffin hissed.

"Godamighty—"

"What ya agoin' to do?"

Another scream split the silence.

"I'm going to kill me a varmint," Cooper spoke as his long legs were eating up the distance to the cabin.

Chapter
Three

Lorna knelt down on the makeshift bed of straw and grass and smoothed the dark curls back from Bonnie's pale, damp face, trying not to let the concern she was feeling show in hers.

"I'm scared, Lorna. It hurts so bad—"

"I know, Bonnie. I've made ready the best I know how. I've got a clean knife to cut the cord and thread to tie it off. There are clean blankets to wrap the babe in and clean cloths ... for you." She wiped the sweat from the young, pain-ravaged face and fought to keep her anxiety from showing. "I've boiled water, too. I've never midwifed, but it's been done for thousands of years so I don't guess there's much to it," she said in an attempt to lighten her own fear as well as Bonnie's. "We'll handle it just fine, and we'll have a babe to fuss over."

"I've seen a few birthin's when I was little and the babe just popped right out." Bonnie paused and gasped; her thin, childlike body with its large humped belly writhed in agony. "Somethin's not right, Lorna! It's ... killin' me ... The Lord's payin' me back," she gasped.

"Don't talk like that. The Lord doesn't pay people back for something that wasn't their fault."

"You've been better to me 'n anybody—Oh! Oh, Lorna! Ahhh—"

"I should've found a woman to help us." A frown wrinkled the smooth skin of her forehead. "But I was afraid Brice would find out where you are. When I saw that loose horse, I was sure someone had followed me here."

"Maybe Brice ain't alookin' for me no more," Bonnie said hopefully.

"Ha!" Lorna snorted. "I'd not chance it. The last time I sneaked home I heard Frank talking to Hollis. They're still looking for you. Brice isn't going to give up something he thinks is his," Lorna insisted. "And do you know what that Hollis said? He said my pa told him he could court me. That filthy, watery-eyed, pea-brained coyote! I'd not spit on him if he was on fire! Besides, I don't think Pa told him any such thing. Do you think you can walk? Would it help?" Lorna inquired, giving her a fixed earnest gaze.

Bonnie rolled to her knees and hung there gasping. "I'll try if you want me to."

Lorna helped her to her feet and put her arm around her. Oh, God, she prayed silently, be merciful to her. She's had nothing but hell all her life. "Put your arm across my shoulders." Lorna's thick, black hair was tied with a string at the nape of her neck and hung down her back to her hips. She pulled it forward to drape down over her breast and Bonnie's thin arm reached out for support.

"Ohh . . . ohh . . ." Consumed by pain, the girl planted both bare feet on the hard earthen floor. The color drained from her face leaving it doughy except for great purple circles under her eyes. Sweat stood in beads on her forehead, collected and streamed down her face. Her eyes were closed and her hand clutched Lorna's shoulder. She clenched her lower lip between her teeth in an attempt to hold back the low, moaning sound coming from her throat.

"Come on, Bonnie. Walk. I heard tell it was the thing to do."

Like a wounded animal, Bonnie swung her head from side
to side, but obediently moved her feet. They lurched to the
end of the room, turned and retraced their steps. Anger swelled
in Lorna until she thought she would burst with it. If she ever
set eyes on Brice Fulton again, she vowed, she'd kill him!
Fear crowded thoughts of revenge from her mind as another
pain struck Bonnie. It made her go rigid and brought whim-
pering sounds bubbling from her lips.

"Ahh . . . Ohh . . . I can't stand it! Please! Please, let me
get down on the pallet. Lorna—"

Lorna eased her down on the straw bed and searched her
memory for any scrap of information she had ever heard about
childbirth. During the night, while she was away, water tinged
with blood had gushed from Bonnie, and pain had been tearing through her since that time. They had thought the baby
wouldn't come for another month and had been sure Volney
would find a place for Bonnie and be back for her by that
time.

Lorna tried to not show her fear when she placed the pads
beneath Bonnie's hips. Blood had soaked her gown and was
running down her legs. *Women died in childbirth.* It was a
common thing. Damn the entire male race, she fumed silently.
Their only thought was for the pleasure of the moment. They
used a woman the same as they used a horse—rode her to
death and when they killed her, they just got another. No man
would use her like this, she vowed. Somewhere in this world
there would be a man for her like Grandpa Light.

Bonnie lifted her knees and planted her feet on the mat-
tress. Her thin, blue-veined hand flattened on her hard, extended belly. Thoughts came to her clearly and she spoke
them aloud.

"I'm going to die, killed by this poor babe. Oh, babe,
don't kill me! I'd never sell *you* to a drunken lout for a broken-
down wagon, a used-up horse, and a few dollars to buy
whiskey. It'll make no matter to me if you don't have ever'-
thin' other folks have. On the inside you'll be the same as

anybody else. But, oh, I'm not ready to die, yet—I've just began to live! For the first time in my life I've got someone who don't make me feel ashamed because—"

A sudden pain rocked through her with such a terrific force that it blocked everything from her mind. She was unaware of the piercing scream that burst from her throat, bounced into every corner of the small room and beyond.

Lorna grabbed her forearms and tried to hold her while she bucked on the bed. Bonnie's eyes were wild as she stared unseeing into her face as the hurting went on and on. The screams from her wide open mouth suddenly subsided and she fell weakly back, her head rolling to the side. Lorna released her arms and looked up.

It was then that she realized the room had darkened because a man filled the doorway. He was a stranger, and big. His hat was pulled low over his forehead and he had a gun in his hand. These things registered in Lorna's mind the instant fear brought her to her feet. She leaped to the corner, grabbed the rifle and turned, barrel out, her finger on the trigger.

"What do you want here?" she demanded. "Get out!" She looked like a small cornered cat.

Shock held Cooper motionless for a minute. Then he holstered his gun. "Sorry, ma'am." He almost choked on the words and began to back out the door.

Another scream filled the room.

"Lor . . . na! Oh, Lor . . . na! Help me!"

Lorna glanced at Bonnie's writhing body and then back at the man in the doorway. She was torn between going to Bonnie and keeping the man at bay with the rifle. Another man, this one hatless, stood there too. She held the rifle in front of her and inched over to stand beside the pallet where Bonnie lay. The girl's head was thrown back, her legs flopped, and blood spilled onto the white sheets.

The fair-haired man held his hands, palms out, in front of him. "We're sorry we frightened you, ma'am. Do what you have to do. We'll not hurt you."

"Get out!"

Bonnie screamed again.

"We'll not hurt you, ma'am," he said again.

"Get out!" Lorna made jabbing gestures with the rifle.

"We'll go. But for God's sake, put the rifle down and help her!" The men started backing from the doorway.

The noises coming from the girl on the pallet were more like those of a helpless dying animal than that of a human being.

"I don't know what else to do!" The words broke from Lorna in desperation. She fell to her knees beside Bonnie, still keeping the end of the rifle pointed toward the doorway. "It's killing her and I don't know what to do!" It was an anguished cry. "I've never helped birth a babe!"

Ignoring the rifle the girl clutched in her hands, Cooper stepped into the room, tossed his hat on the floor and went to kneel down beside the girl. He'd helped to bring many a foal into the world, but had never even been near a woman when she was birthing. There was no room in his mind for thoughts of the stolen mare. The girl had lost a lot of blood. He was sure this wasn't the way it was supposed to be.

"How long has she been like this?"

"It started during the night."

Bonnie opened her eyes and her gaze shifted from the face of the blond man bending over her to the face of the second man who moved in and gently lifted her knees so that her feet were flat on the pallet. She used his dark features as a point on which to focus her mind while her muscles knotted and pulled as if tearing her apart. The pain rolled over her in mighty waves, leaving her gasping and the world reeling.

"I helped with a birthin' like this once down on the Santa Fe," Griffin said quietly to Lorna. "We've got to do somethin' quick or she'll die." He moved confidently in behind Bonnie and lifted her to a sitting position. "Get in front of her," he said to Cooper. "Get 'er up on her knees and hold her upright with your hands under her arms. Ma'am," he spoke to Lorna without looking at her, "strip this thing off her."

Lorna wondered later why she had acted without hesitation and why she didn't feel the slightest tinge of embarrassment exposing Bonnie's naked body to these strangers. Her grandmother always said it wasn't decent for menfolk to be around at a time like this. But she didn't care. She wanted help for Bonnie and if it meant stripping her in front of these men, she'd do it. She placed the gun on the floor beside her. When Cooper slid his hands under the shift and lifted Bonnie, she pulled it up over her head.

"Gawddamn!"

"Godamighty!"

Both men cursed at the sight of the pitifully thin body covered with scars and bruises. Her arms flopped down at her sides and surprise shook Cooper sharply when he saw that there was no hand at the end of one arm; it was rounded smoothly above the wrist.

Lorna saw and unconsciously recorded in her mind the men's reaction to Bonnie's pitiful body and dazed condition.

"Lor...na!" Bonnie's eyes were wild and unseeing as powerful contractions shook her and she had no control over her mind or body.

"I'm here, Bonnie. We've got help, now. You're going to be all right. It'll be over...soon..." Lorna crooned comforting words she didn't believe.

"Ma'am, put 'er arms up on his shoulders." Griffin placed his hands on Bonnie's rock-hard abdomen. "She's too weak to push down. I'll have to do it for her...when I feel it's time."

After several minutes, Bonnie's screams became weaker, but they still filled the stillness with regularity.

"You'll kill her!" Lorna gasped. "She'll bleed to death."

"She can't take much more. She'll die if we don't get it outta her," Griffin snapped. "Spread her legs 'n see if it's comin'. If it starts we'll have to pull it out."

Cooper never felt so helpless in his life. He felt a cold, deadly rage at whoever had mistreated this girl. To be born a cripple was bad enough, but she had been beaten, cut, and even burned. Godamighty! The man who did this should be horse whipped! She moaned like a wounded animal and quivered in her agony, not knowing or caring who was doing for her. Her head fell to his shoulder and her arms clutched him, the nails of her hand digging into the skin of his neck.

"I see a . . . foot," Lorna gasped.

"Ya gotta help me, girl." Griffin spoke sharply into Bonnie's ear. "Take a deep breath 'n push down. I know yo're hurtin' somethin' awful, but ya gotta help me." He placed his palms on the hardened mound of her abdomen and waited for another contraction. "Hold 'er up!" he said to Cooper, and when he felt the quiver of weak muscles, he pushed down.

Bonnie was held erect and the world retreated as the crushing pain rolled over her. She sagged in the hands that held her.

"It's just hangin' there! Oh, God!" Lorna gagged.

"Lay 'er down," Griffin said urgently to Cooper, and they quickly laid the unconscious girl on her back. "Straddle 'er and hold 'er legs up 'n out." He moved quickly, picked up a cloth, grasped the protruding feet and pulled the tiny, motionless being from its mother's body.

"It's out! Oh, God—it's dead!" Lorna gagged again.

Griffin grasped the knife, cut the cord, and tied it with the string. He began to massage Bonnie's stomach with strong knowing hands, and after a short time the afterbirth came with a fresh flow of blood.

Cooper's stomach convulsed, but he managed to wrap the mass of decaying human flesh in the cloth and take it outside.

"Ma'am!" Griffin's hand reached out to touch Lorna's shoulder. "Are you all right?"

Lorna looked directly into his face for the first time and was shocked by how young he looked despite the stubble of light brown whiskers on his face. His curly hair fell down over his forehead and his brows were wrinkled with concern. Gray-green eyes took in the pallor of her skin, and he shook her gently.

"Get a hold on yoreself, ma'am. We got to get that mess out from under 'er 'n get 'er cleaned up. I'll lift 'er up 'n ya pull it out 'n put somethin' clean there, if'n ya got it."

"All right. I'm ... sorry. Oh, I'm so glad you came. I ... couldn't have done what you did. She'd have died!"

"She ain't out a the woods—"

"You think she'll die?" Lorna asked fearfully.

"I don't know," he said gently, and lifted the pale and exhausted girl. "She's been through the fires a hell 'n she ain't strong. I could see that right off."

"How did you know what to do?"

"I helped another fellow with a Mexican woman down in Santa Fe. She was a stronger woman..." He left his words hanging. "This one's just skin and bones," he said softly, laying her gently down on the clean bedding and pulling a clean sheet up over her. "You want me to go out while you wash 'er up?"

"Not unless you want to." Lorna brought a pan of warm water to the bedside. "It was so awful."

"Where's her man?"

Lorna glanced at him. He was bathing the sweat from Bonnie's face. "She doesn't have one," she said tersely.

"Who did this to her?"

"It was a dirty, low-down hunk of crowbait who's not fit to be called a man. Bonnie's folks sold her to him because she's a cripple!" Frustrated, frightened and angry, Lorna fairly shouted the words.

The man, who was not much more than a boy, gazed down at the still face of the girl. Finally he spoke, and his muttered words barely reached Lorna's ears. "Poor little thing," he whispered sadly. His eyes moved over her quiet face and down to the arm that lay at her side. He picked it up and lightly caressed the handless stump with his fingertips. "Ya been alivin' in hell, ain't ya?"

Something in his voice and the sad look on his face caught at Lorna's heartstrings. She burst into tears, stood, and slipped out the door to stand with her arm against the cabin wall and her face against it. Racking sobs shook her and she cried as she had not done in many years.

Cooper heard the sound of the woman weeping before he rounded the corner of the house. *The young girl had died!* He wasn't surprised. The poor thing had gone through too much. He'd like to get his hands on the sonofabitch who'd misused her. He wondered what connection Lorna had with the girl. She was crying her heart out. He went up to her and put a comforting hand on her shoulder.

"I'm sorry, ma'am."

Lorna jumped as if he had touched her with fire. She whirled in a crouched position, her head thrust forward, her moccasined feet planted firmly on the ground. She jerked at the knife she wore in the sash at her waist and glared up at him, her eyes as bright and as furious as those of a treed bobcat.

"Don't touch me! Don't you *dare* touch me, you . . . horny, rutting swine!" she snarled. "I despise you and your kind. Bonnie'll die because of men like you!"

Cooper backed away. This small black-haired woman was set to fight him! She couldn't weigh much more than a hundred pounds dripping wet, yet she held the knife as if she was determined to use it. The silence between them seemed to crackle as though each generated a violent lightning storm. Neither of them moved nor spoke for what seemed an endless space of time. He stared at her, all his senses completely absorbed in her, as if he were wrapped tightly together with her in an invisible cocoon. A tightness grew in Cooper's chest and a numbness came up his neck and rendered him speechless. For an instant, in a small part of his brain, there was a flicker of recognition. It was as if somewhere in time, he had known this woman well. Her face and form were not strange to him, nor were her feelings. The mood would pass in an instant. Knowing that, he waited.

The anger left Lorna as quickly as it had come. She had been unreasonably unfair and she knew it. She looked at the tall, fair-haired man with unabashed curiosity. He was whip-lash thin, yet the muscles of his shoulders, arms and thighs bulged his buckskins. His hips were lean and he wore a gun strapped below his waist, as did most men. But he wore a bowie knife, too. Both knife scabbard and gun holster were tied down. His light sandy hair was straight and thick, his eyes a clear sky blue. There was an amazing quietness about him.

"I'm ... sorry. It was mean of me to blame you for what happened to Bonnie. My name is Lorna." She tucked the knife in her belt and held out her hand.

"Cooper Parnell." Cooper took the step necessary to reach her hand and clasped it firmly. "I understand how you feel," he murmured, and meant it.

Her level brows lifted and her eyes widened slightly. As her features mirrored her changing moods, he felt as if the whole of her character lay quite near the surface. Frankly and openly, observing each detail, she looked him over from the top of his head to the toes of his dusty, well-worn boots. Never before had he undergone such a close scrutiny from a woman. It was done openly, and impersonally.

"What did you do with ... it?"

Her words jarred him back to reality and it took a few seconds for him to answer. "I buried it deep and rolled a rock over it."

"Thank you."

"Ma'am? That girl's been mistreated something awful. Name the one that did it and if I cross his path I'll give him a taste of what he gave that girl."

"Bonnie and I thank you, Mr. Parnell, but I'll take care of it. He'll pay." She looked Cooper steadily in the eye.

He liked the way she stood; her feet planted solidly on the ground, her slim figure erect, head up, shoulders back. Pride showed in the tilt of her chin. She'd made a statement of fact. It was no idle threat. He believed her, and deep within him something warm and sweet grew strong and tall.

"Where do you come from?" he asked, but he was thinking, What a woman. What a glorious, wonderful woman!

She was turning away, but she said over her shoulder, "From Light's Mountain."

Evening came and still Cooper hadn't mentioned the reason he and Griffin had come to the cabin. He chopped a supply of wood for the small fireplace and carried fresh water up from the stream. The girl, Bonnie, lay on the pallet as still as death, her face almost as white as the sheet that covered her. Late in the afternoon she had opened her eyes, sought Lorna's face, then reassured, wearily closed them again. Griffin and Lorna had taken turns sitting beside her, making sure she was covered, even in the warm room. Griffin had said that due to the loss of blood she might chill. Cooper had came to realize that the young nester had more than a normal amount of doctoring knowledge and wondered where he had learned it.

"Mr. Parnell." Lorna came out of the cabin when Cooper brought the two horses up and tied them to the corral posts. "Are you leaving?"

"I hadn't thought to, ma'am, not till some of your folks come to help you with the woman. If it's all right we'll put our horses in the corral and camp down by the creek."

"I'm obliged to you for staying." She walked past him toward the pole corral, lowered the bar gate, and went into the shed. She shoved aside a door at the back of the shed revealing a cave in the cliff, and whistled softly. Cooper heard an answering nicker and a big, gray horse with a white streak that extended from beneath its forelock to its nose came to her and nuzzled her shoulder. She patted the sides of its big face and murmured unintelligible words into the straight, peaked ears that twitched back and forth.

A second horse moved out of the shadowy cave and Lorna went to it, rubbed its nose and then slipped her arms around its neck. She talked to it, making soft little sounds. The horse bobbed its head up and down, almost lifting her light body off the ground. Then, holding it by its mane, she led the second horse out into the light.

Cooper had been leaning against the cabin wall. He straightened and blinked in surprise. Goddamn! It was *his* mare she was leading from the cave! A wave of sickness rolled over him. *She* was the thief! But— His mare was only half broken in, and she was leading this one out of the corral and down to the creek with only a handhold on her mane. The gray followed closely behind her, giving her shoulder an affectionate nudge from time to time.

Cooper watched, almost disbelieving what he was seeing. This docile horse couldn't be the spirited animal he'd bought, and yet all the markings were the same and this mare, too, would obviously foal soon. In hard-eyed silence he stalked after them. There was one way to tell if the mare was his or not; the letters CP would be under her mane on the right side if she were his. He always branded his breeding stock with a small iron he carried in his saddlebag.

A stillness of diffused sunlight and dense shade hung over the timbered valley—a quiet so complete that the rush of the water traveling over stones on its way south and the plaintive song of a mountain thrush seemed surprisingly loud in that impenetrable quiet. He walked up to the mare and she skittered sideways away from him. The big gray reared and whirled to lash out at him with his deadly hind legs.

"Watch it," Lorna cautioned, speaking softly. "This one's half wild and Gray Wolf thinks you may hurt me." She kept a tight hold on the mare's mane, and extended her hand out to the gray. "It's all right. He's a friend. Come, boy." She made small smacking sounds between words. The gray calmed, came to her hand and nuzzled it with his nose. "Go on and drink, my sweetings," she crooned. "I'll be right here." With a pat on the rump of each horse she sent them into the stream. She stood at the edge of the water with her back to Cooper. "Gray Wolf is very protective. It'll take a little time for him to get used to you."

Long minutes went by while Cooper's mind groped for an answer. She seemed an unlikely person to be a horse thief, yet when the mare skittered sideways and bobbed her head, he'd seen the brand he'd put on her no more than a week ago. What had Lorna done to the horse to make her docile? Had she fed her the leaves of that hemplike plant that had such a calming effect? While the horses were drinking she made the little smacking noises with her lips, occasionally murmuring soft words when they raised their heads and looked at her. To Cooper's utter dismay, they came out of the water and to her when she lifted a hand to each of them.

"Have you had enough, my beauties?" she asked in a whispering voice. "I didn't want to leave you in that dark, old cave all day, but I was afraid someone would see you. We don't have to be afraid, now. We have friends with us. Did you eat all that sweet grass I cut for you? Come now, back to the corral." The two horses followed her into the enclosure. She rubbed their noses with gentle fingers and spoke to them as if they understood each word she said. "You be nice to her, Gray Wolf," she said to the big gray. "She's going to be a mama soon. If our friends are still here tomorrow and if Bonnie is better, we'll go out to that high, sweet grass and you can eat your fill."

Lorna left the corral and replaced the bar gate. The two followed her and stood with heads over the poles. She gave each a final pat and went to where Cooper had tied Roscoe and Griffin's horse. Cooper was startled out of his dreamlike, confused state when she patted Roscoe on the neck and moved to go behind him.

"Lorna! Don't—"

She smiled at him over her shoulder. "He'll not hurt me."
With her hand on Roscoe's rump she passed behind him and
Cooper held his breath. Roscoe could batter down the side
of a barn with his powerful hind legs. Cooper stood rooted
to the ground while she crooned and stroked each animal.
Then she came toward him, her face pale and calm, and he
felt as though he were drowning, the waters closing over him;
to his dying day, he would not forget this moment.

"You'd best not put your horses in the corral, Mr. Parnell.
Gray Wolf will be jealous and fight them."

"He didn't fight the mare."

"No. He took to her right away." She smiled while she
was speaking and then sobered. "He understands the mare is
with foal. He'll look out for her."

"The mare is mine. My brand is under her mane." Cooper
blurted the words lest he hold them back forever.

Lorna's answer was accompanied by a gentle, musical
laugh. "She's yours? Well, I'm glad of that! I was afraid she
belonged to someone else."

Cooper gazed at her, bewilderment in his eyes. "Why did
you take her?" he asked quietly.

"Because she was running free. I thought that maybe Brice
or some of his friends had come and would find where Volney
and I had hid Bonnie."

He looked down into her luminous face, soft mouth and
brilliant eyes. He wanted desperately to believe her, yet he
had to persist with what he knew to be a fact.

"I staked her out while I fished in the river."

"She was running free," Lorna said calmly. "I climbed the
cliff and looked off down the valley. I saw her among the
trees. When I was sure she was alone, I went to her."

"You went to her? She let you walk right up to her?" An
edge had crept into Cooper's voice. If Lorna noticed it she
never let on.

"Not at first," she explained patiently. "I talked to her for
awhile. Then I rode her around the mountain. It was a long

way. I didn't want to be gone from Bonnie for so long, but I couldn't bring her down the side of the cliff."

"You want me to believe that you rode a half broken horse for a good fifteen or twenty miles—at night, without a saddle or bridle?" What she was saying was impossible and disappointment knifed through Cooper. The mare could have slipped the halter and run free, he conceded silently, but as for the rest of it . . .

"I don't lie. If you think I do, take your horse and go."

He looked at her and noted the wariness in her eyes and the tightness that had come into her face. "Lorna, I want to believe you—"

She lifted her shoulders in a shrug and when she brought them down they seemed to slump, as if she, too, was suffering from a keen disappointment. She turned to walk away from him, then paused and turned back.

"'Truth is unadorned, falsehoods are wrapped in cunning phrases.'" She quoted the words quietly and turned away.

The quote had such a familiar ring that Cooper called after her, "Who said that?"

She stopped, but didn't turn around. "I did," she said firmly, and walked rapidly to the cabin.

Chapter
Four

It was night, and Cooper restlessly prowled along the stony bank of the creek where he had thrown out his bedroll. He debated about building a fire and boiling coffee, but decided against it. A fire, no matter how small, could be seen from the hills above and he didn't want to be the cause of bringing more trouble down on Lorna and Bonnie.

He thought of the glitter that had come into Lorna's eyes and how her face had tightened when he insinuated she was lying. But, godammit! How could he think anything else? Now, after he'd thought about how she'd handled the horses, he wasn't so sure that she couldn't have done exactly what she said. It was uncanny how still Roscoe had stood when she went up to him. The stallion didn't like strangers, women in particular, yet he didn't turn a hair while she patted his rump and swung his tail. Was the woman a . . . witch? If not, she certainly was a charmer.

Just thinking about Lorna made him uncomfortable and warm. It hampered his thinking, as sensuality assumed dominance over his mind. He knew very little about women, but he knew men and their ways. Since he was a boy he'd been able to pick the ones who dreamed and created from the ones who raped and destroyed. The only woman in his life had been his mother, Sylvia. He thought of her now, back on the ranch near Junction City. She had really bloomed this last year and all because Arnie Henderson had come calling. Cooper chuckled when he remembered how embarrassed his mother had been at first. Arnie had come out from Illinois to work for Logan Horn, and now Cooper suspected he was urging his mother to move to the Morning Sun spread. He would miss her, but she deserved all the happiness she could get. God knew, she hadn't had much when she was young.

His thoughts came back to the present. He had found his mare. The sensible thing to do would be to take the horse and ride out. Griffin would stay with the women, so he'd not have *that* on his conscience. But an unnerving, alien thing was inside him, pulling at him. Although his common sense told him to go, he wasn't ready to leave just yet.

Cooper sat on a rock, watching the water glimmer and ripple over and around stones worn smooth by its passing. He recalled each word Lorna had spoken and tried to find logic in her explanation. Suddenly something she'd said flashed across his mind: *He would find where Volney and I hid Bonnie.* Surely there couldn't be more than one person in the territory with the unlikely name of Volney!

The Volney Burbank he knew was old and gaunt and suspicious of almost everything and everybody. As far as he knew, Volney was the only bona fide mountain man in this part of the country. The old man was little more than a hermit. He ran a line of traps in the winter and collected bounty on the pelts of various predators he killed. Cooper knew for a fact he had boundless respect for the wild creatures he hunted and almost none for the human race. A couple of times a year his nocturnal wanderings would bring him to the ranch and he would pick up a grub bag, leave a pelt or two, and pass on to Cooper any information he had about a wild horse herd in the area. Cooper was the only one at the ranch he'd pass the time of day with. To everyone else he was an enigma, an unkempt old man with a mane of gray-yellow hair about his thin shoulders.

Cooper liked the old man, although he thought he lived an unnecessarily monastic life. There was little doubt that Volney knew about everything that went on in the territory, but he chose to tell none of it. As far as Cooper could recall, he'd never mentioned anyone by name, or named places he'd been. Up to now Cooper hadn't given it any thought, but could the old mountain man be the Volney Lorna spoke about?

He turned and looked back toward the cabin. Through the open door, he could see a faint glow made by the fire in the hearth. His thoughts turned to Griffin, the young nester he'd saved from hanging and who in turn had saved the girl's life—for the time being, at least. He was a strange one, Cooper thought. He had a dead serious confidence about him and a knowledge that seemed too heavy for his years. Now, he and Lorna were trying to rouse the girl enough to get her to swallow a broth Lorna had made from boiling dried beef. Cooper had little hope the girl would live. She'd looked pale as death the last time he'd looked in on her.

"Is there anything else we can do?" Lorna's voice was low, her face drawn into a worried frown. She placed the half-empty cup on the floor beside her and watched Griffin ease Bonnie back down onto the bed.

"The only thin' I can think of is put 'er hips 'n legs up higher 'n 'er head. I heard tell of that bein' done if there was a lot a bleedin'," Griffin said softly. He had a worried look on his young face as if he really cared about the girl who moved restlessly on the pallet.

Lorna studied him as if seeing him for the first time. "Do you think we should do it? She's not bleeding much, but she needs all the blood she's got."

"I don't think it'd hurt none."

"I'll get a blanket and fold it." Lorna stood and looked

down at Griffin's dark head and on an impulse asked, "What's your other name?"

There was a long silence before he said, "I don't go by it, ma'am, unless I got to write it on a paper or somethin'." He lifted his head and looked up. Even in the dim light she could see the desolation in his eyes.

"I'm sorry for prying." Lorna placed a hand on his shoulder. "I don't care who you are or what you've done. I'm grateful you're here with me now."

"I've done time in Yuma, ma'am. I killed my first man 'cause I wanted to, the rest of them was atryin' to kill me—"

"Don't tell me you've done bad things," she said quickly. "I won't believe they weren't forced on you. My granny said the best men are the ones who've been tested by the fires of hell. Sometime I'll tell you about my granny and my Grandpa Light."

"I been to hell, ma'am. I spent five years there. I'm not wanted by the law, now. That's not the reason I don't say my name. It's that I'm kind a shamed, but I'll tell you. It's Fort. Fort Griffin. My ma was a whore there, 'n not knowin' which of the men was my pa, gave me the fort's name. I think she thought it was a joke on the men." He watched her closely, as if trying to see whether she made light of what he was saying.

Not a flicker of emotion crossed Lorna's face, although she never felt more like crying. "There's no need for you to be ashamed of your name," she said softly but firmly. "Your pa may have been the bravest, most honorable man at the fort. Besides, you don't have to live in the shadow of what your ma, your pa or anyone else has done. You're living now, and the kind of man you make yourself to be is up to you. A name has nothing to do with it." When she finished speaking he nodded and looked away from her intense gaze. "Griffin? Do you mind me asking why you wear an empty holster?"

"No, ma'am. I was roped 'n pulled outta the saddle by

some fellers pushin' nesters off open range. They took my gun 'n my knife 'n hung me so I'd die slow. Parnell cut me down. I'm ridin' with him to help find a mare stole from him, then I'm agoin' back to a spot I picked for myself. And I ain't bein' pushed off it like I was trash." Anger and determination laid a sharp edge to his voice.

"Mr. Parnell's mare wasn't stolen. I found the mare running free and brought her here. Mr. Parnell doesn't believe me. More than likely he'll take the mare and ride out at dawn."

Griffin looked up quickly. "I believe you if you say that's how it was. I owe that gent plenty, ma'am, but I ain't aleavin' you here with this sick girl. That old man you was atellin' me 'bout might not come back."

Lorna's hand found his shoulder again. "Thank you, Griffin. I'd be obliged if you'd stay."

"Is she married to the one who done this to 'er?"

"I'm sure she's not. Her folks were on their way to California when Brice bought her from them. She said he got a preacher to marry them. Some preacher!" she said crossly. "Bonnie said Brice got him out of a saloon. She'd fought, cried and tried to run away until then."

"Brice? Is that his name? I'll kill him if'n I come onto him," Griffin said in a tone that clearly stated he meant what he said. He picked up Bonnie's thin, blue-veined hand and looked at the broken nails, the cuts and scratches. "Poor thing. She's had to do ever'thin' with this one little hand. If she can do that, I oughtta be able to bear up with a name like Fort Griffin."

"Oh, Griffin! You're a good man," Lorna breathed, caught by the emotion in his voice and the sadness reflected in his eyes. Her voice was tight, almost choked. "I'll go down to the creek and wash," she said suddenly. "Then I'll sit with Bonnie while you sleep."

Lorna left the cabin. She was a solitary person and needed time to be alone. She walked out into the light of a half moon that rode high in the clear sky. She could see the outline of the man sitting beside the creek with his face turned toward the cabin and deliberately went toward him so he would see her, then moved behind him and on down the rocky bank of the creek. She could feel his eyes on her, but she wasn't afraid. He'd not follow her. The image of his face came to her clearly out of the darkness. She knew him long ago, in another place and time. The thought flashed through her mind and for the space of a dozen heartbeats her steps were unsteady. Granny said she'd felt that way about Grandpa—she said Maggie knew when she first set eyes on Light that she was his woman. Lorna had known Cooper Parnell before. She didn't know when or where, but they were together, just the two of them. The thought was not startling and it hung stubbornly in her mind. She made no effort to shut it out. It didn't matter, she told herself. Only this life mattered, and she would know if he was the one.

Cooper saw the shirt in Lorna's hand and knew she was going to bathe. He also knew her reason for coming toward him when she could have saved steps by going directly to the creek; she wanted him to know that it was her out there in the darkness and not someone trying to sneak up on the cabin. Good thinking, Cooper thought, but how could she have known that he'd not follow her and have his way with her? She was the most disturbing, baffling, exciting woman he'd ever met.

He sat on the rock and time passed slowly. He drew a deep breath and tried to calm the unease that had been fermenting in his breast. Down the valley he heard a coyote call to his mate and her answer echoed in the stillness. The soft music of the cicadas and crickets mingled with the sound of the rippling water along with the faint hoot of an owl and the twit of a scrappy nightbird. He strained his ears for the sound of Lorna coming back.

Suddenly, drifting gently on the night breeze, he heard the sweetest sound he'd ever heard. It was as if the wind were singing. He felt a tingling start low at the base of his spine and travel upward to the nape of his neck where his hair tingled. His face felt as if it was being pricked by a thousand needles. He found himself on his feet, straining his ears, listening with awe and wonder. He'd never heard anything like it before. The voice had a wild, unearthly quality, like the wind. It was full of love and pain, joy and sorrow, yet strong, sweet and powerful. He couldn't distinguish the faint words, but he was sure Lorna was praying in song. It didn't occur to him to wonder how he knew. He could scarcely keep his feet from moving toward her as he listened to the music that seemed to be spun from the air. When it stopped he could feel the thud of his heart beating against his chest, and he let his breath out slowly.

After a few long moments of quiet, he moved a dozen yards in the direction she had gone and stepped up into the dark shadow of the trees, making himself invisible if she should pass. She shouldn't have come out here alone, he told himself, needing an excuse for being there. There could be a cougar, or a two-legged varmint prowling around. He leaned against the trunk of a tree and watched for her to come around the bend in the creek.

She began to sing very softly again and Cooper felt once more the tingling thrill he'd felt before. He was closer to her, and could hear the words clearly.

"When my hair has turned to silver,
   and my eyes shall dimmer grow.
I will lean upon some loved one,
   through my twilight years I go.
I will ask of you a promise,
   worth to me a world of gold;
It is only this, my darling:
   that you'll love me when I'm old."

Cooper listened while she sang verse after verse of the haunting little song, and then another. She was singing for the pure pleasure of it now, comforting herself in song. Although he felt like an intruder, his feet were leaden and he stood beside the tree as if planted there.

There was a long moment of utter stillness when she stopped singing. Then he saw movement coming along the creek bank. She walked slowly, confidently. She wasn't tall, but looked taller because of her carriage, her shoulders squared, her chin tilted. His eyes clung to the slim figure that moved so lightly along the rough path. When she neared the place where he was standing in the shadows, she paused.

"Good night, Mr. Parnell," she called softly with a trace of laughter in her voice.

Cooper was so surprised he couldn't answer. How could she have possibly known he was standing there? He cursed under his breath, more angry at himself than at her. He felt like a child caught looking through a keyhole, and it wasn't a comfortable feeling.

Cooper did not ride out at dawn as he had planned. After restless hours in his bedroll he had fallen into a light sleep. Before dawn he awakened when he heard his name.

"Parnell."

He was instantly alert, threw back the blanket and sat up. "Griffin?"

"Yeah."

Cooper heard the crackle of brush under bootheels before he saw him.

"I don't like to come up on a man in his bedroll without him knowin'," Griffin said and squatted down beside him.

"You can get your head blown off doing it," Cooper said dryly.

"The girl's still asleepin'."

"Do you think she'll make it?"

"I don't know. That woman in there's aworkin' her head off to see that she does."

"There's not a doctor in a hundred miles."

"There ain't no time to get help for 'er. She'll come outta it today or she ain't agoin' to. She's weaker'n a cat—ain't got no strength a'tall." Griffin picked up a twig and twirled it between his fingers. "You aridin' out this mornin'?"

"I'd figured on it, but—"

"I'm stayin'. I want ya to know I'm obliged for what ya done for me. If a time comes 'n I can lend ya a hand, it'd be a favor if ya'd ask me."

Cooper let a long, thoughtful moment pass before he spoke. "You're thinking you owe me and its not sitting easy on you. Is that it?"

"It's part a it. If we'd ever come down across the fence from each other, I don't want no beholden strings on me. I'd wanna come at ya—flat out."

"I'd expect you to. But that isn't likely, unless you go maverick and try to take what's mine."

"I told ya I'm no horse thief." He stared fixedly at Cooper. "When I leave here I'm agoin' to get my horses 'n sell 'em, 'n I'm afilin' on that land ole Clayhill run me off of 'n I'm stayin' on it."

Cooper shrugged. "You're biting off a big chaw."

"Ya can choke on a little chaw same as a big 'un."

"What kind of horses you got?"

"Half-broke grullas. Good, strong, work stock."

"The army will take them if you're of a mind to drive them that far. If not, I know a fellow looking for work stock. I sell mine to him or the army, but I can't find them or break them fast enough. Look up Logan Horn at the Morning Sun. He'll give you a fair price."

"Ain't he ole Clayhill's half-breed?"

"You have something against dealing with a half-breed?" Cooper's voice had turned as hard as iron.

"Not against a half-breed, but I sure as hell ain't dealin' with no Clayhill." Griffin hurled the angry words back into Cooper's face.

"It's up to you, but I'd not put the Clayhill name on Logan

unless you're willing to back it up. He doesn't have no truck with the old man any more than—" He broke off when Griffin stood.

"I'll look 'em up if I make it through Dunbar 'n his bunch."

Cooper got to his feet. "Dunbar's out to make his mark with the old man. But I guess you know that."

"I know it, but he can die from a hole in the head same's anybody. Lorna said come up for coffee. I got a notion to go hunt up some fresh meat."

"I saw a good size herd of elk up on the side of the hill when we came down through there yesterday. I'll see if I can knock one down."

"It's good of ya, knowin' yo're awantin' to ride out."

"It wouldn't be right to leave Lorna alone with the girl if she's bad off." Cooper grimaced in self-disgust. He didn't have to give an excuse for not leaving.

"Lorna ain't no slouch when it comes to doctorin'. She's got a basket full a roots 'n thin's she said her granny learned her to use. I tell ya, Parnell, she's the beatinest woman, 'n the best I ever seen with a knife. She can pin a fly to the wall. It was plumb pleasant to hear her atellin' 'bout her great-grandpa 'n grandma back in the olden days. They walked all the way out here from Saint Louie, just the two of 'em, when this country had nothin' but Injuns, bears 'n rattlesnakes."

A sudden stab of anger and hurt pierced Cooper. He faced it for what it was—jealousy. Griffin had been the one to share the night hours with Lorna. He tried to shrug off the feeling by flipping the sand and burrs out of his bedroll and rolling it into a tight roll.

"I'll be up soon as I saddle my horse," he said curtly and headed for the corral.

He could smell meat frying when he led Roscoe up to the cabin and tied him to a rail. The rumbling in his stomach reminded him that he had been eating sparingly for the past several days. He stepped up to the open door and hesitated while his mind absorbed the scene within. Griffin was kneeling on the pallet holding Bonnie up against his arm and trying to get her to drink from a cup. Lorna was beside the fire forking meat out of a skillet onto a tin plate.

"Morning, Mr. Parnell."

"Morning, Miss . . . Lorna."

"There's meat and biscuits to go with coffee. Do you have a cup in your saddlebag? I don't have an extra one."

"Yes, ma'am, I do. I'll get it.'

She looked worn out, Cooper thought as he backed out of the door. Her hair was tied close to the back of her head and again in two more places making a long rope that lay on her back. She still wore the britches, the long belted shirt and well-worn moccasins. She had looked at him directly when she spoke and he could see dark smudges beneath her eyes caused by little or no sleep for the past two nights. His eyes had roamed her face and the strange feeling stirred in him again. *Had he been too long without a woman?*

When he returned, she was sitting on the floor with her back to the wall watching Griffin gently urge Bonnie to drink. Cooper squatted down beside the fire, filled his cup and picked up the plate. He moved away from the heat of the fire and settled down on his haunches to eat.

"Do you think she's better, Griff?" Lorna asked.

"She's adrinkin'. It's a good sign. She needs to eat somethin'. Do ya have anythin' a'tall to make gruel?"

"I used the last of the cornmeal. All that's left is flour for biscuits. I could go home and get more but it's a good day's ride there and back."

"I've got a bag of dried beans." Cooper watched her head turn slowly toward him. "Mexicans swear by beans. They eat them three times a day."

She looked at him with her great, violet-blue eyes for so long that Cooper began to think she would refuse his offer. Finally, when he was convinced she wouldn't speak, she murmured, "Thank you."

He finished the meal and got to his feet. "I'll water the horses before I go," he said to Griffin. "She'd better get some sleep." He jerked his head toward Lorna. The young nester looked up and nodded. Lorna remained quiet, but Cooper could feel her eyes on him as he went to the door. Before he stepped outside he turned. Lorna was looking up at him, her eyes glazed with fatigue. For a frozen moment in time they maintained that pose, their eyes locked. She was a beauty, Cooper thought. She was a woman to cherish. He had a sudden, strong urge to protect her, to hold her and watch over her while she slept. What would she do if he went to her, knelt down beside her, and told her he wanted to hold her in his arms? Would she turn on him like she had last night and try to stab him with the knife she wore in her belt? Someday, he decided grimly, he'd have to find out.

Cooper dropped the leather bag containing the beans inside the door without saying a word. He mounted his horse, cursing himself for being a tongue-tied fool. By God, when he came back he was going to talk to her and see if he could find out what it was about her that made her so different from any of the other women he'd known. In an angry, impatient mood, he kicked Roscoe unnecessarily hard. The surprised stallion sank down onto his powerful haunches and sprang forward, his momentum carrying him to the woodpile. He jumped it with ease and sped down the track.

It was almost noon when Cooper spotted a small herd of elk grazing in a grassy basin. He made a wide swing behind them so that he'd come up on them from downwind. An hour later he had made his kill, taken the parts of the carcass he wanted and left the rest for scavengers. He figured he had doubled back trailing the herd and was now only a few miles from the cabin.

Cooper had always studied his surroundings with an eye for detail, a habit he'd acquired while searching for wild horse herds. He could draw a map showing each river and stream he'd crossed since leaving the ranch a month ago. He paid strict attention to the quality of grass and to the summer water supply and winter shelter. Now, studying the valley, he realized the water supply was almost inexhaustible, the vegetation lush, and the hills surrounding the valley formed a natural barrier against livestock straying too far from the home base. He wondered what had caused the nester who had built here to leave.

Roscoe was almost incapable of ignoring the lush grass and had to stop every so often to snatch a mouthful, so they moved slowly down the valley heading for the stream that flowed alongside the cabin where Lorna and Griffin waited. The animal path he followed had all but vanished in the undergrowth, so he let Roscoe pick his way leisurely while his thoughts strayed back to Lorna.

She had remained on his mind all day, a disturbing but pleasing presence. He could see her as clearly as if she stood before him, even to the cleft in her lower lip. Her skin was pure cream, her mouth soft and red as an apple, and tendrils of glossy black hair curled about her beautiful, heart-shaped face. It was her eyes, deep violet-blue, a blue of warmth and darkness he'd never seen before, that haunted his thoughts even more than her boyishly thin body with the small pointed breasts that nudged at the baggy shirt she wore. She seemed fragile, like a shy, wild deer, poised and ready for flight, but also wiry, like a small cat that would fight if cornered. It was something about the way she moved that made him think this; a mixture of caution and alertness, so finely tuned that at any time she could explode into action. She'd said she'd come from Light's Mountain. He'd heard of it. Wasn't it a two or three day ride southeast of his place; a vast, almost unpeopled mountain accessible only by high Indian trails?

From down the valley a high yodeling call came to him riding on the wind. Cooper pulled Roscoe up sharply. Then he heard the muffled explosion of a six-gun. Tense, he waited and listened. The silence was broken only by the faraway gobble of a turkey and, closer to him, the sound of a squirrel scampering in the dry leaves. Uneasiness touched him and then mounted to fear. The only gun at the cabin was Lorna's rifle and it was not a rifle shot he'd heard. His anxiety transmitted itself to Roscoe, and the stallion danced nervously. Cooper held him in check for a long moment while he listened for another shot, and when there was none, he let up on the tight reins and sent the horse thundering toward the cabin.

The sun was up above the treetops when Lorna took the soiled cloths from Bonnie's bed down to the creek. She went downstream, washed them in the swiftly moving water, and hung them on bushes out of sight of the cabin. Bonnie had roused enough to murmur that she was hungry and that she could smell the brown beans boiling gently in the iron kettle. Griffin had fed her bits of biscuit dipped in the honey that Lorna had brought to sweeten their coffee, and then Bonnie had fallen asleep again.

Lorna walked slowly back to the cabin, problems nagging her mind. She had to find a place for Bonnie. Brice would come for her sooner or later and there would be nothing she could do, short of killing him, that would prevent him from taking her. She had thought of taking her to White Bull's village, but this time of the year her Indian friends were in the north. She hadn't mentioned that possibility to Bonnie because the mere thought of Indians scared her half out of her wits. Another worry that nagged Lorna was the fact that Volney hadn't returned. What had happened to keep him from coming back as he had said he would? And there was Frank to worry about. Her father had avoided her like the plague since she had caught him, Hollis and the Bettses with old man Prichard's cows. Lorna knew he was ashamed to face her, but he was too weak to break away from Brice and his influence. She just wished he had more . . . guts!

When she entered the cabin, Griffin lifted his head with a start. He sat with his back against the wall, his chin resting on his chest.

"Why don't you sleep for awhile?" Lorna asked. "You didn't sleep a wink last night."

"I never caught ya with yore eyes shut, ma'am. Bonnie's got no fever 'n she's asleepin'. It's the best thin' for 'er."

"I told her the babe was dead, and all she said was she figured it was. She wanted to know if it had ... everything it was suppose to have. I told her that it was perfect. It eased her mind and she went to sleep. I don't see how she came through all that, Griff. I really thought she'd die."

"She's tough. Hard life's made 'er tough. It'd killed a softer woman. Not that she ain't a sweet, soft woman," he added quickly.

"I know what you mean. As soon as she's well enough to move, I'll have to find another place for her. None of the mountain people I know will take her in. They're all afraid of Brice. I was hoping Volney would come back. He said he'd try to find a place where she could work for her keep without doing it on her back."

"Bonnie's not *that* kind a woman." Griffin didn't know why he said that, or why he felt so strong about it. Then, as if thinking aloud, he said, "She's done what she had to in order to keep body 'n soul together."

It surprised him how easily he could talk to Lorna. He could count on his fingers the number of times during the last ten years he'd talked to a good woman. He'd known the whores in the bordellos south of the border, but they hadn't wanted to talk much. While he'd been here with Lorna and Bonnie, he'd felt decent, almost like anyone else, and he wasn't looking forward to the time when he'd ride away and leave them.

Bonnie woke and looked around drowsily. She didn't appear to be frightened when Griffin slid his arm beneath her shoulders to lift her so she could drink the cup of water Lorna brought to her. She drank thirstily, her eyes on Griffin's face, then closed them wearily and drifted back to sleep.

"You can sleep too, if you like." Lorna sat down on the

end of the straw pallet, untied her long mane of black hair and pulled it over her shoulder. The end of it lay in her lap. She began to stroke it with a wide-toothed heavy comb; lightly at first, until it was smooth enough for the teeth of the comb to penetrate the heavy mass.

Griffin tried to turn his eyes away from her, but it was a sight he'd not witnessed for a long time—a woman combing her long, silky hair. She was as beautiful and serene as the Madonna in the cathedral at Juarez. The feeling that came over him was much like the same feeling he had when he walked into the cool, quiet church after being released from the hellhole that was Yuma Prison, and knelt at the feet of the mother of Christ.

"Griff?"

This Madonna spoke to him. He brought his mind back to the present with difficulty. "Are ya sure ya don't want to sleep awhile?"

"I've got too much on my mind. I'll sleep after Mr. Parnell comes back."

"If you're sure, ma'am." Griffin lay down on the floor with his face to the wall and pillowed his head in his arm. So much had happened in the last few days, yet he had never felt so at peace in all his young life. He was alive, he was here, and he wasn't alone. That was the last thought to register in his mind before he fell asleep.

Lorna combed the tangles from her hair, retied it at the nape of her neck, and then with several strips of rawhide, tied it every few inches down the full length to keep it from tangling. She longed to plunge naked into the creek, but even more so, she longed to get on Gray Wolf's back and ride like the wind to some faraway place, stretch her arms wide, feel the warmth of the sunshine on her face, and release the full volume of her voice in song.

She reached over and laid the back of her hand against Bonnie's cheek. No fever, thank God! She lay down, pillowing her head on her arm. Her thoughts turned to Cooper

Parnell. She had been sure he would ride out at dawn. Why hadn't he believed her when she told him about the mare? And why had she felt almost betrayed that he would think she lied? This morning he had looked at her as if he knew her every thought. Did he know that she wanted to follow him out the door, ride with him on the hunt, be alone with him? Did he have the same strange feeling for her that she had for him? Was that the reason he'd stayed?

She was tired. Her eyelids felt as if they were weighted with lead; she'd close them for just a moment . . . It seemed only seconds later that she came up out of a deep sleep, her mind mixed and unclear, her eyes trying to focus on the men coming through the door.

"There's the sonofabitch! Get 'em!"

Lorna was brought to full wakefulness by the loud, harsh voice. It also brought Griffin up off the floor grabbing at an empty holster. Two men sprang on him and he was flung back by their tremendous weight. Quick as a cat, Lorna dived for the rifle beside the door. A huge hand lashed out and grabbed the heavy rope of hair hanging down her back. She was hauled back with such force that tears of pain gushed from her eyes, but she never uttered a sound.

A man with a red stubble of beard on his face gave a shout of laughter. "Wal, looky here, boys. Looky here what we got. We got us a bonus fer acatchin' our horse thief."

Chapter
Five

Lorna made no attempt to struggle against the superior strength of the man holding her. Even in her near panic, she realized the folly of it. Trying to foresee what future action she might take, she made every effort to conceal the knife in her sash. Fear gave way to a feeling of such implacable hatred for men of this breed that droplets of sweat broke out on her forehead.

Griffin was hauled to his feet, defenseless, but jerking violently at the hands holding him. The first thing he saw that registered in his mind was Dunbar with his arm wrapped tightly around Lorna, her back pulled to his chest.

"Get yore filthy hands off 'er, ya stupid bastard!" he shouted hoarsely and tried to lunge forward. The two men holding him hauled him back and slammed him against the wall.

"Who cut ya down, horse thief? Was it yore woman here?"

"Let 'er go. I ne'er set eyes on 'er till this mornin'."

"Ya shore as hell didn't cut that rope yoreself. If'n I hadn't a got to wantin' that horse ya was aridin' I might a not knowed. It warn't no chore a'tall to track ya here. There ain't agoin' to be no little gal to climb the tree 'n cut ya down this time. We'll hang ya proper, like a horse thief ort a be hung."

"Lorna! Lorna—" Bonnie's voice was weak but loud enough to hold a note of hysteria. Her eyes were wide with fright and she cowered back against the wall, pulling the cover up until it concealed all but her eyes.

"Stay still, Bonnie. They won't hurt you." Lorna spoke as reassuringly as her own fright would allow.

"What's a matter with 'er?" Dunbar's bellow filled the small room.

"She's . . . sick."

"What's she sick of?"

Lorna's busy mind churned and grasped at an idea. "I don't know. She broke out in spots and took a fever—"

"Spots? Fever?" The older of the two men holding Griffin whispered hoarsely and swore under his breath. "Gawda-mighty . . . the smallpox!"

Both men released their hold on Griffin and bolted for the door. Griffin stood there, his eyes on the six-gun Dunbar had pressed menacingly against the side of Lorna's head.

"Ya move a inch 'n I'll blow 'er head off," Dunbar snarled.

"Let 'er go. She's got nothin' to do with this. I forced my way in here."

"It shore looked like it. Ya was asleepin' like a babe."

"I'm tellin' ya, Dunbar—" Griffin held up his hands, palms out, and took a step forward.

"Stay back or I'll blow 'er head off!" Dunbar started backing to the door, dragging Lorna with him. "C'mon. C'mon outta there, horse thief. I ain't awantin' to shoot this purty thin', but I will."

"Lorna—"

"Stay put, Bonnie. Don't move off the pallet and keep covered."

"Has she got the smallpox?"

"I don't know. She may have."

Dunbar pulled her through the door and out into the grassy area in front of the cabin. Griffin came out. Lorna noticed for the first time that he had the remote, careful eyes of a man who has lived much with danger. His quick glance took in the two men standing beside their horses. Lorna knew that he was weighing his chances, and if not for her he would leap back into the cabin and slam the door. It would buy him time, and perhaps Cooper would return. She also knew that he wasn't going to take the risk that Dunbar would shoot her, and her mind groped for a way to help him. Dunbar had her arms pinioned to her sides or she could stab him with her knife and create a diversion. The only other weapon at her disposal was her powerful voice. She took a deep breath and prayed that Cooper or some of White Bull's people—even Brice—would hear her call.

"Wah-eee . . . hoo-oo! Wah-eee . . . hoo-oo! Wah-eee . . . hoo-oo!"

The high clear sound that came from deep in Lorna's throat blasted through the silence. It was so loud, so startling, that it was seconds before Dunbar realized that it was coming from the small woman clamped to his side.

"Shut up, gawddamn you!" His big, rough hand moved up to cover her face and squeeze cruelly. Arms free, Lorna flung one hand up to claw his eyes and the other sought the knife in her sash. In the struggle, the gun barrel momentarily slipped away from her head.

Griffin chose that moment to jump at Dunbar, but the distance was too great. Dunbar shoved Lorna to the ground, raised the gun and fired. Griffin was flung back. He staggered to the wall of the cabin and leaned there, blood oozing through the fingers of the hand he clasped to his shoulder. Momentarily forgotten, Lorna scrambled to her feet and ran to Griffin. Within the time it took to draw a breath she was in front of him with both feet planted firmly on the ground, knees slightly bent, head forward, poised to throw the knife she held in her hand.

"I warn you: I can put this blade in your heart before you can lift that gun to fire again." She was deadly calm, knowing what was coming and settling herself for it. The seriousness of her voice caused Dunbar to pause. He stared uncomprehendingly at her for an instant.

"Ya dumb bitch! Ya ain't agoin' to hold off three guns with that knife."

"It'll not matter to you. You'll be dead."

"I ain't awantin' to shoot no woman, but—"

"Don't worry about it. You'll not shoot me. One of those sorry no-goods might, but not you." She jerked her head toward the men beside the horses, but her cold, steady eyes never moved from his.

Her confidence shook Dunbar. Suddenly he had no doubt that she'd try to kill him. It was in her voice and in the unwinking gaze that never left his face. In order to cover the unease that gripped him, he threw back his head and laughed.

"We got us a little ole spittin' wildcat here, fellers." He turned to include the men behind him.

One of the men snickered nervously. "She might scratch ya, Dunbar."

"The yellow belly's hidin' behind his woman's skirts," Dunbar sneered. "Are ya agoin' to make me hurt this purty little thin', nester? Or are ya agoin' to step out 'n take what ya got acomin' like a man?"

"Stay where you are, Griff. This stupid piece of horse dung is scared I'm going to kill him, and he's trying to cover it with big talk so he won't look so foolish. Don't let him goad you into playing into his hands."

Her words stung Dunbar. "Move in!" he yelled to the men behind him. "I come to get that bastard, by Gawd, 'n no split-tail woman's astandin' in my way."

"Hold on, Dunbar. I ain't ashootin' no woman."

"Gawddamn you, Barrett! I ain't a askin' ya to shoot 'er! Shoot that thievin' bastard ahidin' behind 'er."

Lorna could hear Griffin gasping as he tried to stand erect. "Can you move along the wall to the door, Griff?" There was no answer, so she said, "Just hold on then. The longer they stay the more chance they've got of getting the small-pox."

"We ort a get outta here," Fisher complained.

"Ya chicken shit! We can't get no smallpox from out here. Ya agoin' to let the likes a her keep us from acarryin' out the old man's orders? He said hang the bastard, but he'll settle for us shootin' him."

On the perimeter of her vision Lorna saw movement on the flat grassy trail leading to the cabin. Her eyes flicked from Dunbar's face for the merest instant and then back again. A rider was coming in on a buckskin. It had to be Cooper! He was riding hard. Any second the men would hear the pounding hoofs of the horse coming at full gallop. Lorna saw the two men start their move to flank her and Griffin. She took a long, deep breath to steady herself, threw back her head and let the wild, piercing cry burst from her throat again.

"Wah-eee . . . hoo-oo! Wah-eee . . . hoo-oo!"

The unexpected sound had the same effect on the men that it had before. They seemed stunned.

"What's she adoin' that for?" Fisher asked when he recovered from his surprise.

Dunbar seemed at a loss for words. His face turned a beefy red when he saw the slow smile stretch Lorna's lips. The pressure of her stare unnerved him. For an endless moment he stood staring dumbly at the cold-eyed girl.

Lorna threw her voice out again in full volume.

"Shut up that gawdamned caterwaulin'!" he yelled.

"Make me," Lorna yelled at the top of her voice. "Come on, you bush-bottomed, muddle-headed, son of a buzzard, make a move. I want to see if I can hit the third button on that filthy shirt."

"Dunbar! Someone's acomin'!"

Lorna saw the muscles along Dunbar's jaw round into hard knots. She watched him closely, ready to do what had to be done.

Dunbar glared into cold, dark blue eyes and realized with shock that the woman was going to fight him. He'd have to shoot her, and if word got out he'd shot a woman he'd have to leave the territory.

"Who is it?"

"I dunno. He's aridin' a buckskin."

"Hold 'em off till we get our prisoner," he yelled over his shoulder, and then to Lorna, "We'll take him to the law, ma'am. He'll get a trial."

"To the law? Hell, Dunbar, ya know there—"

"Gawddamn ya, Fisher, shut up! Ya 'n Barrett do as I tell ya!"

Lorna kept her eyes steadily on Dunbar's, but she could tell by the sound of the hoofbeats that Cooper was almost there.

There was the sharp crack of a rifle and dirt flew up in front of Dunbar's feet. He feel back and Lorna saw Cooper come riding at him full speed. Dunbar turned to the side and saw the horse bearing down on him. He lifted his arm to fire the gun and the knife shot from Lorna's hand with deadly accuracy, sinking into his upper arm. He yelled in pain and surprise. He dropped the gun and yanked the dagger from his flesh. Lorna darted in and swooped up Dunbar's gun. Holding it in both hands she pointed it at Fisher.

The buckskin horse reared, pivoted on its hind legs, and lunged for Barrett. Cooper struck him on the side of the head with the rifle and the man went down under the hooves of his frightened horse.

"I'm abackin' off," Fisher yelled as he jerked his gun from its holster and threw it on the ground.

When Cooper's feet struck the ground his gun was in his hand. "Goddamn you, Dunbar. I've had about all of you I can stomach!"

"The bitch cut me!"

"You're lucky she didn't kill you. She can pin a fly to the wall with that knife." There was a glimmer of pride in Cooper's angry voice. He picked up Fisher's gun and tossed it out into the creek, then went to where Lorna was bending over Griffin. He had slumped down to sit with his back to the wall. "You hurt bad?"

"I've had worse."

"Now, looky here." Dunbar was holding his hand over the wound in his arm. "Ya ain't got no right to butt in. Yore ole man told me—"

Cooper's fist flew out and slammed into Dunbar's mouth with such force that it almost lifted him off the ground before he fell heavily. Cooper stood over him in a half crouch, his face contorted with burning rage.

"You're within a second of dying. If you mention me in the same breath as that old sonofabitch again, I'll kill you."

It was no idle threat. The expression in Parnell's blazing, blue eyes told him so. Terror clamped icy fingers around Dunbar's throat, pinching off his voice so that it came out thin and high. "How'd I know—"

"You knew, damn you. Everybody in the territory knows I despise that old man's guts. Now, you haul your ass out of here while you've got an ass to haul."

"I come to get that nester. He's a horse thief. I hung him and that . . . split-tail cut him down."

"She had nothing to do with it. *I* cut him down, you dumb sonofabitch. I ought to horsewhip you for what you did to him." Cooper felt an almost uncontrollable rage rising within. "He works for me and if you, or any of the horseshit that works for that old man, even looks cross-eyed at him, you'll answer to me. Is that understood?"

Dunbar got to his feet. "That's a tall order fer one man to be agivin'," he said cockily, trying to salvage his pride.

"Is there something you want to do about it, Dunbar?"

"I ain't in no shape to be adoin' anythin' about it . . . now. But there'll be a time—"

"Any time is fine with me."

"I ain't afergettin' that woman sunk a knife in me."

"You'd better forget it, if you want to live."

Dunbar felt those blue eyes stabbing into him and he realized how dangerous Cooper Parnell could be. Fear touched him.

"C'mon," Fisher urged. "Let's get outta here. If'n ya mess with him that ol' man'll have yore ass in a sling. Ya know what he done told ya 'bout that."

Dunbar took the handkerchief from around his neck and gave it to Fisher. "Shut up and tie up my arm." When they were mounted and ready to ride out, he called, "Ya ain't heard the last of this, Parnell."

"I hope not." Cooper watched them ride away, then went to where Lorna was trying to get Griffin to his feet. "Here, let me do that."

"Let's get him inside so I can tend to him. He's bleeding badly." She spoke calmly, breathing hard from her exertions.

Cooper picked Griffin up in his arms.

"I can still navigate by myself," Griffin protested weakly as Cooper carried him into the cabin.

Bonnie was half-sitting, half-leaning against the wall. Weak tears streaked her face. "Is he dead?"

"Hell, no, I ain't dead!" Griffin tried to cover his embarrassment with bluster. "I'm just arestin' while I bleed to death."

Cooper eased him down on the pallet and Lorna knelt beside him, cutting away his shirt with her knife. With a competence born of long practice, she dabbed at the bloody wound with a cloth, studied it, then laid several thicknesses of the cloth over it.

"The bullet went through, but there's a bit of your shirt in there, Griff. I'll have to get it out."

"Yes, ma'am. I'm obliged for what yo're adoin' 'n to ya for what ya done. I sure do hate it that I brought my trouble down on ya. They was dead set to hang me—"

"It was my fault, Griff. I went to sleep and let them sneak up on us."

"You sure as shootin' bluffed ole Dunbar."

"It was no bluff," Lorna said quietly. "I was set to kill him if he raised the gun."

"Ya'd . . . a done it?" Griffin asked in a breathy whisper.

"Yes. I would've killed him before I let him shoot you down." She said it with no inflection at all. "We're beholden to Mr. Parnell. I was sure of Dunbar, but I didn't know about the other two." She stood and looked up at him. "How did you know I was calling you?"

"I knew."

Their eyes met and held. She nodded, gripped by a sudden shyness. The eyes looking so intently into hers were the bright blue of summer skies. For a moment they were enclosed in a timeless world, seeming to come close to each other, spirit moving effortlessly toward spirit.

"I'm beholden to you, too, for keeping Dunbar from shooting me," Cooper said.

A smile crinkled the corners of his eyes and brightened a face that needed a shave and was streaked with dirt and sweat. Suddenly, to Lorna, it was a dear, familiar face, and she longed to place her palms on his cheeks and lean against his strength. Her answering smile lighted her brilliant, violet-blue eyes until they shone like stars.

"It was what I was supposed to do," she murmured for his ears alone.

He nodded, and she thought how strange it was that they understood each other. It was as if they spoke a language other people didn't know.

"You're the spunkiest woman I ever met. You'll have to teach me how to throw a knife."

"I will, if you'll lend me yours. I'll need it to get the cloth out of Griffin's wounds."

Cooper handed her the knife, then watched as she carefully wiped it on a clean cloth and placed it, alongside hers, on a stone beside the fire so that the tip was in the flame. She allowed the blades to heat for several minutes and then removed them and waved them in the air so that they cooled quickly. She fascinated Cooper as no human being had ever done before. He saw her tighten her lips grimly; she didn't relish her task, but went at it, confidently picking the fragments of cloth from the wound by pinching them between the tips of the two blades.

From her bent position beside Griffin, Lorna asked, "Cooper, will you bring the pan of hot water?"

Cooper. It was the first time she had spoken his name. A strong, unidentifiable emotion set his hands trembling as he poured water from the teakettle into the pan. He set it on the floor beside her. He felt so right being with her, working with her.

Then a thought struck him like a blow between the eyes. *He was acting like a lovesick fool!* He didn't know anything about this woman, and even if he did, there was no room for a woman in his life right now. Hell, he was almost a hundred miles from home. Home was a horse ranch where he had all he could do to scratch out a living for himself and his mother. This woman who so completely dominated his thoughts had a family somewhere in these mountains. She might even have a husband, he reasoned, but he was sure she didn't. Lorna had had no man.

He heard a gasp of agony come from the young nester, and Lorna's soothing words. The sounds reached him through the heavy fog of his troubled thoughts. He looked down to see Bonnie reach for Griffin's hand and grip it hard. With tightly closed eyes, and jaws clenched in pain, he grasped her hand as if it were a lifeline in a storm. Her eyes looked like two burnt holes in a blanket and her face was filled with compassion. Even in her miserable condition she felt pity for his suffering. A disturbing realization hit Cooper—regardless of who and what you were, everyone needed someone.

Lorna spent the afternoon caring for the two who lay in the cabin on the straw pallet. Cooper dressed the meat and roasted it over a fire he built behind the cabin. Watchfulness was a habit of a lifetime, so periodically he circled the cabin and scanned the area. He didn't think Dunbar would be so foolish as to come back, but the man had suffered a blow to his pride and sooner or later he'd seek revenge.

Griffin needed frequent naps because of his weakened condition, and whenever he woke he apologized again for the bother he was causing. Cooper waited for him to mention the fact that he was kin to Adam Clayhill, the news Dunbar had dropped, but Griffin said nothing; Cooper began to hope he had missed the meaning of Dunbar's words.

After the evening meal of beans and fresh elk meat, Cooper led the horses to water and then staked them out in the knee-high grass to eat. He took clean clothes from his saddlebag and followed the rocky bank of the creek until he was out of sight of the cabin. Behind a screen of wild plum bushes he stripped off his grimy clothes, knelt beside the stream and washed them. Then he washed himself and pulled on the clean buckskins, picked up his wet clothes and went back upstream toward the cabin.

He was hanging his wet clothes on the bushes to dry when Lorna came out of the cabin. Cooper watched her approach. The evening light gave her skin a honeyed look against which her eyes were more brilliantly violet-blue than ever. The effortless grace with which she moved, the lightness of her step, fascinated him. She was beautiful to watch. She had loosened her hair from the thongs and it lay on her shoulders and flowed down her back. The breeze fluttered the dark curls about her face and pressed the loose cloth shirt against her slender figure, revealing the lovely curves of her breasts. For a fleeting moment Cooper was reminded of a verse from the "Song of Solomon":

> Behold, thou are fair, my love . . . thy
> two breasts are like young roes that are
> twins, which feed among the lilies.

Since he had been a stripling he had spent the long winter evenings reading. He had read everything he and his mother could find, which wasn't much. That left the Bible, and he had read it from cover to cover. When he was young the "Song of Solomon" had made an impression on his young mind because it was romantic and sexual. He had read it over and over again.

Hellfire! Why did he think of it now? He hadn't thought of it in years. He stood still and waited for her to reach him, shocked by the thoughts that had spiraled through his mind.

Chapter
Six

Lorna stood before him, her eyes meeting his steadily. "I like this time of day. I call it the golden time."

"It's the lonesome time of the day when you're alone on the trail." Cooper realized he was staring at her and looked away toward the fading light in the west.

"Night will begin in a little while," she said a bit wistfully. "A day is ending that will never return and a night is beginning that will never be again."

"And that makes you sad?"

"Sometimes."

"The moon will be coming up soon. I watched it come up last night." They moved side by side toward the creek. "How are the girl and Griffin doing?"

"They're asleep. I think Bonnie's in better shape than Griff."

"He'll be on his feet in a day or two."

"Then you'll leave?"

"I've got to get back to my ranch."

"Tell me about your ranch. Where is it?"

"It's up near Junction City on the Big Thompson River. It's a good two days' ride from here."

"Is it near the Clayhill ranch?"

Surprised, he hesitated, then said almost gruffly, "No. It's about thirty miles beyond."

"Why did you hit that man when he called Mr. Clayhill your pa? Was it your father that ordered his men to hang Griffin because he was going to file on land he wanted?" Lorna's eyes were fixed unwaveringly on his and there was a terrible intensity in her gaze, as if his answer were a matter of life and death to her.

"Why is it so important to you to know?" His voice was abrupt. "You heard me tell them to leave Griffin be."

"Do you think they will?"

"They sure as hell better!"

"Why do you hate your father?"

"Goddammit, Lorna! Leave it alone!"

"I can't leave it alone. I must know everything about you."

She reached out and took his hand. Her touch was a shock to him. He clasped her hand tightly and their fingers entwined. He sat down on the boulder he'd sat on the night before and made room for her to sit beside him, but she stood close to him, leaning against his thigh, looking into his face.

"I don't . . . talk about it."

"I know. It's buried deep." Her voice was a mere whisper on the breeze that came gently down the valley.

"Yes, it's buried deep. It's something I've learned to live with. I don't think about it or talk about it."

"I know," she said again.

He glanced at her, his brows drawn together in a puzzled frown, but he didn't speak. A minute passed—or an hour—Cooper had no idea which, for he was mesmerized by her gentle voice, drugged by the warm pressure of her body against him. It seemed to him that nothing existed beyond the charmed circle of their closeness. This woman who leaned so trustingly against him was completely without guile. Her large, almond-shaped eyes that focused on his face were as frank as a child's. She was so utterly lovely that he was awed into silence as he stared at her perfectly formed features and milk white skin framed with dark, shiny curls.

"I don't understand you. You're the . . . strangest woman I ever met." They were not the words he wanted to say and he searched for others, but none came to mind. "I don't mean you're strange, I mean—"

She laughed softly, musically. "I'm just a woman, like any other."

"No," he protested. "Not like any other woman I've ever come across."

"Does that mean you like me even if I'm . . . strange?" Eyes that laughed into his sparkled like wild violets after a heavy dew.

"Of course. I didn't mean I didn't *like* you!"

"Oh, Cooper!" She laughed again. The cleft in her lower lip gave her mouth a three cornered shape and he couldn't look away from it. "After you get to know me you won't think I'm strange at all. I feel like I've known *you* forever." She added the last in a quiet, serious voice.

"You don't know me at all. I could be an outlaw—"

"I'm serious, Cooper. There's so many things I want to tell you about myself. I want to tell you about Grandpa Light and Grandma Maggie. I want you to know about my granny and my mother and most of all I want you to know about Light's Mountain where I live. And I want to know what *you* think and what *you* dream about, then I'll know why you hide so much tenderness behind that hard shell."

Cooper felt his heart jump out of rhythm, felt his blood pound and drain away. He let out a snort of a chuckle to hide his confusion.

"You want to know a lot. The telling would take all night."

"We've got all night."

The moon came up over the treetops, but they didn't notice it. Lorna stood beside Cooper, her forearms resting on his thighs, her hands clasped in his. The moon shone on her face. It was merely inches away from Cooper's so that he caught each murmured word. She spoke, lovingly, about her grand-parents and of their love of the forests and the mountains. She told him about White Bull, and about Brice and his cruelty to Bonnie. She told him about Volney bringing them to this cabin, saying he'd be back, but that he hadn't come.

"I know that old codger." Cooper chuckled. "He stops by my place once in a while."

"You do? Oh, Cooper, do you think something could've happened to him? He always does what he says he'll do. He's getting so old—" She giggled looking up into his face and he almost forgot what they were talking about. "He'd be madder than a flitter if he heard me say that."

"Maybe he thought there was no hurry getting back. Maybe he thought to wait till after the birthing."

"No, he didn't think that. We told him it was a month away. He was going to find a place for Bonnie and get her settled before she had the baby. Do you suppose he meant to take her to your place?"

"He might've figured to ask my mother to take her in. She's talked to him some."

"Would your mother have taken her?"

"She would have taken her." She'd have seen herself in that poor creature, Cooper thought, and a shiver of hatred for everything Clayhill ran through him.

Lorna stared into the gloom and Cooper stared at her. When she spoke again it was to tell him about her father who wanted to leave Light's Mountain, and of the shame of know-ing he was stealing cattle. She left nothing out.

"I don't know what to do, Cooper," she said with so much anxiety in her voice that his heart swelled with the need to comfort her. "I don't think my pa has laughed since my mother died. He never had anything much to do with anyone until Brice Fulton came to the mountain. Now, he spends all his time with him and his bunch. If he talks to me at all it's to grumble about being stuck on Light's Mountain. He wants to start a freighting business, and to get the cash money he tied in with Brice. I just know he's ashamed, but he's caught in a trap."

"If he's set on going, the sooner the better," Cooper said quietly. "He'll steal the wrong man's cattle and get himself killed."

"That's what I'm afraid of. I've been wondering if I should give him the cash money my granny gave me. He doesn't know about it. Granny wanted me to keep it. She said for me to keep it hidden until the time came that I really needed it. Do you think I should give it to him and let him go?"

Cooper held her hands in his and gently rubbed the palms together. "Only you can decide that, Lorna. I can only tell you to weigh the odds. What's the worst thing that can happen if he stays and continues to steal another man's cattle? And what's the worst thing that will happen if you give him the money and he goes away?"

Lorna was thoughtful for a moment, then she smiled her happy, three-cornered smile. "Oh, Cooper, I knew you could figure out what to do. Of course, I'd rather he'd take the money and go away, even if I would never see him again, than to have him stay here and be caught and hung for a rustler. I don't need the money. I can always get a little cash money by running a few cows up on the mountain."

For a long while they were silent. There was a smoky smell to the cool air caused by the thin plume of smoke that rose from the chimney of the cabin. The grass in the valley was already wet with dew and the forested mountain shadows on each side of them loomed thick and dark. They watched the flickering fireflies dance their brief life away and heard the far-off sound of a hoot owl. Long habits of vigilance were hard to break, and Cooper lifted his head to listen. The call came again and he relaxed.

"It's peaceful here," Lorna murmured. "I love the night-time, and you like it, too, don't you, Cooper?"

"Yeah, I do. When I was a kid I used to try and count the stars."

"See that star up there?" She lifted her face to the heavens.

Cooper looked up. There were a million stars in the sky, and they had never shone so brightly or seemed so close.

"Which one?"

"That one. It's mine." There was the laughter in her voice. Cooper lowered his eyes and found hers, sparkling like twin stars, looking into his. She was laughing. It was a soft, breathless, happy laugh.

Cooper felt the happy chuckles form deep in his chest, roll up and join her laughter. "If you mean that one, it's mine. I saw it first."

"I like to hear you laugh, Cooper. Does it make you happy to be with me?"

"Godamighty! Of course it does." He felt the air go out of his lungs. Her frankness jolted him—she was a constant surprise, a constant pleasure. "Do you always say whatever comes to your mind?" There was a gentle firmness in his face and his voice.

"I like being with you and I like hearing you laugh. So what's wrong about telling you? Didn't you want to know?" She squeezed his hand with surprising strength and held his eyes with hers until his features relaxed.

"I guess so. Are you always like this?"

"Like what? You mean talking to you like I'm doing? Of course not! This is the first time and this is ... special. I've finally met you and I feel good about it. I knew when you touched me and I turned and looked into your eyes that you would be special to me. You felt it, too. I could tell."

Cooper laughed nervously. "I think you've bewitched me."

"Not enough," she said regretfully, her face sobering. "You're making me do all the telling."

"What do you want to know?"

"Everything. All I know about you is that you've got a horse ranch and that you don't have a woman of your own."

"How do you know that?" he teased, feeling a great swell of joy wash over him.

"Because ... *I'm* your woman, Cooper," she whispered with a tremor in her voice. "I know I am. I feel it here." She took her hand from his and placed it over her heart.

He could see the shine in her eyes and feel her breath on his face. *His woman?* He felt a queer pang of fear. He didn't want to love a woman. He didn't know how to love a woman!

"Lorna! We don't even *know* each other."

"Yes, we do. We know everything that matters about each other, we just don't know what has happened to each other up to now. Tell me, Cooper."

"Aren't you cold standing there?"

"A little. I could sit beside you and you could put your arm around me." She laughed at the surprised look on his face. "I'm not asking you to get under the blankets with me— just put your arm around me."

"Lorna! Are you trying to shock me? Don't ever say that to any other man or you'll be under the blankets before you can take a deep breath!"

"I know that. I've said things to you I've never said to anyone. Now, help me up there."

Cooper lifted her up beside him, wrapped his arm around her, and fitted her shoulder into his armpit. Her thigh nestled against his; her head fit into just the right place on his shoulder.

Lorna snuggled against him, curled into the crook of his arm, warm and content. She felt that this was something she had been waiting for, this time, this place.

Afterward Cooper couldn't remember how he had started talking about himself. Once he started, the words poured out of him and he couldn't seem to stop.

"At first I didn't know what a bastard was. I just knew that I was one. It was, 'get outta my way, ya little bastard,' or the kids would say, 'ma says I can't play with ya 'cause yo're a bastard.' My mother washed clothes at the fort, and we lived in a room beside the laundry. I remember one time her ma and pa came to see her, but they wouldn't look at me. They called her a fallen woman and said that she'd burn in everlasting hell for her sin. My mother was angry and sent them away. Later I heard her crying in the night and I wondered if I was the sin they were talking about."

Lorna made a small clucking sound and hugged his hand to her breast.

"When I was eight, my mother married Oscar Parnell. He was everything to me a father could be. I worshipped him and dogged his footsteps from morning till night. He left the army because my mother was so unhappy at the fort and took a job with a man who raised mules. By this time I was doing a man's work, and we saved enough money to put a payment down on a ranch; but he didn't live to see it. He was kicked to death by an ornery mule. Ma and I came on north and settled on the ranch. We've been there ever since."

Lorna's hand curled around his. She pressed her face to his shoulder. She said nothing; she knew he was moving toward the anguishing part of his story, the hurting part. His arm held her tightly to him and he stared up at the impassive, benign face of the watching moon and then gazed at the ever-moving water in the stream.

"One time I asked my mother about the man who sired me and she said that Oscar Parnell nurtured a seed that was sown in the wind, and that he was my pa in every sense of the word except for a minor one. I understood that. Now I wish to God I'd never found out about Adam Clayhill. He's everything I despise in a man; selfish, greedy, without conscience or principles. He thinks that because he was one of the first to ranch here, the whole territory belongs to him.

"A couple of years ago, in order to prevent a lot of killing, my mother faced him in the middle of the street in Junction City with all the townspeople looking on. She walked out between two rows of armed men and told him the man he was trying to kill was his own son. You see, he had another son—by a Cheyenne woman—who was raised in Saint Louis by an uncle who left him a great deal of money. He came out here and bought up the land Clayhill wanted, and Clayhill and his stepdaughter trumped up a charge against him and tried to get him hanged. He despises Logan because of his Indian blood. But there's not a finer man than Logan Horn. I'm proud to call him my brother."

"It must have been hard for your mother to see Adam Clayhill after all those years."

"It was. She knew he was in that part of the country when we got there, but she avoided him. He recognized her that day she faced him down and called her by name. Then he looked at me—I'd already had a few run-ins with him. Logan knew what she was going to do and tried to stop her, but when Ma makes up her mind, it takes a lot to stop her." There was a smile in his voice. "She went up to Clayhill and smacked him across the face. She told him that she should shoot him, but the slap would have to do. It was the first time she'd come face to face with him in all the years we'd lived there. I was never more proud of her, but I can't tell you the feeling I had when I realized that Clayhill was the man who had caused my mother so much pain. I went a little crazy and smashed into him with both fists, knocked him to the ground and spit on him. My mother and Logan made me see that he wasn't worth the trouble it would cause me to kill him."

"Your mother was right. Oh, I'm so glad you didn't kill him." Lorna's arm slid around his back and she hugged him to her. After a short silence, she asked, "How does he feel about you and Logan now?"

"He steers clear of Logan. It galls him that Logan is building a ranch that equals or is better than his, but he's afraid of him, too. Logan walks tall. He bows his head for no man."

"I would like him," she stated simply.

"You'd like his wife Rosalee, too. She married him knowing what life would be like married to a half-breed in this country. They had a boy this past winter."

"And you? Is Adam Clayhill afraid of you?"

Cooper grinned. "Let's just say he's careful around me. At first he thought he'd win me over with the promise that I'd inherit his ranch. The man has guts he hasn't used yet," Cooper said with bewilderment in his voice. "He actually thought I'd be pleased to know that . . . we're blood kin. He expected me to move to the ranch and live with him! I'd not touch anything the old sonofabitch has with a ten-foot pole! He's rotten to the core and that gives me some worry. I can't help it if I look like him, but I don't want to be anything like him!"

Lorna's hand cupped Cooper's cheek and turned his face down toward hers. "You're not like him or you'd have gone bad before now. You and Logan came from strong women and have overcome his bad blood."

"Lorna!" He moved her hand around to his mouth and gently kissed the palm. "Lorna," he said her name again. "You're . . . just so sweet and fresh." He stared down at her face somberly. It was pale and calm, her eyes seemed to burn with a blue light. "I've never talked to anyone as I've talked to you."

"I'm glad," she whispered.

"I heard you singing last night."

"I was singing for you."

Her arm slipped around his neck. He gave a long shuddering sigh and wrapped her in both of his, hugging her close.

"Oh, Lorna!" he whispered in an agony of confusion.

"Don't try to understand it, my love. Just be glad we've found each other."

"I don't want to think about it. I just want to look at you and hold you."

She smiled a smile of pure enchantment. "I'd like for you to kiss me . . . if you want to. Do you?"

"You know I do!"

"Is that why you're trembling?"

"I guess it is," he said helplessly.

He bent his head and his lips moved gently but insistently

over her hair, her closed eyes, and down to her cheek. She turned her head so that their lips met. His mouth closed over hers and moved with supplicant pressure until her lips parted, yielded, accepted the wanderings of his, then became urgent in their own seeking. Her mouth was warm, sweet beyond imagination, but he held back, unwilling to spoil the mood by demanding more than the instant of sharing. He raised his head and looked down at her, his lips just inches from her lips, her breath in his mouth. Each sensed a mystery and loneliness and aching beauty that was precious beyond their comprehension. Their lips met again, clung and released, clung again and parted reluctantly.

He shifted his body slightly to form a more comfortable cradle for her, and she leaned her head back against his shoulder. The moon shone on her face and he could see that her eyes were closed, her lips slightly parted. He was certain, now, that she held some part of his heart.

"Tell me that I've made you happy," she whispered.

"You've made me happy. In all my life I've never been as happy as this. I can't resist you."

"No more than I can resist you. Oh! I'm so happy! I'm so happy I want to sing!"

And she did. Her voice came to his ears softly, beautifully, from where her head rested on his shoulder. He could feel the drag of her hair on his chin when she tilted her face to watch his while she sang.

"Life's morn will soon be waning,
And its evening bells be tolled.
But my heart shall know no sadness,
If you'll love me when I'm old."

When she finished the song, she sat up so she could look into his eyes. "Light and Maggie loved each other more than life. My granny said they loved the same when they were old as when they were young. They even died together. It could be the same with us, my love."

His hands lightly gripped her shoulders and held her away from him. He looked down into her face. Oh, God! She was so beautiful.

"Tonight I've felt things I never dreamed of feeling, but it's too soon, Lorna." He lifted a hand to stroke the hair back from her face with fingers that trembled. "We can't let the attraction we feel for each other get out of hand. I won't tell you I'm as sure about this as you are. God knows I've got a hunger for you that makes me ache. But I'll not pour soft words into your ears and take you to . . . satisfy that hunger. I can't do that to a woman like you—"

"It's all right. Don't fret about it. You need some time to get used to the idea," she said soothingly, and stroked his hair in an age-old maternal gesture of understanding. She slipped down off the rock and stood looking at him. "We've got time. We've got the rest of our lives." She placed a kiss, as soft as the touch of a feather, on his lips, then turned and ran, as fleet as a deer, up the path.

Puzzled and troubled by confusing emotions, Cooper watched her until she was safely inside the cabin. She was like someone who wasn't quite real; a fairy, or a shadowy woman out of a dream. On the heels of that thought came another—she was a real flesh and bone woman. He'd held her in his arms, felt her small warm body against his, kissed her sweet mouth. She was soft and feminine, and yet he'd seen her hold off three men with her knife. At that moment she was deadly. That soft, gentle, sweet little woman would have killed Dunbar if he'd made a move.

He sat with his puzzled thoughts until the moon disappeared behind the old, scarred pine at the western rim of the valley. A restless lobo howled his frustration at the night's failures and his defiance was heard and answered by another of his own kind.

More out of habit than the need to rest, Cooper threw out his bedroll and stretched out on it and looked up at the stars.

"Lorna. Lorna..." He wasn't even aware of saying her name. Only the winds heard and moaned softly in the treetops above his head.

Chapter Seven

It was dawn.

Lorna opened her eyes. Her awakening was instantaneous, none of her usual meanderings in the trance world between sleep and sensibility. This morning, her adolescent dreams had become a reality that jolted her mind and muscle into vivid awareness. *Cooper! Cooper! Oh, my love!* She stretched and curled her toes in pure delight. She'd never felt so happy in all her life. Her future was with Cooper. This morning she felt an awesome kinship with her Grandma Maggie, and wanted to be alone in the forest they both loved to think about it.

She stepped out into the cool morning and stood beside the door. A gray squirrel paused briefly to glance at her and scold before scurrying off for the nearest tree. A bluejay chattered angrily and flew in furious indignation to a branch of an oak tree and from that vantage point hurled insults at the old black crow searching in the berry bushes for a scrap of food. Bold in his hunger, the crow added his own croaking comments before flapping to a more productive berry bush, where he ignored both the jay and the woman. Lorna stood as still as a stone, absorbing the familiar morning sounds, listening for an alien one.

Satisfied all was as it should be, she ran toward the bluffs behind the cabin and began the steep climb to the top of the wooded shelf. She followed her own trail, holding to branches of scrub trees to keep from falling. Halfway up she stopped to look back toward the place where Cooper had thrown his bedroll, but she couldn't see it for the thick tangle of berry bushes. She continued her climb. At the top of the bluff she surveyed the area with quick knowing eyes before she showed herself. Nothing moved. Always cautious, she ran several hundred feet to the right and stopped beside a large blue spruce to look and listen. She darted from tree to tree until she'd circled the place where she had come up from the cabin.

Confident that she was alone with only the creatures of the forest to observe her, she went to the edge of the bluff, straightened to her full height and stretched her arms to the rising sun. She was free. Here there were no confining walls around her. Here she could pretend she was at home on Light's Mountain. She ran a few steps, jumped and twirled around and around with graceful abandon. She dipped and swayed and laughed aloud. She was happy, so *happy*! She wanted to dance and sing, giving herself up to the sheer bliss, the wonder of knowing she had found her mate for life. She *had* to sing. The feeling inside her had to have an outlet, a celebration of this wonderful discovery. She no longer feared Brice would come and take Bonnie. Cooper was here. He'd stand with her against anyone.

The song she sang was an old one Maggie had taught her granny. It was about a very young girl who waited for a lover who had gone wandering over the sea to seek his fortune, but returned home when he realized the treasure he was seeking was his own true love. It was a haunting love song with a compelling little tune. Lorna sang softly and swayed from side to side, her voice, sweet and clear, filled the air around her and carried on the breeze to the cabin below.

Cooper, coming up the stony path beside the stream, paused and listened. He felt his heart still. A spell of enchantment engulfed him as if the sweet, lilting notes clinging to the fresh morning air were coming from another world. He was pulled toward the sound, irresistibly drawn by it. His feet seemed to have no will of their own. As he strode past his bedroll he dropped his hat and ran his fingers through his wet hair.

He scaled the bluff behind the cabin, following the prints of small moccasins on the steep, narrow path that wound around boulders and gnarled mountain pine. He paused to catch his breath, digging in his bootheels to keep from sliding, then hurried on. As he climbed the singing grew louder. When he pulled himself up the last few feet so he could see over the edge he found himself looking into laughing, blue-violet eyes. Lorna held out her hand; he took it and stepped up onto the grassy plateau.

She whirled and left him, jumping and spinning, her hair whipping around her. Her feet scarcely seemed to brush the ground as she skimmed over it, twisting and turning to the tune of the music that came from her throat. "Tra-la, tra-la, tra-la-la-la." Her arms reached to welcome the morning sun that glistened on her blue-black hair, and then swept low to the ground as though she performed some pagan dance.

Cooper watched every delicate movement, heard the trilling music, and could not believe what he saw. Could this beautiful, happy woman dancing with such innocent abandon be real?

In all his life, he'd never seen such beauty as she possessed. It was more than physical. It was in every delicate movement of her small, slender body. It was in the melodious sound that came from her throat, in her triumphant, happy smile, and in her eyes that gazed at him in open admiration. Her cheeks and lips were red against her pale skin and her glorious, blue-black hair danced around her face and tumbled down her back to her waist in reckless abandon.

A fierce rage of longing, an enormous desire, began to stir in Cooper's body as he watched her twisting in a final, joyous spin and stop before him, her eyes glowing up into his. The soft, breathless laugh that came from her lips was as dearly familiar to him as if he had heard it a thousand times—he didn't understand it, or know what was happening to him. He backed away and tried to view her as others would see her—a girl in worn Indian moccasins, britches, an old cloth shirt that hung to her hips and a cloth sash wrapped tightly around a waist he could span with his two hands.

"I knew you'd come." She reached for his hand and held it in both of hers.

"How did you know?"

"I don't know." She laughed up at him. There was no pretense in the eyes that moved lovingly over his face.

Cooper's head was spinning, reality was slipping farther and farther away. He felt a tremor running through him, as if the earth were going to part under his feet. He had to say something, but what?

"You're up early."

"I love the morning."

"Last night you said you loved the night."

"I love everything—now that I've found *you*."

"Lorna—"

"Oh, Cooper, Cooper." She came close to him, wrapped her arms around his waist, and pressed her cheek against his chest. The top of her head fit snugly beneath his chin. His hand came up and stroked the full length of her hair. He'd never felt anything so silky, so alive. His fingers refused to leave it. She tilted her face, smiled up at him, and asked mischievously, "Do you think I'll break if you hug me?"

"I'm afraid you're not flesh and blood."

"If you kiss me, you'll know that I am."

"Lorna! Oh, wild, sweet, Lorna—" The words came from his tight throat in a tormented whisper.

She lifted her lips to meet his. The pressure of his mouth threatened to whisk her to the edge of blackness. The bitter-sweet taste of tobacco and the roughness of his cheek as her nose pressed against it did nothing but fan the flame that was growing inside her. The pressure of his lips parted hers and she felt the tip of his tongue exploring the inner surfaces of her lips. She was enveloped in a whirling velvet mist of sensations that made her knees weak and her body sag against his tall frame. His mouth left hers momentarily, then hungrily returned to capture her in a soul-searching kiss as an insidious, primitive desire grew in both of them.

These wanton, abandoned feelings were strange to Lorna, but she loved them and had no desire to stop them. Instead, she wanted the physical gratification of Cooper's possession and pressed herself against the hardened evidence of his aroused body.

It was Cooper who drew back and held her away from him. His hands moved over her shoulders and back in trembling caresses as he peered down into her flushed face.

"You don't know what this is leading to, Lorna." His voice trembled.

Almost blindly she looked at him, compelling herself to concentrate on what he was saying, but the movement of his firm lips was more enticing than the words coming from them. She was learning how primitive and powerful desire could be. Her soft, feminine body had instinctively responded to the mating instincts of his.

"Yes, I do! It's mating! I always wondered what it would be like to couple with my mate."

"Lorna, Lorna," he groaned, his words muffled in her hair. "We can't . . . I can't—"

"I'm your woman, Cooper." Her voice was low and she was frowning. "Don't you know that I'm your woman?"

Cooper felt a strange, bittersweet warmth. He stared down at her for a long, aching moment. Her lips were red and swollen from his kisses and a few tendrils of soft black hair curled at her temples. She was a dream, a mirage, as pure as an angel's breath.

"You're sweet, untouched—"

"I'm untouched," she admitted with a three-cornered smile. "I've been waiting for you, Cooper. I'm your woman. I know it, but it's too soon for you to know, isn't it?" Her hands cupped his cheeks and she looked deeply into his eyes.

"You don't understand how it is with a man? I want you. God knows I do, but—" He could read the loving acceptance in her eyes. Oh, God, she was so sweet, so tempting. "You can't . . . give yourself to a man you've known for so short a time!" he said tersely.

"I've known you forever. But it's all new to you, isn't that it, Cooper?"

"Yes, it's new to me," he snapped almost angrily. "I can't take a woman like you just as a passing pleasure. It would have to mean more than that." He felt as if he were strangling.

"We'll mate, my love. I'm sure, so very sure." She spoke reassuringly, as if she were comforting a child, and stroked his cheeks with her fingertips. "When we do, we'll take each other."

He stood silently, his eyes searching her face. Then he began shaking his head in denial of his thoughts. She seemed to understand what was going on in his mind and rose up on her toes to brush his lips with hers.

"Light didn't understand either—at first," she whispered.

Cooper shook himself out of what now seemed to be a trance. "What were you doing up here alone? Dunbar or some drifter could've ridden in here and found you." He spoke gruffly in an effort to bring them both back to reality.

She laughed. "After you've been with me a while, you'll not worry about me getting caught out. Come. We'd better go see about Bonnie and Griff. They'll be hungry for their breakfast."

She scrambled down the side of the bluff as agilely as a mountain goat and waited at the bottom for Cooper, who came slowly and cautiously. When he reached her, she took his hand as naturally as if she had been doing it every day of her life.

"Now can you see how I found the mare and had to ride her the long way around?"

He nodded his head in answer to her question, then scolded, "You could have broken your neck coming down the cliff the way you did just now."

"Oh, Cooper, you care. You *do* care!" She hugged his arm and danced alongside him.

"You're damn right I'd care if you broke a leg. How'd I get you out of here?" he said, deliberately misreading the meaning of her words.

"We'd have to stay here then. Just you and I. I wouldn't care a bit."

"I'd pull you out on a travois," he threatened, and unable to resist her infectious happy mood, grinned down at her. "That would be a mighty bumpy ride."

"I know. That's how Volney and I brought Bonnie here." She had to skip to keep up with his long strides. "I'm worried about him, Cooper."

"Volney can take care of himself. He's caught the scent of a cat with a pelt that would bring him plenty of hard cash and he's after it. He'll be back."

"I don't know what to do with Bonnie if he doesn't come back. I can't take her home with me. Brice would get her."

"I'll take her home with me. Ma would be glad for her company."

"Would you do that, Cooper?" Sharing this sweet intimacy with him made Lorna almost heady with pleasure.

"How soon before she can travel? I've got to be getting on home."

"I don't know when she can ride astride. That babe split her something awful."

Cooper felt the color come up from his neck and looked away from the serious, unabashed eyes looking into his. There didn't seem to be any subject too delicate for her to talk about openly and honestly.

"We'll . . . ah . . . see how she gets on."

* * *

In the afternoon Griffin moved out into the sun to expose the wound in his shoulder to the warm air. Lorna had fashioned a sling for his right arm to prevent movement from disturbing the healing flesh. He seemed strangely withdrawn. Although he spoke readily to Lorna, he didn't direct any conversation to Cooper unless forced to answer a question.

Cooper waited until the young nester was alone, then moved over beside him and squatted down.

"I have a feeling something's eating at you."

Griffin looked steadily at him. His eyes were cold, the pupils shrunk to hard points. "What's yore game, *mister*?"

"I figured you'd latched on to what Dunbar said. Well, *nester*," he spat out the word and got to his feet, "I'll say this one time: I feel the same about that old man as my brother does. Any man that puts me in the same pocket as him, or puts his name to me had better be ready to back it up, because I'll call his hand." The finality of the words lifted his voice to a warning note.

Griffin stood and spread his legs to steady himself. "I'm obliged to ya fer what ya done, but it goes down hard bein' beholden to one with your name."

"Name's Parnell. Cooper Parnell. My pa was Oscar Parnell, as fine a man as ever lived. It was him that raised me, taught me to be a man. That old sonofabitch has got no claim on me, no matter what he says, Dunbar says, or anybody else says!"

Griffin stood stiff and defiant. "I aim to keep what's mine if'n it means akillin' him."

"It's what I'd do."

Cooper stood there waiting for some response from the still-faced Griffin, but none was forthcoming. The man had retreated for the moment while he considered his words. The silence went on and on while hard green eyes bored into hard blue ones. After a long while Griffin nodded his head.

"If'n it turns out I'm wrong 'bout ya," he said softly, "I'll not waste time amakin' it right."

Cooper looked into eyes as cold and green as icy water. "How'll you go about that?"

"By killin' ya." Griffin spoke each word clearly and distinctively. "'N I'd make sure ya take a long time adyin'."

"Like Dunbar, huh?" Cooper looked at the slim, young cowboy as if seeing him for the first time. "You'd try it, wouldn't you?"

"There'd be no *tryin'*," Griffin said with a wintry smile. "I'd do it, 'n not like Dunbar. Ya'd not even know who done it, 'cause I don't hold with no rules a fair play. When somethin' needs killin', I kill it, 'n it makes no never mind to me how it's done." His young face was as hard as stone. "I lived five years 'mong the meanest, filthiest scum this side of hell. They tried ever'thin' from stealin' my food to abuggerin' me. It wasn't easy to stay alive, but I'm here. A lot of 'em ain't."

"I'm obliged to you for telling me what to expect. Now, if you've got it all out of your craw, sit down and listen. I have a proposition to put to ya."

Lorna sat with her back against the wall and watched Bonnie twist her hair into a rope and fasten it to the top of her head with two heavy wire hairpins. It amazed her that Bonnie could do so much with only one hand, and she told her so.

Bonnie laughed weakly. "It ain't hard, Lorna. I never had two hands 'n had to do thin's right off with one. Ya don't miss what ya never had." The exertion of pinning up her hair had tired her. She rested her back against the wall and watched Lorna with large brown eyes that seemed unusually dark in her pale face. "Ya told me the babe had ever'thin', didn't you, Lorna? I didn't dream that ya said it?"

"I told you that. It had the right number of feet and hands, even fingers and toes. It was perfect, Bonnie." Lorna hoped to God she was telling it right. The truth was, she had only briefly glanced at the pitiful mass of human flesh.

Bonnie seemed relieved and smiled wanly. "I was 'fraid it'd be like me."

"When you're able to leave here, Cooper's going to take you to his ma. He said she'd be glad for your company."

The old frightened look came back into Bonnie's eyes. "I don't want to go off with him, Lorna."

"You'll have to for awhile. I'm thinking that when Cooper comes to Light's Mountain you can come, too. He'll stand up to Brice. Cooper'll not let Brice be mean to you ever again."

"Ya like him, don't ya?"

"Yes, I do. He's my life's mate," Lorna said in a proud, positive tone.

"Lorna! Are ya agoin' to marry him?"

"He hasn't asked me, but he will."

"You'd leave Light's Mountain?"

"Of course not! I'll never leave Light's Mountain," Lorna said firmly. "My home's there. I could never live anyplace else."

"But . . . Lorna—"

"Cooper will come."

"To stay?"

Lorna laughed. "Of course. It's too soon to talk about that now. It's enough to know that he'll take you home with him and take care of you till the time comes that both of you come home to Light's Mountain."

Lorna was facing the open door and her eyes sought the mountains beyond. She was getting homesick. Despite the wonder of being here with Cooper, she longed for home. She wondered if Frank was worried about her, if her dogs, Naomi and Ruth, missed her and if Moose and Woody had returned from their prospecting trip.

"But . . . Lorna, Cooper might not want to live there—"

"He will! As soon as he sees it, he'll know that's where he ought to be." The words came out with a touch of hostility in them.

Bonnie looked with surprise at Lorna's tight features and knew that her friend wasn't *sure* Cooper would go to Light's Mountain. She didn't understand Lorna's attachment to a place that held so many fearful memories for *her*. But then she'd never lived in one place long enough to become attached to it, she thought ruefully.

Lorna left the cabin and went to where Cooper was hunkered down in front of Griffin drawing a map in the dirt with a sharp stick. She wanted to be with Cooper, to touch him. She stood close beside him and placed her hand on his shoulder. He looked up with questioning eyes. She smiled at him and shook her head. He looked back down at the map he had drawn and for several minutes appeared to be studying it before he spoke.

"This place is not so far from my ranch as the crow flies," he said. "But in order to get through the pass I have to go north." He scratched out the place marking the pass, then the town of Junction City, then his ranch. His eyes made a sweeping tour down the valley and to the surrounding mountains before meeting Griffin's. "This here's the best place for a horse ranch I've come across this side of Thompson Valley where my ranch is."

"Somebody started up here, 'n couldn't make it or got run off," Griffin said, looking far down the valley at the waving grass. "If'n he didn't make it, he didn't give it a good try. There's ever'thin' here a body'd want—natural boundries, grass, water aplenty. My guess is somebody didn't want 'em here 'n run 'em off."

"Mine, too. And I have a good idea who it was. If the land isn't bought we have as much right to it as anyone. What say we make a trip into town and find out?"

Griffin didn't respond at once. Finally he said, "All I got is that horse herd. Maybe forty head."

"From what you say about them, Logan will buy them. I have a little hard money put back. If we need more, we can put it to Logan to stake us in return for his pick of the horses."

"Do ya think he would?"

"We won't know till we ask him. He's running a mighty big herd of cattle and he's got no time to break and train his work stock."

"Do ya figger to go partners?"

"That's the size of it." Cooper held out his hand and Griffin clasped it with his left one, his young face serious.

"I want ya to know right off, Parnell, my friend'll share with me, if he's of a mind to stick 'round. Me 'n him's been in a few tight spots together. He's saved my bacon more 'n once."

Cooper shrugged. "We can always use a man good with horses, there's no two ways about that. What you do with your part is your business."

Lorna studied the map and listened. Excitement bubbled in her so strong she could scarcely contain it. Cooper's ranch was not as far from Light's Mountain as she at first believed. *Oh, Glory! It was probably a day's ride!* She took the sharp stick from Cooper's hand.

"There's another way to get across the mountain without going north, Cooper. Volney showed me the way. It's the way we came from Light's Mountain when we brought Bonnie here. We're here." She made a scratch in the ground with a stick. "And if we go south along the creek, then cross over and follow the timber line, it'll take us past that peak yonder." She pointed toward a snow covered mountain peak. "On the other side, there's a narrow pass that runs along on a shelf that comes out here." She had drawn a line that resembled the letter L with the bottom line tilted. "If that's where your ranch is, it's not so far from where I live."

"How long did it take you to get here?"

"It took a long time when we brought Bonnie here. But after Bonnie was on her feet, I went back home a couple of times to get some things we needed—"

"That's rough country. You rode through it by yourself?"

Cooper asked sharply and got to his feet to look down at her with a puzzled frown on his face.

"Of course." Lorna laughed. "It takes about eight hours of hard riding to get there. I took out before daylight and I was back by midnight. I'd have made it sooner, but wanted to give Gray Wolf time to rest up."

"Back by midnight?" Cooper echoed, his expression going from amazement to anger. "There are Indians out there just itching to take white scalps. And even worse, there are the white and Mexican outlaws that'd just love to get their hands on you. Do you mean to tell me your pa let you ride off at night?"

She ignored his questions and his anger. He wasn't ready yet to understand that she roamed where she pleased.

"Nothing can catch me on Gray Wolf," she said with a shrug. "Going this way will be shorter than going north, Cooper. The trail's a little rough in spots, but I can show you the way. When we leave here, we'll travel together." There was finality to her words as if the decision was made, and Cooper frowned, bringing his brows close together and narrowing his eyes.

"I wasn't figuring on you leaving here by yourself. I was figuring on Griffin staying here with Bonnie while I saw you home," he said stiffly, angrily.

She stood slim and proud, her face tilted up to his, smiling at him, still confident that her decision wouldn't be questioned. "Griff won't have to stay with Bonnie. We'll all go together," she said matter-of-factly, and looked away from him as if the subject was closed.

"*I'll* decide when and how we leave here, Lorna." His tone told her not to argue, but she did.

"I don't want to leave Griff and Bonnie here alone. Dunbar could come back here while we're gone, Cooper. Griff's in no shape—"

"I said, I'll decide."

"I know this country better than you," she said in a tight, persistent voice.

He stared at her for a long moment, then let his hard-held breath out like a sigh. "I'm not denying that. Your way may be better, but I'm going to think on it."

"There's nothing to think about—"

"Lorna! Don't crowd me!"

Griffin looked from one set face to the other, pulled his shirt up over his wound and stood up. "Guess I'll—mosey on in for a drink of water."

He walked away and Cooper would have followed, but Lorna took his hand. "Why are you acting like this? Why are you so angry?"

Cooper swore under his breath. "I've gone my own way for a long time. I'll not have you or anyone else telling me to do this or do that. I do my own deciding."

"I'm only trying to help. You know I'm right about that pass. How else could we have gotten here?"

"Lorna, I'm not saying your way isn't a shorter, better way. I'm saying I make my own tracks. I don't follow after anyone till I think about it!"

"Not even *me*?"

"Not even you."

"Oh, so that's it!" Her voice came out in a throaty rush. "You're all up in the air because I knew about that pass and you didn't. That's mean and little of you, Cooper, and I'm disappointed in you. You're just like all the other men I know. You think that because I'm a woman I don't know *anything*."

"I didn't say that. Now get this straight, Lorna: you may be the prettiest woman I've ever seen and the . . . sweetest, but that doesn't give you any reason to be calling the shots— Oh, hell! I'll water the horses."

Cooper walked away from her, a guilty flush on his face. What had gotten his back up and caused him to snap at her was the confident way she had tried to take over and ramrod things. The stricken look in her eyes when he'd failed to fall in whole hog with her plans had unnerved him. It seemed that part of him resented the spell she'd cast over him and the other part was wildly happy because of it.

Of course he could simply get on his horse and ride away. That thought brought a dull ache that spread through him until it occupied every part of his body.

He wasn't stupid enough to believe he'd fallen in love with her. He was a man like any other. A man had strong hungers that had nothing to do with being in love. And yet— he thought very carefully about this now—he'd had a strong yearning for her from the very first, and it was entirely different from the yearning to go to bed with a woman. One dismal truth alone had significance: he'd come here in search of his mare and met a woman who got into his mind and his blood. But by God, he cursed softly to himself, she wasn't taking over his life completely.

It had been five days since Bonnie had given birth to the dead baby. She had bounced back from her ordeal faster than Lorna had thought possible. She was weak and trembly, but for the last few days her attitude about herself was different. She no longer cringed or looked down when Cooper spoke to her but answered readily. Her eyes shone and she smiled, even laughed occasionally, a sound Lorna had heard very few times since she'd known her. Bonnie had always been neat with her person but now she seemed to take extra care with her hair. She brushed it and pulled it into a bun on the top of her head. Lorna was sure the change in her had been caused by Griffin.

Cooper acted as if they had never had the argument about the pass, and Lorna wisely refrained from mentioning their departure from the cabin. Both of them concentrated on getting Griffin and Bonnie strong enough to travel by feeding them well. Cooper brought in fresh meat and fish and Lorna cooked thick stews. They worked together during the day and in the evenings they walked beside the creek. Lorna would slip her hand into his and he would hold it tightly. They talked of many things. She told him about childhood escapades and he told her about the wild horse herds he'd seen in the mountains south of his ranch.

Each night, before going into the cabin to sleep beside Bonnie, Lorna slipped her arms up around his neck and they kissed. They were sweet, almost chaste kisses, because Cooper kept a tight rein on his passion. Even when Lorna showed her hunger for him, he gently put her away from him and said good night.

At first Bonnie had been so shy with Griffin she couldn't look at him, much less talk to him. And then, as they spent long hours alone together, shyness left both of them, and they began to carry on short conversations that developed into long ones. Once they started to talk, it was as if they would never say all they wished to say to each other. At times they would be so engrossed in their conversation they completely ignored Lorna and Cooper. Cooper would catch Lorna's eye, wink, and they would head for the door.

One morning Lorna and Bonnie stood in the yard in front of the cabin and watched Griffin and Cooper ride off down the valley.

"Griffin said Cooper thinks this here's a good place for a ranch—better 'n what Griff picked out up north. He said if 'n the land ain't took, he 'n Cooper are agoin' to try 'n buy it." There was a wistful note in Bonnie's voice. "This'd make a tight cabin with some fixin' up."

"I don't want Griff to stay here." Lorna's eyes followed the two horsemen until she could no longer see them. "He can't fight off Clayhill men by himself. They almost hung him once and as soon as Cooper leaves they'll be back."

"Ain't it somethin' 'bout that mean ole man bein' Cooper's pa?"

"Don't mention anything about that to Cooper," Lorna said

quickly. "He gets as riled up as a scalded cat everytime that name is mentioned."

"I won't. Lorna, do you reckon I *ain't* wed to Brice?"

"I'd bet my bottom dollar on it. What kind of a preacher would be in a saloon? He didn't give you a paper saying you're wed to Brice, did he?" Lorna turned to find Bonnie looking down at the hand she clasped over the stump of her arm. "That Brice is a dirty, low-down hunk of rotten . . . horse dung, Bonnie. You should know that by now."

"I know it, Lorna. I knowed it right off. Do ya think I could marry somebody else, 'n it'd be all right?"

"Are you thinking of Griff?"

"No!" Bonnie's face turned a bright red. "What e'er give ya a thought like that?"

Lorna laughed. "I'm not blind. You like him, don't you? It shows plain as sin." Lorna laughed at the startled look that came over Bonnie's face.

"It shows?"

"Of course it shows. It's nothing to be ashamed of. It's the natural way of things. I knew right off Cooper was my man, and told him so."

"What'd he say?"

"Nothing. Men have to think they're doing the hunting. I backed off, but I'm not running." She laughed again. "Cooper knows he's my mate, but he's fighting it because he wants to think he's the one to do the choosing. Men are like that, Bonnie. They have more pride than horse sense sometimes." She stepped into the cabin. "I'm going to get those rags of yours and wash them while they're gone."

"No. I'm adoin' it today. I can't let you be adoin' my nasty washin'—"

"Oh, no, you're not," she said over her shoulder. "My granny always said keep out of cold water when your time's on. Besides, it's no chore at all. I just take them downstream and poke one end under a rock and let the fast water do the washin'. Later, I'll get them out and spread them to dry."

"But the men'll see—"

"They won't see anything. And if they do, it won't matter. They have to know you use them. I'm not wanting you to get a back-set, Bonnie. You've got to get well enough to travel. Cooper wants to leave here tomorrow or the next day."

"I'm scared to leave."

"Cooper won't let Brice get you."

"Griff asked me about my folks and about Brice. He said Brice'd not ever hurt me no more. There was somethin' scary in his face when he said it, but somethin' . . . nice, too. Like he thought I was worth somethin'."

"He's had trouble aplenty, Bonnie." A sad expression settled on Lorna's face, and she clicked her tongue against her teeth in maternal sympathy. "My, my, my—imagine him being in that prison and him just a boy. He's had to claw and scratch and kill to stay alive. But it made a man of him— and I'm thinking he'd be a mighty good man to tie to, too."

"It's what I think," Bonnie said, and again there was the wistfulness in her voice.

"I wonder what Cooper's mother is like. It's been so long since I've been around a woman—it scares me, Bonnie. What if she doesn't like me?"

"Cooper don't 'pear to be a man who'd let his ma choose for him."

"No, he doesn't," Lorna said thoughtfully. She looked down at the britches and the worn moccasins she wore, and for the first time in her life wished for a pretty dress.

Chapter Eight

Sylvia Parnell carried the dishpan of water to the end of the porch to throw it out into the yard and saw three riders coming up the lane toward the house. She tossed the water, wiped the pan with a cloth, and set it on the bench beside the door.

With shaky fingers she tucked the loose hair blowing about her face into the knot at the back of her neck. The smoothing of her hair was not due to vanity, but to nervousness. She wished Cooper were there. In the next breath she was thankful he wasn't. When he and Adam Clayhill came together she was never sure that either of them would live to see another day.

This was the third time in the two years since she'd confronted him in the street at Junction City that Adam had come to the ranch and the first time she'd had to face him alone. All these years she'd carried a hatred in her heart for this man who had seduced her at sixteen and left her to face the disgrace of being unwed and with child. Now she told herself she neither hated nor feared him, that he was like a patch of thistle, just something there to be endured, but she knew it wasn't true.

Sylvia stood waiting, a slender, fair-haired woman in a

faded blue dress. The breeze behind her billowed her skirt and lifted strands of hair from the top of her head.

The riders paused at the gate and one of them got down and opened it. The white-haired man on the big, white horse passed through alone and came toward the house. He pulled his horse to a stop at the hitching rail and got off. He was a big man with broad shoulders and long arms. His waist had thickened over the years, but he was not unattractive. His white hair was full and sprang back from a broad forehead. It was carefully trimmed, as was the white mustache beneath his high-arched nose. He shrugged out of the long duster he wore to protect his black serge suit and threw it over the saddle. He came to the edge of the porch, took off his felt Stetson, and flicked the dust from the brim.

"Morning, Sylvia. Fine day."

Sylvia stood with her arms crossed and deliberately ignored his greeting. "Cooper isn't here, and if he was, he wouldn't want anything to do with you. If you keep on runnin' after him, he'll kill you."

Adam laughed. "That's how it's goin' to be, is it? I always like crossing swords with a flippity woman. Kill his own father? He's my son and he's too smart to kill the goose that lays the golden egg. I've had a long ride, Sylvia. Fetch me something cool to drink."

"There's a horse trough out back and a creek on your way back to town."

"Oh, my. You're still holding a grudge after all these years. Look at it this way: I gave you a fine son—you've got nothing to bitch about." He sat down on the edge of the porch and fanned his face with his hat.

"Nothing to . . . bitch about?" Sylvia sputtered, forgetting she had promised herself she wouldn't lose her temper. "All those years I did laundry at the fort to support my son— hearing him called a bastard! Cooper had to grow up in a place where his mother was known as a fallen woman! I could kill you myself for what you did to that boy!" Sylvia's voice trembled with anger. "You . . . make me sick to the stomach! I don't want you here! Leave, or I'll scream and the men will come from the bunkhouse."

"Stop playacting and sit down. There's only one man around here. We passed the other one fixing the fence down at the far end of the valley. And don't play the ravished virgin with me, Sylvia." He pulled at his handlebar mustache and eyed her with eyes as blue as her son's. "You got what you wanted. You were wild for me. You were a little bitch in heat and I serviced you. That's all there was to it."

Sylvia's mouth dropped and color drained from her face. She spun on her heels to go into the house.

"Sylvia!" His commanding voice was like a lash on her back. "You'd better stay and hear what I've got to say if you want that farmer who's courting you to stay in one piece. What's his name? Arnie Henderson? And doesn't he come out here on Saturdays and Sundays? It'd be a shame if he fell off his horse and broke his legs in so many places he'd never ride again—a horse that is." He looked at her over his shoulder to be sure she caught the meaning of his words. Her crimson face told him that she did and he laughed nastily. "Is he as good as I was? You were lousy in bed, Sylvia. You'd never have made it as a whore, but you were all that was available at the time."

"I don't know how anyone as rotten as you can live." Sylvia was beyond anger, beyond tears. His insults had shaken her to the very roots, but she refused to allow him to see the effect of his cruel words.

"I live very well in a house that makes this one look like a pigsty. I've got servants who jump when I holler, and money in the bank. I was the first white man to come to this northwest territory. I drove off the stinking redskins and the riff-raff who follow the trailblazers to a new land. The vultures weren't going to feed off me! I'm a lusty man and take my fucking where I can get it. If that's being rotten, I'm rotten, but I'm rich rotten!"

Sylvia took a long, slow breath to steady herself. "If Cooper knew you were saying these things to me he'd horsewhip you."

"He isn't going to know because you'll not tell him. I want to talk to you about Cooper and I want to look at you when I talk, so sit down."

"I'll not be ordered to sit down in my own home," she said with quiet dignity.

"Very well," he said tiredly. "I'll stand up." Adam got to his feet, turned to face her and leaned against the porch post. He looked at her for a long moment through half-closed eyes. "You're a tiresome woman, Sylvia, but not bad looking for your age. However . . . I don't care for the loose skin and sagging tits of older women." His eyes roamed her figure insolently.

She regarded him unflinchingly, refusing to allow him to intimidate her.

"At one time during the last couple of years I entertained the idea of marrying you and bringing you and my son to live at Clayhill Ranch. Then I realized what a drawback you'd be to a man who expects to be governor of this territory."

"I'd sooner be wed to a rattlesnake." She spoke quietly with no emotion. "You did me a favor, Adam, when you slunk away in the middle of the night like a yellow belly. It opened my eyes to what you are—a taker, a spoiler. I shudder to think about the influence you'd have had on my son when he was growing up."

For an endless moment Adam stared at the cold-eyed woman, aware that behind the calm mask was lethal hatred. Then he shrugged his broad shoulders.

"What's done is done. This is now. I want my son, Sylvia. Cooper is my son. You have only to look at him to know he's a Clayhill. I want him to come and make his home at Clayhill Ranch and take his proper place in running things."

"He'll never do it."

"You're going to see that he does."

"You're out of your mind. Cooper despises you!"

"You're goin' to change that, too. You're goin' to persuade him that it's to his advantage . . . and yours, that he forget the past and think of his future."

"He'll never do it," she said again with a shake of her head.

"I want that boy—"

"My God! Can't you get it through your stupid head that he's not a *boy*? He's a twenty-six-year-old man with a mind of his own."

"When I was twenty-six I had a good foothold on this land. What's Cooper got but a piddly horse ranch that isn't worth diddley squat? Where are your brains, woman?" he asked harshly. "Don't you want anything better for him than . . . this?" Clayhill's eyes roamed the house, the corrals and outbuildings with disdain, and his lips, beneath the white mustache, twisted in a sneer.

"He built up this *piddly* ranch with his own two hands without walking on anybody or hiring killers to run people off their land, which is more than you did with yours."

He ignored her outburst. His cold, steel blue eyes bored into hers. "I want him as a foreman-manager of Clayhill. He's a Clayhill through and through. I'll take him to Denver, introduce him to men of influence, make him a big man in the territory."

Sylvia shook her head with disbelief. "Why Cooper? Why don't you try to *buy* your other son, Adam? Did you know that you have a grandson?"

"Gawddamn you!" His fury burst forth in a strangled shout and his face turned beet-red with anger. "Don't mention that sonofabitchin' redskin to me. He's not a Clayhill! He's a gawddamned fucking red ass Indian."

"Logan's not a Clayhill? How did you manage that, Adam? He's got the Clayhill crooked finger, and Cooper says your grandson has it, too. By the way, did you know that they named him Henry Grant Horn, after Rosalee's father and your brother, Henry, who raised Logan like his own son after you deserted him and his mother? Cooper's very fond of little Henry. He says he's got black hair like Logan's and blue eyes like Rosalee's. Cooper says—"

"Gawdammit!" Adam roared and anger poured out of him. "I don't give a gawddamn what Cooper says!"

"I thought you did," Sylvia said sweetly. "I thought you'd want to know that Logan despises you every bit as much as Cooper does, and being an Indian, he'd think no more of putting a knife in your back than he would killing a mad dog if you were a threat to his family. That family includes me and Cooper, now. The two men have become close friends since they discovered they are half brothers."

Anger unfailingly turned Adam's face a mottled crimson, and when he was angry, as he was now, he invariably struck out at something. His fist hit the porch post with such force the tin on the roof rumbled.

"That bastard hasn't got the guts," he roared. "If he makes a crooked move the army'll be on him like flies on a pile of fresh cow shit and he knows it."

Sylvia's smile had a hint of secrecy to it. "If you say so, Adam."

He slammed his hat down on his head and pointed his finger at her. "You start working on seeing that Cooper comes to see things my way, or else—"

"Or else what?" Sylvia lifted her apron and folded her arms in it.

"Or else that farmer you're fucking gets a hole right between his eyes!" Adam jutted his chin out as he spoke and his eyes were like cold steel.

Pride and dignity caused Sylvia to lift her chin a little higher. "When all else fails, you dip down into your dirty mind for a weapon. You're a poor excuse for a man."

"What you think means no more to me than a pile of horse shit. I mean to get my way in this . . . one way or the other. I'll give you until the end of the month."

With a murderous look on his face, he mounted his horse and stabbed his luckless mount with his spurs. The gelding's powerful haunches propelled it forward into a hard run as it sought relief from the punishing jabs. Adam's men saw him coming and hurried to open the gate. He plunged through it going at full gallop and was soon out of sight.

Sylvia leaned against the wall of the house and watched the men close the gate and ride hard to catch up with Adam. Then she began to tremble, as she always did after each confrontation with him. She'd didn't understand his obsession with her son. It had to have something to do with his male pride, in the fact he'd sired an offspring as handsome and as well thought of in the territory as Cooper. He'd lost considerable face that day in Junction City when it was made known he had a half-breed son who had bought the government land Adam had been using, cutting his holding almost in half.

Sylvia wondered if she would have acted as she did that day, if she had known what the outcome would be. Yes, she thought, she would have. What else could she have done with armed Clayhill men lined up against Logan's armed crew who had just come out from Illinois to help him build Morning Sun Ranch? Adam had been determined to get rid of Logan one way or the other. The whole town heard her tell him Logan was his son. He'd called off his men because his ambition to be governor outweighed his desire to kill the Indian. Of course, in the process, he'd recognized Sylvia as the girl he'd ruined twenty-four years earlier. And Cooper— to her dying day she'd not forget the look on his face when he realized Adam Clayhill was his father. She'd been proud of the way he handled himself that day and during the two years since that time. She'd burdened him with the knowledge that Adam was his father, but she'd also given him a brother he could admire and respect.

Sylvia glanced toward the forested mountain slope and fervently wished that Cooper were home. He should have been back several days ago, she thought with a frown. It wasn't that she worried about him. He was capable of taking care of himself. She was worried about Adam carrying out his threat to shoot Arnie, and she was worried about Cooper's old friend who lay out in the bunkhouse with a crushed hand and foot.

There was a lot the old mountain man wasn't telling about the "accident." Old Volney Burbank was too trail-wise to let an accident like that happen to him—if it was an accident. A week ago he'd come riding in on that little dun horse of his, barely hanging in the saddle, asking for Cooper. The two ranch hands had lifted him off the horse and carried him to the bunkhouse. She'd done the best she could for his broken hand, but Arnie'd had to work on his injured foot, even taking off three of his toes that were hopelessly mangled.

At noon, Sylvia ladled a thick soup into a bowl and set it on the tray she'd made from a flat baking sheet. The old man had eaten very little, and to tempt his appetite she added biscuits, fresh churned butter, and plum jam.

He appeared to be asleep when she entered the square room with the bunks nailed to the outside walls and the pot-bellied stove in its center. She tiptoed to the bed and set the tray on the box she had placed there. The part of Volney's face not covered with straggly gray beard was dark and leathery. His eyes were sunken and now they peered up at her from beneath bushy brows.

"You were playing possum," she accused.

"I heard three horses 'n jist one come on in. What'd he want?"

Sylvia smiled down at him. "There's certainly nothing wrong with your ears."

"I ain't dead 'n I ain't no half-wit!" he replied tartly. "What'd he want?"

"It was someone to see Cooper."

"What was he ayellin' for then?"

"My, my, my." She shook her head dolefully. "You're sharper than all get out today." She made a clicking sound with her tongue. "If you'd pay as much attention to getting some food in your stomach as you do to what goes on around here, you'd be up and out of here in no time at all."

He turned his face away from her. "I'm awaitin' for Cooper. When's he comin'?"

"You've asked me that every day. Now stop being so cantankerous and eat. You're so skinny now the wind could blow you away. Pretty soon you won't even make a decent shadow."

He glared at her. "It ain't seemly for a woman to speak so of a man's limbs."

"I'm not a seemly woman, Volney Burbank. I'd have to be blind not to see that that union suit of Cooper's would go around you a couple of times."

"That ain't seemly neither. Ya ain't ort a speak of a man's drawers!" Volney looked pained, but there was the merest twinkle in his eyes.

"I opéned a fresh jar of plum jam just for you. I hope it sweetens you up some."

"When's that Henderson feller acomin' back? He's sweet on ya, ain't he?"

His remark brought the results he intended and Sylvia's cheeks turned a bright pink.

"You're a meddlesome, nosy old man. Now, you get to eatin' or I'll feed you myself."

"I asked you a civil question, woman. When's he acomin'?"

"Probably on Saturday or Sunday. It's a long ride from Morning Sun."

"Are ya agoin' to wed up with 'im?"

"That's none of your business," she said with a sassy tilt to her chin. "As long as we're asking questions, I have a few of my own to ask. How did a trail-wise old coot like you manage to get a hand and a foot smashed at the same time? Why are you so eager to see Cooper? Who is the Lorna you spoke about while you were out of your head? Is she the poor little cripple you were talking about?"

Volney looked pained and then a cold mask dropped over his features. His eyes, staring up at her, were hard and flat and completely unreadable. "What else did I say?"

"Nothing else. You were concerned," she said gently. "I'm sorry for prying."

The gaunt old man lay there glaring up at Sylvia. All his life he had studiously avoided close association with all except the Lightbody family. And now, for some reason that he couldn't readily understand, he was actually beginning to like this kind, pleasantly pretty woman. He'd never given a thought to whether he liked or disliked her son. He'd traded information about wild horse herds to him for a grub bag. But somehow, he trusted him or he'd not have come here when he needed help. He'd never asked a favor of a man in his life, but when Cooper Parnell came back, he was going to.

Sylvia lifted the cloth from the tray and moved the spoon around to the side of the bowl so he could reach it with his good hand. "When I come back that bowl better be empty."

"And if it ain't?"

"I'll do more than talk about men's drawers and skinny limbs," she threatened. "I'll bring out a bottle of castor oil and talk about . . . bowel movements."

"Humph!" he snorted.

She waited to see if she could get a smile out of him and when she couldn't, she moved toward the door and stepped out into the sunlight. For the first time the old man had shown some spirit. It was an encouraging sign.

Sylvia's eyes automatically went toward the direction from which Cooper would come. Nothing moved on the horizon; but an eagle soared in the sky, glided on the wind currents, and then plunged out of sight behind the hills.

Back at the house she stooped to pull a few weeds growing among the morning glories she'd planted to run up the porch post. She stood there for a long moment, almost dreading going back into the house. Adam's demands and threats buzzed in her head like hornets. She tried to not think about them, but it was only during the brief visit with the old mountain man that she was able to push the dark warnings to the back of her mind.

Then her thoughts turned to Arnie Henderson. During the war he had fought with the Illinois Regulars. Logan had been his captain. An unbreakable bond of friendship had developed between Logan and some of his men. After the war Arnie had gone home to find his wife dead and his farm taken over by carpetbaggers, so he'd come west with other men who had served with Logan to work for him on Morning Sun.

He was a quiet, home loving type of man, a couple of years younger than Sylvia's own forty-two years, but he seemed older and she allowed his maturity was due to his experiences during the war. She'd gotten to know him and enjoy his company when he came to the ranch to get the horses Cooper had sold to Logan. Arnie had very little formal education, but he was well-read. They discovered they both had a passion for reading, and soon he was bringing her books and newspapers with regularity.

Sylvia had endured considerable good-natured teasing from Cooper. Her son delighted in making her blush like a silly schoolgirl. Regardless, she eagerly looked forward to Arnie's visits. He would be out tomorrow or the next day. Should she tell him about Adam's threat or should she just discourage him from coming out for awhile? Cooper's hatred for Adam Clayhill was even deeper than her own. He'd sooner die than do as Adam suggested—and it was unthinkable that she would ask him to, even to protect Arnie. So where did that leave things? She had to warn Arnie and she had to tell Cooper. They were levelheaded men and they would know how to handle it.

"I've got to believe that," she murmured aloud. "If I don't, I'll lose my mind."

Adam Clayhill went back to Junction City and spent the night in the small house he used when he was in town. He was in a dark mood. At times like this he needed release from the frustration of dealing with his son. He thought about Cecilia, the Mexican girl he used at the ranch, and he thought about his stepdaughter, the beautiful Della. Despite his bad mood he had to grin when he thought about Della. If he'd had a daughter, he was sure she would have been like Della. There was a woman who knew what she wanted and went about getting it; just like him, he thought.

As far back as fifteen years ago he'd begun planning to be Territorial Governor. He'd gone back East, found a respectable society matron, married her, and brought her ten-year-old Della and her fourteen-year-old son out to the ranch. He and the boy never got along and it was a relief when, after a few years, he struck out on his own. The boy had kept in touch with his mother until she died ten years ago. Nothing had been heard from him since.

Della was another matter. She was beautiful and knew how to use that beauty; a born courtesan with a sexual appetite to go with it. She and Adam had *discovered* each other several years ago and it had been good . . . for awhile. She was a hot little piece of tail, Adam mused, too hot to be satisfied with any one man. Her weakness had been her passion for the forbidden. She had been determined to seduce the Indian, Logan Horn, and had failed. When that happened Adam had realized she was far too open in her activities for Junction City and had set her up in a house in Denver. She had opened a gentlemen's club where the rich and influential could drink, play cards, gamble, and in secret rooms upstairs indulge in all kinds of carnality. Secretly, Adam was kind of proud of her, and since she used her father's name, her business cast no unfavorable reflection on the Clayhill name.

Adam ate a meal brought to him from the restaurant and went to bed. He lay with his arms folded over his head and wondered how the crew, headed by Dunbar, was doing. He'd sent them to get the nesters off the west range. He was buying that land as soon as he got some money out of government bonds he held. In the meanwhile he couldn't take the chance that some of them might file on the land. The method that always worked was to hang a few of them so the others would get scared and leave. Adam was aware that Dunbar was a stupid man, and had no more brains than to stick his head in the fire if he told him to. He was just the right man for the purpose he was now serving.

Adam's thoughts turned, with resentment, to his brother, Henry. Henry had left his fortune to the *Indian*, giving him the means to buy up land equal to Adam's own. Why hadn't the bastard gone to Texas or Arizona? Why did he have to come here? Because of that sonofabitch things hadn't gone well for him the last couple of years. His status in the territory wasn't what it once had been. He had to do something about it, something to establish his respectability once and for all. Cooper was the answer. There was a son any man could be proud of. Not only did he resemble his father in size and coloring, he had an air of authority about him, didn't back down in a fight and was a natural born leader of men.

"By God, he came from my seed," Adam muttered aloud. "There's got to be something of me in him somewhere. Things would change damn fast with Cooper by my side, running Clayhill Ranch, meeting with the Republicans down in Denver, courting their daughters."

Adam's thoughts spiraled. Goddamn! He'd worked too hard for what he wanted to get sidelined now.

Adam was still in a bad mood when he left Junction City at noon. His nerves were jumping. He sat in the buggy beside his driver, rigid as rock. He'd taken to using the buggy for trips to town. He thought it commanded more respect; was more appropriate for a man of his position. He'd ridden horseback to the Parnells' yesterday because it was faster. Today his sore joints tormented him and he was as prickly as a cactus.

The southwest road meandered along the dry creek bed before turning toward the foothills. The country around them lay utterly still. The only sound to disturb the eerie peace of the road was the jingle of the harness and the thump of horses' hooves. Adam sat scowling, his brow silhouetted in bold profile against the horizon. He'd not moved since he sat down in the corner of the soft, leather seat and propped one booted foot upon the guard rail. The trail was full of holes and jagged pieces of sandstone, which Jacob, the black servant, skillfully avoided lest he incur the wrath of the big, brooding man beside him.

The road passed within hailing distance of a large, white frame house with flowers growing beside the door and a white wash flapping on the clothes line. The place was simply known as The House. It was the only whorehouse within a hundred miles and possibly one of the most *respectable* ones in the territory. It was run by Bessie Wilhite who had, at one time, worked at the saloon as a singer. Every man in the northwest territory knew about The House. It was not only a whorehouse, but a place where a man could go, sick or hurt, and be taken care of regardless of whether or not he could pay. To say anything disrespectful about Bessie or The House was almost like cursing a man's own mother. It just wasn't done.

Adam had long since decided that it was to his best interest to ignore The House, its proprietor, Bessie, and its most popular whore, a mouthy, skinny broad by the name of Minnie Wilson. He knew he didn't have a man who didn't visit The House, and it was all right with him. It kept them from taking off every so often and going farther afield to get their itch scratched.

The Clayhill ranch house was a big, square, two-storied frame building with a wide, railed veranda on three sides. It was surrounded by a white picket fence that no ranch hand dared to step within without being invited. Long windows opened up onto the verandas on both the upper and lower floors. Stained glass panes adorned the upper part of the windows as well as the double doors. The elegant house looked as if it belonged on a shaded street in Denver rather than in the wilds of the northern part of Colorado Territory.

A cluster of outbuildings and a network of pole corrals were set far back from the house, partially screened by a thick grove of junipers. They had been built of stone, log and roughly hewn plank. Compared to the house, they were a mishmash of ramshackle structures.

The horse pulling the buggy stepped briskly up the circled drive and stopped beside the gate. Adam stepped down and the buggy moved on. It was good to be home. He liked the quiet elegance of the house, but of late it had been lonely. He wanted his son to come here, marry a woman of good breeding and have children to carry on the Clayhill name. He would be the beloved patriarch of the first family of Colorado Territory, the natural choice for the highest office of the land—

"Mr. Clayhill."

The voice broke into Adam's daydream and he turned with a scowl to see Dunbar, favoring his right leg, hurrying toward him. The man had made an attempt to make himself presentable by scraping off his whiskers and wetting down his hair. The sleeve of his shirt was rolled up, showing a bloody bandage.

"Did you do what I sent you to do?" Adam demanded without preamble.

"Yes, sir. Ain't nobody living on that range now."

"Good. Did you hang that nester?"

Dunbar's eyes shifted from Adam's steady gaze and he leaned against the fence to take the weight off his sore leg.

"Wal, we hung him, but—"

"But what?" Adam asked curtly. "You did or you didn't."

"We did, but a feller cut 'im down afore he was done in."

"Cut him down? What were *you* doin'? Standing around with your finger up your butt?" Adam roared.

"No, sir. We gone on off. When we went alookin' fer his

horse, we saw he'd been cut down. We trailed 'im to that place down on Blue where we run off that nester last year."

"Well?"

"Cooper Parnell was there. 'Twas Cooper that cut 'im down," Dunbar blurted. He wanted to hurry and get the unpleasantness over with. "He sided with the nester."

"Cooper? What was he doing over there? Did you have a run-in with him?" Adam spit out the questions through lips suddenly tight with anger.

"No, sir," Dunbar lied. "No siree! We know how ya feel 'bout that."

"Then what happened to your arm?"

"The nester cut me up some when we caught up with 'im to hang 'im." He winced and shifted his weight, hoping for a little sympathy. He hoped to hell Fisher and Barrett would keep their mouths shut about the girl.

Adam didn't so much as glance at the injuries. "You didn't say anything to Cooper about me telling you to hang the nester?"

"Oh, no, sir. I said we was after a horse thief."

"Good, good . . . you were. The bastard stole them from somebody. Did you bring them back?"

"Wal, you see . . . we'd left 'em in a boxed canyon while we was trackin' the nester, 'n they was took—"

"You dumb ass!" Adam bellowed. "The nester led you off on purpose. Can't you do anything right? Your bungling's cost us several thousand dollars worth of horseflesh!"

"We'll get a hold a the nester 'n he'll tell us where they is, by Gawd, afore he swings."

"What was Cooper doing there?"

Dunbar saw a way to make things look a little better and grabbed at it. "It shore did look like he'd come to do some horse tradin', 'n we had to back off."

Adam's mind clicked into gear. He wanted those horses. If Cooper paid out hard money for them, so much the better. The sooner Cooper went broke the sooner he'd come to him.

"I want that horse herd and I don't want Clayhill riders suspected of having anything to do with taking them. Understand? Hire a couple of drifters to do the job, then get rid of them."

"I'll get 'em, Mr. Clayhill. Yes siree, I shore will. I won't have no trouble afindin' somebody to do the job."

"It's what I'm paying you for. You say that range is bare?"

"Bare as a babe's butt." Dunbar grinned.

"Any Indian sign over there?"

"Nothin' to speak of."

"Take six men and drive the herd on Baldy Flats out there. Set up headquarters in that place on Blue. I want it made clear that I'm taking over that range. Cooper'll be gone from there by now, but if you see him, don't tangle with him."

Dunbar nodded and Adam went through the gate, slamming it behind him. The man standing outside the fence stewed, the pain in his arm and his leg feeding his anger.

"Goddamn sonofabitch treats a man like dirt!" he muttered. "All he cares about is that bastard of his'n. Wal, if'n I gets *his* bastard in my gunsight, 'n there's nobody 'round to tell the tale, I'll blast *one* of his bastards outta his flea-bitten hide!"

Chapter Nine

It was a morning with no rosy glow in the east. Mists hung over the valley like a curtain as if loath to allow the sun to shine on the group making ready to leave the cabin beside the Blue.

The night before Cooper had questioned Lorna about the mountain pass she and Volney had used. She told him the facts, wisely withholding her opinion until he asked for it. He discussed it with Griffin and with her and Bonnie, saying the decision would effect them all. They decided to take the southern route, but because Griffin and Bonnie were still in weakened conditions, they would travel slowly, taking the whole day to accomplish what Lorna had done in eight hours.

Bonnie sat sideways in the saddle on Gray Wolf's back and Lorna on a folded blanket on his rump. Cooper led off, followed by the women. Griffin on Firebird, with Lorna's rifle in the holder on his saddle, brought up the rear.

They followed alongside the stream straight south. Very shortly after they left the cabin, the stream became a lively trickling run, and when it widened they left it and turned toward the mountains. For an hour they held to a course just below the crest of the foothills.

Despite the dreariness of the day, Lorna was wildly happy.

Every instinct within her was keenly awakened. The colors were more vivid, the sounds more vibrant. A funny little quiver danced down her spine. *She and Cooper were on their way home to Light's Mountain.* Well, not quite, she amended to herself. But when they reached the place where the trail led north to Cooper's ranch, Light's Mountain would be an hour's ride to the south. Cooper figured at that point it would take him a good day of hard riding to reach home.

As the morning progressed, the sky darkened. The wind made itself known first in small puffs and then in growing gusts. Cooper began to wish they'd stayed another day in the cabin on the Blue. He kept going even when he knew they should stop for Bonnie to rest. The trail led upward, sometimes so steeply that Lorna had to reach around Bonnie and hold onto the saddle horn to keep from slipping off Gray Wolf's back. At other times they brushed so close to towering rocks that she and Bonnie held up their legs lest they be scraped by the stone.

A little more than two hours after they left the cabin, Cooper stopped. He chose a spot where a sandy bench was formed between two overhanging shelves of rock. He tossed the mare's lead rope to Griffin and motioned for them to stay mounted while he walked to the edge of the rim, being careful to give himself a background where he would not be outlined against the sky. With his hat pulled low over his eyes he surveyed the area in all directions. It was rugged, lonely country where stunted cedars and gnarled oak clung to ridges of canyon and where red boulders stood, stark and defiant, as they had done since the beginning of time.

With sharp, alert eyes Cooper scanned the area methodically. The only movements were those of two huge jackrabbits who jumped out of a tuft of grass and zigzagged down the slope in smooth, even, bounding motions. Had Cooper's mind been less occupied with the task of their safety, he would have thought them beautiful to see. At the top of each leap their paired ears stood straight up. They disappeared and all was still.

A low roar swelled into rolling thunder. Lightning jabbed downward spitefully, and Cooper felt a decided chill in the wind. He hurried back to the shelter of the overhang.

"There's nothing moving out there but the wind and the jackrabbits," he announced. "We're in for a storm. This is as good a place as we'll find to weather it."

Lorna slid off Gray Wolf and held onto Bonnie when Cooper lifted her down. When Bonnie, stiff and sore, was able to stand alone, Lorna pulled the saddle off Gray Wolf, removed the bridle and slapped him on the rump.

"He'll come when I call him," she said in answer to Cooper's unspoken question. "He can take care of himself."

Griffin led Firebird and the mare to a place where they would have shelter from the south wind, and Cooper jerked the saddle off Roscoe. He placed it beside Lorna's, took a blanket and stretched it out, urged Bonnie to sit down, and hurried to help Griffin with his saddle.

A dazzling bolt of lightning flared, followed by a clap of thunder that sounded as if the very sky above them was being ripped from end to end. The air was filled with a sulfurous stench. The horses whinnied and tossed their heads nervously. The men sank down on the blanket with the saddles to their backs and the women between them. Cooper produced another blanket and an oilskin that he spread over them. He pulled Lorna's back to his chest and wrapped his arms around her.

A torrent of rain struck in a driving sheet. They were sheltered from the mighty blast, but sprayed by the rain sliding off the overhang. Cooper pulled the oilskin up until only their heads were above it, and Griffin did the same on his side. A flash of lightning revealed low, massive thunderheads above the mesa's black rim.

"Are you afraid of storms, Lorna?" Cooper's lips were close to her ear.

A quiver of pure pleasure went through her at the way he spoke her name. She had never felt so wildly happy in her life. It wasn't from fear of the storm that she trembled.

"No. I love storms." She turned her head and whispered against his cheek. "Cooper?" She could feel his breath on her face and smell its faint tobacco scent. "Will you think I'm crazy if I say that storms are exciting?"

"Is that why you're trembling?" His voice was a soft purr in her ear, and she felt the vibrations when he chuckled. Being so close to him caused her heart to thunder and little shivers to run down her back.

"You know it isn't." She giggled and brought her hand out from beneath the blanket to push the hair back from her eyes. Turning her head, she burrowed her face in his neck. The arm around her tightened and she snuggled contentedly against his wide chest.

"You're shameful." The voice in her ear was lazily teasing, but underneath there was a hint of gentle possessiveness.

"So are you for thinking it."

She both felt and heard his chuckle. She couldn't stop the happy laughter that brimmed up in her throat. It was all so new, this wonderful intimacy; being free to tease him, touch him. She caught his hands with hers and pressed them up under her breast. She was alive, soaring, her entire existence focused on him and exulting in being held close in his arms. She filled her lungs with the scent of him. *Oh, blessed storm, please go on forever!*

Wrapped in her own special enchantment, Bonnie was scarcely aware of anything except the man who had turned his back to the wind and the rain and put his arms around her, sheltering her. Rain was sliding off the overhang in a solid sheet. She reached around Griffin to make sure his back was covered with the oilskin and pulled it up to shield the back of his head.

"Am I hurtin' your shoulder?"

"No." Griffin was silent after the one croaked word. He wanted to say something, wanted to tell her the feel of her small, warm body so close to his was like no other feeling he'd ever had. *Bonnie, Bonnie!* It was hard for him to believe he was here with her, and that she was worried his back was wet or that she was hurting him. This sweet, gentle, child-woman, so like a little lost rabbit, was in his arms, pressed against his heart—where she belonged. The realization brought a gentling smile to his hard mouth.

The hand behind his back tugged at the oilskin to make sure he was protected from the rain, and the stump of her handless arm burrowed into the folds of her dress. She was always careful to keep the sleeve of her dress down over it, to keep it out of sight. Poor little girl, he thought. She'd had a hard old row to hoe, but she'd not put up with that fellow, Brice, anymore. He would make sure of that. Griffin felt a tremor go through her and his arm automatically moved to draw her closer into the hollow beneath his arm.

"Are you cold?" he murmured.

Bonnie shook her head. Suddenly it was hard to breathe. She wasn't conscious of the hard ground, nor the soreness between her legs, nor her cramped position. She was aware only of the man with the boyish face and seeking eyes, his arms, the pull of his whiskers on her hair, his breath on her face. Was that his heart or hers thumping so determinedly between them? She closed her eyes, suffused with joy and wonderment, experiencing a strange sense of peace. He held her gently but securely, holding the storm at bay with his wiry body. She wanted to record in her memory this wonderful feeling so she could bring it out and relive it again and again during the bleak days ahead without Lorna's companionship. She thought longingly of spending every day of her life with him, making a home for him, having him with her during the long, lonely nighttime hours—

Bonnie was jarred from her trance when she felt Griffin's hand on her shoulder begin to slide down her arm. Her heart clenched. She made a small, urgent grunt of protest when it reached her forearm. She tried to pull it away. His fingers tightened and then worked their way into the folds of her dress, then into her sleeve and closed around the end of her arm. He held it gently but firmly until she stopped struggling, and then his rough fingers began to lightly caress her. Bonnie thought her heart would stop beating. A lump rose in her throat too large to swallow. Tears spurted and flooded her eyes. She turned her face into the warm skin of his neck.

"Shh . . . shh . . ." She barely heard the sound that was murmured in her ear, but she definitely felt the lips that lingered there. It was a moment she would remember forever.

Almost as suddenly as it had come, the rain ceased. The dark clouds rolled on as if chased by their enemy, the sun. It was as though nature were showing off for the group beneath the overhang. Even as they stood and stretched, blue sky appeared and a rainbow, vivid and magnificent, arched the sky. The sun reappeared with all its intensity, making the green of the washed foliage, the red of the huge bluffs and the white of the snow-capped mountains beyond vivid.

Bonnie stood on weakened legs, keeping her eyes averted from Griffin, but knowing that now there was an awareness between them that hadn't been there before. She felt light and almost giddy with happiness. He had touched her arm, had held it. It didn't seem to be a thing of shame to him. He wasn't repulsed by it! But then, she cautioned herself, he'd only touched it. He hadn't looked at it and he hadn't seen how she used it, pushing and nudging, and carrying a pail of water in the crook of her arm. A little of the joy left her when she thought of Brice saying it made him sick to see it, and she glanced quickly to be sure her sleeve was down.

Lorna called to Gray Wolf and he came galloping up the trail, kicking and frolicking; his spirits high. Her laugh rang out into the freshly washed air as she watched him. Cooper saw her run to the big horse and lovingly pat his face, hang

onto his neck, and murmur into ears that stood straight as he
listened, and then twitched, as if he understood every word
she said. Cooper lifted her saddle and flung it on the gray's
back. His big eyes rolled and the skittish horse would have
danced away if not for Lorna's hand in his mane.

"You're going to have to learn to trust him," she whispered
in his ear. "He's my mate." She turned to Cooper with a
bright smile of thanks and pulled the girth strap beneath Gray
Wolf's belly and cinched it up. She slipped the bridle over
his head and the horse took the bit easily, as if eager to go.

When they were mounted, Cooper led out, leading the
mare. The trail went upward and was difficult to follow, but
there simply appeared to be no other way to go except straight
ahead. The trees around them were mostly Rocky Mountain
nut pine and scrub oak. Occasionally when they rode out onto
a bare shelf they could see the peaks and ridges of the timberline, and above that the white streaks of snow on the rocky
mountain peaks.

Cooper led the party onward and upward, over rugged
rock and along deep cuts until he came to an arroyo with
brush-covered sides. A swift stream flowed over smooth rock
and they rode alongside it to where it cascaded down from
the sides of sheer gray cliffs. Past the waterfall they came
out onto a high plateau. The air was thin and cool. Cooper
set an easy pace. He calculated how far they had to go and
how long it would be before they reached the narrow pass
through the mountains. He took a sack of tobacco from his
pocket and began to build a smoke. It was then that he saw
the Indians.

There were four of them and they came like ghosts out of
the shadowed trees, riding single file. Each Indian was starkly
outlined against the sky as he made his way downward toward
the trail. The dark, alert eyes swung toward Lorna's group
even as the rifle leaped into Cooper's hands. The Indians
wheeled and raced back into the thick stand of fur trees.

Cooper gave a sharp command to the others and spurred

his horse to race for cover among the boulders on the down side of the trail. He jumped from the saddle as the others joined him.

"Don't shoot," Lorna said sharply, forgetting her resolve to not interfere with Cooper's leadership. She slid from Gray Wolf's back and came to peer over the boulder. "I got only a glimpse of them, but they could be Arapaho. If so, they may be friends of White Bull."

"And they may *not* be Arapaho." Cooper cocked his rifle and glanced at her. "Keep your head down," he hissed. "Since the massacre at Sand Creek the chiefs don't have much control over young braves who're still out seeking revenge. Not that I blame them. I'd like to get that bastard, Chivington, in my own gunsight."

Griffin helped Bonnie down, handed her the mare's reins, and took a position beside Cooper with Lorna's rifle in his hands. He waited, rifle ready, but there was no movement or sound.

Cooper cautiously studied the terrain on each side of them and as far as he could see ahead without exposing himself. There was the chance the Indians might retreat down the trail, but there was a greater chance they would make a fight of it. Cooper doubted that the four of them could last long against an all-out attack with only the two rifles. The very silence worried him, because the Indians knew exactly where they were and that there were two women in the group. Of even greater value to the Indians were the four exceptionally fine horses.

"Cooper," Lorna's hand on his arm caused him to looked down into her face, "I'll try and find out who they are—"

"Good God! You're not going out—"

"No, of course not. I'll sing. Almost every Indian in these mountains has heard of me. They think I'm . . . special because my voice carries. I've done it before to identify myself."

"They'll not be the only ones in these mountains to hear you. There are white and Mexican outlaws, too. What about the one that's after Bonnie? He'd know right where to find us."

"I'm not worried about *him*. He'll not show his hand with Indians here. He'll think they're White Bull or some of his people." Her lips curled contemptuously. "He only fights women or someone weaker—"

The sharp crack of a rifle and the sound of the bullet hitting the boulder halted her words.

"They're atryin' to get us to fire back so they'll be sure we're still here," Griffin muttered. "They want to keep us occupied while they flank us. They must think we're stupid."

Cooper looked down into Lorna's upturned face. He lifted a hand and gently brushed the hair from her cheek. It was the loveliest face he'd ever seen. He wanted to hold her, shield her, take her inside himself so she would be forever safe. His hand moved to the back of her head and his fingers stroked her hair while his eyes held hers.

"Go ahead, sweetheart. It's worth a try," he whispered shakily. He couldn't stop himself; he bent his head and laid his lips gently on hers. The softness of her parted lips was undeniably sweet. When he raised his head her eyes were closed, but they opened slowly and looked deeply into his.

She nodded. He'd called her sweetheart! She'd never felt more like singing in her life. She reached for his hand and turned her face upward. Around them the air was filled with her voice. They could hear nothing else. The notes were achingly pure and strong, each word crystal clear, although her companions did not understand them. She sang in the language of the Cheyenne.

"Hear me, brothers of my father, White Bull.
I am known as Singing Woman to all the tribes.
My grandfather was the man the Wasicuns called
Light, but to his Indian brothers he was known
as Sharp Knife.
We cross this land seeking the home of my grandfather.

Let not the blood flow among friends.
Let not your women sing the death song in your village.
Let me not sing the death song for my husband, brother
to Logan Horn of Morning Sun.
My husband is brave and will fight until he dies.
Then I will die. The spirits will no longer hear
the songs of Singing Woman."

A long quiet settled over the area when she finished. There
was not even a birdsong to break the silence or the buzz of
an insect or the rustle of a leaf. Even the wind seemed to lie
down to rest and the puffy white clouds stood still. Between
them and the earth a giant vulture soared silently, waiting for
death below to provide a feast.

Cooper gently disengaged his hand from Lorna's so as to
lift the rifle again to readiness. "I liked your song," he said
in an attempt to make her smile.

Her face was still and pale. Her great eyes met his and he
knew she was aware of the gravity of their situation. There
wasn't another woman in all the world like this woman, he
thought. She wasn't only lovely and proud, she was calm,
intelligent, and plucky beyond all reason. The thought of a
man, red or white, putting his hands on her caused his to
freeze on the rifle, his muscles to quiver, and a feeling close
to panic to knot his stomach.

Lorna glanced behind her to see the horses, ground tied,
standing patiently. Bonnie, standing well back among them
where Griffin had placed her, with the reins of the mare in
her hand, watched with huge and frightened eyes.

The silence seemed to go on and on as if it would never
end. Finally it was broken when Lorna's horse, Gray Wolf,
squealed in protest when Roscoe edged closer to the mare.
And then, as if through the crack made in the silence, the
Indian's voice reached them. It was strong with authority. He
spoke in the tongue of the Cheyenne, but with a different

dialect. Lorna strained her ears and stark lines of concentration creased her face as she strove to understand.

"We have heard of the Wasicun called Singing Woman. I will talk to the daughter of White Bull of the Cheyenne."

"Who is it that seeks to speak to Singing Woman?"

"Blue Feather of the Arapaho."

Lorna turned to Cooper. "They're Arapaho and they want to talk to me."

"I'll go with you," he said as he unbuckled his gunbelt.

"Of course."

Lorna stepped from behind the boulder and Cooper followed, moving up quickly to walk beside her. Two Indians emerged from the woods and came to meet them. One, obviously the leader, had magnificent blue feathers hanging from his braids and a belt of beaded deerskin around his tunic. The other wore a flat-crowned brimmed hat. They approached to within a few feet of Lorna and Cooper. If they were surprised to see the woman with the big voice dressed in men's clothing, their expressions did not reveal their thoughts, but the eyes they turned on Cooper were alive with hate. They looked at him long and hard, then ignored him.

"Singing Woman, your songs please the ears of the Arapaho. We make war on the Wasicun, who steal our land and kill our people, but we no make war on Singing Woman, daughter of White Bull."

Lorna kept her face carefully composed. She didn't look at Cooper, but tilted her chin upward and began to speak, slowly, in case they had difficulty in understanding her.

"To make war on the Wasicun, my husband, and on the Wasicun, my friends, is to make war on Singing Woman."

"We have heard of Logan Horn, the Cheyenne. How is it the Wasicun, your husband, is brother to Cheyenne?"

"Their father is the same, their mothers not the same."

The looks the Indians flashed at Cooper glittered with hatred. He knew that something Lorna had said had angered them. He had caught the name Logan Horn, but that was all of the conversation he understood.

The Indian in the hat now spat an angry word and brandished his coupstick at Cooper. He spoke rapidly to Blue Feather, his voice shrill as he argued for killing the Wasicun and taking the horses.

Lorna crossed her arms over her chest and listened politely while Blue Feather talked to his companion, stating firmly that Singing Woman was the beloved daughter of the Cheyenne, and that he, Blue Feather, would be forced to kill him if he tried to harm her. He said, in no uncertain terms, that *he* would be the one to decide the fate of the Wasicun. His dark eyes, full of contempt, swung around to Cooper and went over him from the top of his head to his boots before he again spoke to Lorna.

"It is said the father of Logan Horn is Clayhill, the Wasicun, friend of Chivington who killed our women and children at Sand Creek."

"Lorna—" Cooper was beginning to understand what they were talking about.

Lorna placed her hand on Cooper's arm without taking her eyes off Blue Feather's stern face. She lifted her head haughtily.

"Is it not said Logan Horn despises his father, the Wasicun? My husband, Cooper Parnell, does not take his father's hated name. He also despises him. My grandfather, Sharp Knife, was friend to the Arapaho. He said every man makes his own tracks. Is this not so with the Arapaho warrior? Are the Arapaho so fond of making war on the Wasicun that they no longer hear the stories of Sharp Knife?"

"There is the other Wasicun, who is not your husband. Why does he hide?" Blue Feather asked scornfully.

"He does not hide. He stayed with the woman who has no hand."

"We will see him."

"*We* will see the braves who hide in the forest," Lorna said, the firmness in her voice matching his.

Blue Feather studied her face. Finally he nodded and without turning he called out a sharp command. When Lorna saw the two Indians coming from the woods, she called out to Griffin.

"Griff, leave your guns, bring Bonnie and come out. Be sure she's got the sleeve of her dress rolled up so they can see she has no hand. They'll think it's a sign she's blessed or she'd have been killed when she was born." She looked up at Cooper. "I think it's going to be all right." She quickly explained to him about the Indian's hatred of Clayhill and told him the next time she used the name while talking to Blue Feather he should spit on the ground. Cooper squeezed her hand and grinned.

Griffin and Bonnie came to stand beside them. Griffin had rolled up the sleeve of Bonnie's dress, exposing the smooth end of her forearm. His hand cupped her bent elbow. He could feel her cringe as four pairs of eyes honed in on the stump at the end of her arm and scrutinized the smooth, scarless flesh.

"Griff, I'm scared."

"Don't show it. Hold yore head up . . . honey. Show some spirit," Griffin muttered. "There ain't a man jack among us that can do with one hand what ya can do. Look the bastards in the eye. Ya ain't got nothin' to be shamed for."

Pride and determination to make Griffin proud of her stiffened Bonnie's back and tilted her chin. All her life she had been made to feel she was some sort of a freak. Now, although her nerves were strung tight as a bowstring, she looked into Griffin's eyes that were almost on a level with her own, and smiled.

"That's the way to show 'em, Bonnie girl. Smile at 'em. They're either agoin' to fight us or they ain't. And if they do, I'm agoin' for the mean one with the hat, 'cause I ain't got one."

Bonnie felt light and airy and unafraid. She could face anything as long as she was with him. The Indians looked at her with dark, curious eyes. Something broke loose inside her and she wanted more than anything in the world to show Griffin that she could stand beside him. She gently shook loose from his grip, lifted the stump on the end of her arm to smooth her hair back from her face and poke the hairpins more securely into her hair. The Indians watched in fascination as she reached over to tie the lacings on Griffin's shirt with her one hand.

"Yo're somethin'," Griffin whispered. "Yo're really somethin'."

"Will my father's brothers share our cookfire?" Lorna asked suddenly. "My husband wishes to share meat and tobacco with friends of his wife."

To her surprise, Blue Feather nodded without hesitation. Lorna smiled up at Cooper. "I hope you've got more tobacco than what you've got in your pocket, because they're staying for a meal."

When Cooper and Griffin would have helped build the fire, Lorna quickly shook her head. This was squaw work, she explained. The Indians would lose respect for them if they should help. The small fire she built was more for ceremony than anything else. Cooper and Griffin sat around it with the four Indians. Lorna passed out meat that had been cooked the evening before. The Indians wolfed down the food as if it had been a long while since they had eaten. She and Bonnie stayed in the background while the men were eating. When they finished, she whispered to Cooper to pass out the tobacco.

Cooper went to his saddlebags and took out three small sacks of tobacco, the last of his supply. He placed them on the ground in front of Blue Feather. The Indian sniffed at the bags, and his eyes sparkled with pleasure. He produced a pipe, filled it, and brought a twig from the fire to light it. He lifted the pipe to his lips with dignity, and after taking

several long meditative puffs passed it to Cooper, who puffed
at it and passed it on to the Indian in the hat. The pipe made
a complete round of the circle. When it came back to Blue
Feather he carefully placed the feathered pipe before him.
He looked directly at Cooper and spoke.

"How is it you do not walk in the footsteps of your father?"

Lorna, sitting behind Cooper, made the translation. She
could tell by the way his back stiffened he was surprised and
angered by the blunt question.

"For the same reason my brother, Logan Horn, does not
walk in our father's footsteps." Cooper looked straight into
Blue Feather's fiercely proud eyes when he spoke and then
spit on the ground contemptuously. He waited for Lorna to
translate.

"Logan Horn is Cheyenne."

"He has as much of our father's blood as I have."

"Why do you hate him who is your father?"

"That's none of your goddamn business, you prying shithead!" Cooper spat out angrily.

Lorna translated his words to say, "It is because he dis-
honored my mother."

Blue Feather seemed to ponder this, then nodded gravely.
His fiercely dark eyes studied Cooper with less hostility in
them. Lorna waited for him to speak again, but he did not.

In the silence that followed the Indian in the hat spoke.
He was younger and more belligerent than Blue Feather.

"I will barter for the woman with no hand." He had scarcely
taken his eyes off Bonnie. Now he looked fiercely at Griffin
and made the offer.

Lorna repeated the words and heard the gasp that came
from Bonnie and the angry snort that came from Griffin.

"Don't be angry," she cautioned. "He holds her in high
esteem. Make the price so high he can't possibly pay it."

Griffin was surprised, but his face didn't register the feeling. He appeared to be considering the offer. He turned serious eyes on the brave, measuring him. The brave stared

back at him haughtily. He held up his coupstick and waved it to show his worth. Griffin looked back over his shoulder at Bonnie. Her eyes were a mute testimony of her anxiety. His left eyelid drooped in a wink to reassure her, and his lips lifted slightly at the corners.

Griffin turned back to the Indian. He rubbed his chin with his fingers, deliberating. "She cannot skin a rabbit," he announced reluctantly, and Lorna translated.

"My first wife builds the fire, my second wife skins the rabbits."

Griffin lifted his shoulders indifferently when Lorna told him what the Indian said. "My woman is lazy."

"She will give me a son with one hand that can do the work of two. It will be a good omen for all to see." He craned his neck to get a better look at Bonnie's slim body. "Is she good on the blanket?"

Griffin seemed to be considering this. "Well . . ." He looked back at Bonnie again, his eyes dancing with mischief. She had drawn her lower lip between her teeth and her eyes sparkled angrily. He turned back and shook his head sadly. "No papoose."

"No papoose?" The Indian's shoulders slumped, then he stiffened them and his dark eyes moved to Bonnie and glittered with contempt before returning to Griffin.

"One pony," he said.

"*One* pony for a woman with one hand that can do the work of two?" Griffin said scornfully. "Look at her hair. Take it down, Bonnie."

"I'll do no such thing, Fort Griffin," she spat at him and jabbed him in the back with her elbow.

"One pony and three beaver skins," the Indian countered, and his expression changed to arrogance.

"Four ponies and six beaver skins," Griffin said firmly.

"No!" The Indian jumped to his feet. The curve of his lips spoke his contempt for such a price for a worthless woman. He gave Griffin a look of disgust and vaulted to the back of his pony. He sat there, his eyes burning hotly, spitting out rapid, angry words.

Finally Blue Feather lifted his hand in an impatient gesture and the Indian in the hat fell silent.

"There are men seeking the yellow stone in the waters you will pass," he said to Cooper. "We did not kill them. They are known to us as friends."

Lorna translated this and then added, "It could be Moose and Woody. They're friends of mine, too."

"I will see Singing Woman to her home, then I will go north to my home on the Thompson."

Lorna hesitated before she translated Cooper's words. He didn't know she had told Blue Feather he was her husband.

"We will go to where my grandfather, Sharp Knife, lived," she said with her hand on Cooper's arm. "Then north to the Thompson."

Blue Feather poked the bags of tobacco and the pipe inside his tunic, uncrossed his legs and got to his feet. He held out his hand to Cooper, ignoring everyone else. Cooper shook it solemnly. Blue Feather turned, mounted his pony, and without a backward glance wheeled and trotted down the trail. His braves fell in behind him.

Chapter Ten

The heat of the dying day was cupped in the sheltered valley and the golden gloom of evening was making itself known. Side by side Lorna and Cooper rode down the timbered hillside and onto the green sward. Unspoken in both their minds was the thought that after today it would be a long while before they would be together again. Cooper welcomed this. He needed time away from this woman; time to get his feeling for her into perspective. Too much had happened too soon.

"I'm glad you came with me, Cooper. I want you to see my home on Light's Mountain." Lorna shortened her reins and turned east, speaking over her shoulder.

Cooper did not reply, but rode along in silence for another little while. Suddenly he spoke, a half smile creasing one corner of his mouth. "I don't think Griffin minded stayin' with Bonnie at all. They seemed to be *took* with each other."

"I know she's *took* with him. She's not had much kindness in her life and I guess Griff hasn't either." Lorna was silent while the powerful gray horse made a dozen cantering strides onward. "I wasn't one bit scared about leaving Bonnie with him. He'll take care of her. Griff needs to have someone trust in him. You trust him, too. You left your rifle and the mare—"

"I couldn't very well leave them holed up without a way to protect themselves, even for just a few hours."

"A few hours? Won't you stay the night?" she asked anxiously.

"Your pa may not make me welcome. Have you thought of that?" Cooper gave her a measuring glance and continued to watch her as he continued. "If my daughter had been gone more than a week and came riding in with a stranger there'd be hell to pay."

"Don't worry about that." She gave him a warm smile. "Frank's used to my coming and going. He knows I've got Bonnie stashed someplace where Brice can't find her and that I've been with her."

Cooper's brows lifted in a puzzled arc. "Why couldn't you have kept her here?" He paused, hating to ask the next question, but asked it anyway. "Wouldn't your pa stand up to the man?"

"Brice convinced Frank that he had married Bonnie, and Pa won't stand between a man and his wife."

"Even if he was killing her?" Cooper asked with impatience in his voice.

"I don't know," she said so softly that Cooper barely caught the words above the rhythmic thud of hooves. She indicated a mound to the southeast. "We're almost there."

They moved over rough terrain and into an upper valley. When they reached it Cooper was convinced that Lorna was a born horsewoman. With her feet lightly resting in the stirrups, she sat a reaching trot, the roughest of all gaits, as smoothly as if the long-striding stallion were moving at a leisurely walk.

"Where did you learn to sit a trot like that? I've seen a few that could do it, but they were mostly Easterners or from Europe." Admiration was evident in his voice now, just as impatience had been while they were discussing her father.

"Frank taught me a long time ago. He said if I was going to ride I'd do it right. That was before . . . Mama died."

Cooper said nothing for awhile. Roscoe broke stride in order to stay with the powerfully moving gray that sensed he was near home. "Your pa's from back East?"

"I think he came from Scotland when he was little, but he doesn't talk much about himself, so I'm not sure."

"Is he a hard man?"

Lorna shook her head. "No..." She drew the word out thoughtfully. "It's just that since Mama died he's wanted to leave Light's Mountain. He doesn't have much to do with me. He... just puts up with me and—" She broke off, embarrassed at having shown him this intimate glimpse of her deepest longing for a more loving relationship with her father.

They skirted the hill and quite suddenly Cooper spied the homestead. It sat back in the pines and looked as permanent and peaceful as the mountains that surrounded it. Smoke curled upward from one of the two stone chimneys. He glanced at Lorna and found her looking at him with a tremulous smile on her face.

"This is my home, Cooper," she said simply, her eyes holding his steadily.

Cooper gave her a searching look and then looked back at the homestead. Quite suddenly they had nothing to say to each other. It was a fact that came to them simultaneously and made them feel awkward. Their glances met and fell away. When he looked at her again he found her watching him closely, as if his reaction to her home was very important to her. She led the way along a well-worn trail to the homestead. Cooper followed and studiously examined it and the surrounding area as if searching for something. His mind absorbed the fact that the homestead was built to withstand an attack and well laid-out. The sheds and pole corrals were situated so that the run-off flowed downstream from the building.

As they neared the house two huge dogs leaped from the porch and in long bounding strides came to meet them, barking their pleasure. The dogs' warning clamor brought a man to the porch. He stood there, loudly cursing the roaring dogs as the two riders came into the yard. He stepped to the edge of the porch, his whistle at once bringing the dogs back to him.

Cooper and Lorna pulled up a dozen feet away and sudden tension gripped Cooper. Below heavy brows and a thatch of dark red hair laced with gray, the man's eyes gleamed with hostility. He was of medium height, stockily built, with wide shoulders and long arms. Cooper returned the man's hostile gaze with no show of emotion. Nor did he speak.

"Who in hell air ye? What ye be doin' here?"

"Pa!" Lorna swung from the saddle and stood, feet spread, her hands on her hips.

Her father's glance went to her and then back to Cooper.

"I asked who ye be 'n what ye be doin' with my lass." His voice was deep and rough with its strong Scottish accent.

"You've got a strange way of greeting a stranger, mister. I'm Cooper Parnell," Cooper said with deceptive mildness. "If you've a decent set of manners to your name, you'll thank me for bringing your daughter home."

Frank gave a snort of disgust. His bright gaze remained unwinkingly on Cooper. "She needs be looked oot fer 'bout as much as do a grizzly."

"I invited him here, Pa. Can't you be decent for *once*?" Lorna's clearly etched features were perfectly composed and wholly cold, belying the fact she was mortified by her father's behavior.

Frank turned his angry gaze on Lorna. "Where ye be gone to, lassie? If it be a mon ye be huntin', there be aplenty here what'd step in an' be *lord* of Light's Mountain if'n ye but say the word." His words were laced with sarcasm.

"You know where I've been and what I've been doing. There isn't a *real* man on this mountain, Frank. Not one who'd stand up to Brice Fulton. *I* had to do it."

"She be his wife!" Frank roared.

"She's not his wife and you know it!" In the tense silence

Lorna's voice sounded unnaturally loud, although she held it to a level pitch.

"I'll ride on, Lorna," Cooper said curtly.

"No! Please stay, Cooper." Her cry of protest came out sharply. She dropped Gray Wolf's reins and came to stand beside Roscoe. Suddenly she was on the verge of tears; she couldn't bear the thought of his leaving. She blinked rapidly to keep the tears from disgracing her. "Don't go, Cooper. I'm sorry my pa is so lacking in manners. He's a rude and bitter man. I should've prepared you for him. Please stay. I'll fix you some supper."

She stood in troubled silence while Cooper looked down at her. He couldn't help but wonder how she had managed to turn out so sweet and loving, living with this angry, bitter man. She stood stiff and proud, her fine-boned profile set with the effort not to betray her tears.

"I don't want to cause trouble between you and your pa. But if you're sure it's all right, I'll stay." He grinned at her. "Roscoe would like a rest. Where shall I put him?"

"I'll show you—" She broke off as the dogs again erupted into violent outcry directly underfoot. Lorna's low command held them where they were, and she turned to look at what had set them off. Two riders filed out of the woods and came steadily toward the house. It was nearly dark, but Lorna recognized Hollis and Billy Tyrrell. Anger showed in the way she straightened her back, snatched up Gray Wolf's reins, and started toward the back of the house.

"*You've* got company, Frank," she called over her shoulder in a scathing tone.

It was dark by the time they had fed and watered the horses. Lorna's joy at being home and having Cooper here with her eased away some of the strain created by her father's unhospitable greeting. She took Cooper's hand and led him to the house. On a shelf beside the back door was a bucket of water, a tin washbowl and a towel.

"You can wash up here, Cooper. I'll wash in my room and then fix us some supper."

"Lorna...I don't want to stay if it'll cause you trouble later on."

"It won't cause any trouble. I want you to stay!" There was a husky note of desperation in her voice. "I'm sorry Frank acted the way he did. He can be mean and hateful when he's in a bad mood. But he's not a bad man, Cooper. I think he's worried that he's in trouble and that you've come to see about the rustling—"

"It's not my stock they're stealing. I'll not give him any trouble, Lorna, unless he pushes me."

"Oh, Cooper! I know that." Lorna slipped her arms about his waist and pressed herself against him. "Hold me for just a minute. You'll be gone tomorrow. I...don't want to think about it."

Cooper hugged her close and buried his lips in her hair. "You can come home with me, meet my ma, and see Bonnie settled." The words came out before he realized he was even thinking them.

"I can't. I've got to see what Frank's up to. Will you come back soon? Please say you'll come back soon." His body was big and hard and warm and he cradled her to him with a gentleness that brought tears to her eyes. Lorna felt the tension in her muscles loosen.

"I can't promise you that I'll be back *soon*," he whispered regretfully.

She took a shaky breath, her voice very low. "But you will come back?" She pressed her face against his shoulder and closed her eyes tightly against the words that were sure to come.

"I'll come back." He lifted her face and kissed her trembling mouth with incredible gentleness. He kissed her eyes, tracing the outline with sensual, delicate caresses. Then his kisses moved slowly down her cheek to the corner of her mouth, his tongue moist and probing. Lorna was swimming in a haze, aware only that she was pressed tightly against him, his mouth warm and tantalizing against her skin. Then he was holding her away from him. "You'd better get in there and fix me something to eat before I carry you off and . . . have my way with you." His whispered threat was edged with desire and a shudder of longing worked its way down his body.

Lorna's laugh was low and joyous. "That doesn't scare me, my love."

"Well, it better," he said sternly.

She held his arms and looked up into his face for a long while. "Oh, Cooper, what scares me is that if your mare hadn't gotten loose, and if I hadn't climbed the cliff that day—" She shuddered and held onto him tighter while she pressed her face to his shoulder. "If you hadn't come looking for her, I'd have missed meeting up with you. It might have been years before I found you again."

She tilted her head to look up at him with undisguised hunger. He had placed his hat on the bench before he kissed her and she could see the thick, crisp hair that covered the tops of his ears and fell onto his forehead. Her hand moved to smooth it back.

"Oh, my love," her heart cried, "will you learn to love me as I love you?"

Cooper could feel the strong vibrations of his pounding heart. He was fascinated by the soft, sweet smile that curved her lips and was reflected in her eyes. He had never felt less articulate in his life. All that he wished to say stayed inside his head. She was a witch, a child-woman. She would take over his heart, his soul, and all his waking moments if he gave in to her.

She moved her hands to his shoulders and raised up on her toes. Her nose nuzzled the hair back from his ear, and warm lips caressed the lobe. "Shall I tell you something you've not thought of yet?"

"How can I think of anything with you doing that?" He

held her away from him and his eyes devoured her smiling face.

"We'll make beautiful, strong children, my love, and... lots of them," she whispered, and then with a giggle she left his arms and darted into the house before he could reply.

Lorna stood inside the door of the darkened house for a moment because her wildly racing heart was making her breathless. He was her dear love. They would have lots of children who would grow up and have children. They'd all live together right there on Light's Mountain.

She could hear the low murmur of voices on the porch and was grateful that Frank hadn't brought Hollis and Billy into the house. She lit the lamp in the kitchen, stoked the fire in the cookstove, and added a few sticks of wood from the woodbox. When she was sure it had caught she hurried to her room and slipped out of her clothes and washed in the china bowl on the washstand. She loosened her hair, brushed it and tied it back with a ribbon, then rummaged through the chest at the end of the bed that held her mother's clothes. She brought out a black skirt and a yellowed, white blouse with large mutton sleeves and a high neck. She slipped them on and buttoned the blouse up the front with nervous fingers. The blouse was too big and the skirt too short. She hadn't worn the outfit since she went to a burying on the other side of the mountain more than a year ago. She dressed hurriedly and slipped her feet into the new pair of moccasins White Bull had given her on his last visit.

The kitchen was empty when she reached it so she went to the door. Cooper was sitting on the end of the porch. She could see the glow of his cigarette and the arc it made when he flipped it into the yard.

"Come on in, Cooper." She stood back when he came into the room. Her hands were clasped in front of her and her violet eyes anxiously searched his face. At first there was nothing; then a smile that started at the corners of his lips spread into a broad grin.

"By jinks damn! Look here! I almost didn't know you without the britches."

"Oh, you—"

"You're a woman after all, and as pretty as a bluewing teal." He laughed with delight at her reddened face, covered her hand with his, and gripped it hard.

"Sit here and behave yourself." She pulled her hand from under his and gestured toward a cane-bottomed chair beside the table.

His eyes held hers for several seconds before he moved. Her heart began thumping in her neck as his low, chuckling laugh surrounded her and warmed her. He cupped one big hand under her chin, gave it a shake and said, "I'm as hungry as a bear and you look good enough to eat."

Lorna took a deep shuttering breath, her joyful heart shining in her eyes. She was almost lightheaded with happiness. "I'd give you a belly ache—"

"I reckon you would." His eyes were still wrinkled at the corners, his lips still twitching.

"I'll fix you a mess of eggs. My hens have been laying lately, and we've eaten eggs till they're coming out our ears. I'm surprised Pa even gathered them."

"Eggs will be fine. I haven't had anything but meat since I left home more than a month ago. I've missed my ma's cooking," he said and grinned in the boyish way she loved.

"You're anxious to get back home?" It was a silly question and she wished she hadn't voiced it.

"Yeah. I left some mares in foal. I'm anxious about them, and about how Ma fared while I was gone. Not that I worried about her, I know she's all right. But I miss being home."

There was a longing in his voice that caused Lorna to feel a sudden emptiness in the pit of her stomach.

She stood uncertainly beside the chair. His home was important to him, maybe as important to him as hers was to her. A new emotion rose up in her as acute as pain—fear he would return to the home he was so eager to get back to and never again come to Light's Mountain.

"How do you like your eggs?" she stammered, desperate to shake off this feeling of desolation. "Fried, or boiled and put in gravy? I'm not the best cook in the world, but most anybody can cook eggs or boil greens and fat-back. Hoppin' John's my specialty. I can just about put meat scraps, peas and peppers together blindfolded. That's easy compared to making doughnuts—I'm just no hand at all at making doughnuts. They come out hard and flatter than a flitter—"

She smoothed her skirt down with the palms of her hands and looked into eyes, warm, bright and . . . twinkling! Color came slowly up her neck and turned her cheeks crimson. She put her palms against them.

"I'm just rattling on like a looney!" she wailed. "Dammit, Cooper! You've got me so nervous and jittery that I'm making a fool of myself."

He put his head back and laughed. Violet eyes, wide with distress, clung to his face. He tugged on her skirt and pulled her closer to him.

"You're the prettiest thing I've seen in quite a spell. I'm glad to know there's a real woman inside those britches you've been wearing and that you can get nervous and jittery."

"I *am* a real woman, Cooper. Don't I kiss like a real woman?"

"Uh huh, you sure enough do!"

"Do I kiss as good as town girls?"

"Well, now . . . I'll have to ponder on that."

There was a silence, then she jerked her skirt from his grasp and stood glaring down at him. "Don't ponder too hard or you might strain what's between your ears!" Eyes that held a trace of hurt and a definite glimmer of irritation met eyes that twinkled with amusement.

"With a little more practice, you'll be a fair-to-middlin' kisser."

She gazed into laughing eyes as blue as the sky and her

brief spurt of anger drowned in their sparkling depths. Then, lightning fast, her fingers reached inside his shirt and she gave a hard yank to a thick tuft of golden hair on his chest. She sprang away when he yelped and reached out his long arms to grab her.

"I'll see if I can find a man willing to let me practice on him," she retorted sassily. Her merry laughter filled the room.

How wonderful, she thought, to have him here in her home, laughing, teasing. He belonged here! He belonged here with her! The thought flitted through her mind like a melody and soft musical notes escaped from her lips. Smiling, she whirled away to start the meal, but the smile on her face died a sudden death when she saw her father, Billy and Hollis watching from the doorway.

Cooper turned his head to follow Lorna's gaze. In the silence that followed, he watched the men come into the room. He had seen men of their caliber in every saloon in the territory; sleazy, hard-faced men, looking for an easy dollar. There was cruelty in the face of one who pushed ahead of the others, a harshness that seemed to spring from some inner source of malice and hatred. He wore a gun tied down and had a knife in his belt. The other man stood slightly behind him and there was an odd similarity in their faces.

"What're ya doin' here, mister?" The harsh voice sprang boldly into the room. Cooper raised up out of the chair and stood facing the doorway, but didn't speak.

"I ain't alikin' ya messin' round my . . . intended."

Lorna let out a muffled gasp of fury. "Damn you, Hollis!"

"Hush, woman. This's men business."

"Why you . . . stupid clabberhead! You dumb . . . hog! Don't be telling me to hush up in my own house! I'm not, and never will be, *your* intended! It would be a cold day in hell when I marry up with trash like you." She reached behind her and grabbed a quirt from the peg on the wall. "Now get out of here or I'll take my whip to you!"

"Hush up yore mouth, I said!" Hollis's small, bright eyes

stared at Cooper while he spoke. "There'll come a time when I'll learn ya to keep a civil tongue in yore head."

"Hold on, Hollis!" Frank roared. "Ye'll not be causin' no trouble in me own house, 'n I'll be havin' ye to know my lassie ain't yer intended 'n *ye'll* be keepin' the civil tongue in yer head."

Small furious eyes swung to the stocky man who stood with his hands on his hips. "Gawddamn ya, Frank! Ya said—"

"I said if me lassie was willin', is what I be sayin' to ye. It 'pears she ain't wantin' ye fer her mon 'n that's the end of it."

Hollis reacted as if Frank's harsh voice had slapped him across the face. His face turned blotchy red and he clenched his fists. He took a step forward as if he would strike him, then rocked back on his heels as if an invisible hand held him. He turned his hate-filled eyes to Cooper.

"I asked ya what're ya doin' here? What're ya sniffin' round Lorna fer?" He turned to stare fixedly at Frank. "It ain't fer nothin', Frank. Ya wantin' a outlander to come in here anosin' round yore gal? If you can't take care of this here drifter 'n send 'im on his way, I reckon I can do it, 'n without no help from you."

"He brung me lassie home, 'n he be welcome to a meal. I'll not be havin' a mon comin' on me place atellin' me to send a mon packin', be Gad!" Frank's voice rose to a roar. Anger was stamped on his face and in every line of his body.

"*Yore* place?" Hollis sneered. "Ya ain't never said nothin' 'bout this being *yore* place afore. 'Twas always *her* place, ya was callin' it." He looked down at the shorter man with an insulting, superior look on his face.

"Get out of here, Hollis, and take that buzzard bait with you." Lorna jerked her head toward Billy Tyrrell. Her voice was sharp and hard and quivered with anger.

Hollis ignored her.

"If'n this is *yore* place, Frank, and ya got the say so round here, ya'd do good to put a strap on that gal's butt, 'n she'd do what she's told without no back-talk."

Hollis's words and his sneering voice caused a hurricane of rage to sweep up from deep inside Frank, ridding him of fear and replacing it with pride.

"Hold yer tongue!" Frank demanded in a strident shout. "I be havin' no mon come to me house 'n speak so of me or me lass!" His head jutted forward and his hamlike fist came out as if to strike Hollis. "Ye 'n Brice be doin' things not to me likin', Hollis." He stuttered with the power of emotion, and his voice was heavy with Scottish brogue. "What ye're doin' be no business a mine, 'n I keep me nose outta it, but I be tellin' ye now, ye had no call to be cripplin' an oold mon like ye done 'n I be havin' no part a it on me conscience."

"Holy shit, Frank! What side a the fence ya on, anyways?" Billy spoke for the first time and edged his way from behind Hollis to stand beside him.

Cooper stood loose jointed, his hands at his sides. He was confident he could handle the blowhard in front of him, but he didn't like the confinement of the room, or the fact that Lorna stood a chance of being hurt in a free-for-all. His eyes moved like the swift slash of a knife, taking in everyone, but they rested for a fraction of a second longer on Lorna. She was looking at her father with something like bewilderment on her face.

"If'n ya ain't with us, yore agin us," Hollis said menacingly.

"Aye," Frank said. "I don't be likin' the turn a things. I done tol' ye me lassie was choosin' her own mon."

"Ferget 'er, fer now. I'm a talkin' 'bout this here gent. He ain't had nothin' to say. Ya doin' his talkin' fer him, Frank?"

Frank shot a glance at Cooper, and it came to him like a shouted warning that here was a man who backed down to nothing. This was the man to watch, with his loose-knit frame and the careless way he held his hands to his sides. The air of nonchalance was a trifle too well managed, too pat. The man's eyes were on Hollis and devoid of expression, his features blank and cold as marble.

"I do my own talking when there's something to say or somebody decent to say it to. All that's here, besides Miss Lorna and her pa, is a couple of mangy, flea-bitten polecats. I've got no use at all for polecats." Cooper's voice was soft, but the words fell like stones in the quiet room.

Hollis started to answer, choked, and said in a barely audible monotone, "Gawdamn! Ya Gawdamn outsider—"

His nostrils flared and a faint white mark rimmed his mouth as color drained from his face. He straightened to his full height, then slowly bent forward. The man's fury was real. It pushed him beyond the bounds of reason. His hand flashed down and grasped the gun at his side.

Lorna moved with blinding swiftness. She slashed Hollis across the forearm with the heavy quirt just as his gun was sliding free. The blow brought a yell from Hollis. The gun fell back into the holster and he grabbed his arm as blood sprang from the cut made by the whip. Lorna lifted her arm to strike him again and Cooper, with a muffled curse, leaped forward and jerked the quirt from her hand.

"Mister, you came within a second of getting yourself killed," Cooper said in a coldly wicked voice. "You better be glad you got a cut on the arm instead of a hole in your head."

"Get out of here, Hollis. You step foot on this place again and I'll shoot you," Lorna said, her voice unnaturally quiet; it's very gentleness caused all four men to send her darting glances. Anger had made her eyes brilliant; her cheeks were flushed and her whole body trembled with rage.

"Sheeit, Hollis. C'mon." Billy pulled on his arm. "Ya know where to find us, Frank," the small man said with a show of bravado in his voice. "Brice ain't agoin' to like what ya done a'tall. He ain't forgettin' 'twas Lorna what took his woman 'n hid her off somewheres. He's likely to be acomin' to pay ya a visit."

"Aye, he's likely to come," Frank said. His tone told Lorna that his spurt of courage was leaving him. His shoulders slumped and he followed the two men out to the porch.

As soon as they were alone, Cooper looked at Lorna. Bright shards of anger danced in his eyes. Anger had taken him so completely that he went white and stared at her in terrible silence for what seemed to her an eternity.

"I should use this quirt on you!" he said coldly and threw it from him. "Don't ever deal yourself in on my fight again. Do you understand?"

"He'd have killed you!" She stared back at him, swept by her own rage, her body rigid.

"I think not!"

"He would have. I know him. He's mean and—"

"I had him covered before his hand touched his gun."

"I didn't know that!"

"You didn't look. *You* could've gotten me killed and I don't take kindly to *that*!"

"No! I wouldn't have let him—"

"Can't you get it through that stubborn head of yours, Lorna? The *other* man could have killed me if he'd had a mind to when you distracted me by dealing yourself in!"

"I'm sorry—"

"You're a take-over, headstrong woman, Lorna—"

"I'm not!" she stormed. Her violet eyes, beneath level dark brows, were icy with anger. "I'm not a weak little flower to stand by and let someone else do the fighting for me. I've had to learn to take care of myself or I'd have been taken over long ago by such as Hollis and Billy."

Cooper wasn't satisfied with that. "I'm not talking about taking up for yourself. I'm saying you had no business butting in! It was between him and me. I didn't want you and your pa in on it."

"Hellfire! You're just like *them*! You think a woman ought to be seen, but not heard, whipped and used till they're all broken down like a used up horse, then thrown out. I'll not be like them, I tell you," she yelled. "I have just as much brains as any man I ever saw and a heck of a lot more than most, Cooper Parnell!"

"Oh . . . hell!" Cooper put emphasis on the last word and took his hat from the peg beside the door.

Lorna took a step toward him, reached the chair and held tightly to the back of it. "Are you leaving?" she asked tightly, fighting back angry tears.

"Not till morning. *I'm* not foolhardy enough to ride out and get myself waylaid." He jammed his hat down on his head. "I'll sleep in the shed, if that's all right with you, *ma'am*."

"I'll fix you some supper."

"Don't bother. I've still got some jerky in my saddlebag."

He went out the door and Lorna could hear his bootheels thumping on the porch planks as he crossed it.

Chapter
Eleven

Frank stood on the edge of the porch. He watched Hollis and Billy ride away from the homestead, and listened to the threats they yelled back at him until darkness and distance swallowed them.

"Brice won't like this a'tall, Frank."

"Brice'll be acomin' to see if'n yo're standin' agin us."

"Lorna'd better watch out. I ain't havin' no woman usin' a whip on me like she done."

"That outlander ain't here but fer one thin', Frank, 'n ya know what *that* is."

When their voices faded, Frank's big shoulders slumped wearily. He'd been willing to ignore their lawlessness, not even bothering to tell Lorna he'd had no part in it. All he'd ever wanted of Brice and his outfit of ne'er-do-wells was the companionship they provided; a few games of cards, an evening of drinking, a way to pass the time.

Aye, but time passed so slowly. Every day was a week, every week a year. Spring, summer, fall, winter; all the same.

"Nora, sweet lass, why did ye leave me?" he murmured. "Ye were all that's ever been good in me life. Ye left an empty shell of a mon to mourn ye, a mon who can't stand the sight of his own flesh and blood, for she be the spittin' image of ye."

Suddenly an incredible awareness of what his life had become descended upon Frank and revealed to him his utter uselessness. What a failure he'd been! What an utter failure. He began to tremble, unable to move. He hooked his arm around the porch post for support and clung there, staring out into the darkness. A vision of Nora's laughing face danced before his eyes, or was it Lorna's face? The two had blended into one, of late. He closed his eyes; it was still there. Sweet, sweet Nora with the soft, soothing hands, warm, clinging body, and dainty ways. She'd been a thing of beauty to be loved and cherished. His love for her had been all-consuming and he'd wanted desperately to take her to a home of his own making, but she couldn't bring herself to leave this accursed mountain and he couldn't leave her.

"Accursed mountain?" he said the words aloud and suddenly it was as if the words he'd uttered were blasphemous. Light's Mountain had been his home for more than twenty years; half of his lifetime had been spent here. The only happiness he'd ever known had been here on this mountain. How could he say it was accursed? Could he *really* leave it, as he had longed to do all these years? Could he leave all that was left of Nora?

"Ach! It's looney, I be, to think of it." His whispered voice was rough with emotion and tears filled his eyes and began to flow down his cheeks.

The revelation of his true feelings was so astonishing it brought on a sudden faintness, drawing all the strength out of him. He sank down on the end of the porch. A thousand sweet memories swept over him; memories of lying with Nora in the deep feather bed; soft, clinging arms; whispered words of love; long winter evenings spent before a roaring fire. He thought about the Thanksgivings they'd shared, and the Christmases. The Lightbody family had accepted him for himself, their daughter had loved him, and he had returned so little. He'd not even tried to understand his child; flesh of his beloved Nora.

Frank began to see clearly what he had become. He'd been living in his own world of resentment and self-pity. His boundless pride had made his world a living hell, and refused to let him appreciate what he had. He'd spent wasted years longing to make his own mark as Light had done. Dear sweet Jesus! He'd done what he'd been destined to do. He'd made his woman happy and together they'd created a bairn who would carry their flesh and blood on into the next generation. He'd had more happiness during the few short years with Nora than most men had in a lifetime.

Frank lifted his head and listened to the sounds coming from the house; sounds made by his Nora's bairn. He hadn't really looked at the girl or listened to her for so long that she had grown into a woman without his realizing it. Now, a man had come, a stranger, and his bairn was in love with him. It was the same as when *he* came to Light's Mountain, a stranger, and Nora had fallen in love with him, not knowing or caring about where he came from, or where he was going. She had merely looked at him and he at her, and they both had known he would stay with her forever.

Frank stood and walked out into the yard so he could look back at the house. The lamplight shone from the kitchen window. For once, he felt no bitterness or shame for what he hadn't accomplished. Pride, anger, even his grief, were self-centered preoccupations for which there was no room in his thoughts at this moment. No other course was open to him now but to dedicate himself, humbly and honestly, to this place so future generations would know where they had come from; something, he thought, he'd never know about himself because he only started to live when he came there.

He walked slowly across the plank that spanned the creek and up the hill toward the burial grounds. He'd walked this path many times in the dark of the night, when peace would come to his troubled mind only while he sat beside Nora's final resting place. He reached the grave and stood for a moment with head bowed, then eased himself down onto the ground, wrapped his arms around his bent legs and rested his head on his knees.

"Nora, Nora, me darlin' lass, me heart is sore 'n weary. I know it's wrong I been to push our bairn from me. Dinna be lovin' me the less fer it, fer my heart had no room but for ye. It's sorry I be..."

Frank felt the warm, thick flood of tears rising to his eyes and he was helpless against them. They rolled down his cheeks and fell onto the abundance of wild flowers he'd planted years ago and since had tended with loving care. Unashamed, he allowed them to fall, for there was no one to see or care; no one but... Nora.

Lorna had never felt so desolate in all her life. The quarrel with Cooper had put such a strain on her that she felt faintly ill with weakness. A lump rose in her throat. She swallowed it with difficulty and looked down at her hands that were clamped to the back of the chair. She'd ruined everything! she thought miserably. A shiver passed over her when she realized how little time she had to try and make things right with Cooper. *Damn Hollis and Billy! Damn Brice Fulton!*

Through the fog of despair that hung over her, Lorna's thoughts turned to her father, and how he had stood up for her against Hollis. She felt a spurt of affection for the moody, gruff Scot who, at times, was like a stranger to her. Was it possible he'd been worried about her during the days, weeks, she'd been away? Was his anxiety for her the cause of his rudeness to Cooper? On more than one occasion she had been away from home visiting White Bull's camp or out panning for gold with Moose and Woody and he hadn't seemed to notice she'd been gone. *He showed more concern for her tonight than he had for years.* The thought was a pleasant surprise to her troubled mind.

Lorna stood quietly for a moment, staring at the shadows

on the floor made by the lamplight. Then, with extraordinary clearness of mind, she began to put things in their right perspective.

There would be time, she reasoned, to settle with Hollis and Billy for embarrassing her in front of Cooper. And there would be time to find out if Frank really had had a change of mind about getting tangled up with Brice Fulton and his outfit. Right now, she had to fix a good supper for Cooper and take it to him. He was too angry to come back to the house tonight, and come daylight he'd ride out. The thought of him leaving was almost too painful to think about.

Lorna lifted the trap door to the cellar, set the lamp on the floor, then went quickly down the steep steps. She filled a small tin bucket with fresh milk, thinking the cellar was as neat and tidy as when she had left it. Frank, for all his grumpiness, was neat and clean in both his person and the house, and for that she was thankful.

Back in the kitchen she checked the basket to be sure the hard-boiled eggs had not rolled on the fried mush and that the hot biscuits were not next to the butter. She blew out the lamp. While she waited for her eyes to adjust to the total darkness, she smoothed her hair back with her palms and took several deep breaths in an attempt to slow her racing heart.

The cool night air felt good on her face, flushed from the heat of the cookstove, and reminded her that it was early September. Soon the nights would turn cold and the sky would be filled with the long streamers of southbound geese and ducks. During the next few weeks she would be busy preparing for winter as had her mother, grandmother and Maggie before her. She would smoke venison, elk meat and dozens of turkeys, render bear oil and fill crocks with nuts and berries imbedded in goose fat.

There would be the hunt for a honey tree. That thought brought Volney to her mind. Her old friend had, for years, told her where to find the honey tree. Something her pa had said came instantly to her mind: *Cripple an oold mon like ye done*. Had Hollis and Brice hurt Volney? Her steps quickened and by the time she reached the shed she was almost running.

"Cooper? Are you in here?"

"I'm out here."

His voice came from the side and she spun around to see the glow of a cigarette in the darkness beside the woodpile and went toward it. Cooper was sitting on a log Frank had dragged down from the hillside to cut up for firewood.

"I brought your supper." She stood hesitantly before him. "And I'm worried that Brice and Hollis have hurt Volney," she blurted. "They would if they thought he'd helped me get Bonnie away."

"Why don't you ask your pa?"

"I will." In the darkness she could see only the tilt of his head as he looked at her. "Cooper, I'm sorry."

He didn't answer immediately, then he said, "You're the most irritating woman I've ever met up with. One minute I want to swat your bottom, the next minute I want to kiss you senseless." His hand came out to clasp her arm and pull her closer to him. "What did you bring me to eat?" he demanded gruffly. "If it's good, and there's plenty, I might decide to let you off with only a pinch or two."

"It's as good as I could do on short notice." His teasing words lifted her spirits. She put the basket on his knees and sat down close beside him, holding the pail of milk in her lap with one hand and hugging his arm with the other. "Oh, Cooper! I'm so glad you're not still mad at me."

"Hellfire! I didn't say that. I need to eat and get my strength up in case I decide to whip your hind." He popped a biscuit in his mouth. "Not bad," he said with his mouth full. "What's this? Fried mush? Fried in grease from something smoked."

"Hot fat," she said happily. "We smoked one last winter. I keep the grease in the cellar so it won't get rancid."

"Uh huh."

Lorna wisely remained silent while he was eating, content

to be sitting close to him, holding the milk pail he occasionally reached for. She could feel his lean, long body against hers and was conscious of his upper arm and shoulder where she could rest her head if she tilted it the slightest bit. A slice of moon, on its way across the night sky, appeared from behind a cloud. She could see that he was looking at her and that his unswerving gaze was like a caress. The look in his eyes took her breath away and left her trembling with happiness. This was heaven, she thought, nothing better could exist in this world, except—to be with him wholly and completely.

She handed him the small tin bucket when he reached for it. He drained it and wiped his mouth on the back of his hand.

"Mighty good. I'd almost forgot how good milk is."

"Did you get enough?" As soon as the words were out of her mouth they were punctuated by a loud growl from her stomach.

"What's that?" Cooper turned to peer down into her face. "Did you eat?"

"I will later. Cooper—"

"Silly woman, you must be starving. Here." He pushed a biscuit into her mouth and while she was eating it, he buttered another. "I could smell that cooking clear out here and my stomach was doing some growling of its own."

"Would you have come back in if I hadn't come out?" she asked with feminine curiosity.

"After I stomped out, mad as a coon with his tail caught in a crack?" His lips were folded together, deepening the lines down his cheeks, and his eyes shone with laughter. To her delight he put his arm around her and pulled her against him. She nestled happily in the crook of his arm. "I don't know if I would've or not. I was thinking on it. Eat the rest of these biscuits," he ordered gruffly. "I don't want you to swoon when I kiss you."

"Are you going to?"

"I'm sure planning on it."

"Maybe I don't want you to," she whispered faintly, and suppressed a giggle.

"But you do." He made the statement confidently and lifted her chin with a forefinger. "Don't you?"

"It's mean of you to make me say it."

"You going shy on me?" His mouth was tantalizingly close to hers. "You *want* me to kiss you. Don't you?" he repeated.

"I think I'll die if you don't," she said recklessly.

"We sure don't want that to happen," he said, but he didn't kiss her. He set the basket down beside the log and put the milk pail in it. "Come on." He took her hand. "I don't like sitting out here in the open now that the moon's up, and I'm afraid if I start kissing you, I'll not care if the world tilts, the sun's up, or who's watching."

She walked beside him so happy she was unaware her feet were touching the ground. They crossed the yard toward the darkness of the forest that surrounded the homestead and stopped beneath a large oak tree where a braided vine rope hung from a limb. Lorna gave it a gentle push.

"Frank made this for me a long time ago. He made a loop on the end so I could put my foot in it and swing." There was a poignant longing in her voice, and for just a moment all the years rolled away and she remembered her father as he had been, a quiet man, but one who had built the swing, taught her to ride, and who had taken her small hand in his while they had hunted frogs along the creek bank.

The oak leaves moved in the slight breeze and their whisper seemed unusually loud in the quiet night. An acorn dropped to the ground. With no other noise, the smallest sounds were audible. Lorna tried to see Cooper's face in the shadows, but the outlines were gone, and she could see only that he was standing there beside the tree.

"Will your pa be able to handle those two if they come back looking for trouble?"

"I don't know what he'll do. He was different tonight. He usually doesn't have much to say about anything, especially anything about me. But I'm not worried about Hollis and Billy. They're sneaky and mean, but they've got no backbone. Brice won't do anything, either. He's afraid of White Bull. He knows he'll come in here and burn him out if he bothers me."

"Tell me about White Bull."

"His father was a blood brother to Light, as White Bull was to my grandfather. I've known him all my life. His tribe spends the summer up on Wind River, spring and fall here, and winter down south. They're peaceful, but sometimes I worry they're going to be pushed too far, then all hell will break loose." She moved over close to Cooper. "More and more people are coming and the Indians are losing their hunting grounds. Something's bound to happen sooner or later."

"This country is filling up, that's sure. The land west of here is hard and lonely and it'll take hard men to tame it."

"You like it here, don't you, Cooper?" She stood motionless, staring at his shadow, transfixed, literally shaking inside as she waited for him to answer.

"Sure. You've got a good place here, Lorna. It's as solid a homestead as I've ever seen."

"Frank's always saying he wants to go on west, but he keeps things fixed up, just like Grandpa did."

"I can see that."

"We have a clear title for just about all of this mountain."

"That's a tidy piece of land."

Lorna got no satisfaction out of his words. She tried to think of something more to say on the subject, but couldn't think of anything except to come right out and tell him it would all be his if only he would stay. Somehow she knew that would be the wrong approach with a man like Cooper. Finally, she found her voice.

"What's your mother like?"

"Ma? I don't know. Why would I want to talk about my ma when there's a pretty girl standing this close? Come here." His arms reached out and drew her to him. Her palms, pressed against his chest, slid up to his shoulders. She looked up at him, into his eyes. He studied her white face, the unruly black hair, and her trembling mouth. "Lorna, girl, you're awful pretty," he whispered huskily.

"Cooper . . . I'm afraid you'll not come back," she said in a low, stricken voice.

"We'll meet again." He leaned his head forward, kissing her reverently on the forehead. His voice was a mere breath in the night.

The softly uttered words sent a shiver of dread down Lorna's spine. They were so . . . impersonal! He could have said them to anyone. A sound, half groan and half sigh, exploded from her. Her arms slid up to encircle his neck, then she raised up on her toes and pressed her slim body to his in a desperate attempt to get closer to him, to hold him. She couldn't let him go until there was some kind of understanding between them.

"I don't want you to go. I love you!"

"Sweet Lorna . . ." His whisper warmed her lips. He looked into her eyes and watched as her tongue came out to moisten her lower lip.

"I *do* love you—"

"Shh, don't say anymore," he cautioned. "You can't be sure."

"Why do you say that?" She was near tears. "I *am* sure."

"How many men have you met on this mountain, Lorna?" he asked sternly. "Is what I saw tonight all you've had to choose from?"

"It's you I want! I knew it back there on the Blue. You wanted me then, too. Why are you acting like this? Is it Frank? Is it because I'm not like town women? Kiss me, Cooper. Kiss me and I'll show you I'm—"

His mouth, hard and commanding, fastened on her mobile lips, stealing her breath away and swallowing her words. There was nothing gentle about his lips. He was using his mouth as a means of shutting hers. His kiss was a dark, sweet eternity of firm lips and warm breath.

The small fire kindling deep within her and the pounding of Lorna's heart made her realize that his lips had softened, and that she was cradled in his arms and her lips had been irresistibly forced apart. The tobacco taste of his mouth, the woodsy, musky smell of his face as her nose pressed his cheek, and the hard strength of his embrace made her head swim—she was only vaguely aware of the hand that traveled down the length of her spine and grasped her firm buttocks, pressing her fiercely, impatiently, against his body.

Something warm and powerful began to throb in the area below her stomach and she inadvertently whimpered and moved restlessly against the urgent hardness pressing into her belly. Her unrestrained response seemed to trigger a deeper need in him and the quality of his kiss exploded into a persuasive, sensuous, passionate demand.

Her soft mouth was sweet against his ruthless one and he kissed her thoroughly and at length, wanting so much more that his body trembled with restraint. Finally his lips freed her mouth and came to rest on her cheek.

"You're enough to drive a man out of his mind." His voice was a deep rumble. He moved his face so that he could look at her. Her eyes were damp and wide and her mouth puffy and trembling. "I've never seen anyone like you. You're like a beautiful flower growing on a rocky cliff—slender, bending with the wind, but tough."

The desire Cooper felt for her was a deep pain gnawing his vitals. No other woman had ever come close to making him feel like this woman did, but he'd not let her rule him, he'd not let her call the shots! His mouth set stubbornly and Lorna's eyes riveted on it.

"There's a lot I like about you, Lorna. I like the way you laugh and sing. I like the proud way you hold your head." He brought up his hands and cupped her face. "Most of all I like your eyes and your . . . mouth. No man has ever kissed a sweeter mouth." His lips sipped at a tear that suddenly rolled down her cheek. "What I don't like is a woman telling me what to do or butting into my affairs without my asking. Can you understand that?" he asked in a hard, firm voice. Then, to soften his words, he kissed her gently on the mouth.

"I don't understand you," she whispered. "I want to be your mate, like Maggie was to Light. I wanted to help—"

"I don't understand me either," he said with great certainty. "I don't even know what I'm doing here in the first place. I should have been home a week ago." The hardness left his face and he smiled down at her. "I guess I wanted to be with you a little while longer."

His words brought her a delicious breathlessness. She searched his eyes, now tender and teasing, and laughed happily through her tears, her mouth making the three-cornered smile. Her fingers caressed his face, her nose nuzzled his chin, before she placed her lips sweetly on his.

"I want to be with you . . . forever."

"You're a stubborn little woman and will take strong handling. I don't know if I'm up to it." He leaned against the tree, his long legs spread wide, and pressed her against him intimately. "You'd better get back to the house," he murmured, but his arms tightened around her even as he said the words. He kissed her throat just behind her ear. "Mmm . . . your hair is as soft as down." He nuzzled it again. His lips moved to her face, his hands to her hips.

"I like hearing you say soft words . . ." Her mouth moved to meet his and the words came from the center of her being. Their mouths met with equal fervor—hot, searching, insistent. She clutched him to her, desperate in her desire to possess and be possessed.

Under his stroking hands, Lorna's body went slack with sensuousness and pressed wantonly against him, pressing into every crook and curve of his body. Instinctively, she rubbed her softness against his hardness. Hungrily, blindly, she sought his mouth, and her kiss conveyed the deep heat inside her which was a new and delicious feeling. Whatever the future held, she thought, tonight was hers. Tonight she'd know the joy of coupling with her mate.

His lips played seductively on hers and desire flooded his mind, obliterating all reason. The powerful tug of her beauty set him ablaze with hunger and his hands roamed her body boldly, pulling her blouse from the waist of her skirt and finding one firm, small breast and squeezing it possessively. Both her arms were about his neck. He bent slightly and lifted her off her feet, capturing her thigh between his and holding it tightly for a long delicious moment. His breathing was harsh and Lorna could feel his hard body tremble against hers. She felt a shock of eager excitement to know that he was aroused as much as she.

"Sweetheart?" He lifted his head, his eyes, very close to hers, flaring with warmth and desire. His face had an intense expression. "We've got to stop—" His voice was ragged with emotion.

"No! I don't want to! I ache for you—"

"If we don't stop now I'll not be able to!"

"I'm yours. I'm your woman."

Her face was raised to his. He took her mouth, teased it with his tongue, parted her lips, and let his tongue mingle with hers. He moaned into her open mouth, one large hand on her back, the other on her hips pressing her flat stomach to the evidence of his passion.

With his hands under her hips he lifted her waist high and sat down in the soft grass with her astride his lap. Her arms were about his neck, her legs encircling his hips. He leaned back until his shoulders rested against the tree trunk and she lay against his chest while his hands lifted her to pull her skirt from between them and spread it over them. And then his hands were beneath her skirt and into the wide legs of the split undergarment she wore, kneading, stroking her naked flesh. It was the most wondrously exciting moment of her life.

A heavenly frantic feeling began to build as his fingers touched her soft wetness and searched for her moist depth. She strained against them, gasping for breath, feeling a thousand tiny thrills dance in her stomach. Her response was so convulsive that Cooper growled deeply in his throat as she writhed against him.

"I want to touch you. Let me..." Her hand burrowed between them, seeking, touched the wrist of the hand giving her pleasure, and felt for the elongated hardness that reached up to his flat belly. She humped her back to give her better access. He grabbed her wrist and groaned in protest.

"Lorna...baby. You don't know—"

"Yes, I do."

"You don't have to—I'll pleasure you," he breathed desperately.

"Don't you want to put it inside me the way you're supposed to?"

"Oh, God! You know I do!"

"Then help me."

"This is your most precious gift," he whispered as if in deep pain. "I can't take it—"

"You're not taking it, darling. I'm giving it. Help me—"

"Witch woman!" he said almost angrily. "You've put a spell on me. I can't resist you; you draw the very soul out of me!"

His hands beneath her skirt worked frantically at the lacing on his buckskin britches until his burning flesh was throbbingly erect in her grip. He was seized with an excitement that left him trembling and constricted his chest until he thought he would suffocate. Borne beyond restraint, his hands moved beneath her, his fingers seeking the warm dark entrance, and then he lifted her until the tip of that portion of him that throbbed as if it was a separate part of him entered the gate of her moist opening. He held her there for endless seconds while little spasms of exquisite pleasure sent rippling quivers through her. Then, holding her buttocks in his hands, he slowly let her down, giving her time to draw away, but she met his flesh eagerly and impaled herself on his throbbing warmth. He slid slowly into her until he felt what he'd never felt before—the membrane guarding her virginity.

It was a moment he'd never forget. Sitting upright in the soft grass, with this sweet woman astride his lap, he savored the feel of it. His heart thundered against hers and the hands on her hips pressed her soft belly against his hard one. She clung to him, her arms around his neck, her legs bent back, her knees in the soft grass.

"Cooper?" There was uncertainty in her voice and she began to kiss his face frantically.

"Don't you . . . know?"

"Know what?" She pressed her nose against his cheek and rolled her face back and forth in an agony of need.

"There's a skin there. I'll have to break it."

"Is that all that's wrong?"

"All women have it until they've been with a man."

"Oh, I thought there was somethin' wrong with *me*."

"Darling girl . . ."

"Tell me what to do."

"Ahh . . ." The sound came from deep in his throat as she lowered herself to impale herself more completely. He probed urgently, turning this way and that. Then suddenly, unexpectedly, there was a pain-pleasure so intense that she cried out his name. She clung to him, heedless of the pain now, aware only of that thrusting, pulsing rhythm increasing unbearably to a tempo that brought her higher . . . higher. She wanted what they were reaching for and quivered with expectation. She was speared on a pinnacle of pain and ecstasy. Cooper's body jerked repeatedly and she was flooded with a healing warmth. From somewhere in the blaze, she heard a soft, triumphant, "Oh, God!"

Lorna came languidly back to reality and found her hands clasping Cooper's head to her breast, her face in his hair. He was still huge and deep inside her, but the waves of frenzied pleasure that had ripped through her were subsiding. In their place swelled a burning desire to comfort him. She caressed his back and shoulders and stroked his damp hair back from his forehead.

Holding him, Lorna looked up at the stars, thinking that they had never seemed so big nor so brilliant. He turned his face to her breast and his mouth moved against her.

"You . . . tie me in knots." He flexed his hips and she felt it in the center of her being.

"Cooper . . ." His name was a caress on her lips. All the adoration she had saved was given to him now. She murmured his name as her lips glided over straight brows, short thick eyelashes, cheeks rough with stubble, and to his waiting mouth. It was glorious to feel this freedom to love and caress him.

"Oh, sweetheart! Be still . . ." he breathed in gasps when she began to move on the spear that pierced her. Then he grasped her hips and moved them urgently in a circular motion, being careful to not press too deeply inside her. "Sweetheart!" he whispered helplessly, and with a long breath he thrust at her full force with frenzied urgency. She felt the warm flow of his release and held him shuddering in her arms.

Feeling wonderfully loved and relaxed, Lorna allowed him to lift her from his lap and pull her skirts down over her legs. He lay down with her in the soft grass and cuddled her in his arms. Almost instantly she was asleep.

Chapter Twelve

Cooper lay staring up at the stars. Slowly his thoughts assembled and sorted themselves out. His intentions had been to talk to Lorna, hold her, and . . . maybe kiss her. What man in his right mind *wouldn't* want to hold her? he reasoned. He hadn't meant for a few kisses to lead to the intimate, soul-stirring, gut-stomping experience they'd just shared. He admitted, reluctantly, that the idea of being with her in just that way had crossed his mind. Every night since he'd met her he'd fantasized about holding her, warm and naked, in his arms. He was a man with strong hungers, and he'd occasionally had them satisfied by women who made it their business to dull the ache that sometimes tore at his groin. But none of the experiences he'd had, not even with the most expensive whore in Denver, could come close to what this little mountain sprite had given him. She'd given herself openly, completely, and the thought of parting from her in the morning gave him an acute feeling of despair.

Here's a woman he could share his life and his heart with, he thought, even though, at times, she was so irritating he wanted to shake her. Living with this fairylike creature would never be dull. The thought brought a silent chuckle that shook his large frame when he recalled talk he'd heard about physical love being distasteful to so-called *refined* women. Aroused to full womanhood, this wild child had taken an uninhibited pleasure in their mating. She'd certainly make the long, winter nights something to look forward to. The corners of his wide mouth lifted; he pressed it to her forehead, tasted the clean sweetness of her flesh, and snuggled her small body closer into the hollow of his.

Lorna lay soft and warm against him, her breasts pressed tightly to his chest. He felt an almost overwhelming desire to feel the softness of those young, firm breasts against his naked flesh, but he fought down his desire and lay quietly, hoping the pounding of his heart wouldn't awaken her.

The ribbon that had held her hair to the back of her head had come loose and the silky, dark curls lay in a tangle over her shoulders. A wave of tenderness washed over him as he felt the yellowed shirt beneath his palm, and smoothed the faded black skirt down over her hips. He'd known the moment he'd seen her in them that they were the only female garments she owned and that she'd dressed herself in them to please him. She'd lived on this mountain all her life, he mused, and since her granny died five years ago, she'd not had the company of a woman until Bonnie. It was no wonder she'd been so protective of the girl.

He'd take her home with him, Cooper told himself. He'd wed her, and they'd have the strong, beautiful children she said they'd have. Then a thought struck him with the force of a sledgehammer. Oh, dear God! He emptied himself in her not once, but twice! He may have already planted a seed in her body that would grow to be his son. The guilt he felt as a child for having disgraced his mother by being born came rushing back painfully. That settled it! he thought with grim determination. They'd ride directly to Junction City and get married. No offspring of his would ever be called bastard and grow up to despise him the way he despised Adam Clayhill!

In the quietness of the night, Cooper reflected on his life

up to this point. He realized that it would be changed from this time on. Lorna had been unexpected. He'd dreamed of meeting a woman someday who would walk beside him, but it was always in the future when he had a secure life to offer her. He was a man with a lot of hopes and few illusions. He had a clear and definite idea of the way he wanted to live. He wanted to work his ranch, saddle his own horses, fight his own battles, and walk his own trail. Oscar Parnell had worked hard for the money they paid down on the ranch and anyone who tried to pry him loose from that ranch would have a fight on his hands.

Lorna, he realized with sudden certainty, had dreams of her own. The story of Light and Maggie had caught her romantic imagination and she dreamed of reliving their lives right here on Light's Mountain. He had been aware of it almost from the first. Her numerous references to her grandparents, and the way she had watched him when they were approaching the homestead told him how anxious she was that he be favorably impressed.

Lorna was due a rude awakening. No man worth his salt would be satisfied to settle in here and try to live up to the legend of Light and Maggie Lightbody. Perhaps that had been her father's downfall. The man was soured on life. He had no hopes or dreams. A man needed a plan, needed direction. If he didn't have that, he had nothing.

When the birds began to stir in the branches above his head, Cooper knew dawn was not far away. He rose up on his elbow and peered down into the face of the woman pressed so tightly against him. He was reluctant to awaken her. He had never held a sleeping woman in his arms. It was pleasant to feel her small body against his, depending on him for warmth and protection.

A rush of blood through his veins spread an unwanted arousal through his body. For a long while he hung over her, looking at her. Reason dissolved the hunger that gnawed at him. Her body would be sore, her private parts tender from

his intrusion. There would be other times. She was his . . .
now. Her violet-blue eyes, her lips with the three-cornered
smile, her small round breasts and slim, tight body . . . all
his. She fit perfectly against him, as if she had been made
to be tucked beneath his heart. He felt he knew her as he had
never known anyone before. He knew her mind, her soul,
her spirit, her secret place. She had never known the touch
of another man. He alone had possessed her. The thought at
first awed him, then sent another quiver of desire through
him. He pressed his nose against her cheek to smell the
freshness of her skin and stroked her hair back from her face,
then tenderly kissed her forehead time and again.

"Wake up, pretty girl," he whispered as he shook her
gently. "It'll be daylight soon."

"I'm awake," she murmured, but didn't open her eyes.

"You were playing possum," he accused.

"Uh huh. I liked what you were doing when you thought
I was asleep." Her warm breath hit his face with small puffs
and he knew she was laughing silently. She was like a little
girl in a fully bloomed woman's body. Her arms slipped
around his neck, her fingers cupped over his ears. "Brrr . . .
your ears are cold. I'll kiss them and get them warm."

"You'll get to the house is what you'll do," he said gruffly.
"Your pa will be out looking for you."

"I don't want to go to the house. I want to stay here and
kiss you." She reached for his lips and placed hers firmly
against them. He kissed her back, slowly, sharing a moment
of sweetness with her.

When at last he lifted his head, he looked down at the
pale luminous oval of her face framed in the mass of tumbled,
dark hair that was soft and shining in his fingers. Her smile
was pure enchantment and he said the first thing that came
to his mind.

"Your eyes have lights in the dark. Did you know that?"

"Like a cat's eyes?"

"I've heard tell of blue-eyed housecats."

"I feel wonderful!" She stretched herself to her full length and snuggled against him. "We mated, didn't we, my love? It was grand! Do you think we made a baby?" Her frankness left him speechless, but she didn't seem to notice. "Bonnie said it was hurtful and she hated doing it, but she'd only done it with Brice. One time he sent her off to meet Billy, but I found them and lashed Billy's butt with my whip. Now it's funny to think of him running into the brush with his pants down, but it wasn't funny then. Oh, poor Bonnie. Sometime I'll have to tell her how grand it is doing it with the man you love. It was like flying, Cooper. There wasn't anyone in the whole world, but you—"

"You talk too much."

"You know how to shut me up."

"And I know what it will lead to." Cooper pulled his arms free, got to his feet, and pulled her up beside him. "We've got things to do before we leave this morning and we'd better get to doing them. You can take what we can pack behind our saddles unless your pa will give us the loan of a pack-horse."

Lorna looked up at him, her smile replaced by a puzzled frown. "What are you saying, Cooper?"

"I'm saying, little feather-head, that we're leaving here and heading for the preacher in Junction City."

"Now? I can't leave here now," she sputtered. "I've been gone too long as it is. I've got to dig the potatoes, pick the beans—I've got to see what Frank's up to. If he goes, there'll be nobody here to look after things and the place could be wrecked by the time we get back."

"We're not coming back, Lorna, except for a visit," he said slowly and plainly so she didn't misunderstand. "And I'll not be able to bring you back for a good long while. I've got business to tend to. We'll get married and get you settled in at my ranch. You'll like my mother and she'll love you."

Lorna looked as if he had struck her. "I . . . but, I'm not.. "

She began to shake her head vigorously. "I'm not going to live on your ranch. *This* is my home!"

"It *was* your home, sweetheart. When we marry, you'll make your home with me." His hands came out and grasped her shoulders. In the dim light he could see the stricken look on her face and he was sorry to hurt her, but it was best she understand, right from the start, how things were going to be.

"Cooper!" She tried to wrap her arms about his waist, but he held her from him so he could look into her face. "There's everything *here* a man would want. It will all be yours!"

"Now, what are you saying, Lorna? Spell it out. Let's put our cards on the table."

"I'm saying that this land is clear, the grass and water good—the cabin is the best in these mountains. You can do everything here you can do down on the flatlands. This can be yours, Cooper, all yours."

Cooper looked at her for a long moment before he spoke.

"Usually when a woman marries she leaves home and makes one for her man. What about your pa, Lorna? Wouldn't he feel like he's being crowded out?"

"He doesn't want it. He hates Light's Mountain."

"I don't want it either, sweetheart," he said gently to soften his words. "Have you ever wondered why your pa hates it here?"

"He just . . . hates mountains! He wants to go west to the ocean."

"That's what he says," Cooper said patiently. "But my guess is he hates it because it's not *his* place and he feels like an interloper here, as I would."

"It can't be *his* place! He's not a Lightbody," Lorna said as if suddenly out of patience with the senseless exchange.

"And *you* are. Is that it?"

"Of course I am. But—"

"But what? But your Lightbody blood makes this place more yours than his, despite the fact he married your mother and he's your pa? You said he'd been here for more than twenty years. Don't all the work and sweat he's put into this place amount to something?"

"You don't understand. Light left this homestead to his son, my grandfather, who left it to my mother, and she to me. There have been Lightbodys on this mountain for more than sixty years."

"And so this hunk of dirt and rock belongs only to the Lightbodys because your grandpa was here *first*? God-amighty! I've heard this same stupid thing a hundred times. If that's the case, Lorna, the Indians were here *first*, and the mountain belongs to them." Cooper's voice grew harsh as his frustration mounted. "Understand this: I'm not coming here to live. This place would *not* be mine. It's your pa's. He's earned this homestead by right of sweat and possession. If you've got the sense you were born with, you'd see that, turn loose of this place, get on with your life, and let him get on with his."

"Well!" The word exploded from her lips. "I guess I don't have the sense I was born with, because I don't see *that* at all! I'll not turn my back on Light's Mountain for you or anyone, Cooper Parnell. Light and Maggie spent their lives building this place for future Lightbodys, and I'll not leave it for Frank to squander away." Her cheeks were suffused with color, her balled fist evidence of her anger.

"What makes you think he'd do that?"

"I just know, that's all. My place is here—" The tremor in her voice angered her all the more. Dammit! she cautioned herself, she'd better not cry!

"Don't be too sure of that, little spitfire. After tonight, you could be pregnant and your place will be with me."

"I hope I am!" she shouted to keep from crying. "Then sure I'll be there'll be another Lightbody to carry on." In her anger she had unconsciously picked up her father's Scottish brogue.

"It would not be a Lightbody!" Cooper bellowed in his

rage. "Get that through your thick, stubborn head. It would be a *Parnell*."

"Don't you mean a *Clayhill*?" Lorna shouted back, her aroused voice dangerously near breaking.

Cooper raised his hand as if to slap her. He used all the self-control he could muster to still his hand. She neither cringed nor showed fear. Her eyes were bright with shards of anger and looked unusually large in a white face rigid with rage.

"Don't ever say that again, for I might not be able to keep from striking you." Cooper's voice climbed shakily above his fury to speak calmly. "Now, I'm telling you once again, we'll go to the preacher and be wed. I'm not leaving a bastard of mine on this mountain."

"And I'm telling you, Cooper Parnell, when I wed, I'll do my own choosing and in my own good time!" In all her life she'd not felt such crushing anguish, but pride stiffened her back and held her head erect. "I'll not leave my home and all that's dear to me knowing I'll just come back for a *visit*. I'm staying right here on Light's Mountain and if that means having *your* bastard, so be it!"

"You'll not have *my* bastard! I'll make sure of that. I'll be back, and if you've *took*, I'll drag you to the preacher by the hair of your head, if that's the only way to get you there, and wed you proper."

"You'll not know if it's your bastard or not!" she spat out spitefully. "I'll sleep with every man on this—"

"And I'll break every bone in your body!" he roared, looking down at her with his anger beating through his eyes, trying to glare her down, but there was no give to her. When he spoke again his voice came out on a lower, more persuasive, note. "I'm asking you to be sensible and stop trying to make me into another Light and yourself into another Maggie. They're dead, Lorna, and we are two *different* people with more than half of our lives yet to live."

She jerked her shoulders from his grasp. "If you think I'm

trying to do *that*, you're crazier than a drunk hoot owl! Go on back to your ranch, Cooper. It will take you sixty years to build it to what I've got here."

"No," he said tightly. "I'll not have what you've got here if I live to be a hundred. I'll have something I built myself, not something handed to me on a platter. And I'll have my self-respect, which is more than you Lightbodys have left your pa."

Cooper turned his back on her and began to walk toward the woodpile where he'd left his hat. Lorna followed and persisted with her argument.

"Not many men are offered an improved homestead, Cooper."

"Don't you mean the loan of it, Lorna?" he asked without looking back. "Now I'm sorry I took what else you offered. I thought you were giving it freely, but it was just a little bait thrown out to keep me here so you could try and fit me into another man's boots."

"It wasn't that! You know it wasn't! I knew you were leaving this morning. You've promised to take Bonnie to your mother, and I thank you for it. And I know you've got to go see the land man about the land on the Blue for Griff. But when you get all that settled, you could come back." She was unable to keep the hopeful quiver out of her voice.

"I'll be back. You can bet your bottom dollar on it. I'm coming to look at you and see if you're growing my kid. You'll not know I'm within fifty miles unless you look like you've swallowed a watermelon. Then, by God, you're coming with me to the preacher. After you've given birth you can do as you damn well please." There was no gentleness in his tone and she wanted to cry.

"Damn you! You . . . pissant! I love you!" she shouted, her temper splintering again.

"Yeah? You don't know what love is. Love is giving, not strangling!"

"I know more about love than you do! At least Frank loved

my mother," she said cuttingly. After a knowing silence, she drew in a sharp, hurtful breath and her palms flew to her cheeks. She would have given anything in the world to be able to take back the words. "I'm sorry, Cooper. I didn't mean that."

"You meant it." He turned to look at her, his hurt mirrored in his eyes. "I *am* a bastard," he said slowly, deliberating on each word. He placed his hat on his head and pulled it low over his eyes. "Nobody knows what it means to be a bastard more than I do. But I knew the love of a good man and so did my mother. He told me that what happened was no fault of mine, or ma's, but it took me a long time to understand that. I promised myself that I'd never beget a bastard and there's been no danger of it until now. If you have an offshoot of mine, Lorna, I'll take it, keep it, and I'll raise it up right. I'll not hamstring it by forcing my ways on it, either. I'll teach it to cut its own path. It'll be free to make it's own mistakes and be whatever it's got the guts and the brains to be."

He went into the shed and came out with his tack. He dropped it beside the pole corral and whistled for Roscoe.

Lorna's face mirrored her anguish. Although she had known Cooper for a short time, she was certain of one thing: nothing she might do or say would sway him from his course. She felt tears burn her eyes, and after a long look at him, she turned abruptly away and stood staring out into the early morning light, listening to the sounds he made saddling his horse.

His attitude boiled down to one thing, she decided. He didn't love her. The words echoed in her brain. She began to tremble and her legs became so weak they could scarcely support her. How could she have been so wrong about him? She'd been so sure that he was the one for her. She was just a dumb, gullible, backwoods, mountain girl, she scolded herself. Why would he want her when he could have a woman who knew about petticoats, pretty dresses and how to smell nice? What she had here didn't amount to anything compared to that. He'd probably done what they did last night with a lot of women! The thought brought a lump to her throat and a pain to her heart.

Thunder and damnation! Pride forced abject misery to the back of her mind. She wouldn't let him see he'd put a knife in her soul and twisted it. She'd tell him to get the hell off her mountain. She didn't need him! Her eyes filled with tears and she blinked rapidly. Damn, damn him! She'd not let him know he'd just knocked the wind out of her. Oh, Lordy, she'd have to put on a good face when she said good-bye. She lifted her chin, flung her hair back over her shoulders, and turned when she heard the creak of saddle leather.

Cooper had pointed Roscoe toward the trail, but suddenly he turned back and stared down at her for one brief instant, as if to carve on his memory forever the features he would never see again.

"I'm obliged to you for helping Bonnie. Tell her I'll see her ... sometime—" She stared up into Cooper's face, her features curiously devoid of expression, and willed reality to return and change that cold, hard face to the tender, loving one she had known just hours ago.

He nodded, his lips clamped so tightly that lines showed on each side of his mouth. Then, with one final look, he lifted the stallion with a feather-light hand in a pivot that set it squarely down on its back trail. Its forefeet hit the ground running. Moments later his horse's hooves struck dull echoes through the morning stillness. As the measured beats faded in the distance, it was replaced by a low sobbing wail that came from Lorna's throat as she ran to the house.

The door closed behind Lorna and she was alone. She could cry now. It was both a relief and a sickening misery in one. She lay down on the bed. The tears came in an overwhelming flood. They poured from her eyes, rolled down her cheeks, and seeped between her fingers that were pressed hard against her face. Presently she roused herself long enough to take off the blouse and skirt and slip beneath the quilt. Her mind longed for rest and she sought the sweet oblivion of sleep although the sun was heralding a new day.

Sometime later she awakened, vaguely conscious that there was someone standing beside the bed. She opened her swollen eyes and tried to focus on the person bending over her. With listless disinterest she wondered what Frank was doing in her room—he never came here. The thought seemed to travel a million miles from her brain to her lips, and finally she voiced it.

"What are you doing here?"

"Air ye sick, lass? It's the middle of the day."

"No, I'm not sick, just tired."

"If that be the case, I leave ye be." He went out of the room and closed the door.

Wide awake now, her level black brows drew together in a puzzled frown. She tried to think of a time since her mother had died when her father had come to her room to see about her, and not a single instance came to mind. Did he know she had been with Cooper until dawn? Oh, Cooper! The thought of him brought a flood of tears to her eyes. With him she had reached her greatest happiness and her greatest despair all within a space of a few hours.

A desperate feeling of loneliness possessed her, a loneliness that was her future. Turning on her side, her eyes roamed the room, taking in the wooden chest, the walnut table, the washstand her grandpa had made, and the settle beside the fireplace. Throughout the years, an abundance of love had gone into the making of this home. She loved it, but that was all the love she had in her life.

She sat up on the side of the bed, waited for a sickening, spinning feeling to leave her, then washed in the bowl on the washstand. The cold water felt good and cleared her head. After she dressed in britches and shirt, she nudged the black skirt and the white blouse under the bed with the toe of her moccasins, vowing silently to never wear them again. When she left her room she went directly to the kitchen. It had been almost twenty-four hours since she'd had anything in her stomach but a couple of biscuits.

Frank was dishing up something from a kettle on the stove. The aroma assailed her nostrils, making her acutely aware of her hunger.

"Beans and ham," Frank said as if speech was an effort. He carried his bowl to the table, sat down, hunched his shoulders over it and picked up his spoon in one hand and a piece of cold cornbread in the other.

Lorna filled a bowl and sat down. They ate in silence, which was their usual way, but today Frank's eyes strayed often to his daughter's white face. Her cheeks were hollow, her skin so pale it seemed to be transparent, and her violet eyes were swollen and rimmed with dark circles. His daughter was hurting. It was plain to see.

Lorna looked up and was surprised to see the shadow of pain in her father's eyes. She looked away quickly and continued eating. As the minutes passed, the tension between them came alive. She felt emotion begin to infiltrate the icy barrier with which she protected herself when she was with him. The bitterness she had felt for so long due to his indifference seemed to dissolve in one long shuddering sigh, leaving only emptiness. She'd cut him loose, she thought suddenly, and make it possible for him to go to California. He didn't want or need her! She didn't need him. She didn't need anybody! She stared at him for the space of a dozen heartbeats, her eyes dilated with pain.

Not one to dawdle once a decision was made, Lorna got up from the table and pulled a chair over to the brick chimney. She stood on it and stretched to her full height, but couldn't quite reach the loose stone that hid the opening to her secret hiding place. She stepped off the chair and looked around the room for something to place on the chair to give her more height. She heard the scrape of her father's chair on the floor as he got up from the table. He stepped up on the chair beside the chimney, removed the loose stone and reached for the leather pouch. Lorna caught it when he tossed it to her.

"Is this what ye be wantin', lass?" There was no way Lorna could hide her surprise. "Not a coin be missin', if it's what ye be thinkin'," Frank said on seeing the shocked and suspicious look on her face. He sat back down at the table.

"It's just that . . . I didn't know that you knew it was there," she said wearily, placing the bag of clinking coins on the table beside his bowl.

"Years ago, yer mother told where 'twas stashed. Did ye think I be stealin' from me own lass? Is that why ye didn't ne'er speak of it?"

Lorna's cheeks tinged with color, but she held her head erect and looked him in the eye. "Granny said hold it back till times were real bad."

Frank looked at her from beneath thick, bushy brows. "Times be bad fer ye, do they, lass?" There was something agonizing in her eyes that tore at him. They were like Nora's eyes when she knew she was dying.

"Not for me, but they are for you. Take it and leave Light's Mountain before you get yourself hung for cattle stealing." Lorna felt as though someone else was speaking the words for her. She heard them, but couldn't feel them in her mouth. An incredible numbness had settled on her like a dark shroud.

Frank placed the spoon carefully on the table beside his bowl. Lorna forced herself to meet his eyes levelly.

"Ye be thinkin' yer pa's a thief? Is that what ye be thinkin'? Or be it yer mon won't stay if I be here?" He spoke hastily, as if he didn't want to say the words, but they had to be said.

"He's got nothing to do with it. I don't want you hung."

"Why, lass? Then I be gone and out of me misery."

"I don't want you hung," she repeated tiredly. A huge sigh shook her entire body. The last few hours had been unbearable. The most unbearable of her life. The pain and the pressure seemed endless. Why didn't he take the money and go? It's what he always wanted to do. "You've been talking about getting in the freighting business. You don't have to steal cattle to get the money. Here it is."

"A mon's got to have somethin' to talk about, somethin' to dream on. There be naught to dream on here."

"Take the money—"

"Ye be throwin' good money after bad, lass," he said, hurt and anger in his voice.

"I don't care about the money. I just want you away from here before a posse comes riding in."

"If ye be wantin' me gone, I'll go. I have me pride, though 'tis sadly worn. But I be tellin' ye this," his voice rose to a roar and he gulped down spittle and air, "I dinna measure up to the Lightbodys, but I be no thief, by Gad!" He reared up out of his chair, sending it crashing to the floor behind him. His hamlike fist came crashing down on the table with a violence that jarred the heavy crockery bowls. "By holy hell, I no be havin' me kin put the name thief to me!" His face was twisted with bitterness and smoldering anger.

Lorna had no idea how many seconds went by while she stood and stared at him, his words echoing through her mind. She was shocked speechless. For him to deny his part in the rustling was the last thing she expected. Anger had made his face red, yet he looked tired, old; there were deep creases on each side of his mouth and around his eyes. She'd not noticed before how gray he was. She looked searchingly at him for a long moment. Then the shock was over. She was able to speak calmly.

"You don't have to shout. I'm not deaf. I saw you with Hollis, Eli and Luke. You were driving old man Pichard's cows."

For an endless moment Frank stared dumbly at the cold-eyed girl. His face was suffused with crimson and he opened and closed his mouth as if strangling.

"No!" he managed to say. "Ye dinna see me drivin' the ol' mon's cows!"

"You were there to meet Hollis and Eli. You knew what they were doing."

"No!" he was shouting again. Then, "Aye! I ken they be stealin' fer weeks on end! Ye come down from the hills a ridin' that gray devil straight at 'em, and I ride to head ye off, afore ye get yerself killed, so foolhardy ye be!"

"That's the only reason you were there?"

"I be sayin' it."

"You think they'd kill me to keep me from telling?"

"Aye. I be tellin' ye that."

"They'd not dare!"

"Ye think not, lassie? It's hard mon, they be."

"Brice has got a cruel streak in him a mile wide. He's mean to everything he owns—horses, dogs, women. And Hollis is of the same cut."

"Aye. He is that. And 'tis sure I am he be killin' to save his own neck if there be one to point the finger at him."

Lorna was beginning to feel faintly giddy with relief, yet not daring to completely believe her father had no part in the rustling that had been going on for months. They stared at each other across the table and finally Lorna sank down in the chair.

"But they're friends of yours. You're down at Brice's night after night." Her eyes were sharp and penetrating, her lips were set defensively, but she prayed he could convince her he was innocent.

Frank was still. Only his eyes were alive, and they examined every line in her face.

When he didn't say anything Lorna continued, "Granny always said birds of a feather flock together. What was I to think when you were gone for several days at the same time Brice and Hollis were gone, and I'd heard about the nester being killed?"

"Aye. I took meself off when I knew they'd be gone from the mountain. But 'twas not what yer thinkin'. Ye wanted to think me no good 'cause yer granny did think it," he said tiredly. "Aye, 'tis true. I be not a mon the likes of Lightbody. I could'na come to this land an' built this place wid only a wee lassie by me side. But it mattered not to yer mother. Be yer own mon, she says, and that I try to be." His voice rose defensively. "Weak, I be, but I no be a thievin' mon!"

Lorna saw anger, yet pleading, in his face. Somehow he looked both vulnerable and strong. But it had been so long— so many years had passed since they'd said this many words to each other at one time.

"If you didn't go with them, where did you go when you were gone for a week at a time?" Lorna persisted. It had gone this far; she had to know all of it.

"I dinna ask ye where ye go," he snapped, and his jaw set stubbornly. "But I'll tell ye. This be a lonely place with only the likes of Brice an' his kind to while away the time. Ye canna say I dinna do me work about the place, so 'tis no business of yers, lass, if'n I take meself to town to blow the cobwebs from me brain, an' ease me achin' some. Me Nora knows how 'tis—" Suddenly, huge tears filled his eyes, but he held his head erect and refused to look away from her.

Lorna looked at him as if she had never seen him before. Somehow she couldn't equate this big, proud man with tears rolling down his cheeks with the moody, surly man he had become the last few years. Her granny had thought him lacking, and although she had never said as much, her attitude of cold silence toward him had spoken for her. Lorna had known from an early age that she tolerated him because her daughter had loved him and married him.

Why, he'd been lonely, she thought. All those years when she had Granny he didn't have anyone. He'd lived here silently and somberly, never letting her get to know him.

"Pa...I'm sorry!" She spoke over the lump that rose in her throat. Tears blinded her, but she got to her feet and made her way around the table to him. "I'm sorry, Pa. I'm truly sorry." She moved into his embrace, circled him with her arms, and put her head on his shoulder.

Chapter
Thirteen

It had been difficult at first for Lorna to talk to her father. She carefully kept the conversation on safe topics and he followed suit. She said nothing more about his association with Brice Fulton, and he didn't mention Cooper or his abrupt departure. Instead he told her about a cougar he'd shot after it had brought down one of their cows, and that he had caught the scent of a wolverine in the shed a few days ago. He told her he planned to put a new roof on the smokehouse and that if she planned to keep all the pumpkins from the garden they'd have to either dry some of them or dig out more space in the cellar.

Lorna asked her father if there were more green beans in the garden to string and dry, and if he'd spotted a honey tree. She offered to help bring timber down from the hills to cut for firewood. She told him about Bonnie and how she had suffered giving birth, and saw his eyes go dark with pain as he remembered her mother dying during childbirth. Finally Lorna told him about the mare she had found running loose, about Cooper and Griffin coming to look for it and their part in helping Bonnie.

"Cooper has a horse ranch near Junction City and he and

Griffin are thinking of filing on land down on the Blue and starting another one."

"'Tis for certain he be a mon who knows horse flesh, if what he be ridin' be an example. I ne'er seen a finer animal fer strong hindquarters." Frank seemed younger, more relaxed, as if the weight of the world had been lifted from his shoulders. He even smiled occasionally.

"Have you seen anything of Volney? He said he'd find a place for Bonnie and come back for her. He didn't come. It isn't like him."

"Aye, lass. 'Tis sorry I am to be tellin' ye, but I think the oold mon was sorely used by Brice. Mind ye, I just know what was let slip by Billy. 'Twas said a rock fell on the oold mon, but I be thinkin' they broke his legs when he would'na tell where ye took the wee cripple lassie."

"Oh! Damn that Brice! He'd better not have hurt Volney. Where is he? Did you look for him?"

"Aye. He not be on the mountain. 'Tis sure I am of that."

"Moose or Woody might have seen him," Lorna said hopefully.

"Aye. They be comin' soon to make ready fer winter." Frank filled his pipe and looked at her over the light he held to the bowl. "Ye be watchin' yerself, lass. Ye braced up to Hollis, and ye scored a mark agin' Brice. They be not forgettin'."

"I'm not afraid of them. They know White Bull will kill them if they harm me."

"Aye. 'Tis glad I am the Indian is fond of ye."

"He and his people will be coming back through soon," she said wistfully, suddenly longing to see her old friend.

"Aye." Frank got to his feet. "I be taking meself down to the corn patch to see if the blasted coons have been in it again."

Lorna watched him walk down the hill toward the low land where he had planted the corn. She couldn't recall a time when she'd ever heard him say where he was going or give a reason for going there. This new closeness between them was comforting and fragile and ... precious.

Evening came early. The shadow of the mountain crept down over the ranch buildings and the air became cooler. Lorna sat on the porch working a churn dasher. The kitchen was spotlessly clean; the trestle table, workbench, and washstand had been scrubbed vigorously with a stiff brush, dried, and oiled. The seasoned old wood gleamed after being polished with a soft cloth. The wood ashes had been hauled out and saved for making soap, the floor scrubbed, the glass chimneys washed.

She had worked hard, hoping to keep her thoughts at bay and ease the ache in her heart, but all she could think of was Cooper and the complete, unforgiving disgust she had seen on his face when he left her. She relived the moments they had spent together, even the ones when she had been angry with him. Now, the thought of his arms, his kisses, the sweet smell of his breath and his soft voice in her ear brought a wave of sickness rocking the pit of her stomach. Her heart ached for her lost love, but her pride was wounded as well. She had been so sure her love had been returned.

Lorna was jarred from her reverie by the dogs, Ruth and Naomi. They shot out from beneath the porch and raced toward the edge of the clearing. A rider came out of the timber and Lorna's heart fluttered hopefully until she realized that it wasn't Cooper returning. Cursing the dogs, the rider bore down on the house. Lorna stepped to the edge of the porch, her whistle at once bringing them back to her.

Dust boiled thickly beneath the horse's hooves as Brice Fulton jerked on the reins. The horse stopped a dozen feet away, but danced nervously as the cruel bit cut into its mouth. Below the brim of his battered hat Brice's eyes blazed with hostility. He studied her with a cold, impersonal intensity. Her incredible self-possession was a thing he had never before encountered in a woman. To him she appeared to look down on everything and everyone. She had an untouchable air about her that had irritated him since the first day he'd set eyes on her. It was as if she were a queen and he a lowly peasant. She had the power to make him feel inferior, and when she looked at him as if he were a nothing, it was like pouring salt on an open wound. By God, he'd shake the bitch, he vowed. Someday she'd come crawling to him and lick his hand!

Lorna said nothing. She had learned that to say nothing was more unnerving to a man like Brice than to curse him or hurl accusations. Her intense hatred of him was like a festering boil, but the emotion rioting through her was wholly concealed behind the noncommittal expression on her face.

"Have ya got my woman here?"

Lorna's violet, thick-lashed eyes flicked over him contemptuously. "No."

"No," he mimicked. "Then where the hell's she at?"

"Where you'll never find her. You're not fit to live with a hog, much less a sweet, gentle girl like Bonnie." Her voice was coldly wicked and cut Brice with the clean precision of a finely honed knife. She turned and walked into the house.

"Gawddamn ya for a fuckin' bitch!" he shouted. Anger boiled up out of him causing him to lose all reason. "Don't turn yore back on me. I want that whore back, by Gawd, 'n I'll get 'er if I have to tear down this gawddamn place ya set such a store by."

Lorna took a coiled whip from the peg just inside the door. Holding it behind her she stepped back out onto the porch.

"A whore gets money for what she does. I didn't know you paid Bonnie."

For an endless moment Brice stared at the cold-eyed girl, so embroiled in his anger and resentment he didn't notice the look of lethal hatred on her face. He took off his hat and wiped the sweat from his brow with the sleeve of his shirt.

"Ya'd better tell me where she's at, by Gawd, or I'll kill ever' blasted thing on this place that's walkin' on four legs."

"You're all talk, Brice. You won't do anything," she contradicted him calmly. "You're too much of a coward, beside being a back-shooting, cattle-rustling woman beater," she told him with a chill smile.

"If ya was a man . . . I'd kill ya—"

"No," she contradicted again. "If I was a *man* you'd not have the guts to face me."

It clearly required all Brice's self-restraint to refrain from leaping from his horse and knocking her down. His face turned crimson and his mouth worked as he spat out silent oaths. He took his frustration out on his luckless horse and jerked on the reins, causing the animal to rear and spin on its hind legs, stirring up a cloud of dust. He dropped his hat and cursed loudly. Excited by the commotion, the dogs came bounding out from under the porch, leaping and frolicking and yipping happily. Ruth grabbed Brice's hat between her huge jaws and shook it playfully.

Without warning, Brice pulled his horse around in a smooth pivot. In the same instant his right hand lifted as swiftly as a striking snake, the gun in it glinting dully. The crashing report of the two shots fired from the heavy Navy pistol echoed back and forth through the hills before falling finally into a complete silence.

A look of pure shock settled over Lorna's face as she stared wordlessly down at Ruth and Naomi. Ruth's wiry body had toppled and lay still; she had been shot through the head. Naomi, making pitiful whining sounds, blood pouring from her lower body, crawled on her belly, trying to reach her dead sister.

Brice shoved the gun back into its holster and got off the horse to retrieve his hat. "That's a start," he said in a tight, thin voice.

"That's a mistake," Lorna said flatly.

Moving slowly but decisively, Lorna stepped out into the yard, the uncoiled whip dragging through the dust behind her. She faced him squarely. With the ease of long practice she willed herself to keep loose and to not allow her temper to force her to make a foolish move.

"I done told ya—"

"I owed you for what you did to Bonnie, and now for Ruth and Naomi." The words were spoken as casually as if she were speaking about the weather.

His eyes dropped to the whip. "Ya get a thought of usin' that whip on me 'n I'll treat ya like I'd treat a man."

"Don't you mean like you'd treat a woman?" she drawled with heavy sarcasm, and lifted her straight black brows in a way that infuriated him even more.

Brice had scarcely time to blink his eyes before she acted. She took a step back and cast the fourteen foot strip of leather with a flick of her wrist. The tip of the bullwhip caught him on the chest. He let out a yelp and backed up rapidly. The reins slipped from his hand and the horse shied away.

"Ya . . . bitch!" His voice was a strangled scream.

"Mule's ass! Filthy hog! Son of a mangy . . . polecat! I'll take your flea-bitten hide off, inch by inch!" she shouted. Half-mad with fury now, she crouched; feet spread and firmly planted, her small, slim body poised for action. She watched his every move with eyes made brilliant by her anger.

Brice realized the danger confronting him. She was like a small, striking rattlesnake. He grabbed for his gun, but he was a second late. The end of the lash bit into his wrist and the gun flew out of his hand. For an instant he stared at the gash cut to the bone, unable to believe that she would dare to do this. When he regained his senses, he lunged toward her.

Lorna understood what he intended to do—get close, which was the only defense against a bullwhip. She backed away. A good whipcracker had to strike with the tip only for maximum damage. As soon as it wrapped around a man's arm or body, the whip could then be seized and taken away.

A muleskinner had spent a winter on Light's Mountain recovering from a near scalping. He had taught Lorna to handle the whip, and being one who had to furnish her own amusement she had spent many hours practicing with it, as she had with the knife, until she could balance a potato on a stump and cut it in half.

Lorna shagged the whip backward.

"Ya gawddammed slut!" Brice lunged forward again, his face white with rage. "Ya shit eatin'— Yeeow!"

This time she caught him on the hairline. Hair and blood flew and he staggered backward, bellowing his rage, blood streaming down his face from where the forked tip had taken away the skin. She snapped the whip again, catching him across the shoulders. He yelped and spun around. She ripped open the seat of his trousers, drawing a bloody line across his bared buttocks. He let out a helpless bleat of rage and tried to run. She hooked him around the ankle, tripping him, and stripped him twice across the back as he scrambled to his feet and flailed his hands to catch the whip, but he might as well have been trying to snare a striking snake.

She was careful not to use too much force. With the fourteen foot whip she could easily break his leg and she didn't want to do that—just yet. And she used care not to let the whip end wrap more than twice because she had to free it before he could grab it.

"Ach, lassie! Have ye lost yer mind?"

Lorna was vaguely aware that her father had come running into the yard and was calling to her. She paid him no mind and went after Brice with a vengeance, remembering the whip and burn marks on Bonnie's body, and the dogs lying dead in the yard, and the possibility he had injured an old man. Each time he tried to break away and run, she tripped him. And as he struggled to get to his feet she lashed his back, buttocks and thighs, now wet with blood.

He could hear the sibilant rush of the whip as it came down across his back like a white flame, and yelled under its searing pain. He was like a wild man, raging and frothing at the mouth, his eyes glazed. She laid the whip on him until she had cut the shirt off his back and his trousers sagged down around his ankles. Each time he reached for them she lashed his buttocks until they were enveloped in a sheet of white hot agony that brought his voice tearing up from deep inside him.

"This is for Bonnie," Lorna yelled. A wildness filled her and she opened a deep gash on his cheek. "This one's for Ruth, who only wanted to play." The whip snaked out and took the upper part of his ear. Bellowing like a wounded bear, Brice clamped his hand to the side of his head. "This is for Naomi," she shouted and laid the bloody tip of the whip across his bare belly. "And this is for Volney." Anger gave strength to her arm. The breathy hiss of the whip sliced through the air again. The tip struck precisely where she intended it to strike, and flicked the hair from his lower belly.

With a sharp scream, Brice bent double, hands clasped over his dangling private parts, sure that they would be next. The pain was almost unbearable; he lacked the power to stand and his legs gave way. He fell on his face in the dirt and lay there sobbing like a baby.

Lorna went to him, coiling the whip as she walked. She looked down on the bloodied flesh and spat contemptuously.

"You deserve more than this, you mangy cur. Much more." She hooked him beneath the chin with the toe of her moccasins, forcing his head up. "You're rotten, like a sore eating away at what's decent on this mountain. We don't need your kind here. Get off Light's Mountain! Because if you don't, I'll kill you, or White Bull will. And if he does it, you'll be a long time dying!" She spoke in a calm, unyielding voice.

Brice peered up through a curtain of pain. The figure standing over him was a she-devil from a horrible dream. A mass of tumbled black hair framed a white face as hard as stone. Her red mouth sneered at him; violet eyes bored into him like a hot poker. She was a witch that had set him on fire! He cringed. The movement sent rivulets of pain streaming all through him, and he whimpered before this overwashing torture that threatened to fling him headlong into feared darkness.

Her exertions had left her shaken and drenched with sweat. Lorna turned to her father who stood beside the dogs, his face slack with disbelief.

"Are they dead?" Her eyes held his, then dropped to the bloodied knife in his hand, and then to Naomi who lay in a pool of blood.

"Aye. I could'na let her suffer."

Lorna nodded numbly. In a backlash of emotion, her face suddenly crumbled, tears filling her eyes and streaming down her cheeks.

"They thought he was funning and wanted to . . . play—" Her voice was husky with tears and grief. She knelt down and patted the still, warm bodies. "Bye, Naomi. Bye, Ruth. You were good dogs and minded when told to behave. I'm sorry I didn't see what he was up to till it was too late."

A chill touched her and held her motionless. Intuitively, she knew when her enemy moved. She jerked erect and turned. Brice, holding his britches up with one hand, had gotten to his feet and was staggering toward his horse.

"No!" she shouted, and sprang forward, striking the horse on the rump with the coiled whip. The squealing, frightened animal bolted out of the yard. Without breaking stride and stumbling blindly, Brice turned and followed, cursing and sobbing with pain.

"Ye've done it now, lass. 'Tis a fact Brice can'na take that 'n ever hold up his head again."

"What other way was there for me? I didn't want to kill him and I couldn't let him go." She tipped her head forward so he'd not see the tears that again welled in her eyes. "I thought of killing him. I could've put my knife in his heart before he reached his gun, but I've not killed a man, Pa."

"Aye, lass. 'Twas my place to handle this." He went to her and stood hesitantly, wanting to comfort her, but not knowing if she could accept it. "'Tis sorry I be I let it come to this."

Lorna reached for him and laid her head on his shoulder. It was so good to lean against his strength. "You didn't know."

Frank sighed. "He'll hate ye fer this, lass. He'll not make foot till he's had his comeback." He put his arms around her. *Where had the time gone? It was only yesterday she was a wee lassie. Now she was the size of Nora!* "I'll kill the mon if he touches a hair on yer head," he said with lusty gruffness. A chill touched him and he trembled at the thought of the danger that lay ahead for her.

Lorna raised her head and looked at him. "Oh, Pa—what would I do without you?" She wrapped her arms about his thick waist and hugged him hard. Her heart ached with a physical pain almost too hard to bear. The grief she'd held inside her burst out like water through a broken dam. Her body convulsed and she began to sob great shuddering sobs.

Frank didn't understand this daughter of his. One moment she had the nerve to face an armed man with a bullwhip, the next she was crying like a child in his arms. He didn't know what to say to her so he just held her and stroked the length of tangled hair that flowed down her back.

Cooper rode away from Light's Mountain so angry he was several miles away before he remembered to be cautious. He pulled his blowing horse to a stop and then walked him to cool him off. Usually he traveled like an Indian, taking the longest route if it was the easiest on his horse. This morning he had let his anger cloud his judgment and Roscoe had been the one to suffer from it.

Cooper was puzzled by his own feelings of hurt and frustration, and dearly wished he could place the blame for his predicament on Lorna, but knew the fault was his and his alone. He could have backed off at any time. Instead, he had allowed himself to become more and more involved with her and finally the inevitable had happened. He could have no more turned down what she offered than could a man turn down a drink of water when he was dying of thirst. He groaned aloud, remembering.

The sweet innocence of her giving was something he would cherish all his life. All the more reason why he'd not allow her to bear his child alone—if there was a child. Even now, when he was so angry with her, he wanted nothing more than to hold her, love her, and take care of her always. But she'd not twist him around her finger! he thought with a spurt of resentment.

"I'll be double damned if she will!" he exclaimed aloud, and the sound of his own voice shocked him. Good God! She'd even gotten him talking to himself!

He was sure he loved her, and in her own way she loved him. But to live a peaceful, happy lifetime together would take more than love. It would take thoughtfulness, consideration and respect. He could not accept what she wanted him to do; give up all that he'd worked for and take up another man's leavings.

His thoughts veered. Hollis was a dangerous man. A stupid man who knew how to hate was always dangerous, and Cooper had seen the hatred in Hollis's eyes when he looked at Frank and later at Lorna. It was a hatred born from his humiliation. Would Frank be able to handle him and protect his daughter? And what about the man, Brice? Hollis and Billy seemed to think he was the big man on the mountain. Perhaps he shouldn't have left Lorna there—but what else could he have done other than hog-tie her and throw her over his saddle? Somehow he was certain Frank wouldn't have stood for that. He'd seen the concern in his eyes when he looked at her. There was love there, even if Lorna was unaware of it.

The sun rose behind him and swept the shadows from the broad land. Cooper saw the peak near the high mountain pass, many miles away, turn to gold; the valley became green and still under the sun. He saw a buzzard soar, a covey of quail scutter beneath the brush, a swarm of honey bees settle onto a patch of blue mountain flowers. A skunk waddled onto the trail and paused in the sunlight. Cooper pulled Roscoe to a halt and waited for it to pass and wondered if it was sick because it was a nocturnal animal not given to daytime wanderings. He heard the far off coo of a mourning dove and the lonely, plaintive call did nothing to lift him out of his depression.

At the end of a short, steep strip of loose shale, he turned Roscoe and rode down the canyon toward the place where he had left Griffin and Bonnie. He was eager to get them and get on home, yet strangely reluctant too.

He saw smoke from a fire, but it was thin smoke . . . the kind a cautious man like Griffin would allow to drift upward. Smoke could be either a warning or an invitation, and in this country where you never knew if a man was friend or foe, smoke could be an invitation to trouble.

Oscar Parnell had taught him that a man was never free from danger, and Cooper had grown accustomed to watchfulness. It was something that had ingrained itself deeply. It didn't show, but it was there in all his actions, and he was alert as he drew near the camp.

Bonnie was feeding small twigs into a fire. She got to her feet and backed away, her eyes wide and apprehensive, and silently watched him approach. She reminded Cooper of a cowed little pup that expected to be kicked, and fury at the man who had mistreated her knifed through him.

Griffin climbed down out of the boulders, the rifle in his hand. He came to where Bonnie stood and leaned weakly against a small sapling.

"Ya done good, Bonnie. Ya was cool 'n natural like." Then he said to Cooper, "We wasn't sure it was ya. Yore a mite early."

"I got an early start." Cooper got off his horse and slipped the bit from its mouth, but let the bridle hang around its neck. Gratefully, Roscoe began to clip the short grass. "Everything all right here?" His eyes took in the fresh blood stain on Griffin's shirt.

"Fine. I got a mite rambunctious climbin' them rocks." He grinned apologetically.

Cooper saw the alarm in the woman's eyes when she looked at Griffin. She quickly delved into a pack and brought out a clean cloth which she folded into a pad, slipped it inside his shirt and pressed it against the wound. Griffin's eyes clung to her face and hers to his, as if they were the only people in all this vast land.

Lordy, Cooper thought, watching the intimate touch of their hands. Something had happened between them while he was gone. They had taken to each other like a duck to a pond. They were in love! He wondered how that would work out. Old Clayhill would do his level best to hang Griff, and that Brice fellow would be after Bonnie. Poor kids, he thought. And they were not much more than kids. It would not be easy. They had nothing and nobody but themselves. Hell! he thought with a spurt of satisfaction. They would have each other, and friends pulling for them. It was more than some folks had. They'd get by.

"I'll have a snort of coffee, then we'll make tracks for the ranch before we get caught in these mountains and have to fight our way out." Cooper spoke almost gruffly and settled down on his haunches beside the fire, his hands curled around the cup, uncaring that his companions looked at him strangely and exchanged puzzled glances as they began to break camp.

Chapter
Fourteen

In the middle of the afternoon Cooper began to see familiar landmarks and knew the distance to his home was narrowing down considerably faster than he had expected. He rode through a sunlit afternoon, sitting lazily in the saddle, his right hand resting on his thigh, his keen eyes studying the terrain ahead. They had stopped only one time since early morning. Bonnie was tired, but she hadn't let out so much as a murmur of complaint. Griff had padded his saddle with blankets, and Cooper had lifted her up to ride in front of him. The mare was too skittish for either of them to ride in their weakened condition, but Firebird was a strong horse, and seemed not to mind the extra weight.

Off and on all day, Cooper had heard the low murmur of voices behind him and would have been surprised to know that their talk was mostly of him and Lorna.

"He's tore up 'bout somethin', Griff. I hope it ain't that Brice give him trouble."

"If'n he did, my guess is he could handle it. He ain't a man to be fooled with, 'n if'n somethin's started he'd see the end of it. It's my bet he's up in the air over somethin' Lorna done."

"Lorna ain't no rattle-head—"

"She's used to thin's agoin' 'er way."

"There ain't ever been no one to tell her different. Lorna ain't scared a nothin'.'"

"Ever'body's scared a somethin'."

"What're you scared of, Griff?"

He chuckled. "Ya put my back to the wall, didn't ya, girl?" He was silent for a moment, then he said, "Wal, I guess I allus feared I'd be old 'n sick 'n die by myself with nobody knowin' or carin'.'"

"Oh, Griff!" Bonnie turned to look at him. "I been scared a that, too."

"Ya don't need to be scared a that no more, girl. I'd care. Fact is, I'd wanna die too."

Tears spurted in Bonnie's eyes. "I ain't never had nobody but Lorna to . . . like me. Maybe my ma did when I was little. Pa always shamed her 'cause a my arm. Then when I got bigger she didn't seem to like me no more, leastways she'd a not let Pa sell me off to Brice like she done."

"Ya got to fergit about that, honey girl. Ya got me, now. I aim to take care of ya from here on. Ain't nobody agoin' to hurt ya, less'n they go through me first."

"'N ya got me, Griff. Ya ain't never agoin' to be by yoreself when yo're sick. 'N when yo're old I'm ahopin' I'll be with ya—"

"Now don't we make us a pair?" he whispered huskily, and there was wonderment in his voice.

"We shore do." Bonnie leaned her head back against his good shoulder. "Oh, Griff, I wish Lorna could be happy like me. I'm just scared thin's didn't work out for her 'n Cooper like she was ahopin' they would."

"I was athinkin' that he was smitten by 'er the way he looked at 'er when she wasn't lookin'.'"

"She liked him. She told me she did. She wanted him to come back 'n settle on Light's Mountain, but I'm athinkin' he'd not want to."

"He ain't goin' to be pushed to do anythin' he don't want to do, that's shore."

"I wish she'd a come with us. There ain't nothin' on Light's Mountain for her to choose from. If'n she stays there her pa might make her marry up with one a them no-goods like Hollis or Billy. 'N I'm 'fraid Brice'll hurt her 'cause she helped me be shed of him. She don't know how mean he kin be when he's riled."

"If'n he does, I'll kill him. I aim to, anyhow, fer what he done to you."

"Oh, Griff, no! I don't want you tanglin' with him. He'd not fight fair, 'n he's got Hollis 'n Billy—"

"I ain't got it in mind to fight *fair*. When a snake needs killin', ya kill it. Ya don't stand there 'n give it a chance at ya."

Griff shifted to ease the ache of sitting on the horse's rump and Bonnie turned to look at him. The expression on his face was one she'd not seen before. His cheeks were drawn in, his eyes narrowed, his face frozen into immobility. He had withdrawn into himself and seemed to be a million miles away from her. The hair on the back of her neck rose and she felt a chill of apprehension. With a frantic eagerness to ease the tension, she began to chatter.

"I'm awonderin' how far now to Cooper's place. Yo're tired, ain't ya, Griff? Yo're just frazzled to the bone, ain't ya? Is yore shoulder ahurtin' ya again? When we get there, I'll smear it good with lamp black." Her young face showed her concern for him.

His face relaxed and he grinned at her. "It ain't bad. The pine resin ya put on this mornin' stopped the bleedin'. How're ya doin'?"

"All right now we're on even ground. It was scary acomin' down that steep place back yonder. I almost pulled all the mane outta this poor horse aholdin' on," she admitted with a breathless laugh. "Griffin—" She turned back facing the trail so he wouldn't see the worry that clouded her eyes.

"What if Cooper's ma don't like me? What if she can't stand
to . . . look at my arm? I was in a store once 'n a lady come
in 'n saw it. She screeched."

"There ain't no chance a that happenin'. Ain't no chance
a'tall. Cooper wouldn't a had ya come if'n he'd thought there
was. But don't ya worry none. I'm atakin' ya with me when
I go back to the Blue. But first we'll find us a marryin' man,
like I told ya last night."

"Griffin! 'Bout marryin'—I don't 'mount to much—"

"Hush up that talk! Ya 'mount to aplenty. Yo're my woman,
'n my woman's the best there is."

"Ya might not think so, later on."

"When?" he breathed in her ear. "When ain't I goin' to
be thinkin' that yo're the sweetest, lovin'est, prettiest woman
I ever did see?"

There was a burning ache in Bonnie's throat. She was like
someone feeling her way along a dark, narrow path.

"I reckon when it's too late for ya to back out." She was
compelled to look back at him. He was grinning. His eyes
were smiling, too. He looked young, boyish. Even his beard
was soft and fuzzy. It struck her how young he was and how
hard his life had been up to now.

"Ya mean when we're sittin' on the porch hollerin' at our
grandkids to come help us to bed? Even then I'll be athinkin'
yo're grand 'n wantin' to hurry 'n get ya under the covers."

She turned back and closed her eyes tightly. She could
still see his face. His lips nuzzled her ear, and she fervently
wished her galloping heart would behave so she could think
of something to say. When his arms tightened around her and
she felt the touch of his lips on her cheek, she giggled helplessly despite her tiredness.

"Oh, Griff! Stop that! Cooper might see."

They were bone weary.
The evening sun had set when Cooper got down to open
the gate that enclosed the ranch buildings. He had ridden for

the last hour with his mind empty, his ears hearing only the hoof falls of his horse, those behind him, and the creak of saddle leather. Roscoe knew he was home and fidgeted anxiously. Firebird could smell the mares in heat, and Griffin issued stern commands to keep him at a smooth walk. Cooper could see the flutter of his mother's blue dress as she waited on the porch.

It was good to be home.

Sylvia stepped off the porch when Cooper rolled from the saddle. Her eyes were only for her son, although she had glanced briefly at the two riding double on the flashy big sorrel with the light mane and tail.

"Howdy, Ma."

"Hello, son. You look all tuckered out. Did you have a hard trip?" She reached up and kissed his cheek.

"You might say that. How are things here?"

"Things are fine. After you've washed and had a decent supper I'll tell you what all's happened."

"I brought somebody who needs some looking after for awhile, Ma," Cooper said for her ears alone. They exchanged a look of understanding before he went to lift Bonnie down from the saddle. "This is Bonnie," he said, keeping his hand under her arm until Griffin slid from the saddle. "And this is Griffin. He had a little bad luck a few days back and ran into a bullet. You might need to take a look at it, Ma. It opened up on him again this morning."

Bonnie looked at Cooper's mother, and her fears grew with leaps and bounds. She was so soft, so pretty and clean. Her dress was freshly ironed, her white apron spotless, her hair combed to the top of her head and coiled in neat swirls. Oh, mercy! she thought. This woman wouldn't want *her* here! Her heart felt like a rock sinking to the bottom of her stomach. Bonnie wanted nothing more than to hide so Cooper's mother wouldn't see the stump on the end of her arm, the soiled, ragged dress, and the shoes that Griffin had patched last night with a thong. She nervously lifted her hand to push back the heavy strands of hair from her face and secure the pins in the knot on her neck. All the while she held her handless arm behind her. She felt Griffin's hand on her shoulder, gently urging her toward the woman who came to meet her. She turned beseeching eyes on him.

"Griff—"

"It'll be all right," he murmured.

"You poor child!" Sylvia exclaimed. "You're worn down to a nubbin' and pale as a ghost. I'm guessing you're hungry, too. Cooper won't quit a'tall when he's on the trail. It's a good thing he's got Roscoe 'cause he'd ride a weaker horse right down to its knees in a day's time," Sylvia chattered, seeing the panic in the girl's eyes and hoping to give her time to collect herself. "My goodness gracious, but it's been a spell since I've had a woman to visit with. Come right on in."

"Thank ya, ma'am."

Sylvia's blue eyes went from Bonnie to Griffin and she saw the anxious look on his face as he watched the girl who clutched his arm.

"She'll be just fine with me, Mr. Griffin," she said, and smiled at him. "I'll look after her. You go on and take care of your horse, then come in for supper. I made a berry pie, Cooper. I had a feelin' you were comin' home today."

Bonnie's eyes pleaded with Griffin not to leave her, but he gripped her shoulder reassuringly and followed Cooper toward the buildings behind the house. She watched him until he was out of sight, then turned to see the sweet-faced woman smiling at her.

"My name is Sylvia."

"I . . . I'm sorry to mis put ya, ma'am. I can go to the barn with Griff—"

"You'll do not such thing. You're not mis puttin' me at all. Come on in. You don't know what a treat it is for me to have another woman in the house."

Bonnie stood as if her legs were knee deep in mud. She

was afraid to move. She hadn't been able to change her padding since morning and she could feel a warm wetness running down her legs. Oh, Lordy! she thought helplessly, wishing fervently that Lorna was with her. If she went in the house it might gush out on the floor, then what would she do? Despite all she could do to hold them back, tears spurted in her eyes.

"Ma'am, I cain't—"

"Land agotion! What's wrong?"

"Ain't . . . nothin', ma'am. I—"

Sylvia caught a whiff of a recognizable odor and saw the agony of embarrassment on the girl's face. Understanding of her predicament dawned. "Is your time on you?" she asked gently.

Bonnie nodded mutely and worked to keep her face from crumbling.

"It's a cross we women have to bear. We'll get you fixed up in no time. I'm not using my pads, now. They're clean and folded—"

"I cain't go in there." Tears streamed down Bonnie's face.

"Why not, child? Why ever not?" Sylvia was dumbfounded.

"I'm . . . dirty—"

"Why, of course you are. I don't see how you can be on the trail and not be dirty. But that's no reason—"

"You ain't seen my arm," Bonnie blurted.

"Your arm?"

"I ain't got no . . . hand on it."

"Landsakes! What difference does that make? I saw it when Cooper lifted you down from the horse." Sylvia put an arm around Bonnie's waist and urged her toward the porch, but the girl held back.

"It don't make ya . . . sick?"

"Of course it don't make me sick. Whatever gave you an idea like that?"

"But . . . yo're a *lady*! A real one."

Sylvia looked at her tear-streaked face, trembling mouth,

and her enormous soft brown, dark-circled eyes swimming in tears. Her skin was drawn tightly over her high cheekbones and she was thin to the point of gauntness. Her brown faded dress was ragged and patched, and the wet spots on the bodice told her the girl had recently given birth and her breasts were leaking milk. The man with her was little more than a boy, but they had looked at each other with a world of love in their eyes. Where in the world, thought Sylvia, had Cooper picked up these two young waifs?

"Now, listen to me, Bonnie. I like to think of myself as a lady, but not a *prissy* lady," she said gently. "I'm a woman who's been through the mill. I've known hard times. I've been down to where I had one dress to my name and washed men's dirty drawers from mornin' till night to put food in my little boy's mouth. There's not much that I've not seen or heard, so it takes a heap to make *me* sick. I don't know where you've come from or where you're goin', but my son brought you here and you and your young man are welcome. You're very welcome. Come on in, now, so we can get you cleaned up before the men come in for supper."

Cooper paused in the door of the bunkhouse to allow his eyes to become accustomed to the dim light. One of his men had told him Volney Burbank, the old mountain man, was here, and how he'd come riding on in on the dun horse, his hand and foot mangled and barely conscious enough to hang onto the saddle horn.

"Ya finally come back, did ya?"

Cooper's eyes sought the far corner of the bunkhouse where the old man lay. "Finally," he said as he went across the plank floor. "How're you doing, Volney? Louis says you came in here looking like you'd tangled with a wildcat."

"Why I'm adoin' jist fine. Cain't ya see I'm jist alayin' here takin' my ease?" the old man asked waspishly. Two hostile blue eyes glared up at Cooper from beneath bushy brows and a tangle of yellow-gray hair.

"I'm glad to hear it. Do you want to tell me how you came to be in such a fix?"

"No, I don't want to tell ya nothin', 'cause it ain't none a yore business. But seein' as how this here's yore bunkhouse, 'n I been chowin' down on yore vittles, I will. I snagged my toe on a stump."

His grumpiness touched off Cooper's impatience. "Don't be stubborn and proud, Volney. Somebody worked you over and I have a fair idea who it was."

"Ya ain't got no idea a'tall, young scutter! Mine yore own dadgum business. Kill yore snakes 'n I'll kill mine."

"If that's how you want it, I'm sorry for prying." Cooper was turning away when Volney's voice stopped him.

"I been awaitin' fer ya to get back. Ya sure took yore own sweet time."

"I'd no reason to make a beeline home."

Volney heaved himself up to lean against the wall, breathing hard from his exertions. "I got me a good 'mount a pelts stashed in a cache not far off. They'd brin' in five, six hunnerd or more." The raspy voice subsided, and the gaunt old man's piercing eyes stared up at his still-faced friend. Cooper waited, knowing what was coming and knowing how difficult it was for Volney to ask for assistance. "They be yores . . . 'n yore ma's. She's a smart alecky woman, yore ma is."

"That she is," Cooper admitted with a grin. "Was she after you to take a bath?"

"Wash yoreself! Shave yoreself! Eat! She perty neigh nagged me to death! She even came sasshayin' out here with a peach can fer me to use as a gaboon!" He spit a stream of yellow tobacco juice into the can beside the bunk. Blue eyes speared up from beneath shaggy brows to glare at Cooper again. There were few things that rankled Volney like being obligated to someone. The pelts would pay for his keep here, but forcing his concern for Lorna on Parnell was another matter. He hated this moment, hated the words he was going to say, hated himself for being so goddamned old and careless that he'd let the thing happen that made it necessary for him to say them. But for Lorna he'd do it at whatever cost to his dignity. "I got a thin' to ask ya—"

Cooper had thought he'd let the cantankerous old man suffer the humiliation of asking for his help, but he could see what it was costing him to ask the favor.

"By the way, Volney, I've got a message for you," he said in an offhand manner, as if what he had to say was of no importance. "I met a friend of yours over on the Blue. She was a right sightly woman, even if she was wearing baggy old britches and carrying a stiletto. She said if I run across a stinking old man that needed a bath and a shave to tell him she and Bonnie had made out all right."

The information took Volney so unaware he opened his mouth, closed it, opened it again, and let his breath out with a whistle. He blinked his eyes rapidly and his tired old shoulders slumped with relief, then straightened, and he glared at Cooper angrily.

"Wal, dadburnit! Why didn't ya say so, 'stead a standin' thar alollygaggin' 'round?" His tone clearly indicated he was surprised. He was also relieved and angry because Cooper had been making small talk when he could have told him, right off, and eased his mind.

"I was going to. But you had your tail in a crack and I thought I'd let you squirm for a bit." Cooper stroked the stubble of whiskers on his chin absently. "It's about time for supper—"

"By jinks damn, Parnell! Was them women all right?"

"Well, I'm no Sir Galahad, but I'd not have left them if they weren't."

"Who's that Galahad?"

Cooper grinned. "Fella I knew once. Have you had your supper?"

"Yo're jist as smart alecky as yore ma! I'm atellin' ya, them women cain't stay thar. If'n Brice Fulton don't find 'em, ole Clayhill's pack a varmints will, 'n it won't be no play party for them women. 'Sides, the cripple gal's time's 'bout on, 'n it won't surprise me none if'n she passed on havin' that youngun."

"She almost did. Most likely the beating she took killed the babe. Quit your fretting, old man. I brought Bonnie here to Ma and took Lorna home. Her pa will look after her."

Volney shook his grizzled head in a denying gesture. "He ain't good fer sheeit! He ain't done nothin' but piss 'n moan since Nora passed on."

"I can't do anything about that." Cooper turned to go.

"Hold on fer jist a goldurned minute, Parnell." Volney swung his good leg off the bunk and sat up. A grunt came from the tobacco stained lips as pain knifed through him. "Yo're shore closemouthed with yore words, mister. I'd jist as soon try to get blood outta a turnip."

"It's the same with you, old man. When did you ever tell me anything that I didn't have to pry out of you?"

"Thar weren't nothin' aneedin' to be told till now. Now, I'm tellin' ya that gal's back thar on Light's Mountain with a bunch what's meaner 'n a pit a rattlesnakes. Brice Fulton ain't agoin' to back up. He'd club his own granny if'n she crossed him. Him 'n them what's got shit fer brains'll be pesterin' Lorna 'bout where Bonnie's at. 'N if'n they catch her off guard—"

"I met a couple of *them*—Hollis and Billy Tyrrell."

"Thar! See thar! They was in on it. They helped Fulton—" Volney suddenly snapped his mouth shut, realizing he'd given out more information than he intended.

A spurt of anger knifed through Cooper and a vow planted itself in his mind that he'd someday even the score for Volney and Bonnie.

"His time'll come, Volney. You can depend on it," he said quietly.

"Parnell?" Griffin spoke from the doorway.

"Come on in," Cooper said. "This is Volney Burbank, the man who took Bonnie and Lorna to the cabin on the Blue."

Griffin came across the room. Volney glanced at him, then back to Cooper. "Did Lorna hear anythin' from White Bull?"

"Not that I know of."

"Sheeit! I was ahopin' he'd come back 'n would be stayin' fer a spell. Who's this bird?" he growled, looking up at Griffin. "What're ya gawkin' at? Ain't ya ever seed a man laid up, afore?"

Cooper glanced at Griffin to see how he was taking the old man's sarcasm. His lips were quirking and he was trying hard to keep a straight face.

"Wal, now that ya speak on it, I ain't ne'er seen one all duded out in a dress like yo're in."

"Consarn it all!" Volney shouted. "Ya be one a them smart ass whippersnappers, do ye? 'Twas that muddle-headed woman what took my britches 'n left this here confounded sack to cover my naked limbs. Ya watch yore mouth, hear? Elseways there'll be a real chicken flutter set-to when I get my legs under me agin."

"I'm plumb sorry I riled ya, mister. No offense intended a'tall," Griffin said humbly, his shoulders shaking with silent laughter. Abruptly his face sobered. "Fact is, I'm debted to ya for what ya done for Bonnie. I want ya to know I'm atakin' her for my woman, 'n I pay the bills for me 'n mine."

"Ya, do, do ya? Wal, now. Ya ain't dry behind the ears yet. Ya best leave the likes of Brice Fulton to a man what's been up the Trace 'n o'er the mountain. That man be me, sonny."

"If'n you say so, ole man," Griffin said quietly.

There was something in his voice that made Volney Burbank take a second look at the slim young man. He met the boy's downbearing gaze. It was steady—unshakable. On widely planted legs, he loomed over him. There was nothing threatening in his stance, only absolute confidence.

After what seemed an eternity to Cooper, who stood watch-

ing, Volney nodded his grizzled head. Griffin dipped his in
reply. It appeared to Cooper as though, at this moment, a
silent bond had been forged between the very young and very
old man.

Chapter
Fifteen

It took almost a week for Cooper to catch up on the work he needed to do around the ranch. It would have taken longer but for Griffin. Although the young nester's shoulder was still sore and stiff, he assisted a mare with a difficult birth, treated cuts, pulled broken teeth, lanced boils and acted as general veterinarian; treating everything that walked on four legs that had a need for it. He had a way with animals and Cooper was impressed with his knowledge of doctoring them and the sensitive, caring way he went about doing it.

The night Cooper came home Sylvia told him about Adam Clayhill's visit, leaving out the gross insults he'd heaped upon her, and told of his threats to waylay Arnie Henderson and cripple him if she didn't persuade her son to go to Clayhill Ranch and take up residence. It was a relief to share this concern with her son. She had already told Arnie, and he had assured her that he would take extra precautions, but that threatening and doing were two different things and he doubted Clayhill would carry out his threats.

"I've been pondering on paying that old sonofabitch a visit," Cooper said with slow deliberation. "This goes a long way to helping me make up my mind." On seeing the look that crossed his mother's face before she could hide her fear,

218

he told her about the place on the Blue and that he and Griffin planned to file for the land. "I want the old man to know I've got a hand in on that place and if Griffin's bothered anymore by Clayhill riders he'll answer to me."

"Oh, Cooper! Right now he wants to claim you as his son, but he could turn against you in the time it would take to bat an eye and have you waylaid and killed. Adam Clayhill is the most unpredictable, unscrupulous man alive."

"Ma, I've told you this before. If it comes to it, I'll kill him before he does harm to me or mine. That goes for anything he does to Arnie, too, as I reckon he'll be part of the family soon. When do you expect him to ride this way again?"

"Probably not for another week." Sylvia could feel the color on her cheeks as her tall son grinned at her. "Oh, you—" she sputtered and stomped into the house.

It took just twenty-four hours for Bonnie to lose her shyness with Sylvia. Her confidence grew as the two women worked side by side in the spotlessly clean kitchen. Sylvia was easy to talk to and Bonnie talked about her childhood, her life with Brice, and meeting Cooper and Griffin as they made preserves, dried apples and berries, apple butter, saurkraut and pickles. She told her about Lorna and Light's Mountain, but was careful not to mention anything about Lorna being attracted to Cooper because she was sure he hadn't spoken to her in that way to his mother. She told about the difficult birth and how the men had found them in the cabin on the Blue.

Sylvia insisted that they make a couple of dresses for Bonnie out of goods she had put aside. One was a light butternut brown for everyday use and the other a blue print she would wear to be married in. Sylvia tried to not show her astonishment when Bonnie, using her one hand, threaded her own needle, tied the knot and made neat small stitches on the cloth. This was clearly the happiest time in Bonnie's life. She was being shown more kindness here, by this woman, than she'd had during her entire life. And she had Griffin, whom she loved with all her heart and soul.

Bonnie took over the care of Volney, taking him his meals, seeing to his wants, and spending some part of each morning and each afternoon sitting beside him. Sometimes he slept, not even knowing she was there. Since Cooper had come home the old man seemed to have lost his desire to hurry and get well so he could get back to the mountains he loved. It was as if the reason for leaving the Parnell ranch was no longer there. Griffin, too, spent considerable time with him each evening, and one time after hearing him fret over his dun horse, Griffin brought the animal to the door of the bunkhouse so Volney could see the animal was being cared for.

Time moved uneventfully down the corridor of busy days until one evening at dusk. Louis, the ranch hand, came galloping his horse into the ranch yard, jerked him to a stop and yelled for Cooper. Cooper got up from the supper table and automatically pulled his hat down on his head before he hurried to the porch.

They spoke briefly.

Louis wheeled his horse and headed for the shed, and Cooper stood on the porch for a moment. He had not been in a blacker frame of mind since the day his mother had named the man who sired him. Hate pushed and shoved at his mind, threatening to block reason. He gazed for a long moment toward the mountain and forced himself to recall Lorna's face, hoping to calm himself and remove the murderous rage that had swept over him before he went back into the house.

He paused in the doorway and looked at his mother, who had risen from the table and stood behind her chair, her hands fastened to the back of it, quietly waiting for the bad news that could only bring the shy ranch hand racing to the house.

"Louis found Arnie." He watched his mother's hands fly

to her cheeks and added quickly, "He's not dead, but he's sure torn up."

"How bad?"

"Louis said he's beaten to a pulp and has a busted leg." Griffin got up and reached for the dusty old hat Cooper had given him when they first arrived at the ranch. "I'd as soon you stay with the women, Griff. Louis and I will fetch him home in the wagon. You can't tell about a dirty, low-down bunch of trash that would hire out to do that to a man. They might just be waiting for me to leave the house and come pay Ma a visit. If they come, shoot the sonsofbitches and talk later. Ma can help you, she's a damn good shot."

"I'll keep a eye out," Griff said, and quietly left the house.

"Adam did just what he said he'd do . . ." Sylvia's voice grew weaker, then ceased altogether.

"Damn his rotten soul!"

"Where's Arnie?"

"Up near the red bluffs where the creek makes a horseshoe turn, Louis says. He saw buzzards circling and thought a mare had dropped a foal or been brought down by a cat. It was a dead horse, all right. They'd shot Arnie's horse right between the eyes."

"Oh, no! Arnie set a store by that horse."

"It's a damn sorry man who'd shoot a horse like that."

"Can you get a wagon in there?" Composed now, Sylvia was back to practical thinking.

"Not all the way, but Louis figures close enough so that we can carry him to it."

"I'll have things ready here."

Cooper went to her and gripped her shoulder. "Arnie's a tough bird. He'll make it."

"It was mean and wicked of Adam to do that to Arnie. I hate it that he's sufferin' on my account. He's a good man—"

"Buck up, Ma. It might just be worth it to Arnie to have you take care of him," Cooper said and pinched her chin.

"Oh, hush your teasin', Cooper, and go get him. They might come back," she said with a worried frown.

"I've been thinking of that and I'm glad Griff will be here with you and Bonnie."

"Take a lantern, son."

"I will. I hope we can find him in the dark. There's no moon tonight, is there?" he added as an afterthought before he went out.

Bonnie had moved back into the shadows, away from the light of the lamp that sat amid the uneaten supper. She didn't understand the underlying meaning of the words that passed between mother and son, but realized the importance of them. Shying away from the leashed violence she sensed in Cooper, she waited until he left the room before she moved to clear away the scarcely touched meal.

The evening wore on. After getting the bed in Cooper's room ready for Arnie and laying out bandages, salves, and everything she considered would be useful, Sylvia took the lantern and went down to the shed to look for a smooth straight plank they could use to set a broken bone. She had no idea if the plank would be needed, but she had to be moving, doing something, or else anxiety would mangle her nerves.

To a woman at home, not knowing if her man was dead or near death, the waiting hours were long and torturous. When she ran out of things to do, Sylvia leaned against the peeled pine post that supported the porch roof and strained her eyes toward the mountains, watching and waiting for a moving speck to appear out of the darkness and listening for the faintest sound of the creaking wagon or the jingle of harnesses. She was grateful for Bonnie's quiet presence and for Griffin who patrolled the perimeter of the ranch yard.

It was after midnight when Griffin's voice came to Sylvia from out of the darkness. "They're acomin', ma'am. I'll be agoin' out to open the gates."

"I don't hear anything," she said and turned her ear toward

the trail. She couldn't hear a thing, not even the young nester's footsteps on the hard-packed ground as he hurried away.

"I don't hear anythin' either," Bonnie said. "But if Griff says they're acomin', they're acomin'. He's the beatin'est man ya ever did see fer gettin' 'round in the dark. Ya want me to light the lantern fer ya 'n build up the fire 'n get the kettle to boilin'?"

It seemed to Sylvia a long time before she heard the sound of the approaching wagon. When she did her heart leaped with relief, then plunged with dread. She reached for the lantern when Bonnie came to the porch with it and stepped out into the yard, holding it high to guide the wagon to the house. She could see that Louis was driving the team and Cooper's light colored hat was bobbing up and down behind the wagon seat. She stood very still, forcing herself to remain calm and accept whatever the next few moments would bring.

"Cooper? Is he all right?"

"He's alive, Ma. He passed out while we were getting him to the wagon. Griff, fetch that new door ya made for the bunkhouse and we'll carry him in on it. We'll get him as close to the porch as we can, Ma, but it'll mean ruining your flowers—"

"Oh, shoot! I don't care about that. Is he hurt bad?"

"Pretty bad. Maybe you should let me and Griffin—"

"You mean he's not a pretty sight? Landsakes, Cooper, you know I'm not squeamish." She lifted the lantern and looked over the side of the wagon. The light fell on Arnie's bloody, battered features. She wouldn't have recognized him except for the thin, graying hair, the handlebar mustache, and the blue and white striped shirt she'd made for his birthday. He'd been so proud of it. Now it was riddled with a hundred tears and was soaked with blood. "Oh! Oh, God in heaven—" Her voice rose in hysteria.

"Ma!" Cooper said anxiously. "You all right, Ma?"

"Yes, son. Yes, I think so. What in heaven's name did they do to him?"

"The goddamn pissants dragged him!" Cooper spat the words out viciously.

"Dear God! How on earth can men be so cruel to their fellow man?"

Sylvia was grateful that Arnie remained unconscious while the men got him on the bed and cut away his shirt and breeches. His boots had been torn from his feet when they dragged him and his feet and ankles were covered with blood and dirt. She inspected the sickening mass of lacerations by the light of every lamp they owned, and wondered whether or not she was equal to the task of caring for him. She was no stranger to the sickroom. Often she had dressed the wounds of severely injured men, but never had she beheld such a grisly mutilation of human flesh.

Don't think about who did this, she told herself, think about what has to be done.

Griffin straightened out the bent leg and swore. "They busted his leg with a rifle butt, I'm athinkin'. The dirty bastards! 'Scuse me, ma'am. See this here bruise, Cooper? It's what they done, all right. They busted it while he was down. Leastways it won't cripple him up like it'd done if'n they'd busted up his thigh bone." Griffin's gentle fingers went over Arnie's body feeling for more broken bones. "This'n's all that's busted. We'd best get it straight 'n tied up good 'n snug afore he comes to, 'cause it's agoin' to hurt like hell."

When Cooper pulled on Arnie's leg and Griffin worked the ends of the broken bone together Arnie moaned, then cried out as the searing pain hauled him up out of the darkness. He fainted again almost immediately, and Griff and Cooper hurried to complete the work on his leg before he became conscious again.

Sylvia turned her attention to the welter of bloody debris coating Arnie's back and chest while Griffin cleaned his feet and ankles. Bonnie kept them supplied with pans of clean warm water. After they cleaned the blood and dirt from his body, they washed it with vinegar water and liberally smeared the tears in his flesh with ointment.

"I heared tell, ma'am, that a dosin' of whiskey 'n honey is good for a man what's lost blood like this'n has," Griffin said when they had finished.

"I've not heard of that, but I'll give him some when he comes to."

"Sugar works the same, but I guess most folks has got more honey 'n sugar. It's somethin' 'bout the sweet—"

"Where in the world did you learn so much about doctorin'?"

Griffin carefully screwed the lid back on the ointment jar before he spoke. "When I got out of Yuma, I took up with a ole man who doctored when he was sober. He'd had schoolin' at some place across the water. I think he said Edinburgh or somethin' like that. He'd been in the war, 'n when he got to athinkin' 'bout all the arms 'n legs he'd cut off, he'd get the willies 'n get roarin' drunk. He'd do all sorts a crazy thin's. I stayed with him for a spell 'n helped him out when folks pressed him to doctor. I'm athinkin' he was a jim-dandy doctor in his prime."

"What happened to him?"

"He died."

"What a waste. Many a good man has drunk himself to death."

"He died a snake bite." Griffin's voice had changed and Sylvia glanced at him. He was staring at Arnie's bruised and swollen face as if his mind were a hundred miles away. "Sometimes when he got drunk he'd think he saw snakes. A couple a galoots thought it'd be funny if'n they was real. They throwed one on a porch where he was alayin', rantin' 'n ravin' 'n thinkin' there was crawly things on him. It bit him afore I could kill it."

The small doses of laudanum Sylvia gave Arnie kept him sleeping for the better part of two days, then she ceased giving him the drug, knowing the danger of its becoming habit forming. He woke one morning in pain, but his head was clear and by evening he was able to give Cooper an account of what had happened to him.

"It was pure ole carelessness to let myself get caught up and yanked off my horse like a trussed up steer. This feller hailed me down to talk and was askin' me the way to town when a rope settled on me and I was hog-tied afore I knowed it."

"Do you know who they were?"

"There was no names called, but I know they was Clayhill men. They said tell Mrs. Parnell the next time it'd be my tallywacker. 'Course I ain't saying nothin' like that to Sylvia. When I see them birds, they'll wish they'd finished up the job."

"How are you feeling?" Cooper asked after a long pause and glanced at Arnie to let him know his mother had come to stand in the doorway.

"Well, I ain't feelin' up to snuff, but I ain't complainin', neither." Arnie turned his head painfully so he could look at Sylvia, then back to her tall son sprawled in the chair beside the bed. "I'm afeared I crowded ya out of yore bed, Cooper. Ya coulda took me to the bunkhouse."

"Ma wouldn't hear of it. She's a bossy woman, Arnie. You'd better know right off what you're in for."

"I'll never have me no prettier boss."

Cooper looked up to see the doorway empty and heard his mother's steps going rapidly across the kitchen floor. He grinned at the man lying on the bed. "I trust your intentions are honorable?"

"'Course they are, boy. Your ma ain't got no doubt about it."

The two men looked at each other for a moment, then Cooper stuck out his hand. "I'm glad, Arnie. Real glad for you and for Ma."

"Ain't nothin' settled—"

"I know. You're more than welcome to come here. This is Ma's home as much as mine."

"I had it in mind to build a little place over on Morning Sun."

"If it suits the two of you, it's fine with me. Arnie," Cooper's eyes sought those of the older man, "do you think you'll be up to sitting on the porch in a day or two? I want to go to town, but I'll wait till you're up to handling a rifle."

"Do you think there'll be a need for it?"

"I don't know, but I don't want to go off till I'm sure you're fit to take care of things. I've not worried about it before because Ma can handle a rifle as good as a man. Louis is a good man, but he's got to be told what to do. Volney's down on his back. I don't know if the old man'll ever get up again."

"Do you reckon it was the same bunch that did me in that worked on the ole man?"

"No. It's not the same bunch at all."

Cooper told Arnie about Clayhill's men hanging Griffin, about trailing the mare to the cabin on the Blue and the run-in there with Dunbar. He told of taking Lorna to Light's Mountain and of his suspicion that Brice Fulton was responsible for Volney's injuries.

"I'm athinkin' that folks is gettin' meaner all the time," Arnie said when Cooper had finished. "It's got to be the times we're alivin' in. Didn't used to hear a things like this till the war."

"Folks have always been mean," Cooper said, remembering his painful childhood at the fort where his mother was a laundress. "They just show it in different ways."

"You mean to take the young feller when you go?"

"I was planning on it."

"He's a cold-eyed youngun. I seen some like him durin' the war. They'd got all the softness knocked outta 'em."

"You'd be surprised about Griff. He's soft as mush when it comes to women or a hurt animal."

"Is that right? Well, give me a day to get used to gettin' around with that forked stick he fixed up for me. Then you go on off with a easy mind. I can't run, but I can shoot."

Lorna had spent a couple of weeks of very hard work, followed by several unprofitable days lolling around the house. The dried beans were in the basket on the porch waiting to be shucked and cabbages were in the cellar waiting to be shredded and made into kraut, but she couldn't get interested in doing any of those things. It had been more than two weeks since Cooper had ridden away and she had whipped Brice with the bullwhip. She hadn't heard from either man; not that she'd expected to hear from Cooper, but she had thought Brice would be back, with Billy and Hollis as backup to seek vengeance.

The news she received about Brice was secondhand. Luke, Hollis's cousin, stopped by and said Brice, Hollis and Billy Tyrrell had left the mountain just as soon as Brice was able to sit a saddle. He said Brice was acting strange. At times he was like a mad dog snapping at everyone, and at other times like a whipped cur. Being around him was like walking on eggs, Luke said, you never knew which way to jump first.

It wasn't thoughts of Brice that troubled Lorna's mind; it was Cooper and what had happened between them. Not that she was completely aware of it, but since meeting Cooper, Light's Mountain had lost some of its magical attraction. The September days were spent as they had been for as long as she could remember, preparing for the long winter months, but the zest with which she had accomplished these tasks was gone. She went about the work automatically, listlessly.

White Bull and his people returned. The old chief came to see her. She told him about the whipping she gave Brice, but carefully refrained from mentioning Cooper, knowing that if White Bull thought she wanted him for her man, he would send a party of braves to fetch him to Light's Mountain. The tribe was planning to move on south, and if she was to visit the village she must do it soon. Not even the promise of that could shake her from her lethargy.

The saving grace of this dark time in her life, she was to realize later, was the new understanding between her and her father. His quiet companionship was her only comfort. Frank seldom left the homestead during the weeks following "Black Sunday" as he called the day Lorna had whipped Brice Fulton.

"He be a mon to seek vengeance," he declared more than once.

"Let him try," Lorna would reply heatedly, looking toward the rock covered mounds where they had buried the dogs Brice had killed.

She missed Naomi and Ruth. She missed them going with her to the barn when she went to milk the brindle cow and their happy yipping when Frank came to the house. Now there was only the clucking of the flighty chickens, the scolding of the bluejays and the caws of the black crows that hovered over the homestead.

Lorna didn't know exactly when the idea came to her to go take a look at Cooper's ranch. The idea was an offshoot of the notion she had to search for Volney. There were two places the old mountain man could have made for; a shack he sometimes used high up on the timberline, or one down on the Thompson River. From there it wouldn't be far to where she thought Cooper's ranch was located. The idea hung in her mind. She mulled it over until one day she thought of something Cooper had said: *I'll get a look at you and you won't even know I'm within a hundred miles*. At that moment the idea solidified into something she could hold on to and pursue, and a tingling excitement began to build within her.

Frank stood in the yard as she tied a bedroll behind her saddle and filled the saddlebags with provisions. Gray Wolf danced nervously, anxious to be away, and she spoke to him sternly. The morning was crisp as only a late September morning could be in the mountains. The smell of frost made the air sharp and tangy.

"I dinna need to be sayin' to ye that I'd as soon ye not be goin'," he said and looped the coiled bullwhip over her saddle horn.

"I know, Pa. Thank you for not arguing against it."

"Ye be a woman grown, daughter. Ye be knowin' yer own mind 'n goin' yer own way."

"I'll be all right. You keep an eye out, hear? Don't let yourself get cornered if Brice and his bunch come back."

"They be halfway to California by now, I'm thinkin'."

"Keep an eye out for Moose and Woody, too. They'll be coming soon. They'll probably be here by the time I get back."

"Four days, ye say?"

"Give or take a day. Pa—" She never called him Frank, now. "Don't worry." She went to him and took the oilskin pouch of food from his hands. "Other times I've gone off and you didn't worry—"

"Aye, I did in me own foolish way, but not like now. Ye be careful, girl."

"Aye, oold mon, 'n ye be careful, too." Lorna imitated his Scottish brogue in an attempt to make him smile, but his dour face remained furrowed with worry lines.

She stored the food in the saddlebag and swung into the saddle. Gray Wolf danced and Lorna laughed for the first time in weeks. In britches, perched atop the big horse with her hair stuffed up under a flat-crowned brimmed hat, she looked like a small helpless boy, but Frank knew she was far from helpless. With the rifle, the stiletto and the bullwhip she would be a dangerous enemy for any man to attack.

"Bye, Pa," she called over her shoulder and gave Gray Wolf rein to set his own pace.

Lorna climbed up out of the valley and into the higher hills to pass over the ridge to the trail that led downward. She traveled by stages, letting Gray Wolf pick his own way for the most part, but here and there she reined wide of an unnecessarily steep climb out of consideration for her mount. She was acutely attuned to her surroundings, turning her head constantly, sending her sharp gaze skittering over the terrain in suspicious searching.

This was her country. She loved the upthrust ridges, the crisscrossing canyons filled with pines and the streams, almost dry now, that would be rioting in the spring, carrying the melted snow to the valleys below. She knew every species of wildlife that lived here: the birds—and she could mimic their song to perfection—the deer, the rodent, predator, and reptile. She could tell what had caused a panic-stricken deer to bound along the trail by the sound of the rustling in the underbrush.

This was her world and she had seldom been lonely in it. There was always the sound of the birds, from the concerted outburst of profanity from bluejays to the soft cooing of the mourning doves and hoot owls, the call of a coyote, the scream of a cat or the chatter from a squirrel to listen to. Now, this day, she was urgently happy to be leaving the mountains for the flat tablelands at the feet of them.

From the moment they left the homestead, Gray Wolf had sensed an urgency in the girl on his back. On the downward trail he traveled faster, as the summons came more strongly to him. Lorna let him go, but slowed him cautiously when the table on which she rode narrowed. On her left was a wall that rose a hundred feet into the air, and to her right the rim of the table marked a fall of nearly twice that distance, making this long and flat expanse a gigantic stairstep carved by nature into the side of the mountain. At the far end of the step the land was a jungle of boulders and it took her the best part of an hour to work her way through them. Once free, she found herself in a land of towering ponderosa pines and dense undergrowth. She and Gray Wolf drifted through it with almost no sound at all.

It was warmer in the lowlands. They stopped by a swiftly moving stream to drink and Lorna cautioned Gray Wolf. "Just a few swallows now, you're too hot for much of that cold water."

She took off the blanket coat she wore, tied it to her bedroll and wiped the sweat from her face. Her head itched beneath the hat and the heavy mass of hair. She took off the hat and massaged her head with her fingertips before carefully tucking the hair up under the hat again. There was no point in flaunting the fact she was a lone woman in case she met someone on the trail.

She reached the Thompson in late afternoon and followed it downstream. Her mind searched for everything Volney had told her about this small log cabin he called headquarters. The mountains were his home, he'd said, but the cabin was a place to go to and winter if the notion struck him.

She saw it in the late evening, just as dusk settled over the timbered bench. It was squat and sturdy, like Volney, and blended into its surroundings so perfectly that her eyes had passed over it the first time they scanned the area. She drew Gray Wolf to a halt and the two of them remained stone still for long minutes while she examined every foot of terrain around the cabin. A squirrel was sitting beside the door, an acorn in its paws, eyeing her, swishing its tail angrily.

"There's no one here. No one, at all." She spoke softly to Gray Wolf. His ears twitched and his nostrils quivered, but he moved slowly forward.

The squirrel cocked his head, then dropped the acorn and scolded before scampering up a tree.

Chapter
Sixteen

Lorna heated water for coffee, then put out the small fire she
had built in the smoke-blackened fireplace. She didn't want
to draw attention to the cabin should there be anyone within
smoke-smelling distance. After she ate she staked Gray Wolf
out in front of the cabin and lay down on the pile of musty
furs Volney used for a bed, confident the stallion would alert
her if anyone approached. She was tired after the hard day's
ride. Tired and disappointed.

She had hoped to find Volney here and that he would be
his usual cantankerous self, scoffing at the idea she would
think a peabrain like Brice Fulton could get the best of him.
She needed to have a visit with her old friend and tell him
about her father and how he had withdrawn into himself after
her mother died and make it clear to him that he'd had no
part in the cattle rustling that was going on. *How could she
have ever thought that about her father?*

She wanted to tell Volney about Cooper, too. It was strange
that Volney had never mentioned being an almost regular
visitor at Cooper's ranch. But then, Volney never felt the need
to tell her anything about his wanderings.

Morning came and she was tinglingly aware that before
the day was over she would see where Cooper lived and

might even get a glimpse of him. She hadn't planned any farther than keeping well out of sight, looking over the ranch and making sure Bonnie was there. After that she'd go back home and hope that Volney would show up sometime before winter set in.

In the middle of the afternoon Gray Wolf lifted his head and sniffed repeatedly. Lorna reined in, keeping the stallion still with a hand on his neck, and surveyed the area. Judging the best screen would be in the junipers to the west, she turned into them, crossed a well-worn trail and rounded the foot of the hill marking the highest point of the valley's southern, outspread arms. She had traveled down less than a half a mile of sloping terrain before she came to another trail. Two shod horses had passed early that morning according to the prints they'd left in the dark red soil. She wheeled Gray Wolf to give him a running start and the stallion easily jumped the trail, leaving no evidence she had crossed it.

She drew rein on a slight rise a quarter of a mile from the ranch buildings. From this position she could see the front of the house, the side of the bunkhouse and all the outbuildings. Cooper's home was a compound of small, neat buildings, a network of pole corrals, and a single-story house with a wide porch. There were flowers, planted in rows, along the front of the house and a wire fence surrounding a vegetable garden on the side of it. The only movement that she could see with her naked eye was from the horses in the corrals, the white chickens picking in the yard, and a wash that fluttered in the breeze from a wire stretched between two trees.

Gray Wolf stood avidly sniffing the air with belled nostrils and busily working ears. He tossed his head excitedly and Lorna hastily moved him back into the trees, fearing he would let loose a shrill neigh announcing his presence to the mares. In a small clearing where the grass was ankle-high, she dismounted, drew off the saddle and fashioned a rope halter for Gray Wolf. She was afraid to ground-tie the big stallion as she usually did, afraid the mares would be too great a temptation for him. She put him on a long lead rope, with one end fastened to the halter she slipped over his head and the other end tied securely to a young sapling.

"I know you hate being tied," she murmured in his ear. "I hate doing it to you, but if you let your mating instinct take you down there, Cooper'll know I'm here. I can't let him think I've come running back to him with my tail between my legs. You understand, don't you, my dearest friend?"

Lorna took the glasses from her saddlebag and went back through the screening junipers. She settled down on the cushion of thick needles with her back against the rough trunk of a tall pine. With pounding heart and trembling fingers she raised the glasses to her eyes.

A man was sitting on the porch. His hair was light, he had a handlebar mustache, and his leg was wrapped and propped up on a box. It wasn't Cooper.

She moved the glasses so she could study the clothes on the line. She saw shirts and Cooper's long-legged pants, but she didn't see anything that belonged to Bonnie. Beyond the clothesline, inside a three-sided shed, a man worked at a forge. He wasn't Cooper, either. In the corral beside the bunkhouse several horses stood beneath a brush arbor, swishing the pesky fall flies with their tails. One of the horses was the mare she had found, the mare that had led Cooper to the cabin on the Blue, the other was a wiry dun horse. *Volney's horse!*

Lorna took the glasses from her eyes and rested her forearm on her bent knee. Either Volney was there, or else Volney was dead and Cooper had buried him and brought his horse there. It was more than likely he was dead, she thought painfully. Oh, poor Volney. She wished she had killed Brice Fulton!

A woman came out onto the porch, but before Lorna could get the glasses in position she had gone back into the house. Then she saw Bonnie walk out into the yard. An old yellow dog moved lazily out from beneath the porch and came slowly to meet her. She stopped to pat its head, then continued on to the clothesline. Lorna had never seen Bonnie looking so grand. She was wearing a tan dress that buttoned down the front. The waist fit snugly and the skirt came down to the tops of her shoes. The only thing Lorna had ever seen her wear was a sack-type dress that had been patched a hundred times and had strips of material sewed on the bottom to make it longer as she grew taller. Something else was different about Bonnie; *both* of the sleeves of her dress were rolled to her elbows.

Now the woman who had first been on the porch came out to the line and took the clothes from Bonnie. She was as tall as Bonnie, but not so slender. Her light hair was not slicked back and fastened in a tight knot as most women wore it. It was puffed and piled atop her head and the wind blew wisps of it around her face. She didn't look old enough to be Cooper's mother, but she must be. After she talked to Bonnie for a few minutes, Bonnie went to the bunkhouse and the woman went back to the house.

Hours passed. A ranch hand rode in from the north, put his horse in the corral and went to the bunkhouse. Lorna hadn't caught a glimpse of Cooper and she began to suspect he was not there. She felt strangely empty, alone and deflated, up there on the hillside looking down at Cooper's home. She felt small and insignificant, an outsider. She *was* an outsider. Fool, she admonished herself. Suddenly she wanted the people on the ranch to know that she was there. She wanted to sing, to sing loud, to let them know that she, Lorna Douglas from Light's Mountain, was there and that Bonnie was *her* friend. Tears filled her eyes, ran down her cheeks, and on to stubbornly held lips. She had never before wanted to sing merely to let her presence be known. What was the matter with her? Was she jealous of poor Bonnie? Did she want to be there with Cooper's mother taking *his* clothes off the line?

"Oh, shoot!" she muttered. "She'd not think much of me

in these britches. She'd want Cooper to have a woman who could sew and dress her hair all fancy. It sure didn't take her long to get Bonnie all duded out in a fine dress."

Lorna sat beneath the tree until the sun retreated behind the western mountains. She saw Cooper's mother bring a plate of supper to the man on the porch and carefully place it on a box beside him. She put her hand on his shoulder for a moment before she went back into the house. Lorna saw Bonnie go once again to the bunkhouse, a covered basket on her arm. Evening light faded rapidly and the glow of a lamp appeared in the window of the house below.

The night wind swept down the valley and chilled the forlorn figure huddled beneath the tree. Lorna got stiffly to her feet. Her stomach growled noisily, reminding her that she hadn't eaten since morning. She made her way back through the thick grove to where she had left Gray Wolf. He was calmly cropping the grass and looked up as she approached. Wanting comfort from some living thing, she went to him and looped her arms about his neck and buried her face in his flowing mane.

"I'm just backwoods, Gray Wolf. Just backwoods like Brice said I was. I don't belong here. I belong on Light's Mountain. But, by jinks damn, I'm not leaving until I know about Volney. I'll slip down there tonight and talk to Bonnie and tomorrow we'll go home."

The night was moonless with only the stars to brighten the sky. Lorna sped confidently through the darkness, her feet making no sound. The thing uppermost in her mind as she approached the ranch buildings was to let the yellow dog know that she was there. She did this by hunkering down and making soft noises in her throat. When the dog's curiosity got the better of it and it came hesitantly to her, she fed it a biscuit and scratched its ears. Then her problem was getting it to stay put and not follow her. Once this was accomplished she darted into the house yard and sped across the open ground to the smokehouse.

She stood with her back to the stone building and listened. Having roamed the woods all her life, Lorna had acquired a quality of stillness and learned to cultivate the art of listening because her life could depend upon it. Lorna's ears were trained to tune out the usual noises, ignoring them. It was the strange sounds she listened for or the lack of the normal sounds.

After a brief pause, she sped swiftly toward the shed where she had seen the man working on the forge, froze against the wall, hunkered down, and waited. After each move she stopped to listen and wait patiently to see if the insects would begin their singing again, or if something not known or understood was near them. When the contented chorus from the crickets began again, she slipped between the poles of the corral and stood quietly between the mare and Volney's dun horse, uttering soft sounds and rubbing their noses with gentle, knowing fingers. After awhile she passed between the poles again and into the next enclosure. Not a sound from the horses had betrayed her presence.

Lorna carefully inspected the corrals, the sheds and the barn. She didn't find Cooper's or Griffin's horses in the stalls where she was sure Cooper would keep the stallions. Nor did she see the black saddle Cooper used, or Griffin's high-backed saddle with the cavalry stirrups. A feeling of disappointment as well as anger at Cooper swamped her. She wanted to swear aloud, but suppressed the desire and snarled, "You . . . horse's patoot! I hope *you've* had a two-day ride to Light's Mountain and found *me* gone."

There were at least two men in the bunkhouse, according to the snores coming through the half-opened door. Lorna peered in. It was darker than the bottom of a well and smelled of dirty feet and liniment. She backed out and quietly moved across the yard to the house.

The yellow dog came to her. She placed her hand on its

head, but before she could reach down and stop it, its wagging tail began to strike a tin box that sat beside the house. Thump! Thump! The tin crinkled noisily.

"Shep, are you after the kittens again?" The voice came from inside the house. "Leave them be, Shep, or their ma'll come back and scratch you up good."

Lorna held her breath and waited. The light from the lamp shone through the door and onto the porch. She watched that light and listened, ready to dart away in the darkness.

"Shep wouldn't hurt the kittens, would he?" It was Bonnie's voice.

"No. He's gentle as a lamb with them. He didn't like cats when he was young and chased away every cat Cooper brought home. Now they chase him." The woman laughed softly.

"That's what happens when ya get to be old 'n crippled up." The voice was male and carried the sound of the far away south.

"You're only crippled temporarily, Arnie, and you're not *old*. Because if you're old, I am, and I certainly don't feel like I'm ready for the rocking chair yet."

The man laughed. "I'm shore glad a that."

"I'll see 'bout Shep, Mrs. Parnell. I'd sure hate it if'n he hurt them little kittens."

"He won't hurt them, dear. But take that ham bone to him. It'll give him something to do. I swan, he used to not let a thing come onto this place without settin' up a ruckus. Now the only thing he barks at is strangers. The other day a bighorn antelope went through here not fifty feet from the house and Shep just laid there and watched it."

Bonnie was coming outside. Lorna patted the dog that was responsible.

"Here, Shep." Bonnie came down from the porch holding out the bone as an enticement. "Here, Shep. Here, Shep."

Lorna held her hand on the dog's head and he stood as still as stone beside her. She waited until Bonnie came around to the side of the house, then indicated with the touch of her fingers that he could leave her. He went to meet Bonnie, his huge bushy tail wagging a greeting.

"There ya are. Looky what I got for ya, Shep." Bonnie let the dog take the bone from her hand and he disappeared in the darkness.

"Psst! Bonnie. It's me, Lorna."

"Oh!" Bonnie jumped back in fright. "Lorna?"

"Shh . . . Come over here. I want to talk to you."

"Lorna! What in tarnation are ya doin' out here in the dark?"

"Waiting for you to come out."

"But . . ." Bonnie's head jutted out as she peered at Lorna. "Ya shoulda just come on in, Lorna. Mrs. Parnell'd make ya welcome. She's real nice."

"I don't want to come in. I came to see how you're doing."

"I'm doin' all right."

"What's Volney's horse doing here?"

"He's here. Volney's here, Lorna. Brice hurt him somethin' awful, but Volney made it here. Mrs. Parnell's been takin' care a him."

"Then he's not dead! Oh, I was so afraid he was. Where is he?"

"In the bunkhouse. His hand 'n foot was smashed, but they's healin'. Me 'n Mrs. Parnell's been atryin' to get him to get up 'n take the air in the sun, but he won't budge from the bed. He just says it's no use."

"Well, for crying out loud! What's gotten into the old coot?"

"Mr. Henderson says it sorta takes the starch outta a man sometimes when he's ole 'n somebody comes down hard on him like Brice done. Mr. Henderson says—"

"Who's he?"

"Mr. Henderson? He's—"

"Bonnie." Mrs. Parnell's voice floated through the open door. "Won't Shep come?"

"Yes, ma'am. He come. I'm . . . jist takin' the air 'n lookin' at the stars."

"Isn't it cold out there without a shawl?"

"No, ma'am."

"Let the gal be, Sylvia, 'n come on over here. She's thinkin' 'bout her feller. It's what you ought to be doin'." The male voice was low and barely audible.

"Where are Griffin and Cooper?" Lorna asked when all was quiet again.

"They went to town. They'll be back tomorry. Lorna, Cooper was fit to be tied when he come back to where me 'n Griff was. He never cracked a smile fer days—"

"I want to see Volney."

"Ya can see him tomorry. Come on inside 'n meet Mrs. Parnell. Ya'll like her. She's the nicest woman I ever met—"

"I'm not coming in, Bonnie, and I don't want anyone but Volney to know I'm here. Least of all Cooper or his mother. Hear?"

"I won't tell if'n ya don't want me to. Lorna . . . Griffin wants me 'n him to get married. Ya said I weren't married to Brice."

"You're not, but that doesn't mean you have to jump right up and marry someone else."

"Ya said ya knew right off Cooper was the one ya wanted."

"Well, I was wrong."

"I knowed I liked Griff a lot, but I waited till he said somethin' first. He says he's agoin' to kill Brice, Lorna. I hope he don't. It'll get him in trouble."

"You don't have to worry about Brice. Pa thinks he's halfway to California by now. He took off like a scalded cat after I gave him a working over with the bullwhip. What did Cooper go to town for?"

"You . . . whopped Brice? Oh, Lorna! He'll kill you!"

"Ha! Let him try!"

"Stay 'n talk to Cooper. He'll be back tomorry. Lorna, I

got to go in. Mrs. Parnell'll be thinkin' it strange me astayin' out here so long. Stay till tomorry 'n talk to Cooper 'n Volney . . . 'n me. Ya been the best to me a anybody 'n I miss ya."

"You have Mrs. Parnell now." The little red devil of jealousy was sitting on Lorna's shoulder and she hated herself for saying that, so she tried to make amends. "And . . . I'm glad for you. She can do more for you than I can."

The thought that Lorna was thinking she'd been deserted came to Bonnie's mind. "If Brice be gone . . . maybe I ought to go back with ya," she said hesitantly.

"No," Lorna said quickly. "Griffin wouldn't want to come to Light's Mountain. You stay with him. He'll take care of you and you'll not have to suffer any more beatings from the likes of Brice."

"We're agoin' back to the Blue when he 'n Cooper get thin's set up. Ya'll come there, won't ya?"

"Of course, I will. But not till spring. Tell Volney to get up off his backside and onto that dun horse of his and come on up to Light's Mountain to winter. Tell him if he doesn't come, I'll be here to fetch him before the snow. I won't have him taking Cooper Parnell's charity when he can have a place with me and Pa."

"I'll tell him." Bonnie threw her arm across Lorna's shoulders and hugged her, then turned and went up onto the porch. She stood there for a moment before she went into the house.

Lorna had never felt so lonely in her life. She ran swiftly and silently back to the place where she'd left Gray Wolf. He made a small welcoming sound when she neared. She threw her arms around his neck and gave way to the tears that had choked her all the way from Cooper's house.

Lorna saddled Gray Wolf as the first light of dawn streaked the sky, mounted and rode south. She came to the Thompson River, forded it at a narrow point, and found a place among the boulders where she could build a small fire. She cooked a thick slice of bacon by letting it hang above the flames on a pointed stick she slanted into the ground, and ate cold beans from a can while water heated for coffee.

She'd put in a miserable night. Her busy mind had refused to be shut off so she could sleep. She wished she'd been able to see Volney. If he was able to sit in the saddle she'd take him home with her. The thought of going back to see him played around in her mind. She'd ride in there, big as you please, and go straight to the bunkhouse. Of course, they'd know that she'd been there before, or else she'd not know Volney was there, but what did she care? Cooper wasn't there.

She remembered some advice her granny gave her a long time ago: In case of a doubt, don't. She thought about that now. After awhile she kicked river sand on her fire to put it out and repacked her saddlebags. She backtracked across the river and drew up on the reins when she came to the place where she would turn south. It was now or not at all. The desire to see Cooper, even from a distance, outweighed common sense. Oh, shoot! she thought. What harm would it do if she stayed another day? Her father wasn't expecting her for two days and she could get home faster than she got here now that she knew the way. She turned Gray Wolf north and they returned to the clearing where they'd spent the night.

Cooper and Griffin rode in just before noon. Lorna saw a small dust cloud and turned her glasses on it. The man sitting so tall in the saddle and riding the handsome, prancing buckskin could be no one but Cooper. Griffin, on the sorrel, rode beside him wearing a new black hat. They were deep in conversation because their heads turned toward each other every so often and they were walking the horses. Lorna had no name for the sensations that poured so strongly over her as she watched this man who had been continually in her thoughts since she'd met him. They worked inside her with majestic wonders and a craving for his invading flesh returned to taunt her.

"Damn you, Cooper! Damn, damn you!"

Lorna saw Bonnie come out onto the porch and stand

beside Mr. Henderson's chair. She was wearing the tan dress again, but today she wore a blue apron over it. Cooper raised his hand in greeting, then went on to the corral. Griffin stopped beside the gate and Bonnie came out to meet him.

When Cooper went into the house, Lorna placed the glasses in her lap and tilted her head back against the tree. She felt as if she had been climbing a steep hill and had at last reached the crest. She sighed deeply. She was tired in both mind and body. She lolled there mindlessly, refusing to let Cooper enter her thoughts, and soon she was sleeping soundly.

While Lorna slept, Cooper came out of the house. As he passed the smokehouse on his way to the shed, he stopped suddenly, looked down and stepped back. After a moment, he squatted down on his haunches and studied the sign on the ground before him. He extended his thumb and forefinger to measure the moccasin print in the dirt. He stayed that way for a long moment before he stood and followed the prints to the house. He saw where Shep stood and saw Bonnie's prints beside the moccasin prints. For a long while he stood at the corner of the house looking toward the hills to the south, then went to the barn to saddle his horse.

The sound of a dog barking woke Lorna. Instantly alert, she lifted the glasses to her eyes and saw Cooper bringing his horse through the gate from the corral. The dog, Shep, was barking and frisking around them. She saw Cooper point toward the house and the dog, his head down, obeyed his command and slunk under the porch. She watched him mount his horse, and to her dismay, he headed straight for the copse where she was sitting.

Lorna was seized by inexplicable panic. She jumped up, slipped behind the tree, and looked once again to be sure he was heading this way, then raced through the trees to where Gray Wolf waited. She didn't take time to erase all trace of having been there. The thought of facing Cooper was more than she could bear right now. In terror, she flung the saddle on Gray Wolf, grabbed up her bedroll and mounted. The stallion, made uneasy by the tension in Lorna, reared and went skittering sideways through the trees. A heel touched his side, he half-squatted on powerful haunches and launched himself into thundering flight, his body stretching longer and lower to the ground with every giant stride.

Lorna's mind was filled with a contradiction of thoughts. *Bonnie had told him!* No, Bonnie wouldn't tell unless he pried it out of her. Had Bonnie told Volney and Volney told Cooper? No, Volney was so stingey with words that he squeaked! Damn Cooper! He knew she was here. But how did he know? How in the world, unless—Oh, for Christ's sake! She'd left prints down there! It hadn't occurred to her that hers would be the only moccasin prints and his sharp eyes would spot them.

She gave Gray Wolf his head and leaned low in the saddle to keep from being swept off by low branches. After a mile climb she slowed him down so they could pass over a particularly treacherous stretch of windfalls and sliding rocks. He'd not catch her now, she thought smugly. At the top of a high craggy rise she stopped, dismounted, lay flat on the rock and peered over the side. She scanned the area with the glasses. After a few minutes she saw movement. Cooper had taken the downward trail instead of the upper one. She chortled to herself happily. *He'd not found where she had camped in the copse!*

An hour later Lorna saw Cooper going back toward home. She watched him through the glasses. He rode slowly, studying the trail, looking to see if she had crossed it. He passed the place where she had jumped Gray Wolf across the track and she grinned with satisfaction. She'd been taught to hide her tracks by the best there was: White Bull and Volney. Why hadn't she thought of prints last night?

Lorna stayed on the craggy rise until it was almost dark. When she estimated that there was about a quarter hour of light left, she mounted and headed Gray Wolf back down the steep grade, letting the horse pick his way, knowing that his eyes were sharper than hers. She didn't even consider heading home from this point. Feeling confident that she could outfox Cooper, she couldn't resist going back to the clearing, and the idea of teasing him began to dance in her mind.

"Griffin and I signed with the land man to take up that land over along the Blue. We're going to see if Logan will want to contract for horses once we get going." Cooper took the meat platter from his mother's hands, helped himself, and passed it to Arnie.

"Ain't no doubt 'bout that," Arnie said. "The captain's needin' stock what with all the cows he's runnin'."

Cooper looked at his mother. "Things are quiet in town. Mable at the eating house sent you a hello. Bessie Wilhite was in the mercantile. She's looking real good. She said she's got a new girl out at The House and that me and Griff and Arnie ought to stop by." He shot an amused glance at his mother and winked at Arnie.

"Cooper Parnell! Hush up that talk right now! I don't want to hear anything about that house," Sylvia sputtered. "I declare, what a thing to be talkin' about at the supper table. But . . . I always kind of liked Bessie . . . regardless."

"Bessie was . . . friendly. Fact is I didn't see any unfriendly people at all. I figure on going back in a few days to take care of some business—"

"Oh, Cooper! Couldn't you just let things lie still for awhile?"

"No, Ma. I'll not let what happened to Arnie lie still, and not what happened over on the Blue, either. After that I've got business with a fellow in the mountains."

"I figure that's *my* business," Griffin said tightly.

Cooper glanced at him, then back to his mother as she spoke.

"Are you goin' to Clayhill Ranch, son?"

"I'm figuring on it," he said curtly. "Arnie, I'm hoping

you'll be here long enough to give me time to help Griffin fetch his horse herd over to Morning Sun."

"I ain't agoin' no place fer a spell, unless I'm ridin' in a buckboard," Arnie said and cast a devilish grin in Sylvia's direction.

"Mrs. Parnell, I'd be obliged if Bonnie could stay here till I get set up."

"I wouldn't hear of her doin' anything else. It's pure pleasure to have her here."

"I'm obliged to ya, ma'am."

Cooper looked down the table to where Bonnie was seated. She had been quieter than usual tonight, and he was pretty sure he knew the reason.

"Lorna didn't stay long, did she Bonnie?" He asked the question casually.

The fork on its way to Bonnie's mouth halted, then slowly returned to her plate. A dark red blush came up from her neck to cover her face, and guilt-filled eyes darted first to Griffin and then to Sylvia.

"Did she see Volney?" Cooper helped himself to a large helping of potatoes.

Bonnie shook her head. Her eyes pleaded with Griffin to help her, and when he looked at her steadily with a puzzled frown, she bent her head and gazed at her plate.

"There hasn't been anyone here, Cooper," Sylvia said. "Arnie was on the porch from daylight till dark and Shep would have let us know if someone had ridden in after that."

"No," Cooper said, looking at Bonnie's downcast face. "Shep wouldn't have let you know if Lorna was here. And she didn't ride in, did she, Bonnie?"

"Lorna?" Sylvia, too, looked intently at Bonnie. "Your friend from the mountain? Volney talked about her, too, while he was out of his head. Well, for heaven's sake, Cooper, are you sayin' she came all that way and didn't let anyone but Bonnie know she was here?"

"That's what I'm saying."

"I can't believe it—"

"You would, Ma, if you knew Lorna. Isn't that right, Bonnie?"

"Yes, sir."

"She knew I wasn't here, didn't she?"

"Yes, sir. But she didn't know where you'd gone. I told her—"

"When did you see her? When was she here?" Sylvia asked, and Bonnie wanted to die. Everyone, even Arnie, had stopped eating and was looking at her.

"Last night." Bonnie almost choked on the words. "She was out there with Shep."

"Well, I declare! What kind of girl roams around in the dark like that? While we were sitting in here, she was out there looking in. It gives me chills to think someone was out there and we didn't know about it. Is she one of those half-wild creatures you hear about once in awhile?"

Bonnie saw the smile that lifted the corners of Cooper's mouth. "Something like that," was all he said, and helped himself to pie.

"Poor girl," Sylvia crooned. "Poor little thing. Well, I guess she's just not used to bein' around folks."

Cooper's eyes took on a glint of amusement. His glance darted from Bonnie to Griffin. There was a quietness on the young man's face, and he looked back at Cooper in much the same way as he had the day they'd talked about Clayhill being his father. He knew that Griffin was remembering the small girl who had crouched in front of him holding off three men with a thin knife. That girl had saved his life at the risk of her own.

Griffin placed his fork beside his plate. "It goes down hard to listen to Miss Lorna being made light of, ma'am. She ain't no poor little half-wild thin'. She's a real nice lady, 'n the spunkiest one I ever knowed."

Sylvia's face reddened and she looked quickly at Cooper. "I wasn't makin' light—"

"Ma's never met anyone like Lorna," Cooper said quietly. "Not many people have. She takes some getting used to. You'll have to admit that, Griff." He looked at his mother and Arnie, who sat quietly listening. "Lorna's lived on that mountain all her life with a bunch of rough men and a pa who's soured on life. She's chuck full of dreams about her grandpappy's ma and pa. I'm thinking it's the only thing she knows that she can hold on to. Her only friends are that old mountain man in the bunkhouse, a Cheyenne Indian, and Bonnie. Her mother and her granny died when she was a little girl, and she's answered to no one since. She's handy about taking care of herself, and can do some things better than a man. I never saw anyone use a whip like she can, or throw a knife, either. And she's got a way with animals that almost makes you think she's a witch. She's as different from any woman I ever met as daylight and dark."

"Miss Lorna's a real fine woman." Griffin's gaze held Cooper's steadily before he looked toward Sylvia and spoke again. "'N there ain't no put-on to Miss Lorna, she can sing like a—"

"She's agoin' to get herself killed is what she's agoin' to do!" Bonnie blurted, interrupting Griffin. Her lips trembled and she looked as if she would cry. "She stripped the hide off a Brice with the bullwhip 'n . . . he'll kill 'er!"

All eyes turned to Bonnie and there was a dead silence.

"Is that why she left the mountain?" Cooper asked quietly.

Bonnie was so worked up she didn't even hear the question. "She said she whopped him good, 'n he took off like a scalded cat. She thinks he's gone, but I know he ain't. He won't go till . . . he gets his own back. He's bad, I tell ya. He's plumb bad, 'n he hates Lorna fer helpin' me get away from him. He'll do somethin' to her. I know he will . . ." Her voice trailed away in a frightened wail.

Cooper stood beside the table, his fists clenched, his usually unreadable face a mask of fury, the half eaten piece of pie on the plate in front of him. *How stupid of him to think she'd come looking for him because she'd had a change of mind about marrying him!* The little spitfire had gotten herself in a fix and had come running to him and Griff to get her out of it. Disappointment fed his anger.

"Jesus, my Lord Christ!" he cursed. "That woman doesn't use a lick of sense! Doesn't she know that whipping a man's worse than shooting him? She's the most bullheaded, confounded—" He stomped out of the room without finishing what he was about to say and not really understanding why he was so angry.

The silence that followed Cooper's outburst seemed to go on and on until Sylvia, eying the half eaten pie, said, "Well, I do declare! What's gotten into him?"

Chapter
Seventeen

Lorna, astride Gray Wolf, her bedroll tied behind her saddle, turned the horse toward the end of the valley where Cooper lived. A warm and comforting thought had stayed with her throughout the evening while she waited for the darkness of night—a thought that hadn't occurred to her when she took off in headlong flight this afternoon. *Cooper had seen her prints and he'd cared enough to go looking for her.* Perhaps there was still a chance that he cared enough to give up the ranch and come live with her on Light's Mountain.

She nudged the horse and they moved down the hill toward the trail that led to the ranch house. She wanted Volney to know she was there. Volney, not Cooper, she told herself. Cooper would have to come to her. But there was a way she could let both of them know that she was still there. She was going to do it and then head for home.

Lorna judged her distance to the house carefully and drew rein well back from the first fence line. She looked behind her, mapping in her mind the way she would go if Cooper should come after her. Gray Wolf, excited by the smell of the mares, resisted, at first, her command to stop. She talked to him in a low soothing voice.

"Shh . . . shh . . . I know you want to be with the ladies

down there, but I can't let you go. Be patient. We'll be home soon. By that time Ginger will welcome you."

The big horse quieted and stood still, although his skin quivered and his ears stood straight and tall.

For a long while Lorna sat staring at the soft glow of lamplight coming from Cooper's house. Was he eating supper? Was he sitting on the porch, smoking and visiting, and not giving a damn that she was out alone in the darkness? Heart of her heart! she thought miserably. *One night of loving, a lifetime of memories.* She had been so sure that theirs had been a union of mind and soul and spirit as well as of the flesh. The only thing left for her now was to go home to Light's Mountain and take comfort from her memories. The sudden need to reach out and touch him, if only with her voice, was a vibrant pressure in her throat that she could deny no longer.

She filled her lungs, lifted her face to the stars, and began to sing, her voice soaring true and clear as a bell out into the dark, moonless night.

"Beautiful dreamer, waken to me,
   Starlight and dewdrops are waiting for thee.
Sounds of the rude world, heard in the day,
   lulled by the moonlight have all passed away."

The melody was ideally suited for Lorna's high soprano voice and she sang the song with more power and sweetness than she had since it was taught to her by the Irish muleskinner who was gifted with a beautiful tenor voice as well as a talent with the bullwhip. Regardless of how she justified it in her own mind, she was singing for Cooper and she felt strangely exultant. The chill, sweet airs of early autumn blew down the valley toward the ranch house carrying her song.

On the porch, where he sat with Griffin and Arnie, Cooper rose up from where he lounged, his back resting against the porch post. The sound of her voice cut him off in midsentence, clearing all thoughts of what he'd been saying from his head and setting his heart to bucking in his chest. The little devil!

Of all the crazy, stupid, things to do! If there was a woman-starved drifter or outlaw within the sound of her voice he'd be looking for her. He'd like to shake some sense in her! No. Right now, at this moment, if he could get his hands on her he'd . . . wring her neck!

"Gawd! What the hell is that?" Arnie said in a low hushed voice.

"Miss Lorna," Griffin said simply, almost reverently.

In the kitchen where Sylvia and Bonnie were doing the dishes, Sylvia was wiping out the dishpan. The clear, sweet melody reached her as if it were floating on the wind.

"Mercy!" she exclaimed. "What in the world?" She dropped the cloth and hurried to the porch. The voice coming out of the night was so hauntingly beautiful it was frightening. She went to Arnie and put her hand on his shoulder. He wrapped an arm about her thighs and pulled her close against the side of his chair.

"She's still here!" Bonnie murmured and followed Sylvia to the porch. "I ain't never heared anythin' prettier than Lorna singin'," she announced proudly.

"I've never heard anything like it in all my life," Sylvia murmured. "Cooper—" She looked around. "Where's Cooper?"

"He ain't here, ma'am," Griffin replied, and tugged on Bonnie's hand so she would sit down beside him. He didn't add that Cooper had bolted around the corner of the house seconds after they heard Lorna's voice.

"I begged her to come to the house, Griff. But she wouldn't. Are ya mad 'cause I didn't tell ya?" Bonnie sat down on the edge of the porch. He reached for her arm and pulled her close to him.

"'Course not."

In the bunkhouse, Volney lay in his bunk. The voice coming out of the night was more than mere music to his ears. His heart began to thump strongly and the dull, hopeless feeling that had dogged him since he awoke one morning to discover he couldn't lift his arm and his good leg was almost useless faded away. He felt as if new life were being pumped into his tired old body.

"Wal, I'll be hornswoggled!" he exclaimed, and began to laugh, a cackling sound, and slap his thigh with his hand.

"What's that I'm ahearin'?" Louis asked, pulling up his suspenders and heading for the door.

"Why, it's my little gal, is what. Ain't a bird in the world that can outsing my Lorna. I knowed she'd come alookin' fer me. I knowed she'd reckon I was here."

Out on the gentle slope of the hill, wrapped in the soft darkness of the night, Lorna finished the song. She listened intently for the sound of a hoof on the sod, the faint squeak of a gate or creak of saddle leather. A velvety silence followed. She closed her eyes and took a long shaky breath. *It was what she wanted, wasn't it?*

Suddenly she hated the silence and wanted to fill it with song. The spirit of sheer, reckless devilment laid a grip on her. Once more, she told herself. She'd sing for Volney. She'd sing his favorite and he'd know she was thinking of him.

"O Shenandoah, I love your daughter.
    Away, you rolling river,
For her I've crossed the rolling water. Away,
    we're bound away,
Across the wide Missouri."

After each verse, Lorna paused for a few seconds to listen. Then, hearing nothing, she would continue. Her singing, like a high, wailing wind, reflected the loneliness that possessed her; her voice rose to the heavens, soared down the valley in a great tumult of pure sound. It seemed to fill the star-studded sky.

"O Shenandoah, I'm bound to leave you,
    Away, you rolling river,
Oh Shenandoah, I'll not de—yeeow!"

The scream of fright came tearing out of her as she was jerked from the saddle by a rough hand that grasped her arm.

"Wolf! Wolf! Hiya! Hiya!" she screamed, and jerked her knife from the scabbard. The stallion pivoted on his hind legs, his teeth bared, his front hooves ready to strike.

"Call him off, damn you!" Cooper snarled. "Call him off or I'll shoot him right between the eyes!" His arm was like an iron band around her waist. He plucked the knife from her hand even as she was turning to use it.

Her concern for her horse calmed her. "Whoa, whoa, Gray Wolf . . . it's all right." She spoke in a normal tone to the big horse and in the same tone to Cooper. "Let go of me, you mule's ass. He'll charge you if I tell him to."

"If he does, I'll shoot him."

"He'll not back off till you let go of me." She was careful to speak calmly. The horse tossed his head, one front hoof pawed the ground, and he squealed with rage.

Cooper grasped her hand and let her stand away from him. With her free hand she stroked the stallion's nose with her fingertips and uttered soft, unintelligible sounds in her throat. Cooper wouldn't have believed it if someone had told him about it, but he was seeing with his own eyes a stallion, ready to lash out with its deadly hooves, calm down and stand quietly under the fingers of this small woman.

"I'm surprised he let you sneak up on me," she said.

"I came downwind."

She turned to look at him. He was hatless and breathing hard. "I guess I was closer to the house than I thought I was."

"A good quarter of a mile. I've not run so far in a long while."

"You can run right back. I'm going home."

His grip on her hand tightened. "Not tonight. You're coming back to the house with me."

"I'm doing no such damn thing! Get your hands off me, you . . . stinking polecat. You've no claim on me!" Even in the darkness he could see the angry lights in her blue-violet eyes. She pulled on her hand, but he refused to let it go.

"I might have."

"You don't! I bled the week after you left," she said spitefully, and moved as far from him as his hold would allow. "There's nothing of ours growing in me so there'll be no reason for you to be sneaking around on Light's Mountain."

"That's a load off my mind!"

His words cut into Lorna like the sharp edge of a knife. Pride kept the tears at bay and allowed her to snap, "Mine, too!" The grip of his fingers was numbing hers. She pulled on her hand again. "I've been . . . looking for Volney. Bonnie says he's here and he's all right."

"He's *not* all right."

"Bonnie said he was healing."

"Maybe. But he's not himself. I think he's had it in the back of his mind that you'd come here. You'll see him in the morning."

"I'll not be here in the morning. I'll be on my way to Light's Mountain by morning."

Cooper grabbed the stallion's reins from her hand and jerked on her other one. "Come on," he gritted. "We'll put this *beast* of yours in a stall, then I'll take you to see Volney. After that I just may find a strap and beat your butt."

With long, determined strides, he started for the ranch house. Lorna resisted and continued to resist even as she was being dragged along. Finally realizing the futility of pitting her strength against his she relented, but she had to run to keep up with him.

"Cooper, I don't want to go down there. No! Please . . . please don't make me—"

"Shut up and come on!"

She set her heels into the ground and tried to dig in. He almost toppled her over as he yanked her along.

"I'll—see Volney," she said and a sob broke her voice. "That's what I came for. I was worried about him."

"Then why didn't you ride in to see him? Or was there another reason for this night visit?"

"What other reason is there? It certainly wasn't to see *you*."

"I'm sure it wasn't to *see* me, only drive me out of my mind. You've got yourself in a fix this time, haven't you, Miss Spitfire? You've got no sense at all."

"What do you mean?"

"You know what I mean! But neither me nor Griff has got the time right now to go up there and finish what you've started. I told you I'd take care of that in my own good time."

"I don't know what you're talking about."

"You don't stop to think at all, Lorna. You just act as the notion hits you."

"I want to go home, Cooper."

"You *are* going home!"

"No! I want to go home to Light's Mountain." She began to cry, silently and hopelessly, as she stumbled along beside him.

They reached the gate. It was difficult for Cooper to open it with one hand, but he managed. He pulled Lorna through and the stallion followed. Gray Wolf's mind was now on the two mares inside the poled corral. He neighed shrilly and danced at the end of his reins. It was all Cooper could do to handle him and retain his hold on Lorna. Griffin materialized out of the darkness when they reached the barn.

"Do ya have a stall that'll hold him?" he asked as if it were an everyday occurrence for Cooper to come dragging a girl by one hand and holding a wildly agitated stallion who had mating on his mind with the other.

"The stall opposite Roscoe's will do it." Cooper spoke jerkily, his breath coming in gasps.

Lorna pulled on her hand, then in a sudden frenzy she saw the walls closing around her. She lashed out with her moc-casined feet to kick at his shins.

"Stop that!" Cooper snarled and almost jerked her off her feet.

Lorna emitted a shrill whistle and the stallion whirled, ready to attack.

Cooper pushed Lorna at Griffin. "Hold her while I take care of this sonofabitch. Don't let her get away from you. She's slicker than a greased pig, and by God, I'm tired of chasing her."

Griffin's arms circled her waist and he held her tightly against him while Cooper wrestled the stallion into the stall.

"Let me go, Griff. Please—"

"I can't, Miss Lorna. Ya hadn't ort to be out there by yoreself. It ain't a bit safe for ya."

Cooper dropped the heavy bar, closing Gray Wolf in. He grabbed Lorna's hand once again as if not trusting Griffin to hold her.

"Are you going to unsaddle him?" Eight hundred pounds of angry horseflesh crashed against the heavy timbers and shook the barn.

"No! I'm not unsaddling him. I told you, I'm going as soon as I've talked to Volney."

"Stubborn to the last, huh, Lorna?"

"Griffin—" Lorna turned to where the young man had been standing, but he was gone.

"Griff won't help you. He knows you've got no business out there by yourself. If Fulton doesn't find you a bunch of woman-hungry prospectors will. They'll be after you like a pack of mangy wolves after a female in heat."

"You're vulgar!"

"This isn't Light's Mountain. You're lucky you got this far. And you're stupid if you think they couldn't corner you."

"They'd be no worse than you!"

"You think not?" He snatched the worn felt hat from her head and the rope of blue-black hair fell down her back. "You'd not *like* what *they'd* do to you!" He heard her quick intake of breath and instantly regretted the words. "What you need is a strong hand to keep you in line, Lorna, the same as that stallion of yours."

"It won't be *your* hand that does it," she spat, and tilted her chin defiantly.

"Don't be too sure about that. Come on. Volney's not deaf. He knows you're out here."

She walked along beside him as they left the barn and went along the building to the bunkhouse door.

"Louis," Cooper called. "Light the lamp and you and Sam skedaddle for awhile. Volney's got company."

"While they waited outside the door, Lorna wiped the tears from her face with the sleeve of her blanket coat and kept her head turned away when the two men came out the door. Cooper pushed her into the bunkhouse ahead of him. The lamplight reached into the four corners of the square room. She saw Volney's matted, gray head lift up off the pillow so he could see her. Feeling herself freed from Cooper's shackling hand, she went to him.

"Oh, Volney! You old buzzard! I thought sure you were dead!"

"Wal, I ain't. So ya can put that in yore pipe 'n smoke it."

His voice was weak, but the old waspishness was still there. Lorna did her best to hide her alarm when she looked at him. His eyes were overly bright and there were two red spots high up on his cheekbones. She felt a stab of fear. In all her life she'd never seen Volney flat on his back. She glanced over her shoulder. Cooper stood watching them, his shoulder planted against the wall. The look he gave her let her know he had no intention of leaving them alone. She squatted down beside the cot.

"Did Brice do this to you, Volney?"

"I ain't ever answered to ya afore 'n I ain't adoin' it now. What took ya so long to get here?"

"I went to the shack on the Thompson—"

"I'd a gone there if I'd a knowed you'd already met up with Parnell."

"What's he got to do with it?"

"Ya was aneedin' a place fer Bonnie, wasn't ya?"

"If this was the place you had in mind why didn't we come here in the first place?"

"How'd I know his ma'd take her in?" He snorted in disgust and leaned over to spit in the can beside the cot.

"I want to take you home to Light's Mountain. Can you sit a horse?"

"Not fer a spell. I'll be all right here. 'N I ain't takin' no handouts if'n that's afrettin' ya. Ya ort to know Volney Burbank ain't beholden to no man. Is White Bull back?"

"Yes, he's back. He'll be around for a good long while." She knew he had changed the subject deliberately and saw the relief on the old man's face when she'd lied about White Bull when the truth was he'd already gone south for the winter.

"The hill trash'll not do ya no hurt then."

"They're gone. Didn't Bonnie tell you? Frank thinks they headed for California. Billy let something slip to Pa about hurting someone. If I'd known for sure Brice had done this to you, Volney, I'd have killed him."

"I ain't ne'er asked ya to butt in on my fight," he said waspishly.

"And I never asked you to butt in on mine and Bonnie's," she retorted in the same tone.

"What ya need is a man. Yo're long past marryin' age, 'n yo're a gettin' too feisty. Ya cain't ride the wind as ya've been doin' up there on Light's Mountain. Times is achangin'. There'll come a time 'n you'll find ya've straddled a whirlwind."

"Then I'll ride it out, and I'll thank you to tend to your own business, old man, and let mine be!"

"Ya like him, don't ya?"

"Like who? Him?" She jerked her head toward Cooper

but kept her eyes on Volney's face. "I can't stand him. I wouldn't have him if he was smeared with honey and rolled in raisins!"

Volney's laugh was a dry cackle.

"What are you laughing at, you old coot?"

"What're you so het up fer? Didn't Parnell jump 'n get all mealymouthed 'n bug-eyed over ya?"

Lorna stood and glared at the bright-eyed old man. She tossed her hair back over her shoulder and her dark lashes narrowed until her violet eyes were barely visible. The color that tinted her cheeks and the way her mouth snapped shut told Volney how near the truth he was.

"There are times when I don't think I like you at all, Volney Burbank. You're a nosey, mean old busybody, and you'd better button up your mouth, or you'll be seeing the backside of me, and I won't be back."

Volney ignored her outburst and darted a glance at Cooper beside the door. He was cleaning his nails with Lorna's knife and trying to hide the grin on his face.

"This'd be a good place fer ya, girl. Parnell's not as bad as some I knowed of, although he ain't what I'd call *extry* smart. If'n he was he'd a had ya to the preacher by now." He paused and looked up at Lorna with an innocent look on his face. "His ma's a bossy woman, but I reckon you can make do with her. I'd not be surprised if'n she didn't strip them britches off a ya 'n put ya in skirts 'n shoes." He laughed and slapped the bed with his good hand. "I'd shore like to see it."

"I'm sorry that I'll have to deprive you of that pleasure," Lorna said stiffly. "If and when you want to come to Light's Mountain, you'll be welcome as always. I'm going home." She felt betrayed and wanted to cry again. She whirled to leave and came up against Cooper.

"She's not going anywhere until I have the time to take her." He spoke to Volney over her shoulder.

Lorna hadn't heard Cooper cross the floor to stand behind

her. He placed his hand on her arm, and she shrugged it off as if it were hot and stepped away from him.

"You can't keep me here if I want to leave. Not even your *sainted* mother would want *me* here."

"What makes you so sure of that? How do you know what my mother wants?"

"I don't *care* what she wants. It's what I want, and I want to go home." There was tension in every line of her body, and her white face looked wan and peaked as she strove to keep the stricken look from her face by drawing her straight brows together in a frown.

"I said I'd take you back in a few days."

"No one *takes* me anyplace, Cooper Parnell. Get that through your thick head!"

"Get this through your thick head, Lorna: I'm not turning you loose out there on the trail by yourself. Men who've been in the mountains all summer are coming down for the winter. A lone woman would be mighty tempting."

"I can take care of myself. I always have." Her violet eyes bored into him like the sting of a bee.

"Come on out of here. There are things I've go to say to you that would make Volney's hair stand up straight."

"Don't pay me no never mind." Volney placed his hand on his chest and was watching them carefully.

"You stay out of this," Lorna spat.

"I aim to do jist that. I'm athinkin' ya've met yore match, missy."

Volney's eyes clung to Lorna's white face. This slip of a girl meant the world to him. He let his breath out slowly and he seemed to sink deeper down onto the bunk. He'd not worry about her now. Parnell had a fondness for her—a great fondness. He had seen it right from the start. The mountain's not the place for her any more, he thought sadly. Times had changed. What Lorna needed was a man to stand between her and the varmints that would ruin her—just as Maggie had needed Light. Parnell wouldn't let her have ever'thing her own way, either. He'd not go to Light's Mountain and walk in another man's tracks. He'd make his own. Volney heaved a sigh of relief and closed his eyes.

the said Jacques and the two said Jacques and the two said
and the said Jacques and the two said Jacques and the said
and the said Jacques and the two said Jacques and the said
and the said Jacques and the two said Jacques and the said

Chapter
Eighteen

She'd made a fine mess of things, Lorna thought as she stomped out of the bunkhouse ahead of Cooper. The instant she stepped through the door his hand clamped onto her upper arm. She stopped, turned, and glared up at him.

"Stop treating me as if I'd come to steal something. I've seen what I came to see. I'm going now."

His hold tightened immediately. "Not yet."

She didn't argue with him, nor did she struggle. She refused to pit her strength against his; but she remained half-turned away, passively waiting for him to release her. They stood thus in an awkward silence, the night wind running chill fingers over her flushed face. Cooper reached out and laid his hand against her cheek and gently turned her face up to him. When she didn't resist, he drew her to him.

"No," she said, and turned out of his encircling arms.

"All right." The hand on her arm propelled her forward.

Lorna walked calmly beside him, trying to blot from her mind the physical awareness of him. She rebelled against it, sensing in it a threat. It wouldn't do to let the hunger that drew her to come here control her now. Yet even as she cautioned herself, she wanted to turn to him and find shelter in his arms as she had on Light's Mountain.

They passed the smokehouse and the privy and walked on toward the shed where she had seen the man working on the forge. Cooper drew her inside and released her arm, but fenced her in by placing a hand on the wall on each side of her. She pushed against his chest.

"Move back, please," she said with quiet disdain. "You were not treated as a prisoner when you came to Light's Mountain."

"I didn't go sneaking in there in the middle of the night, either."

"This isn't the middle of the night and I'm not here because I want to be."

"I realize that . . . now. At first I thought you'd—well, never mind about that. You've got yourself into a heap of trouble, haven't you?"

"What do you mean? If I was in trouble I'd certainly not come to you."

"How about Griff? Were you looking for him?"

"Heavens, no! I've been looking for Volney. Billy let it slip to Pa that they'd hurt him."

"They did that, all right. How did you know he was here?"

"I didn't until Bonnie told me. I wanted to see how she was doing, too."

"Bonnie's doing fine. She took to Ma right off."

"That's just dandy!" Lorna was trying so hard to keep from crying that she let her guard down and the words came out sarcastically.

In the silence that came down between them Cooper's inscrutable eyes tried to penetrate the darkness to reach into Lorna's. After a long time, he moved his hands from the wall, but remained close to her.

"Bonnie's getting some pride back. She's not acting like a whipped pup anymore."

"I'm glad." Lorna's voice trembled.

"Are you?"

Lorna's head came up defiantly. "Of course I am."

"She and Griff are going to marry and settle over on the Blue."

"She told me. It'll be the end of both of them. If old Clayhill doesn't kill them, Brice Fulton will."

"I doubt that."

"It's the truth! You know it." Her patience was waning.

"Lorna, Lorna. I don't know what to do with you!"

There was gentleness and affection in his voice and Lorna had to hold onto her anger and keep it as a shield between them.

"I'm no concern of yours," she snapped.

"Yes, you are. You know you are." He rested one hand against the wall beside her head and with the other he fingered the hair that had come loose and was lying against her neck. "Why didn't you wait for me and Griff to finish our business here? On our way back to the Blue we'd have come to Light's Mountain and settled with Fulton for Volney—and for Bonnie, too."

"I don't wait for anybody to come kill my snakes. Brice deserved more than a whipping. He killed my dogs, Ruth and Naomi, besides hurting Volney. He treated Bonnie like she wasn't even human. He's not fit to live! I thought of killing him. I could've done it easier than whipping him, but I've not killed a man."

"It would have been better if you'd killed him and had your pa drag him off the mountain. A man can take a lot of things, but being whipped by a woman isn't one of them."

Cooper's caressing hand moved to her cheek, and his fingers stroked her soft skin. For a moment she was unable to move or speak, trembling with humiliation because she wanted nothing as much as she wanted to lean into that caressing hand, but she stood perfectly still. She could feel his breath stirring the hair on the top of her head, and he moved still closer until her breasts slightly touched his chest. He smelled smoky, tangy, and of freshly washed clothes.

"Will you please move back and give me room...to breathe?"

Cooper drew a deep breath and moved back a step. "Stay here with Ma and Bonnie, and I'll go settle with him."

"He's gone. He took Hollis and Billy with him."

"I'll make sure."

"No! I don't want you interfering in my business."

"Come on up to the house. We'll talk about it in the morning."

"No!" She tried to slip under his arm, but he grabbed her and pulled her against him. "Let go or I'll cut you with my knife!"

"You don't have it. I took it when I jerked you off the horse."

"You—" Lorna's hand went to the sash around her waist. It was empty. She had not been without that knife since she was a child. What had her infatuation for this man done to her? "Give it back. It was my Grandpa Light's."

"I reckon it's safe enough—now," he said with a trace of laughter in his voice. He took it from his scabbard where he had slipped it in alongside his and handed it to her. "You couldn't cut me any more than I could cut you. Come on, sweetheart. Come to the house and meet my mother, visit with Bonnie and get a good night's rest. We'll hash this over tomorrow and decide what to do." His voice was soft and persuasive now.

Sweetheart. Her heart trembled and her thoughts milled around in wild disorder. In the end she knew that she couldn't go in the house. She had come in the middle of the night, an uninvited backwoods girl in ragged shirt and britches. No! She couldn't face that woman with the neatly piled hair and freshly ironed dress who couldn't possibly understand her and the way she lived.

"I'm not a bit tired," she said spiritedly. "And I've had my visit with Bonnie." Cooper's arm was around her and he was urging her out of the shed. She dug in her heels. "I'm not going in there, Cooper. I'd be obliged if you'd stop shoving me."

"Why not? What have you got against my mother? You've not even met her."

"And I'm not going to, either. I'll not have her looking at me as if I'm something that crawled out from under a rock."

"What gave you the idea she'd do that?" Cooper was clearly dumbfounded. "Was it what Volney said about Ma being bossy? He was just talking to hear his head rattle. He likes her. He fusses at her like he fusses at you. That's how I know he likes her."

"I don't care if he likes her or not. I'm not going in and that's the end of it." Lorna felt the vacant feeling in the pit of her stomach expand to her heart. Everything had gone wrong. The only thing to do was to play out the hand and wait for her chance. "I'll stay until daylight, if it will set your mind to rest." She added the last scornfully. "But I'll sleep in the bunkhouse with Volney."

"No, you can't stay there. Louis and Sam and Griff would have no place and I'll not ask them to go to the barn. Come on." The grip on her arm had loosened, and now his hand merely guided her.

Lorna walked beside him feeling the frantic clamor of her heart. She wished she hadn't come here. Didn't he say that he was going back to Light's Mountain to settle with Brice for Volney? That's what he said, but was he going back to see her, too? Oh, yes, she remembered suddenly. He was going back to see if she looked like she'd swallowed a watermelon!

"I've got to see about Gray Wolf."

"I'll light a lantern."

"I don't need it."

She pulled away from him and went into the barn. Cooper followed. He knew the barn like the back of his hand and seldom needed a light, but wondered how she found her way to Gray Wolf's stall. She must have eyes like a cat. He leaned against the heavy timbers of the stall while she loosened the cinch on the saddle, pulled it off and dropped it on the floor in the corner. There was a long silence. Cooper could see the blur of her white face. She looked so small standing beside the big horse. She began to murmur to Gray Wolf; soft unintelligible sounds. The horse tossed his head, but stood quietly.

"Come on out, Lorna."

Silence.

"Don't think for a minute that I won't come in after you if you don't come out."

"Gray Wolf would fight you if I told him to."

"I know that, and I'd have to shoot him."

There was a long pause.

"Yes," she said, and there was quiet resignation in her voice.

She climbed through the bars and before she could straighten, Cooper swung her up in his arms. He went to the back of the barn, stood her on her feet, and kicked fresh cut grass into a mound.

"You can sleep here."

"I'll need my blanket."

"I'll keep you warm."

"No!"

Cooper chuckled. "No? That's all you've said since you've been here. Lie down. I'm just going to hold you, that's all. I deserve it after what you've put me through." He pushed her down into the soft grass and followed to stretch out beside her.

"Please . . . don't," she said in a voice muffled against his shoulder.

"Don't what? I'll never force you to do anything you don't want to do. Don't you know that?" he murmured with his lips in her hair, and wrapped his arms around her. "Although there have been times, several in fact, when I wanted to strangle you and then twist this pretty little head of yours right off your shoulders. Right now I want to kiss you and see if I like it as much as I did the other times." His breath was a warm tickle in her ear.

"Don't!" She strained away from him, but his arms possessed an incredible strength and he bound her still closer to his hard sinewy body until she felt she must be crushed to death. Slowly, lingeringly, he kissed her mouth before releasing it. She felt a sharp stab of pleasure and a weakening in her determination to resist him.

"Hmm... I like it even better. Your mouth is sweet." He kissed it again, gently.

Tears filled Lorna's eyes. "Why do you want to kiss me? You don't even like me. You said so—"

"No, I didn't. I didn't say that at all. I said you were stubborn, bullheaded beyond reason, and a take-over woman who needed a strong hand. I also said you were spunky and willful, but pretty as an angel. I want to add that you're also the sweetest woman I ever kissed, and you can carry a pretty good tune, too, when you get all wound up." His voice teased; his lips caressed her face, his hands her back and hips.

"You were awfully mad that morning."

"I sure was. I was so mad I was halfway down the mountain before I knew it."

"You're not mad at me now?" She snuggled her face in the curve of his neck.

"Sure, I am. I'm madder than a hornet, but I'm willing to call a truce for awhile." He nuzzled her jaw and ran his fingers into her hair at the back of her neck to hold her face against him. "Ah... girl, you feel so good. Take off that damn coat. I'll keep you warm."

She slipped out of the coat and her arms wrapped around his neck. She snuggled in his arms and felt his heart beating as wildly as her own. *He did care for her! He did!* She tried to speak, but failed. Instead she stroked his face and hair with trembling hands and tenderly kissed his lips before resting her head on his shoulder.

"I love you, Cooper. I love you so much it hurts me here." She brought his hand around to her heart and his fingers closed possessively over her small breast as if they were coming home.

"Ah . . . sweetheart." His voice was the softest of sounds.

All the emotional bruising of their parting and the weeks that followed flowed and melted away under the balm of his lips. Her mouth clung to his in a moment of incredible sweetness.

Very softly she said his name. "Cooper."

He lifted his head and rested the tip of his nose against hers for a moment, then drew back, waiting, letting his eyes, soft with love, drink in her face. He didn't say a word, but kissed her mouth fiercely, passionately. Lorna closed her eyes and moved sensuously closer to him and braided her leg between his.

"Careful, pretty girl. Careful," he cautioned.

His hair was a soft glow in the dark. She felt the feathery touch of it against her skin, then the warm caress of his lips in the curve of her neck. Sudden tears ached behind her eyes. She moved her hand to the back of his head and gently stroked his hair.

"Don't you want to mate with me, my love?" she whispered into the cheek pressed to her lips.

"Ahh . . . More than anything." His voice sounded as if he were strangling. "But . . . I'll wait till we're wed. I'll wait . . . if it kills me. Then, after you're mine, I'm going to drown in you."

Lorna's heart almost burst with joy at knowing how much he wanted her. Her arms tightened and she held him to her with all her strength while she murmured soft words of love against his lips.

"You won't have to wait, my love. I'm as much yours

now as I'll ever be. I'm your woman. Hold me, love me, drown in me if you want to."

His hands roamed over her rounded hips in the heavy duck britches and cupped her small breast in his palm. His mouth closed fiercely over hers, parting her soft lips, urgent in his need. Her body felt boneless as he fitted every inch of it against his, pressing her down into the soft grass. This was Cooper, her mate, her lover. He wanted her as much as she wanted him. She felt herself being swept away on a cloud where nothing mattered but satisfying their need for each other.

"I can't do it! I can't risk it again! I've got to get you to the preacher," he muttered hoarsely. "Oh, God, my sweet, pretty woman! I want you so much—"

"Cooper..." His name melted on her lips and when she tried to speak, her words kept fading, swept away by his kisses. "Cooper..."

"Shh... don't say anything." His lips covered hers before she could speak and she forgot what she was going to say. His voice was a whisper when finally they broke the kiss.

"There are things I've got to tell you. You won't have to share the house with my mother, if that's been bothering you, sweetheart. Arnie wants to marry her and take her to Morning Sun to live." He lifted his head and her arms fell from around his neck. "I've got to put a stop to this while I can! Turn over, sweetheart. I'm afraid I don't have the willpower I thought I had." She turned and he pulled her back to his chest and her hips into the cradle he made with his thighs. "I deserve an extra star in my crown for this," he whispered in her ear, nuzzling her hair with his chin and kissing her on the neck.

His words had left Lorna frozen inside. He wasn't even considering coming to Light's Mountain. He was planning on this being her home. Did he know he had taken her heart? Of course, he did. She had told him she loved him. Did he know he had crushed it? Would his heart be broken, too? He had held her and kissed her as if he loved her, but he had never said the words.

"Do you love me, Cooper?" Her breath came out light and gasping.

His laugh was low and tender. He hugged her and nipped her earlobe lightly with his teeth. "Oh, sweetheart, you've been under my skin since the day I met you, tormenting me, driving me crazy."

"But do you love me?" she insisted in a breathy whisper. She clamped her lips shut and swallowed repeatedly. She was afraid she was going to cry.

"If loving you means thinking about you all the time, and worrying about you so I can't sleep at night. If it means getting crazy mad at you when you've done something foolish, and wanting to beat the daylights out of you and love you at the same time, I guess I do love you."

"You sound like you don't want to."

"I admit that I'd rather have had a more manageable woman," he said with a chuckle. "But I'll settle for the one I've got." He lifted his head and his lips teased at the side of her face. "I know you're disappointed that I won't live on Light's Mountain, but you'll get used to it here, sweetheart. You can pick out some good mares to put to Gray Wolf and watch his offspring grow along with ours. We'll get some hounds to replace Ruth and Naomi. Your pa will be welcome anytime, and maybe when he sees you settled here and happy, he'll not be so sour. I'll take you over to Morning Sun to meet my brother and his wife, Rosalee. And even if you don't think so now, you'll like Ma. She's always wanted a daughter. After awhile you'll not miss Light's Mountain at all."

No! Lorna screamed silently. She would not leave Light's Mountain. This would never be her home, because she'd not stay here and let her grandmother's house go to wrack and ruin. She was a part of Light's Mountain and Light's Mountain was a part of her. Not even for Cooper, her love, would she leave it. He'd come to her, if he loved her. And if he didn't, it was best to know it now. But if he did come, he'd love it, and after awhile he'd not miss *this* place.

"Get some sleep, sweetheart. Tomorrow I'm taking you to town and tomorrow night," his hand slipped inside her shirt and his rough palm caressed her breast, "I'm going to love you all night long." He made his voice low and threatening.

Lorna lay tightly against his body, her head resting on his arm. She couldn't move. She was in an untenable predicament. There was nothing she could do for now. She shivered, his arms tightened, and she wept silently.

She had forced herself to relax, but her eyes had never closed. She was sure that Cooper thought she was asleep, and she tried to breathe as if she were sleeping. Her body was still, but her mind was busy. She prayed an opportunity would arise that would allow her just simply to fade away and not be forced to face Cooper's mother and make a big to-do of not wanting to stay. She would rather die than face her and have Cooper ask his mother to fix her up so she would be presentable enough to take to a preacher. All of those thoughts vied for precedence in Lorna's troubled mind.

The hour was somewhere between midnight and dawn. Lorna had not heard the twittering of the birds in the branches above the barn so she knew dawn was at least an hour away. She lay against Cooper in quiet limbo, her mind searching for the words to say to him when morning finally came. She heard the scuffing of boots and the squeaking of the barn door when it opened, but she never moved a muscle or allowed her breathing to quicken.

"Psst, Cooper."

Cooper lifted his head, then eased his arm from under Lorna and moved away. She felt the cold hit her back, then he was covering her with her coat. He didn't speak until he was a dozen feet away. "What is it, Griff?"

"The ole man wants ya."

"Can it wait till morning?"

"I reckon not."

Cooper looked back toward Lorna. She was worn out, he thought, and his eyes caressed the blur that was her slight body. Even if she did have more spunk than brains, he grinned at the thought, he now knew for certain that she was the most precious thing in the world to him. She had scarcely moved since he had turned her away from him. He listened to her breathing for a moment, and satisfied that she was sleeping soundly, left the barn.

The light from the lantern hanging from a nail on the rafters cast flickering shadows about the room. Sam and Louis were snoring in their bunks. Griff, without a shirt, paused just inside the door.

"I'm athinkin' the ole man's in a bad way. He's had some sort a spell. He woke me up acallin' for ya."

Cooper crossed the room and hunkered down beside the bunk where Volney lay. His leathery face was gray, his lips tinged with blue, and he was gasping for air. Beneath his shaggy brows his eyes appeared to have sunk back into his head, but they were bright and seeking.

"Hit . . . took ya long enough."

"What can I do, Volney? Do you want me to call Ma? She might could make things easier—"

"Naw, I . . . don't need 'er fussin' 'round." He looked over Cooper's shoulder and saw that Griffin still stood beside the door. "I got a . . . thin' to say." He gasped out the words. "At my shack, on the Thompson . . . back uphill 'bout half a mile . . . tall pine . . . topped . . . by lightnin' 'n marked by . . . elk horns—"

Cooper realized with a certainty that the old man was dying. The gnarled hand that lay on the quilt was limp, and the odor of urine and bowels he could no longer control wafted up from the bedclothes.

"Is there something there you want me to tend to, Volney?"

"A cache . . . in cliff hole . . . west of pine. Looks like rock

... slide. Dig in ... it'll take some doin'. Thar's pelts 'n six sacks a gold ... I been ... pickin' it up ... fer years. Some nuggets, some ... dust." He stopped to catch his breath. "Pelts fer yore ma ... fer my keep—"

"She doesn't want pay. She—"

"I ain't got ... no time," he said and shook his head impatiently. "I'd be obliged ... if ya give a ... sack of my gold to the young ... feller, thar. Hit'll ... give 'im 'n Bonnie a start." He stopped again and drew great gulps of air into his open mouth. "The rest is fer Lorna." He paused again to get his breath. His eyes closed and he remained still for so long Cooper wasn't sure if he was gone. After a few minutes, he opened his eyes, and his voice when it came was stronger. "Ya want to marry up ... with my little gal, don't ya?"

"Yes, I do. I intend to marry her tomorrow."

"Hit's what she ort to do. She ain't ... ort to be on that mountain no ... more. Hit's not like it ... was. Spoilers ... air acomin' in—"

"She'll be here, with me. I'll take care of her."

"Marthy ... her granny ... filled her head ... with notions—"

"I know about that. I'm not going to try and fill Light's shoes."

"Hit's good. That time's ... gone." He closed his eyes as if his eyelids were so heavy he couldn't hold them open, but suddenly he opened them wide and looked wildly at Cooper. "Fulton'll come fer 'er—"

"He'll have to go through me to get to Lorna and through Griffin, too. Don't worry."

"She still ... here?"

"She's sleeping. Do you want me to get her?"

"No! She ... ain't ne'er seen me lessen' ... I was on my feet. I ain't awantin' ... her to see me ... now." He closed his eyes again.

Cooper placed his hand over the cold limp hand that lay on the bed. He had never touched the old man in all the years he'd been coming to the ranch. Now he gripped his hand, doubting that Volney could feel his touch.

Griffin came and sat down on the end of the bunk. He moved a box toward Cooper with his foot. Cooper grasped it and pulled it under him. They sat silently, waiting. The birds began to stir and their twitterings signaled the start of a new day. The oil in the lantern began to flicker and Griffin got up to refill it. He came back with tobacco and papers, rolled a smoke and handed it to Cooper, then rolled one for himself.

"Allas . . . thought I'd die by myself . . . Off in the woods . . . with nobody to know." Volney spoke with his eyes shut. Both men were surprised to hear him speak again and leaned forward to catch his words. "'N buzzards'd pick . . . my bones clean." His eyes, glassy and wavering, opened and turned toward Cooper. "Ain't bad . . . adyin' in bed—"

"You'll not be alone, old timer." Cooper lifted Volney's hand so he could see it clasped in both of his.

"She was . . . purtiest little thin' ya ever . . . saw. She'd come . . . arunnin' to meet me—" His voice was a hoarse whisper, his face gray, his eyes blank now. "Ne'er did have nobody . . . hug my neck till . . . she done it. Her hair . . . blacker 'n midnight . . . get all tangled up . . . 'n she'd not let nobody touch hit or comb out the snarls . . . but me. Make me . . . purty, Volney. I want to be purty . . . like mama. When I grow . . . I'm agoin' to be like . . . you. I like you, Volney . . . I like you . . . better 'n anybody. Make me a . . . cotton-tail powder puff . . . Did ya get . . . that ole cat ya was trackin'? Can I go with ya? Please, Volney." The tired old man's chuckle had the sound of dry cornstalks rubbing together. "Ya behave yoreself, youngun. Mind yore mama, 'n . . . I'll bring ya . . . stick candy . . ." His voice faded away.

Cooper held tightly to Volney's hand and was not sure when life left him. Griffin knelt down beside the bunk. He felt for a pulse beneath the tangle of beard that covered Volney's neck and spilled down onto the bedcovers. After a minute he reached up and closed the old man's eyes and got to his feet.

"He thought a heap a Miss Lorna," Griffin said, looking down at the still face.

"I didn't know he was so bad off."

"He had a spell a few days back 'n another tonight. I reckon he knowed he was done for. This mornin' I helped him let water in a can, 'n it went down hard on him to have to ask me."

"He'd want to be buried up there by his place on the Thompson. The mountains were his home. He wasn't a flat-lander. I reckon I'll have to put off the trip to town."

"I'm sure glad Miss Lorna come."

"She's going to feel mighty bad. I guess I'll go tell her and get it over with." Cooper stretched and ran his hands through his hair and fingered the stubble on his chin.

"I can put his clothes on. Your ma washed 'em up."

"I'll give you a hand as soon as I've told Lorna."

Cooper stepped out into the still morning. Dawn filled the sky in changing sheets of color. There was a chill of early fall in the air. He wondered if Lorna had been warm without him. He was anxious to see her, even though he had bad news to tell her. He walked briskly past the shed to the barn.

The door to the barn was closed when he reached it. He opened it to swing it back. Light streamed down the long aisle from the open door at the rear. Even without glancing at Gray Wolf's empty stall, he knew with a sick, sinking feeling in the pit of his stomach that Lorna had gone.

Chapter
Nineteen

Lorna stood in the doorway and watched Cooper and Griffin enter the lighted bunkhouse. What would Volney want to talk to Cooper about? The old coot was as much of a nighthawk as she was. He'd probably slept all day, was wide awake, and wanted to jaw about *her* wild and reckless ways. If his business with Cooper was about her, she didn't want to know about it.

She slipped into her coat and went to Gray Wolf's stall. Talking to him in a low singsong voice to keep him calm, she saddled him, slipped the bit between his teeth and led him out the back door of the barn. Lorna's heart jumped with fright when Roscoe neighed as they were leaving. She clamped her hand over Gray Wolf's mouth to keep him from answering. Moving as swiftly and as quietly as possible, she moved away from the bunkhouse and along the rail corrals where Cooper kept his mares and working stock. Along the way she let down the gate rails. The stock would find the opening as they were, even now, coming toward them, being curious about the strange horse in their midst.

Lorna headed south after she was clear of the homestead. The stock following her would wipe out her tracks and after a few miles they would scatter. Cooper would be furious at her for letting down the gates, but it was necessary. Rounding them up in the morning would keep him and his men busy for several hours, and by that time she would be miles away. She regretted not being able to tell Volney she was leaving. In a week or two, if he didn't come to Light's Mountain, she would ask her father to go see about him. Volney would understand and would get a good laugh over how she'd managed to outfox Cooper. The chance to leave had just fallen in her lap and she had to take it.

It was over. Cooper was not for her. She had made a mistake back on the Blue when she had looked at him and thought he would be forever a part of her and she of him and that they could live their lives together as Light and Maggie had done. He would never have the same feeling for Light's Mountain that she had. It was a hard lesson learned and she was determined to not dwell on what might have been. People didn't die of broken hearts, she told herself sternly, and if others had survived a heartbreaking disappointment, so could she. Something good had come out of the last few weeks—she'd discovered that her father loved her. He'd not come right out and said so, but he did. It was more than she'd had before. After these brief thoughts of Cooper, Lorna blocked him from her mind and concentrated on getting home.

The hour before dawn was the darkest. She rode cautiously and watched the stallion's ears. He had strong survival instincts and his ears would perk up and stand at attention when he sensed any living thing near them. Daylight found them near Volney's cabin. They stopped briefly for Gray Wolf to drink and for Lorna to fill her canteen and then pressed on.

It was midmorning when Gray Wolf stopped and his ears came up, signaling that there were travelers on the trail ahead of them. He made a soft blowing sound and his front hoof stamped impatiently.

"What is it? Do you hear something?"

The horse's ears twitched and he looked fixedly ahead.

Lorna turned him off the trail and into a thick growth of
sumac already turning red prior to shedding its leaves for
winter. She moved back from the trail, lay along the horses
neck and ran her fingers over his mouth to quiet him. Soon
she heard what Gray Wolf's ears had picked up minutes
before—riders coming down the trail. She heard them long
before they came into view. Three men on swaybacked horses,
each leading a pack mule, two riding abreast, the third several
yards behind. They appeared to be prospectors, bearded, ragged and dirty. And they rode as if they didn't have a care in
the world.

"Hand me that thar jug. Ya been suckin' on it fer the last
ten mile."

The man handed over the jug and wiped his mouth with
the back of his hand. "When I git to town, I'm agoin' to get
me the fattest gal I kin find. I'm agettin' me one soft as a
featherbed, 'n I'm agoin' to bounce up 'n down, 'n up 'n
down. Whoopee! Rinky-dink . . . whoop-de-do!" The echoes
of the shout reverberated from hill to hill and were finally
lost far down the valley.

"What're ya agoin' to do that fer? Ya ain't got nothin' to
put in 'er." A good-natured loud guffaw roared down the
trail.

"How'd ya know? Ya ain't ne'er seen it. I weren't called
Big Bull Jenkins fer havin' no itty-bitty thin'. Gimme back
that jug. I'll tell ya 'bout a gal I had oncet down in Podunk-
ville. She was so fat I had to look twice to see if'n she was
astandin' up or alayin' down—"

"Haw! Haw! Haw!"

Lorna waited patiently until the sound of the men's voices
and ribald laughter faded in the distance before she took to
the trail again. She urged Gray Wolf on to greater speed to
make up for the time lost. As they climbed higher the air
became cooler. Without a hat to hold her hair down over her
ears she felt the cold. She set a course for the distant moun-

tain, and after a series of shortcuts she came to the step cut into the side of the mountain that led to the top.

Several more times during the day she had to leave the trail and wait for horsemen to pass. They usually traveled in groups of two or three. Two men stopped not fifty feet from where she was concealed among the dense growth, dismounted and relieved themselves. Their horses were more alert than they were and looked in her direction, ears twitching nervously. She scanned the area and mapped in her mind a plan of escape in case she had to run, but the men mounted and rode away. The mountains were chuck full of people, all strangers to her.

Darkness came quickly as she reached the crest of the mountain. As badly as she wanted to keep going, she realized the folly of taking the dangerous trail down at night. Gray Wolf was tired and she was worn out to the point of being dazed. She found a place where there was a little grass for her horse, and large boulders to shield her from the wind. She wrapped herself in her blanket and with her rifle beside her, bedded down for the night. Sleep came instantly.

Lorna woke to full awareness. There was a thin layer of frost on the grass, but none on the rocky trail because of the heat they had retained from the sun. She was stiff, sore and hungry, and tried to appease her stomach by drinking half of the water in her canteen. She poured the rest of it in a shallow indention of a rock for Gray Wolf.

As she descended to the valley and the familiar trail that would lead her to the homestead, her weary mind dwelled on a hot meal, a bath and bed, in that order. She sat listlessly in the saddle, trusting Gray Wolf to choose the easiest route.

Shortly before midday, when she was only a few miles from home, she caught the faint elusive whiff of wood smoke. She sniffed it again and it became stronger as she traveled toward it. The smoke was heavy and tickled her nostrils. When she realized it was smoke from a smoldering fire, she felt the first tinge of alarm. Her heart fluttered for a moment, then began to pound urgently. She put her heels to Gray Wolf to goad him into a faster gait and they raced toward the homestead.

The sight that greeted Lorna's eyes when she reached the top of the hill would stay in her memory forever. Beside the crooked stream, its green banks lined with berry bushes, she saw the black skeleton of her home. The charred logs of its tumbled walls were spread out like burned ribs and smoke wafted up from a dozen different areas. She stared at the blackened chimneys which towered as silent sentinels over the pile of charred, smoldering logs and an accumulation of more than a half-century of personal possessions.

"Oh, God! Ohh . . . Ahh . . ." The agonized wail that filled the silence was an utterly helpless, hopeless, strangled cry of despair. With wild, reckless abandonment, she sent Gray Wolf scampering down the hill. "Oh, God! Oh, God! Pa! Pa!" The screams that came from her throat excited the big horse and urged him to greater speed, and when they reached the smoldering ruins, he braced his feet and stopped abruptly. Almost wild with fear and grief, Lorna tumbled from the horse. Her feet went out from under her, but she bounced up running, screaming, "Pa! Pa!"

Silence.

The wanton destruction of the homestead was complete. The house, the barn, and the sheds had burned to the ground. The pole fences were pulled down. Hogs lay dead in their pens and dead chickens littered the yard. Ginger, her gentle mare, as well as Frank's horse and two mules had been shot in the head and lay near the burned-out barn. The back and sides of the stone smokehouse stood, without roof or door, surrounding charred hams, sides of venison and smoked turkeys. The tin shed lay in a heap of rubble inside the still-standing support post.

Numbed, Lorna stood amid the death and destruction. Finally the full awareness of what had happened here penetrated into her cumbersome mind. She raised her arms to the sky and a howl of raw, unmitigated anguish tore from her throat. *Maggie! Maggie! I'm sorry! I'm sorry!* She tried to say the words that pounded in her brain, but she couldn't get them out. Her lips formed the shape of them, in speechless agony, in a mute, gut-ripping moan. Her hands turned into claws, and crying, sobbing, wild, she tried to rip the hair from her head. The pain brought her from the depths of horror to reality. Then she was sobbing with a new terror. *Where was her father?* She ran from one burned-out building to the other.

"Pa! Where are you? Oh, damn you, Pa! Please don't be dead!"

From the edge of the clearing someone shouted her name. At first it was merely an echo in her head. The voice was loud and familiar, and she looked up to see a big man with black hair and beard running toward her. He wore heavy boots, his duck pants were held up with rope suspenders and his red-checked shirt barely came together over his protruding abdomen. Lorna ran down the path toward him, her arms outstretched before her.

"Moose! Moose! I can't find Pa—" She threw herself in his arms and the big bear of a man held her to keep her from falling.

"Frank's with us, little purty. Me 'n Woody's got him over at the cabin."

"Oh, thank God! I was so afraid—" Her lips quivered like pink pedals in the wind, helpless, hopeless. The tears flooded her eyes and ran down her cheeks.

"I been awatchin' fer ya."

"It was Brice, wasn't it, Moose?" Lorna looked back over her shoulder. "Brice did it because I whipped him! He said he would. It's gone. Gone..."

"Yep, I reckon it was Fulton. Me 'n Woody heared the shootin'. It was done when we got here. Warn't nothin' we could a done anyways."

"I'll kill him. I swear to God I'll kill him!"

"Hit's best ya come on, now."

"Thank goodness Pa's all right."

Moose turned away, his big, shaggy head bowed almost to his chest. A new fear ripped into her. She grabbed his arm and got in front of him so she could see his face. "Moose? You said Pa was with you—"

"Yep, I did. We ort to be agoin'—"

She shook his arms trying to make him look at her. "He's hurt, isn't he? Is it . . . bad?" she whispered hoarsely, pushing the words out on little spurts of breath.

The big man looked down at her small, white, oval face with large pleading eyes. He lifted a huge hand and settled it on her shoulder. "Little purty thin'. I . . ." He gulped. "I got to say so. Let's get ya on the horse 'n ya can go on ahead."

Lorna whistled for Gray Wolf. When he came to her, Moose gripped her waist and lifted her into the saddle. She kicked the horse and he covered the half mile to Moose and Woody's shack at a dead run. The door to the windowless log cabin was open and propped back with a stick. Woody stood in the doorway. He was a tall, extremely thin, stoop-shouldered man. His long face was serious. Lorna slid slowly from the saddle. Her heart was so heavy with dread that she could scarcely breathe. Woody moved aside and she entered the dimly lit cabin.

Frank lay on a bunk that was nailed to the side of the far wall. His forehead and cheeks were smoke-blackened and blistered, and in front his hair burned to the scalp. A cloth, bright with blood, covered his naked chest. Woody had coated his burned hands with bear grease and they lay on his thighs. Lorna could see that he was suffering horribly. She swayed on her feet when she realized that he was dying. He opened his eyes when she knelt down beside him.

"Pa, I'm sorry—" She choked up and couldn't say more.

"Ach, me wee lass, it's sorry I be for the wasted years."

There was a momentary catch in his breath, followed by a faint moan. It was a steady hurtful sound.

"Don't talk about that, Pa. I caused this—I shouldn't have gone off and left you!"

He waited for another ripple of pain to pass and ran his tongue over dry lips. "'Tis glad I be ye were gone."

"It's my fault. I wish I'd killed him!"

"Don't fault yerself, me bonnie sweet babe. 'Twas me own doin'. I shoulda held me ground before so it dinna come to this—"

"No! Oh, Pa, please don't . . . die." Tears made her eyes sparkling pools of blue water. They spilled over and rolled down her cheeks.

"It's no so bad, sweet lass, but for leavin' ye."

"What'll I do without you?" The cry came from a throat tight with sobs.

"I got ye the cover Nora made wid the wee stitches. It be singed but only a mite." He tried to lift his hand to touch her, but it fell back to the bed. "'N Maggie's wee slippers ye be so fond of—"

"Oh, Pa. You went into the fire for them?"

"Aye. 'Twas little enough, lass. 'Twas all I could get for ye—"

"They're just *things*, Pa. You're what matters to me."

"Nora loved the house." His eyes pinched and a tear rolled from the corner and into his singed hair. "I couldna stop them."

"Were Billy and Hollis with Brice?"

"Aye. But 'twas Hollis who shot me. He wants ye, lass. He means to have ye, 'n he be a mean mon." Frank's voice was weak, but it outranged the small room and spilled out into the bright sunlight.

"He'll never have me. I swear it!"

"Aye. Ye've picked Parnell to be yer mon, have ye?" At her hesitant nod, he sighed. "If there be a mon to stand against the likes of Hollis 'n take Light's place in yer heart, lass, 'tis Parnell."

Lorna found a spot on his arm where she could lay her hand without giving him pain. These were the last few minutes she'd spend with the man who had planted the seed that gave her life. Her father was dying, and all she could do for him was give him peace of mind.

"Aye. Right ye be as usual, oold mon," she said with the accent she used when she teased him and was rewarded by the flicker of light that came to his eyes. "Don't fret about me being alone. I'll be all right. I'll have Cooper. But . . . I'll miss you, Pa. I—I wish you'd be here to see your grandson."

"I be knowin' that 'tis bonnie he'll be if he takes after me lassie."

"I love you. I'm sorry for thinking you didn't love me. You were lonely, Pa. I know that now. I've been selfish and self-centered, going my own way. I wish I was more like Mama." In spite of her resolve to keep calm, her lips trembled so that she could scarcely say the words.

"Ye be her spittin' image, but ye can't be inside but what ye are. I be wishin' I be more like Light. Yer mama said 'twas no matter."

"It didn't matter to her. She loved you so very much."

"'Tis me Nora that I'll be seein'.'" His words thickened and ran together, ebbing slowly out of time, receding like wavelets on the sand.

"Give Mama a hello, Pa."

"Aye."

His eyes sought Lorna's face and he gazed at her. He continued to look at her while seconds turned into minutes, minutes into timeless silence. Lorna's brain knew that he was no longer with her, but her mind refused to accept it. She stayed beside him and silent tears rolled from the violet-blue wells and fell on her hand clasped to his arm. She wept for her Pa, who had come to Light's Mountain from far across the water and stayed with the woman he loved even after her death. She wept for the home that was lost to her forever, and for herself, who was now alone.

When the well of tears ran dry, leaving her empty and a little mad with grief, she leaned over and kissed her father's cheek and gently closed his eyes with her fingertips.

"Good-bye, Papa," she whispered. "They'll pay for what they've done, Pa. I'll make them pay if it takes the rest of my life. I swear it."

Lorna lay down on the bunk opposite the one where her father lay and fell into an exhausted sleep. She woke to the sound of heavy pounding in her head. It was twilight. She sat up on the edge of the bunk and looked across to where her father lay, his hands folded neatly on his chest. Slumping forward, she braced her elbows on her knees and held her face in her hands. The pounding continued and she realized it was coming from outside the cabin. After a moment she got to her feet. The floor rolled and pitched crazily under her. She braced herself against the wall until she was steady, then went to the door.

Moose and Woody were putting the finishing touches on a burial box they had made from odds and ends of boards they had scrounged. Woody was straightening nails on a flat stone, and Moose was hammering them into place. They stopped what they were doing and looked at her helplessly.

"I'm awfully hungry," she said, and braced herself against the door as she felt herself sway.

Woody was a leathery, string bean figure of a man with an Adam's apple that leaped spasmodically up and down. He was an educated man who liked to read and Lorna had often wondered what had happened in his life that drove him to the nomadic life of a prospector. As he came toward her now, his homely face had a worried look.

"Sit here on the doorstone, Miss Lorna. I'll bring you something. You look done in."

"Thanks, Woody. Did Gray Wolf let you take off his saddle?"

"He seemed to know it was a special time, miss. He stood pretty as you please. I gave him a hatful of grain, and Moose pulled off the saddle. We turned him loose, knowing he'd not leave you."

"He won't go far. He's all I have, now, Woody."

"It'll be no chore at all to put up another cabin. We'll have a cabin-raising before winter sets in and ask the folks on the other side of the mountain. It'll take some work, but Moose and I want to help you build the place up again."

Lorna shook her head. "No. Another cabin there would mean nothing to me. What was in it was what mattered, and there's no way to bring that back." She sank down on the doorstone. "I don't ever want to go back, Woody."

Woody made no answer. He thought he'd never seen a face so sad. He held his silence while studying Lorna's beautiful white face. The girl didn't know how lovely she was, even in her grief. Where would she go? What would she do? An unattached woman as lovely as Lorna would have no trouble finding a protector, but from what he'd seen of the men in these mountains, there wasn't much for her to choose from. He stood there staring at her until he couldn't bear what was in her eyes anymore. He couldn't bear to look at that much heartbreak, longing, anguish, all intermixed with such a bleak expression.

"Will you do something for me, Woody?"

"Of course. But first you must eat."

While she ate, she told him about the sack of gold coins she had hidden in the chimney. "I'll be obliged if you'd get them for me, Woody."

"Moose and I will go over first thing in the morning. We were gong to . . . make a place for Frank beside your ma."

Tears filled her eyes, but she blinked them away. "Yes." She took a few more bites of food, chewing slowly, forcing herself to eat, because she knew she needed as much strength as she could get. "If there's anything there you want, take it," she said quietly.

Woody made a growling noise of protest, but remained silent. He went to help Moose carry the box into the cabin. Lorna moved from the doorway and kept her face averted from the box.

"Woody," she said with her back turned away, "cover... Pa with Mama's quilt."

It was Moose who answered. "If'n that's what ya want, it's what we'll do."

The next morning Lorna saddled Gray Wolf and tucked the bag of coins Woody had brought from the homestead in her saddlebag. Calm and clearheaded, she braided her hair in one long braid and tucked it down inside her coat. She didn't have a hat, she had left it at Cooper's ranch. All she had in the world were her horse, saddle, the clothes she wore, Light's knife, her rifle and bullwhip, but it was enough. Moose made a travois, hitched it to their mule, and lashed the burial box to it. Lorna, leading Gray Wolf, walked behind her father's body to the family burial ground. When they came to the stream, Moose and Woody carried the box across and up the hill to the gaping hole they had dug at first light. They lowered the box, then stood back with their hats beneath their arms, their eyes on the sad-faced girl.

"Woody? Will you say something?"

"I'd be honored, Miss Lorna."

He moved to the head of the grave and somberly recited the Lord's Prayer. When he finished he and Moose looked to Lorna for instructions and she nodded. Lorna watched until the box was no longer visible, then went to stand beside the wooden cross that marked her mother's final resting place. She began to sing.

Her voice rang clear and powerful in the crisp, fresh autumn air. It rose with an unearthly quality that reached the sky. Both Woody and Moose stopped shoveling to look at her. She was facing the mountain with her face lifted. They were awestruck, although they had heard her sing many times before. She sang now with such clarity and quality of feeling that it brought tears to their eyes. Her voice on the still morning air was amplified and rendered directionless by the walls of mountains surrounding the small upper valley.

Moose and Woody had never before heard the words or the tune, and Woody felt strongly that no one else had ever heard them either. The words and the music were coming from the shattered pieces of the girl's heart.

"I will meet you over yonder,
    where there is no pain or strife.
I will meet you over yonder, my
    dear ones—who gave me life.
There'll be no more sad tomorrows,
    no more sad good-byes.
I will meet you where the mountains
    meet the skies."

She stood still and staring for a long moment after the last echo of her voice died in the distance. Then, dry-eyed and with a slight smile, she went to Moose and put her arms around his ample waist.

"Thank you," she murmured.

The big man choked up, grunted, and hugged her.

She went to Woody. "Thank you. I'll never forget you and Moose."

"We'll make a marker, like your ma's."

"I'll appreciate it. Someday I may be able to come back, but not . . . soon."

"You take care of yourself, hear?" His Adam's apple was jumping convulsively. He tried to meet her eyes, but could not.

"You, too." Seeing his distress, she shook his arms, then raised up on her toes and kissed his cheek. "I'll be all right. Don't worry."

She turned away quickly and mounted Gray Wolf. Her

two friends watched her, saying nothing, knowing it was useless to try to stop her from leaving. She kept her face turned away from rubble that was once her home, and sent the big gray splashing across the creek and into the woods.

Chapter
Twenty

Cooper spent more than just a few hours gathering up the stock Lorna had let loose before she left the ranch. It took him, Griffin and Louis the better part of the day. He was exhausted and angry—angry more at himself than anyone else.

Lorna Douglas was a selfish, wild, undisciplined little wildcat who was free of any sense of obligation to anyone except herself. He should have known, back there on Light's Mountain, that there wasn't anything she wouldn't do to get her own way. She'd made a regular feather-head out of him with her sweet words and soft, clinging little body. *She loved him! Ha!* It was a game with her to try and bend people to her will; the ultimate result didn't concern her. She could stay on that damn mountain, live there, wallow in the legend of Light and Maggie Lightbody, and die there. He'd not ask her, ever again, to share his life. Damn her! When she left she took a part of him with her, but he was through with her now—or would be as soon as he turned over Volney's gold to her.

When evening came Cooper went to the house for supper. It was a quiet group who sat around the table. Sylvia's heart ached for her son. It was obvious, so obvious, that he'd fallen in love with the little mountain girl with the big voice. He had come to the house to tell her the old man had died, but the fact that he hadn't mentioned that the girl was gone or that she was responsible for his brood mares running free told her more than words how much he cared for her.

Bonnie had cried most of the day. She'd been within hearing distance when Cooper discovered his gates down, and in the first heat of anger the things he'd said about the mountain wildcat, spoiled brat, black-haired devil woman had cut her to the quick. She knew that Lorna was none of those things. She was good and kind and if not for Lorna she would more than likely be dead by now, like Volney. She also cried for the old mountain man. He had been the one man on the mountain who had helped her escape that living hell, and because of it he had died.

"We'll take Volney up to his place in the morning and bury him," Cooper announced to the group in general.

"How far is it, son?"

"With the wagon it'll take most of the day."

"Then you'll be gone a couple of days."

"It'll be more like four or five. I've got something to do after that."

"I'd be obliged to go with ya to do it," Griffin said.

The two men looked at each other for a long while, then Cooper nodded. "Louis can go along and bring back the wagon."

Sylvia looked from the young man to her son. There was more, much more, going on here than they were talking about. The mere fact they were not talking about it made it all the more serious. She studied her son's face. He had worn a worried frown all day. She'd not ask him what was troubling him. He was a man and entitled to his privacy. When he wanted her to know, he'd tell her.

"Can you handle things for a few days without Griff, Arnie?" Cooper asked.

"Sure can. Though I'm itchin' to get to town 'n bust heads."

"Arnie! When is this ever goin' to end?" Sylvia exclaimed.

Cooper looked at his mother. "I don't blame him, I'd feel the same. But I'd be obliged, Arnie, if you'd put off busting heads and look after Ma and Bonnie for a few days."

"I aim to. I aim to look after yore ma till doomsday comes." Arnie gave Sylvia a devilish grin. He enjoyed making the color come into her cheeks. "I'll be alookin' after yore young lady, too, young feller," he said to Griffin.

"It's settled." Cooper got to his feet and left the house. he had scarcely eaten a plateful of food.

It was a long slow journey to Volney's cabin. The trail narrowed at times and the wagon carrying the coffin was forced to leave it and make its own tracks, bumping over stones and bypassing downfalls. They arrived in late afternoon and after a quick meal from the hamper Sylvia and Bonnie had provided, they chose a spot beneath a bluff behind the cabin and placed Volney Burbank in his final resting place. They buried him deep, and just before they yanked out the boulder that would cause a small rockslide to cover the grave, the three men stood hatless and silent beside the grave. It was twilight, and darkness was settling over the quiet, wooded mountainside.

"Good-bye, old timer," Cooper said. "You're one of the last who blazed the trail for the rest of us."

The three men stood silently for a long moment paying their last respects to the old mountain man. Cooper nodded to Griffin who had looped a rope over the boulder. Firebird bunched his muscles and strained. The boulder moved and the rocks came tumbling down and the body of Volney Burbank was given back to the mountains he loved.

Louis hitched up the wagon at dawn and headed back to the ranch. It was then, while they were drinking the last of the morning coffee, that Cooper told Griffin about the cache and the bags of gold dust.

"I'm going to take Lorna's share to her."

"I'd the notion ya was agoin' to the mountain to settle with Fulton."

"That too, if I find him."

"I figger I got more of a reason to settle, 'cause a Bonnie."

"We'll play it by ear. I want you to know that I don't hold with shooting a man in the back, even if he's got it coming."

"I aim to be alookin' him in the eye."

"Fair enough."

They didn't have any trouble locating the pine that had been topped by lightning, or the hole in the cliff covered by a small rock slide. In less than a half hour they had pulled away the rocks exposing a small, natural cave just large enough for two or three men to sit in comfortably.

Air whistled through Cooper's teeth when he saw two stacks of prime furs, each almost four feet high arranged on wooden platforms to keep them off the floor of the cave.

"He said he had furs worth about five hundred. These'd bring a couple of thousand if they'd bring a dollar."

"There ain't no way yore goin' t' get them outta here without a pack train or a wagon," Griffin said, and ran his fingers over the pelt of a silver fox. "The ole man shore knew what he was adoin' when he stretched these hides."

"We'll have to come back with the wagon. I didn't want to mention any of this to Louis. If the word got out about the cache every gold-crazed man in the territory would be digging here thinking old Volney found it right here."

Cooper dug in between the two stacks of furs and pulled out a deerskin pouch. The top was tied with a thong. He loosened it and the pouch fell open. Inside there were six bags, each the size of a man's two fists, one placed on top of the other. Cooper lifted one of the bags and then pulled the drawstring and peered inside.

"Good Godamighty!" A slow smile twitched at the corners

of his mouth. "I didn't expect anything like this. There's enough here to make a man rich!" He tossed one of the bags to Griffin and watched the amazed expression settle on his face as he peered inside. "One of them is yours, Griff. Volney's very words were: 'Give a sack of my gold to the young feller. It'll give him and Bonnie a start.'"

"I ain't ne'er had nobody give me a dime. I ain't sure if I ain't dreamin'."

"You're not dreaming." Cooper held out his hand for the bag and Griffin returned it to him. He put it alongside the other five, then turned back to the dazed young man. "He said one out of the six, Griff. He didn't say which one, so I reckon you've got the right to choose."

"No, I cain't do that. I'm jist so dumbfounded—"

"This will pay for that land on the Blue, set you up in ranching and build a decent house for Bonnie. I'm mighty glad for you, Griff."

"Confound my soul, Cooper. I just cain't believe that ole man'd give me . . . that."

"Well, he did. And he'd given it some thought, too. He knew there'd be plenty for Lorna. Now make your choice. We'll pack the rest in my saddlebags and take it to Lorna. Ma'll have to wait awhile for the pelts. She doesn't know she's getting them anyway, and she'll snort at thinking she's getting pay for nursing Volney."

"Jist gimme back the one I had afore. That's plenty big enough. I ain't agoin' to try 'n do Miss Lorna out of a heavier sack." He took the sack and held it in his two hands. He began to smile. "Dadgum, Cooper. I jist don't know what to say."

"You don't need to say anything to me. It's not my doing."

"Won't Bonnie be plumb surprised? I'm agoin' to get her some dresses 'n a bonnet with blue ribbons on it. 'N shoes, Cooper. Did ya know she's ne'er had shoes bought jist for her? I'm agoin' to fix up that cabin, maybe build on a room or two, 'n buy her a iron cookstove like your ma's." Still grinning and shaking his head in wonderment, he looked toward the place where they had buried Volney. "I sure do wish that ole man knew how tickled I am."

"He'd not want thanks. He'd want us to get on with it and take the rest to Lorna." Cooper went to get Roscoe, led him up close to the cave and packed the rest of the sacks in his saddlebags. "If word of what we've got here got to some of the men coming out of the hills, our lives wouldn't be worth a plugged nickel."

"I've seen men die over a bent spoon—"

"It's a shame, but it happens."

"What'a 'bout you, Cooper? Didn't Volney say anythin' 'bout you havin' any?"

"I reckon he thought Lorna and me would be a team. But there's no chance of that now."

"I'm plumb sorry to hear it."

The men worked silently after that and stacked the rocks carefully over the hole that now held the furs. Cooper led the horses away and Griffin painstakingly swept the ground with a branch, wiping away their tracks.

"Another 'n who'll be tickled 'bout this is Kain," Griffin said when they were mounted. He led off and spoke to Cooper over his shoulder. "Ya know, he's the feller that stayed with the horses when I hightailed it to keep Dunbar's outfit from afindin' where we'd hid 'em. I been awonderin' 'bout him 'n athinkin' I ort to be gettin' on back. I hope he didn't let that outfit get him cornered."

"Where did you meet up with him?"

"Santa Fe. He'd been goaded to fight 'n I stood at his back to keep the bastards from knifin' him. We took outta town on a dead run with six of the meanest hombres I ever did see chasin' us. That was 'bout this time last year. We was in Denver for awhile, then we come on up here. Kain knew the country and was agoin' to help me get a toehold afore he drifted on. He's not wantin' to settle here. I'm wantin' to light somewheres. I'm tired a eatin' beans by a campfire when it's colder 'n a well-digger's ass. I'm wantin' me a warm cabin 'n a soft woman."

"Any chance he'll run out on you?"

"None a'tall. I'd bet my life on it—'n I have a couple a times. If'n he says he'll look after the herd, he will or die tryin'. He's slow to rile, but when he does he's a ring-tailed tooter. If'n he's heard Clayhill's bunch tried to hang me, it'd not surprise me none if'n he didn't ride in there 'n call him out."

"So he's a gunfighter."

"Not no more 'n me. He fights when he has to."

"Most men do," Cooper said dryly. "Or when there's something they want."

Several times during the day they passed groups of men coming down out of the mountains for the winter. The thought crossed Cooper's mind that Lorna might have met up with just such men on her way back to Light's Mountain and that she'd had trouble with them. A lone woman on the trail was easy pickings. He tried to shove the thought from his mind and tell himself that she was no ordinary woman and was able to take care of herself, but the worry hung there, nagging at him.

They stopped for the night before they reached the crest in the mountain, pulled back off the trail into a dense growth of pines and underbrush and found a small clearing for the horses. They staked them close to where they threw down their bedrolls, rolled in their blankets and tried to sleep.

Cooper spent a restless night. He dreaded the confrontation with Lorna and having to tell her that Volney was dead, yet he was anxious to know that she had arrived home safely. He had to get her out of his system, he told himself impatiently, because he couldn't spend the rest of his life with his guts tied in a knot. Thank God he didn't have to worry about her being pregnant—if she was telling the truth. He flopped over and pulled his blanket up around his ears. Damn her! He'd not had a peaceful moment since he met her.

They woke in chilled dawn, saddled up, and rode out without bothering to eat, anxious to cross the mountain and get down to where it was warmer. There was the smell of snow in the air when they reached the highest elevation. In another week or so the summit would be snow-covered. Cooper thought about this and the fact that he would be cut off from Light's Mountain until spring. That was fine with him. Surely by spring he would have come to his senses where Lorna was concerned.

They went down the trail Lorna had taken a couple of days before. Griffin was impressed with the beauty of the country and mentioned it. When he got no response from Cooper he kept his thoughts to himself.

Cooper was occupied with his own thoughts. The fact that he would see Lorna soon afforded him little pleasure. He wondered what she would do with the gold Volney left to her. Most women, if they were suddenly rich, would move to town, get themselves all duded up, travel, and take in the sights. Somehow he doubted the sudden riches would change Lorna at all. Even dressed in britches and her father's old shirt, she was more woman than any he'd ever met. The natural pride and grace of her bearing, her rapture as she sang and danced in the woods gave her an inner beauty that had nothing to do with what she was wearing. God, if she was any prettier in a fancy dress than she was in those old britches, he didn't know if the world could hold her.

Cooper estimated they were about three quarters of a mile from the homestead when he became aware of a stench in the air. He sniffed, trying to recognize the odor. It became stronger by the minute, and finally Griffin mentioned it.

"It smells to me like somethin's dead—a whole bunch of somethin'. I smelled the same thin' once when me 'n Kain came onto a place where stampeded cattle had gone over a cliff. Phew! I ne'er smelled anythin' so rotten in all my life."

Cooper had a nagging feeling that something wasn't right about the same time Roscoe pricked his ears and tensed under him, not liking the odor or the eerie quietness. A few minutes later they came out of the woods and Cooper saw the mass destruction that had once been Lorna's home. He and Griffin reined in and sat there in stunned silence. There was not a building or a fence standing, except for the stone walls of the smokehouse. Not a living thing moved on the homestead. The dead animals that lay among the ruins were swollen and covered with flies. Tiny whiffs of smoke still drifted occasionally from the blackened rubble.

"Jesus, my God," Cooper muttered. "Lorna set such a store by this place—" He put his heels to Roscoe and they moved swiftly toward the ruin.

"Gawddamn!" Griffin called from behind him. "Is this where Miss Lorna lived?"

Cooper didn't answer. He'd heard a pounding and caught a glimpse of a red-checked shirt across the stream in a small pole-fenced area. He reined in and studied the area carefully. Griffin was doing the same. Their eyes caught and Cooper tipped his head toward where the man, ignoring them, pounded on the stake. Griffin nodded and indicated he would circle the homestead.

The man was big. He had black hair and a bushy black beard. If he knew anyone was approaching, he didn't let on. Cooper walked Roscoe toward him. He continued to drive the wooden cross into the ground. When Cooper saw the freshly filled grave his heart did a flip-flop in his chest. Almost breathless with fear, he moved his horse around so he could read the inscription on the cross:

> FRANK DOUGLAS
> husband of
> NORA
> father of
> LORNA

It was Lorna's father buried there. Cooper took a deep breath of relief.

"Where's Lorna?" he demanded without preamble. The man ignored him and continued pounding, then kicked dirt around the base of the flat board and stamped it down. "Where's Lorna, damn you!" Cooper shouted, and his voice bounced off a distant mountain and came back to him.

The man picked up his rifle and turned toward him. "She ain't here."

"Where is she?"

"Gone."

"Where'd she go?"

"Who wants to know?"

"I do, damn you. Cooper Parnell."

"Never heared of ya."

Cooper ground his teeth in frustration; the hold on his temper was deteriorating rapidly. His anxiety made him lash out recklessly. "Listen, you pile of horseshit," he bit out between jaws rigid with anger, "I don't have time to be hee-hawing around. You'd better tell me if that woman's all right or not, or I'll get off this horse and stomp the shit out of you!" He made a move to dismount.

"C'mon, if'n ya think ya can." Moose gripped his rifle by the barrel and prepared to swing. He was a giant of a man and from the looks of him, he was not one to back down.

"Hellfire, man, I don't want to fight you. I just want to know if the bastards that did this got their filthy hands on Lorna."

"She was all right when she left."

"When was that?"

"Yesterday morn."

Cooper felt a deep, swelling relief. His fingers trembled as he pulled the makings for a cigarette from his pocket. "Smoke?" he asked.

"Naw. I got a chaw." Moose spit a yellow stream of tobacco juice onto the ground. Although he appeared to be relaxed, he was primed and ready to fight and Cooper knew it.

"I'm Parnell," Cooper said as if he hadn't told him his

name before. He knew that if he was going to get any information out of this giant he'd have to go at it in a different way.

"Name's Moose. Got other names, but don't rightly need 'em."

"Is your partner's name Woody?"

"Yep. How'd ya know?"

"Lorna. She said you're friends of hers."

"Yep."

"What happened here?"

Moose leaned on the rails that surrounded the small burial ground. He spit again, looked off down the trail, then over at the ruins of the homestead. He watched Griffin ride up and peer inside the smokehouse. Cooper waited patiently. Moose looked at him, his black eyes taking in everything about him, sizing him up, measuring him, and finally deciding the tall, fair-haired young fellow was a decent sort.

"Air ya here alookin' fer Lorna?"

"I am."

"What fer?"

Hell! None of your goddamn business! Cooper wanted to shout. He took a long pull from his smoke, then said calmly, "I owe her some money. What happened to Frank?"

"One of the fellers that tore up the place shot 'im. Me'n Woody got 'im on down to our place, but there warn't much we could do. Lorna got here afore he passed on."

"She wasn't here when this happened?"

"Nope. Happened day afore she got here."

"Who did it?" Moose didn't answer. He took a hunk of tobacco from his pocket and cut off a slice with a long thin knife. "Do you know who shot Frank and burned the place down?" Cooper prodded gently.

"I reckon I do."

"Then I'd be obliged if you'd name them. I mean for them to face a reckoning."

"I'm thinkin' Brice Fulton came to burn 'em out 'cause

Lorna 'bout whopped the skin off 'im. He's a mean'un, that Brice is. Frank tried to reason with 'im, 'n Hollis Johnson shot 'im down. They's plumb crazy, both of 'em. Billy's jist a dumb kid. He ain't got the sense God gave a goose. Frank said there was four of 'em, but he didn't know the other'n. They fired the house 'n shot ever'thin' that moved. Shot like he was, Frank went in the house to get somethin' fer Lorna. The fire drove 'im out 'n they shot 'im agin fer pure cussedness. Hit's a pure wonderment he lived the night out." Bit by bit, Moose told the whole story. He finished up by saying, "Woody 'n me is agoin' to clean the place up a mite. The little gal knows she can winter with me 'n Woody if she's of a mind to. She might be back, though she says she ain't."

The heat of unremitting rage washed over Cooper. "Did Lorna say where she was going?"

"Nope. Warn't my place t'ask."

"Which way was she heading?"

"The way ya was acomin' from, I reckon."

"I'm obliged to you, Moose. If Lorna comes back tell her I was here and that I've got a message for her about Volney Burbank. If I don't find her, I'll be back."

Cooper and Griffin went back up the trail toward the pass where they'd crossed over the mountain. A few miles from the homestead they stopped to fry bacon and boil coffee.

"I sure do feel bad 'bout Miss Lorna losin' her home," Griffin said sorrowfully. "Her heart must be busted in a dozen places."

"It wasn't an easy thing to face. That and losing her pa."

"I aim to kill 'em, ya know. I just wish I could a done it afore they did what they done."

"I aim to find Lorna. Then I'll settle with Fulton and Hollis Johnson."

Cooper desperately hoped that Lorna had gone to his place. She was alone now, her home and her father gone. There was nothing to keep her on Light's Mountain. He would see to it that after a while the pain of losing the home Light and

Maggie had built would ease and she would come to think of the ranch as her home.

Arnie Henderson saw the rider coming toward the house when he was a mere moving speck on the horizon, but he waited until the sorrel horse turned up the lane before he called out to Sylvia.

"Rider comin' in, Sylvia. You women stay in the house."

"Someone's coming? I'll do no such thing, Arnie Henderson," Sylvia sputtered from the doorway.

"Stay in there or I'll spank yore butt—when I'm able."

"Well, I never! You're getting mighty bossy." She could hear him chuckling while she was taking the rifle from the pegs over the fireplace. She crossed the room to stand just inside the door. "Who is he?"

"I dunno."

Bonnie watched Sylvia with large frightened eyes. She lived in constant dread that Brice would find her. She peeked out the door and relief slumped her shoulders when she saw a man with slim waist and hips sitting tall in the saddle. He wore a dark, peaked hat and a tan leather vest over his shirt. It wasn't Brice or Hollis or Billy Tyrrell.

Arnie watched the man approach. Watched him lean from the saddle to open the gate, pass through, and close it with a shove from his booted foot. He rode up to the hitching rail, but didn't dismount.

"Howdy," he said to the silent Arnie. "Is this the Parnell ranch?"

"It is."

"I'm looking for a young fellow by the name of Griffin. I was told in town that he came in with Cooper Parnell."

"Who might you be?"

"My name is Kain—"

"Kain?" Bonnie slipped out the door. "Are ya the one who's alookin' after Griff's horses?"

"I'm the one."

"Griff told me 'bout him. He's a friend of Griff's, Mr. Henderson."

"Wal, then, climb down 'n come on in," Arnie invited.

"Thank you."

Sylvia stood the rifle beside the door and came out onto the porch. She eyed the stranger while he hitched his horse to the rail. He was Cooper's age or a little older. His boots were of the best leather and not run-down at the heels, his clothes clean and he rode a good horse. He also wore two tied-down, silver-handled revolvers. He came to the porch and removed his hat.

"Ma'am."

"I'm Mrs. Parnell, Cooper's mother. This is Arnie Henderson, and this is—" She turned, but Bonnie wasn't there. She could see the hem of her dress just inside the door where she had fled. The girl was so shy Sylvia's heart went out to her. "Oh, I guess Bonnie is seeing to something on the stove. Step up on the porch and have a seat, Mr. Kain. Would you care for a nice cold glass of buttermilk? Bonnie and I just finished churning."

"Thank you, ma'am. It would be a treat." His dark face broke into a smile. His eyes were amber, his lashes brown, his cheeks clean shaven and he had extremely white teeth.

When Sylvia returned with the buttermilk they were talking about Arnie's leg and Arnie was saying the worst part of the whole thing was having the darn thing itch and not being able to reach in to scratch it.

"'Course, sometimes when night comers I can sweet talk Sylvia into takin' off the wraps 'n scratch it for me."

The man's eyes took in the flush on Sylvia's face, and saw her reach behind her and pinch Arnie's arm. He drank the milk and returned the glass.

"That was mightly fine. Thank you. As I said, I'm looking for Griff. It seems the young lady knows him?"

"Yes. We've all become quite fond of him. Excuse me,

Mr. Kain, I'm putting the noon meal on the table. I'll set a place for you."

"Don't bother, ma'am—"

"It's no bother at all. A friend of Griffin's is more than welcome."

"I'd sure be pleased to know where that Griff has been all these weeks. If he's been here eating home cooking while I've been eating beans over a campfire, there's going to be a reckoning." Sylvia recognized that there was no threat in his words, but rather a fondness for Griffin.

"I'll leave the tellin' to Arnie. Cooper always says I make a mountain out of a molehill, anyway."

"That's the truth," Arnie said, and grabbed her skirt when she passed. "Sylvia gets her mouth agoin' 'n she's liable to tell ya it's rainin' when the sun's shinin'."

"Arnie! You make me so mad!" Sylvia hissed and yanked her skirt from his grasp and flounced into the house.

"I ain't e'er had such fun as I get teasin' that woman. She be pure pleasure, 'n that's certain." Arnie emitted a chuckle that went on and on. Finally he stopped and leaned forward. "Did ya have trouble findin' the place?"

"No. The land man pointed it out on a map."

Sylvia heard the low murmur of the men's voices and was thankful to leave it to Arnie to judge what to tell the stranger and what not to tell him. He wasn't at all the type of man she thought would be a sidekick to Griffin. He wasn't down on his luck, according to his clothes and his horse. He was older, educated. If she were to judge him, she'd say that he was no ordinary man, just as she had known Logan Horn was not an ordinary man when she first met him. There was a confident air about him that said he was not to be fooled with but that he'd be a good man to have on your side.

Bonnie was so nervous she wanted to melt inside herself. This was the friend Griffin had talked about; the one who had helped him steal his horses back from Clayhill. Griffin thought a lot of him. Bonnie suddenly saw herself as Kain

saw her and was afraid that she'd not measure up and somehow he would change Griffin's mind about marrying her.

Kain helped Arnie to the table. After they were seated
Arnie said the blessing and the food was passed. Bonnie kept
her head bowed and the end of her arm among the folds of
her dress. Sylvia kept a conversation going and Bonnie stole
shy glances at Kain. He had washed at the washbench and
combed his hair. It lay in dark waves straight back from a
part on the side. He was mighty handsome, but he couldn't
hold a candle to Griff, she thought. His fingers were long
and slender, his nails cut close and clean. It was fascinating
to watch him handle his knife and fork. They worked together,
but not one time did she see him put his knife in his mouth.

When they finished the meal, Kain helped Arnie get back
to his chair on the porch. He didn't ask why he was sitting
there with a rifle within easy reach, and Arnie didn't tell him
how he came to have a broken leg and a face full of scabs
and bruises.

It was evident to Sylvia that the two men had sized each
other up and liked what they saw. She smiled fondly down
at Arnie. He was a *good* man and he had certainly added zest
to her life. She would make a home for him over on the
Morning Sun, and Cooper could raise his family here. Sometimes things did work out as they should, she thought, and
placed her hand on Arnie's shoulder.

"You're welcome to stay the night, Mr. Kain," Sylvia said
when Kain mentioned that he should be getting on back to
town.

"Thank you, ma'am, but I'll be going. I have an envelope
in my saddlebag for Griffin. It's the money for his horses.
Tell him that I got a good price from the army and that they
even came and got the entire herd. I'll be in town for a few
days, then I'll be moving on."

"I wish you were staying," Sylvia said, and shook her
head sorrowfully.

"I plan to set Adam Clayhill straight about Griffin and the

place on the Blue before I go, ma'am." There was no overt change in Sylvia's expression, only a faint grimace of her full lips. Kain's admiration grew for this woman who had endured so much with a head held high.

"Can you do that? He's a hard, vicious man who will do anything to get what he wants. Anything at all."

"I know that. Not much happens in the territory that isn't talked about in a saloon."

He continued to look straight at her, but Sylvia knew he was talking about Arnie's leg and the fact that Adam Clayhill had set his thugs on him. She realized, too, that Kain knew Adam wanted the son who despised him to come to Clayhill Ranch. Sylvia drew in a deep hurtful breath. Her shame was known throughout the territory.

Sylvia stood beside Arnie and watched Kain ride away. Bonnie had refused to come to the porch, but now she stood in the doorway watching him too.

"Did you tell Kain that Adam's men would have hung Griffin if not for Cooper?"

"No. I tole him Cooper 'n Griff had gone to bury the ole man. If Griff wants him to know, he'll tell him."

"I think he knew anyway. I think he knows all about us, Arnie. I wonder who he is."

"I take him for a man what uses his eyes 'n ears 'n what's atween. 'N he don't let no moss grow on him anywheres, that's shore. I'd say he'd be a good one to tie to in case a trouble."

"I wish he'd stay," Sylvia said again.

Late the following evening, Cooper and Griffin rode in. Their horses were tired and the men almost worn out from a hard two-day ride without sleep. Sylvia met Cooper at the gate.

"Is Lorna here, Ma?"

"No, son."

"Has she been here?"

"No."

"Fix some supper, will you? I'll be ridin' out in the morning." Cooper wheeled his horse and headed for the barn. Sylvia could have cried when she saw the look of disappointment on his face.

Chapter
Twenty-One

Lorna headed straight for the Johnson place. If anyone knew where Hollis had gone it was his cousin Luke. She rode into the yard, saw Luke's slatternly mother indifferently draping wet clothes on the bushes beside the washtubs, and reined over to her.

"Howdy, Mrs. Betts."

"Ain't ya sinkin' mighty low acallin' on us poor hill trash?"

Lorna felt her insides quiver hotly. Pearly Betts, at thirty-five, looked twice her age. Her sallow skin sagged and hung in pouches along her jawline and her hair, stringy and dirty, clung to her sweat slick face. She looked like what she was, a bitter, worn down woman. Lorna felt a faint pity for her, but knew it was a wasted emotion.

"I'm looking for Luke."

"What fer? Ya ain't never give my Luke the time a day." A smug smile of satisfaction came over her face. "I did hear ya had a fire over at yore place. I sure hope it didn't hurt that fancy house of yores none."

"You'll be happy to know, Mrs. Betts, that it burned to the ground."

"Oh? My, my. Ain't that a shame. Are ya awantin' Luke

311

to help ya build it up agin? Well, he ain't agoin' to. 'N I ain't atellin' ya where he is, neither."

Lorna wondered why she had ever felt a spurt of pity for this woman. She turned her horse and rode in a leisurely jog until she dipped from sight on the trail, then let Gray Wolf run for half a mile.

The idea of going to Brice's cabin played on her mind. She knew he wouldn't be there; even Brice wouldn't stay on the mountain after what he'd done. There was a chance that Luke and his father might have gone there to salvage what they could from what Brice left behind. While she was trying to decide what to do she heard the sound of horse coming fast. She pulled off the trail and waited. It was Luke.

"Miss Lorna—I saw you talkin' to Ma."

"I was looking for you. She wouldn't tell me where you were."

"I didn't reckon she would. I'm plumb sorry . . . 'bout ever'thin'."

"Where did they go, Luke?" she asked softly.

"Pa'd kill me if I told—"

"He'll never know."

"He said it ain't no business of ours 'n I'd better not be ashootin' off my bazzoo. But it warn't right to burn up a place like they done."

"They killed my pa, too, Luke."

"Frank? Lordy! They didn't say nothin' 'bout that."

"Hollis shot him. Twice."

"I'm plumb sorry—"

"Where did they go? Who was with them besides Billy?"

"Billy didn't want to do it, Miss Lorna."

"But he did. Who was the other man?"

"Dunno. Hollis said they'd met him in town 'n he was askin' 'bout a woman named Lorna who lived down this way. He said you'd done some caterwaulin' 'n you'd stuck him with your knife."

"Did he have red hair?"

"I dunno, Miss Lorna. I never did see him. Hollis said he was some high muckity-muck's right-hand man 'n that he was plumb tickled to run on to men like him 'n Brice. He had work for 'em. Good payin' work."

Lorna's mind absorbed this information. The fourth man had to be Dunbar, the one who had come to the cabin on the Blue and tried to hang Griffin. He'd be just the type to take up with the likes of Brice and Hollis.

"Did they go to Junction City?"

"I cain't say, Miss Lorna—"

"You take care of yourself, Luke. If you ever want to get out of this hog wallow, go to the Parnell ranch up on the Thompson. You're a good man with horses. Cooper Parnell might give you a job."

"Ya think he would?"

"You never know till you ask. Thank you, Luke. You're about the only decent thing left in these mountains. You and Moose and Woody." She reined over and held out her hand.

"Bye, Miss Lorna. Ya . . . watch yerself. Hear?"

Lorna rode east and north, coming down off Light's Mountain on the eastern side. Cooper had told her Junction City was straight north of the place where they had turned to go to Light's Mountain when they had left the cabin on the Blue. She followed the canyon, riding cautiously. Her rifle was reassuring in her hand, and she held it ready. She was now in a vast and empty land, and she rode into uncertainty with no one beside her. Gray Wolf alone was confident. He was on a trail and he held to it.

At sundown she paused to water her horse, to fill the canteen and to prepare some food for herself. At this place she rested, and for an hour she slept. More comfortable on the trail at night, she mounted up and went forward with extreme caution, pausing often to listen. At any time she might come upon someone who had rolled up in his blankets for the night or another night rider like herself.

The walls of the canyon closed in and darkness enfolded her; the wild cliffs rose up, rough, old, and silent. A river roared through its confining cliffs beside the trail, and its bellowing echoed against the canyon walls. It was a relief to look up at the narrow band of sky, with its stars.

Lorna lost all sense of time. Somewhere ahead, in Junction City, were Brice and Hollis and the man named Dunbar whom she had knifed on the Blue. Her granny had always told her that birds of a feather flocked together. She never really understood the full meaning of that until now. Her granny had also said that nothing brought men closer together than to be united against someone. It appeared that her enemies had joined forces.

Hours passed. Suddenly Gray Wolf lunged upward, scrambling hard on the lip of a cliff. The cool night breeze hit her face and she knew she was out of the canyon and on the flatland.

When dawn was breaking, she left the trail and rode into the dense woods. She was exhausted from the long hours in the saddle, and Gray Wolf was tired, too. There was no sound but that of the walking horse and the twittering of birds. Within her there was a vast emptiness, for every moment of the long ride she had been acutely aware of what lay ahead. She had been to a town only two other times in her entire life. Just walking her horse into town was going to take all the courage she had. She'd need a clear head and to have that she had to rest and think.

She woke after a few hours of sound sleep. The air was cold, and she threw off the blanket reluctantly, rolled it, and tied it behind her saddle. She filled her hands with water from her canteen and splashed her face and dried it on the end of her shirt. After combing and rebraiding her hair, she saddled Gray Wolf and turned him toward town.

The first thing she was going to do was to buy herself a hat. She felt the weight of the gold coins in the pocket of her coat and blessed her granny for saving them. Use them when times were hard, she had said. Times had never been harder than now, right this minute, as the long street lined with buildings loomed ahead.

Junction City was a town of pot holed, muddy streets, frame buildings and a few rawly new brick buildings, spread out along one main street, with two streets branching off on either side. Houses, set like small boxes, lined these streets. At the far end of town, looming gauntly above the houses, was the church with steeple and cross unfinished.

To Lorna it looked like a metropolis. She reined in on the edge of town to look. For a moment she sat deliberately taking in the smells and sounds, which were wholly different from what she had known, and watching the activity in the street. Her father had said that Denver was many times bigger than Junction City. She couldn't imagine it, or how people could live in such a crowded place. Smoke drifted upward from at least fifty chimneys, dogs roamed the streets, horses stamped at pesky fall flies, and merchants stood in open doors or visited with customers on the board porches.

Lorna saw a mercantile sign above a store at the end of the first block, and feeling more frightened and unsure of herself than she ever had in her life, she headed for it. A dog ran out from beneath a porch and nipped at Gray Wolf's heels. The nervous gray lashed out with his hoofs and sent it rolling in the dust. The cur picked itself up and slunk back under the porch. Lorna scarcely noticed the interrupted gait.

There were a few horses on the street and a few people on the boardwalks fronting the stores, but no one paid any attention to the small figure on the horse, and for that Lorna was thankful. She stopped at the store, sat for a minute, then slid from the saddle. She dropped the reins on the ground in front of the horse, looped her bullwhip over her shoulder and took her rifle from the scabbard.

"Don't let any of this fuss get you excited, Gray Wolf. I'll be back in a minute. I have to start somewhere," she said and rubbed his nose with her fingertips. "This place is good as any."

Lorna stepped up on the porch and went through the open door of the mercantile. She paused and looked around. As soon as her eyes accustomed themselves to the dim light, she saw an astonishing array of goods. Here was everything from dress goods to harnesses to crackers and dried apples. Rope, chains, buckets and a variety of tools hung from the rafters. The aisles were choked with kegs, boxes, tubs, pickaxes and bags of flour, salt and sugar. Lorna sniffed the air and smelled a mixture of leather and spices, new wood and coal oil.

"Howdy, young feller. I didn't hear you come in." The booming voice came from somewhere among the coats, jackets, pants and blankets that were stacked against one wall. Lorna watched the man come toward her. He wore a white shirt and had a striped apron tied about his middle. Beneath an almost bald head, his face was round and pleasant. "'Scuse me, ma'am. Lookin' against the light, I thought—"

"I need a hat," she said, almost defensively. She shifted her rifle to her other hand and reached into her pocket for the bag of coins.

"Right over here. I've got ever' kind a hat a young lady'd need."

Lorna followed him to the hat counter. Sitting on blocks of wood was a selection of bonnets; straw hats decked with ribbons; velvet hats with peacock feathers; and satin hats in every color of the rainbow. She wanted to cry. It was all so confusing. All she could do was shake her head.

Mr. McCloud had been in business for five years, and he was certain that in all that time he had never seen a more beautiful face than the one before him. It was a white, perfectly formed face surrounded with shiny dark hair that she had tried to slick back to conceal beneath the collar of her coat. Almond-shaped eyes beneath straight dark brows were of a color he'd seldom seen. The lower red lip that was slightly trembling had a cleft, giving her mouth a three-cornered shape.

There was almost a pleading quality to the violet-blue eyes that looked back at him.

"I think I know what you need, young lady. Come this way." He led her to the men's wide-brimmed, peak-crowned hats. "I don't know as I blame you a bit for wanting to hide, if you can, the fact you're a pretty young woman. This town is full of toughs and if you're planning on staying long, it's best you keep a sharp eye out."

McCloud talked as Lorna looked over the stack of hats. Finally she placed the rifle on the counter, lifted a dark hat from the pile and put it on her head. It came down over her ears.

"Too big," McCloud said. "I'll find your size." He shuffled through the hats and came out with one. "Try this. There's a mirror back over here."

Lorna went to the big mirror. She didn't recognize herself at first. The mirror she'd had at home showed only one small part of her face at a time. She grimaced at what she saw. She wished she was bigger, heavier, and her face wasn't so white or her lips so red. Oh, well, she couldn't do anything about that. Her hair went into the crown of the hat easily, and she tilted the brim low over her eyes. Back at the counter she picked up her rifle and tossed down the bag of coins.

"Take what you need," she said and turned her back to look at the bullwhips that hung from a peg.

McCloud was dumbfounded. "I don't want to do that, ma'am," he said gently. "Let me tell you a few things, miss. You must keep your money in your pocket and only bring out what you need or someone will snatch it and be gone."

"I guess you're right," she said gravely and opened the bag. "How much for the hat?"

"Three-bits." He took the coin she gave him. "I'll get your change. I haven't seen you around here before."

"I've not been here before. I'm from Light's Mountain."

"Light's Mountain? Is that a town?"

"No, it's a mountain," she said, turning away and blinking

rapidly. Her eyes were clear when she looked at him again. "Mister—"

"McCloud." McCloud held out his hand.

"Lorna Douglas." Lorna shifted the rifle and put hers in it. "I'm obliged for the advice. I guess you can tell that I've not been to town much. I'm looking for three men. Do you know Brice Fulton or Hollis Johnson, or a man named Dunbar?"

McCloud watched Lorna carefully. There was an aura of sadness about the girl and now a deadly intensity while she waited for him to answer.

"I never heard of the first two. There's a man named Dunbar that works for Clayhill Ranch."

"Does he have red hair?"

"I believe so. Is he a friend of yours?"

"No. Can I ask you something else? Do you know if he's in town?"

"He was last night, miss. But he probably went on back to the ranch this morning. Adam Clayhill don't give his men much time off."

"Is there a lawman in town?"

"No, ma'am. The marshal from Denver comes up once in a while. There's talk about incorporating the town and hiring a sheriff. Most folk want law and order, but some are fightin' against it."

Lorna nodded thoughtfully. "How do you get something to eat here?"

"There's a eatery right up the street. It's run by a woman named Mable. Just walk in and sit down and she'll dish up what she's cookin'."

"Is that all you have to do?"

"When you finish, give her one of those coins like you did me, and wait for the change."

"Thank you. There's one more thing. Do you know Cooper Parnell?"

"Sure do. There's not a finer man around than Cooper.

He was in here the other day and said he was going partners with a young feller down on the Blue. Do you know Cooper?"

"That old Clayhill will run them out of there," she said heatedly, ignoring his question.

Lorna went to the front of the store and McCloud followed. He felt uneasy about her. "Are you staying the night in town?"

"I don't know, yet."

"If there's anything I can do for you, come on back in."

"You've done plenty, thanks."

"That Dunbar's a rough man, miss, he hangs out with the town toughs. Are you sure you want to find him?"

"I'm sure."

"Well, in that case," McCloud said with a deep sigh, "take off that hat and ride down the street with all that pretty hair flyin' loose, and in a hour every man in town will be on the street to get a look at you. Word will spread about the new woman in town and Dunbar'll find you."

"That's a good idea. Thank you, Mr. McCloud."

"You can tie your horse out behind, if you like. Give him a scoop of grain."

"I'll pay—"

"Stop in before you leave town and we'll settle."

McCloud watched Lorna lead the horse between the buildings. It was as fine an animal as he'd seen in a long time and his curiosity about the girl grew. She was a lovely, well-mannered young woman, but oh, so unworldly. What could she want with a man like Red Dunbar? He wished he had a way of getting word to Cooper Parnell before Dunbar came back to town.

He stood in the doorway of the store and watched her come back from between the buildings. She carried her rifle in her hand and had the bullwhip looped over her shoulder. Instead of going down the boardwalk to the restaurant, she went down the middle of the street. At first glance she appeared to be a slim lad, but on second glance anyone could tell she was a woman, and McCloud had no doubt as to what

the reaction to a woman in britches would be. He scratched
his head. He couldn't think of a time when he'd seen a woman
come to town in britches since a freighter and his woman
came through several years ago. He watched to make sure
Lorna was going in the right direction, then went back into
the store.

It was no easier walking into the restaurant than it had
been to enter the store. There was one long table down the
center of the room and several round tables at the back. One
diner, a man in a dusty flannel shirt, sat at the long table with
his back to the door and another man, in a tan leather vest,
sat at one of the round tables. Lorna hesitated. Was she really
hungry enough to go in?

"Come on in, youngun." The woman's voice came from
the back and a round face looked through a hole cut in the
wall. "Find ya a seat. It's a beef 'n dumplin's today."

Lorna despised having to walk between the tables to get
to the back where she could sit facing the door, but she did
it as quickly as possible. She perched on the edge of the chair,
with the rifle across her knees.

"Take off yore hat!" The voice boomed from the back.
"Ain't ya got no manners? No man eats at *my* table under a
hat."

Lorna's face turned a fiery red. Both men turned to look
at her and she wanted to crawl under the table. Her eyes
fastened on the woman coming through the doorway. She
was very fat, her dark hair was parted in the middle and
pulled to a tight bun on the back of her head. She was fanning
her flushed face with the tail of the apron wrapped about her
waist. Lorna snatched the hat from her head and her hair
tumbled around her face and the braid fell forward onto her
chest. She gripped the hat in one hand and the rifle in the
other, and wished she hadn't been so foolish as to come in.

"God love ya, dearie!" The woman stopped and stared. "I
thought ya was one of them trail busters that's been eatin' at

the end of a wagon fer so long they ain't got no manners a'tall. Here ye be, a pretty little gal. Hungry, air ya?"

"Yes, ma'am. I can pay."

"I got the fixin's all ready. It's a mite early fer the noonin'. So ya can eat 'n be gone afore the crowd pops in."

"I'm agoin', Mable. Ya want to take my money now?" The cowhand at the big table got to his feet as he spoke.

"Ain't ya got time fer more pie, John?"

"It's mighty good pie, but I'd better be lightin' a shuck for the ranch."

"Wal, now, if ya hurry, ya might have time to stop by Bessie's on the way." The fat woman laughed uproariously.

"If ya wasn't so busy cookin' up larrupin' grub, I'd not have to go to Bessie's." The cowhand dropped some coins on the table and pinched Mable's cheek.

"Go on with ya, John Nelson. Stop the tomfoolery or I'll tell Logan to kick yore butt off Morning Sun." Mable slapped at his hand, picked up the coins and put them in her pocket.

"If'n he did, it'd give me more time with you, darlin'."

Mable reached for the broom and the laughing cowhand raced for the door. She was chuckling when she brought out the granite coffee pot and refilled the other diner's cup.

"You wantin' anything else, mister?"

"No, thank you. I've had plenty."

"Ya sure do look like somebody I know, but I can't place the when or the where of it."

"I was in here yesterday."

"Lordy mercy! I knowed that. I mean—"

The man laughed and Lorna's eyes were drawn to him. He was clean shaven and his hair was combed neatly. Although he was seated she knew he was tall. He reminded her of Cooper and she turned her eyes away. She didn't want to be reminded of Cooper. She didn't want to be distracted from what she had to do. Besides, she told herself sternly, this man's hair was dark and Cooper's was light. His voice wasn't soft like Cooper's and his eyes weren't blue like Cooper's, and—

"DeBolt," he was saying. "Kain DeBolt."

"Name don't mean nothin'," Mable said. "I must be gettin' old. Time was I could name ya ever' handsome man fer twenty square miles." Mable laughed and her belly bounced in rhythm. "I'll be gettin' your dinner now, honey," she called to Lorna and went back to the kitchen.

The man finished his coffee and was placing his money on the table when Mable returned with a plate of food and pan of bread.

"Bye. Come on back, now," Mable called.

"Thank you, I will."

"Ya want coffee?" She put a plate of beef and noodles in front of Lorna. Lorna nodded and began to eat. Mable returned with the coffee pot and two cups. "Do ya mind if I set with ya a spell? The rush'll start 'n I'll not get a chance to get off my feet. Lordy, they do hurt 'n I've got a pile of dishes to do."

"I'll do them for you." An idea had hit Lorna. Everybody had to eat.

"Bless ya, honey. Ya lookin' for work?"

"No. I'm looking for some men who burned down my house and killed my pa."

"Well, landsakes!" Mable panted and wiped her eyes on her apron as if better to see Lorna. "What'll ya do with 'em when ya find 'em?"

"I'm going to kill one of them. I've not decided about the other three." She spoke in a calm unruffled voice and took another bite of food.

"Child! Do ya know what yore sayin'?"

"Yes, ma'am, I do. And I'm not a child. I'm almost twenty years old."

"Where're ya from, ch—miss—"

"Douglas. Lorna Douglas. I'm from Light's Mountain."

"Is that up near Cheyenne?"

"No, ma'am. It's south." Lorna lifted the fork again and chewed the food slowly. She decided suddenly she wasn't as hungry as she thought she was. She placed the fork beside her plate and looked the woman in the eye. "Miss Mable, I'll wash all your dishes if you'll help me. I need to get myself fixed up in a dress and my hair all prettied up on top of my head like pictures I've seen. I need to get a parasol and shoes with heels and something to make me smell good. How can I do that?" she asked so innocently that Mable's mouth fell open.

"Well . . . I don't know if there's a store-made dress in town. I guess yores got burned up in the fire." She clucked her tongue against the roof of her mouth sorrowfully. "Poor little mite."

"I didn't have any dresses. I never wear them. But Mr. McCloud at the mercantile said if I let my hair down and walked down the street, word would get out about a new woman in town and the men would come to look at me. I thought if I had on a pretty dress, they'd come faster. I don't want to stay here very long. I want to do what I've got to do and get back. I need to find a place to winter."

"Yo're thinkin' the men yo're lookin' for will come to ya?"

"It's what Mr. McCloud said."

Mable made a mental note to tell McCloud to keep his big mouth shut and his advice to himself. Aloud she said, "Do ya know anybody around here?"

"Ah . . . no."

Mable fanned her face with her apron and gave Lorna's hand a reassuring pat. Her single-mindedness was unshakable, she decided. With or without her help she'd do what she'd set out to do. The only way she could help her was to delay it a little if she could.

"I'll tell you what. Have you heard of The House?"

"No, ma'am."

"A friend of mine, Bessie Wilhite, lives out there. She's

got some girls 'n one a 'em, Minnie Wilson, is 'bout yore size. Go 'n tell Bessie what ya need. I'll write a letter for ya to take to 'er so she'll know ya ain't job huntin'." Mable laughed and Lorna wondered why.

"I can pay—"

"Honey..." Mable gazed at the beautiful young face and the violet-blue eyes. There were men here who would die for this innocent young woman, and others who would kill to get her. "This is a mean town. Every drifter, outlaw, deserter, and just plain no-gooder wanders in and out of here. Why don't ya just give this up 'n go back home?"

"I can't, Miss Mable." Tears flooded Lorna's violet eyes and beaded her thick dark lashes. "I just buried my pa. I can't let 'em go."

"All right, honey." Mable squeezed her hand. "Ya tell Bessie what yo're up to. Bessie's been in more 'n a few tight spots. She'll know what t'do."

"I'll wash the dishes before I go."

"You don't need to—"

"I want to. You've been kind."

"I ain't got the heart to say no. But ya ain't payin' fer yore meal."

Lorna washed dishes all through the noon meal, glancing through the opening in the wall every time she heard the screen door slam, hoping to see one of the men she was searching for. The men came in, removed their hats, sat down at a table and helped themselves from the large bowls of beef and noodles and platters of cornbread. They laughed and talked, but there was no loud swearing and no spitting on the floor. Mable carried a large coffee pot from table to table, joking with the customers and filling coffee cups.

Lorna looked at each face, but none of the men were Brice, Hollis, Billy, or the red-headed Dunbar. By the time the last man left the dining room, Lorna was doing the last of the dishes. She dried her hands on the roller towel, put on her coat and carefully tucked her hair up under her hat.

"Here's the letter." Mable slipped a folded paper in her coat pocket. "If ya change yore mind ya can winter with me 'n work fer yore keep."

"Thank you. It's good to know I've a place to come back to."

"Ya bet your bottom dollar ya have, honey," Mable boomed. "Ya know where yo're agoin', now?"

"Straight north along the creek. White house with flower boxes in the windows."

"That's it. I told Bessie in the letter to keep ya the night. I ain't awantin' you hurt, child."

Lorna picked up her rifle and her whip. "I'll be all right."

But she wasn't so sure when she crossed the porch and stepped into the dusty street. There were people and movement everywhere. The town was alive with horses and wagons; some covered, some loaded with freight. A handsome buggy sped past her, driven by a black man in a black coat and square, high-topped hat. She barely had time to get out of the way. She could hear music and loud laughter. The dust was offensive to her eyes and nose and the noise to her ears.

Halfway down the block a teamster was having trouble with a balky mule. He was shouting curses and trying to back the mule into a three harness hitch positioned beside two other mules. The animal was frightened and the louder the man cursed and yanked on the bit the more the animal resisted. Finally the man began to beat the mule with a flat board. The mule squealed and tried to sidle away. The animal was scared and suffering. It was more than Lorna could stand. She broke into a run.

"Stop that!" she shouted and hung onto the man's arm.

The big, burly teamster shoved her away with a sweep of his arm and brought the board down against the side of the mule's head. Lorna regained her balance and before he could strike the animal again, the tip of the bullwhip caught the teamster between the shoulder blades. She put just enough strength behind the blow to sting him and get his attention.

"What the hell!" he spun around. "What the hell are you doin'?"

"Don't hit that mule again, mister."

"Why you goddamn, snot-nosed brat! I'll hit that goddamn mule when I want. It's my mule."

"Not while I'm here, you won't. I'll put the mule in there if you can't do it."

"Who said I couldn't?" The teamster's face was a mask of fury. He spit toward Lorna and lifted the board. She cast the whip and the board flew out of his hand. "Yeeow! Goddamn you to hell and back!" He yanked a wood splinter from the palm of his hand, swore viciously, and lunged for Lorna. She sidestepped his charge easily.

"I don't want to hurt you," she said and backed away. "I just don't want you hurting that mule. Back off, mister."

"You meanin' to fight me?" The man looked at her with disbelief.

"If I have to."

"Jesus Christ! I can break your scrawny neck!"

"I can put your eye out with this whip if I've a mind to."

"Hey, some of you fellers step on the end of that whip. This kid needs his ass busted."

Lorna hadn't realized a crowd had gathered. She glanced at the circle of men who were waiting, grinning.

"I'd like to see what the sprout can do with that lash, Freiden. Ya got two eyes, ya don't need both of 'em." There were loud guffaws from the men behind her.

"Hell! I ain't fightin' no kid what's still shittin' yellow."

"Ya sure it ain't you what's yellow, Freiden? Air ya 'fraid of a wet-eared kid?"

Lorna turned. The man talking was standing on spraddled legs, a wicked grin on his whiskered face. He was an agitator, a troublemaker, one of those who stood on the sidelines and urged other men to fight. It stuck out all over him.

"At least he's doing honest work, and he's smart," Lorna

said. With a flick of her wrist she cast the whip and whisked the hat from the agitator's head.

Now it was the teamster's turn to laugh. The rest of the spectators joined in. The agitator picked up his hat, beat the dust from it against his thigh, and slammed it down on his head. His face had turned an angry red and Lorna knew she had made an enemy.

"The lad's all right," the teamster said. "He's got guts. I'll bet you five dollars against that whip, kid, you can't put that mule in line."

"I'll take that bet." Lorna coiled the whip and looped it over her shoulder. "Hold my rifle," she said to the teamster.

She went to the big, brown mule and put her hands on each side of its face and spoke softly. "Did he hurt you, big fellow? You're just scared, and that big, old, dumb man doesn't know it." She put her arms around the mule's neck and pulled its head down so she could whisper in its ear. She patted its sides and flanks, then came to the front and pushed gently. The mule obediently backed up and Lorna maneuvered it into place.

The watching audience was quiet, and when she walked behind the mule to hitch the harness to the leveler, she heard the teamster gasp, "Don't!"

Lorna finished hitching the mule and patted the big face affectionately. "You're a nice fellow, you are. Behave yourself now." She reached for her rifle and the dumbfounded teamster gave it to her.

"Wal, I'll be hornswoggled! That's the meanest damn mule this side a hell."

"No. He was scared."

"Here's your money, lad. Do you need work?"

Lorna's hat was suddenly snatched from her head. She sucked in a painful breath and turned. The surly cowboy sailed her hat far out into the street, bent and thrust his face close to hers.

"Ain't no lad, a'tall, Friedman. Hit's a split-tail in them britches."

"Wal, by jinks damn if it ain't."

"Purty 'un, too." The cowboy's big rough hand closed over the braid of thick dark hair.

Lorna stood perfectly still and held him with her eyes. "Get your hands off me," she said calmly.

"Make me." The cowboy laughed, showing yellow teeth. He glanced at the men ringing them. "Looky here, boys. I think I'll whap me a soft, little ole round bottom."

"Leave her be." The teamster grabbed the cowboy's arm.

"Ya wantin' her fer yoreself, Friedman? Yeeow! Gawd-damn—" He grabbed at his belly and his hand came away bloody. "You cut me, you bitch!"

"I'll cut you again if you don't back off."

"Leave the lady alone." The commanding voice came from behind Lorna, but she didn't turn. She held the knife ready. The cowboy backed away, but his face was ugly and he kept his eyes on the man behind Lorna.

"Butt out," he snarled. "Butt out or—"

"Or what? You're about to get yourself killed, mister. I don't hold with manhandling ladies."

"Ladies? Ya ain't callin' this split-tail in britches a lady."

"That's exactly what I'm calling her. Now back off or make a stand, it's up to you. And while you're deciding, get the lady's hat."

The crowd was suddenly quiet. The cowboy looked around for support from the onlookers, but found none. He hesitated, then went to the middle of the street, returned with Lorna's hat and slapped it against her chest.

"I'll be lookin' for ya," he mumbled, turned on his heels, and shouldered his way through the small crowd.

Lorna slipped the knife in her sash, and put on her hat, not bothering to poke her hair up under it. It was no use closing the barn door after the horse was gone, she thought, and turned to face the man who had come to her rescue. She wasn't in the least surprised to see the man in the tan leather vest who had been at Mable's. He was taller than average, wide of shoulder and chest, but with a lean trimness. His tawny colored eyes moved slowly but constantly. They crawled up and down and over the crowd like live things, missing nothing. His stance told her that he was poised and ready for action. Lorna's eyes flicked to the two tied-down revolvers. *This was no two-horn drifter. This man was as dangerous as a rattlesnake, and the cowboy knew it.*

"Thank you," she said, walked around him, and started for the store where she'd left her horse. The man fell in beside her and she said, without looking at him, "You don't need to walk with me. I'll be all right."

"I mean to make sure. That rowdy is a braggart and a troublemaker. You set him down pretty hard, and he'll cause you trouble if he can."

"I can take care of myself."

"I think you can ... most of the time. You're handy with the whip and the knife. What else can you do?" They had reached the store and turned in between the buildings. Gray Wolf watched her approach with ears peaked.

"I can sing," Lorna said simply, shoving her rifle into the scabbard and mounting.

"If you'll wait, I'll get my horse and see that you get out of town without being bothered."

"No one can catch me on Gray Wolf." It was a statement, not a boast.

"Which way are you going?"

"North. I'm going to The House."

"The H-House?" Kain had stammered only a few times before in his life.

"Yes. Have you been there? Do you know Bessie?"

"Well ... ah ... yes, I guess I do."

"I heard you tell Mable that your name is Kain. I'll tell Bessie that you helped me." She turned Gray Wolf toward the street and was gone.

Kain stood for a long moment, and then shook his head
and grinned. The world was full of surprises. Who would
have thought that innocent looking little baggage in that shirt
and old patched britches was a whore? She sure had him
fooled. By damn, but she was a good actress. She ought to
be on the stage.

He walked to the end of the building, lit a long slim cigar,
and watched Lorna ride out of town. God, he thought, he
hadn't been so wrong about a woman since he was sixteen.
He would have sworn, when she walked into Mable's, that
she was fresh from some backwoods homestead and it was
her first trip to town. Instead she was from The House. *She
was one of Bessie's whores.* All dressed up, she'd be an
eyeful, there was no doubt about that. But why in hell was
he so disappointed? he asked himself. She didn't mean anything to him. Pretty women came out of the hills all the time
and were dazzled by the money they could get in town for
what they'd been giving away at home. It was just one more
lesson in human nature. You couldn't really tell by looking
at the outside of a person what was on the inside.

Kain stepped up on the porch, nodded to the merchant
who was standing in the doorway, and headed for the saloon.
It had been two days since he'd been to the Parnell ranch
looking for Griff. He'd wait one more day and if the boy
didn't show up, he was going to shake the dust of this two-
horse town and head west.

Chapter
Twenty-Two

Cooper and Griffin rode into town from the south not a half hour after Lorna rode out to the north. Cooper's face was set with worry lines and he was tired from a sleepless night. The night before he and his mother had hidden Lorna's portion of Volney's fortune in the cellar at the ranch. They had decided that if he took all that gold to the bank in town, word would spread like wildfire and attract every gold-crazed man in the territory. As soon as he found Lorna, Cooper would take her and the gold to Denver where she could decide what she wanted to do with it. But first he had to find her—before she found Brice Fulton and Hollis Johnson.

They rode down the busy street to the bank and Griffin handed over enough of his gold to pay for the land on the Blue and to repay Cooper for the money they had used as a down payment on the land. Cooper had persuaded him that it was no longer necessary for him to have an active partner, but that he would remain a partner in name only, until Griffin could establish his credit with the merchants.

Griffin also carried in his pocket the money Kain had left at the ranch for the horse herd. He was eager to see his friend, but more than that, he felt a burning desire to even the score

with the man who had tried to hang him and with Brice Fulton
for his cruel treatment of Bonnie.

When they reached the Federal Land Office, Adam Clayhill's landau was parked in front, and his driver stood at the
head of the team. Hatred knotted Cooper's guts as it did each
time he was near him.

"The old sonofabitch is here," he said softly, coldly. "No
doubt he's heard the news that more of his free range has
been bought up. He hasn't lost any time getting to town to
find out for sure."

Cooper and Griffin stepped quietly through the open doorway and stood unnoticed just inside the door.

Adam Clayhill was an imposing figure with his white hair
and mustache, his large frame in a dark suit, white ruffled
shirt and string tie. He was livid with anger, jabbing his finger
against the territory map that hung on the wall of the office,
shouting and cursing at the small man in the visor cap who
stood with his hands clasped in front of him as if praying for
deliverance from the tyrant who raged at him.

"I've been using that range for twenty years, you pea-
brained, shithead bastard. I told you a month ago I was going
to buy it and for you to hold onto it for me. I'm not giving
up land to every addle-brained fool who can rake up enough
cash for a down payment on range I took from the goddamn
Indians and held on to when there wasn't anything but a half
assed platoon of cavalry in all this territory. I held on to it
then, and by Gawd, I'm hanging on to it now! Gawddamnit!
Don't you have anything but shit between your ears?"

"It's government land and my job is to sell it to whoever
has the money to pay for it. I couldn't hold it for you just
because you told me to." The clerk's voice climbed shakily
above his fear of the big man who towered over him. His
narrow shoulders were bent under their burden of humiliation,
but he was gamely trying to hold his own. "This is government
property you're on and I'm a government official. The law
says—"

"To hell with the law!"

"I'm just doing my job, Mr. Clayhill."

"Your job? You fucking bastard! Your job's to see that this territory isn't taken over by the scum that couldn't make it back East and come out here to get *free* land!"

"The land's not *free*—"

"How many acres did they get?"

"Ah ... I couldn't say right off," he hedged.

"Don't try to bullshit me, you little weasel." Without warning Adam grasped the man's shirt front, and with a convulsive heave he slammed him against the wall with a violence that shook the frame building. The man's head cracked against the boards behind him and his visor cap slid down over his eyes. "How long have you been here? Six months? That's long enough for you to know who runs things around here."

"I ... I couldn't help—they told me in Denver to sell." Terror burst from the small man in a choked sob as he righted his cap and stared up into the furious eyes above him.

"Did you know that Cooper Parnell is my son?"

"Yes, sir. I'd heard—"

"Is that why you sold him the land?"

"No, sir," the clerk said determinedly. "I sold it because the law says I have to. Mr. Parnell and his partner had the money to put down. Lawyer Schoeller fixed up the papers. They paid a third down and will pay the rest in ninety days."

"I don't give a gawddamn about what that crackpot Schoeller drew up! Who's Cooper's partner?"

"Young feller named Fort Griffin."

"Fort Griffin? Jesus Christ, what kind a name is that?"

"I don't—"

"How much money do they owe?"

"I'm not sure." The clerk's agonized eyes darted from Adam to the men beside the door.

"You can lose your job for giving out confidential information." Cooper took a couple of steps into the room as he spoke.

Adam's hand dropped from the clerk's shirt and he spun around. The scowl dropped from his face like a curtain. "Cooper, my boy—"

"Don't *boy* me, you rotten hunk of horseshit! I'm not your boy. I'm not *your* anything." Cooper took a long step forward. "I'd rather have been sired by a mangy warthog than you." Cooper spoke softly, but his every word struck Adam like ice, and with each one his finger jabbed into Adam's chest.

"Now, Cooper, you don't need to get in a huff. I naturally wanted to know—" Adam backtracked a few steps, but Cooper followed.

"You wanted to know how your plan to hang Griff didn't work? Luck. Pure luck. I happened to be there to cut him down."

"I didn't know anything about that. I swear." Blood stained Adam's face and his breathing deepened.

"Bullshit! I suppose you didn't go out and threaten my mother, either. If you ever come to my place again, or speak to my mother, or have your hired thugs waylay and beat up one of our friends, I swear to God I'll cut your rotten, black heart out and poke it down your throat."

"Did she tell you that?" Adam's face was a brick red, but he tried to appear unruffled. He smoothed his shirt front and flicked dust from the dark sleeve of his coat. "Don't you know by now that she—"

Cooper hit him in the mouth with his clenched fist. It was a lightning blow that caught Adam by surprise. He staggered back against the wall; blood spurted from his split lip and stained his white mustache. He hung there, stunned with surprise, until his head cleared.

"Say one thing about my mother and I'll kill you here and now and be done with it. Stay away from her, stay away from me, stay away from the place on the Blue. How much plainer do I have to make it?"

"You-you . . . She's—" Adam sputtered.

Cooper hit him again and Adam's head bounced against

the wall. Cooper grabbed his shirt front and slapped him hard across the face with the back of his hand. "Say it," he gritted as if he were strangling. "Say it and I'll stomp your guts loose."

Adam looked at him with pure hatred in his eyes. He couldn't recall a time when a man had talked to him in such a manner. Two years ago when the whole town heard he'd slept with a squaw and sired a son, the humiliation had brought him low for weeks, but he'd lived it down. Now this, and by a son he'd hoped to claim.

Cooper shoved Adam from him. He staggered to regain his balance and took a handkerchief from his pocket to dab at his mouth.

"You'll be sorry for this."

"The only thing I'm sorry for is that I didn't kill you two years ago. I will yet, if you bother my mother or if anything more happens to Arnie Henderson, or if you lift a finger against Griffin. Do you understand what I'm saying, *old* man?"

"You've just made the biggest mistake of your life," Adam said with cold deliberation. His blue eyes were steel hard and focused unflinchingly on Cooper's face. He knew that within an hour it would be all over town that Cooper, his son, had beaten him. The humiliation kindled a hatred, like a white-hot heat, that surged up from his toes and worked its way through him. "I could have done a lot for you. My name carries weight in Denver."

"You've already done a lot for me. You've saddled me with a shame I'll never be able to live down."

Adam looked pointedly at the clerk as if daring him ever to repeat the words he'd just heard. The small, nervous man fidgeted and looked at the floor. Then Adam looked at the man who leaned carelessly against the wall, meaning to intimidate him as well. Griffin stared back at him, his young face a mask of cold contempt.

"You're *Fort* Griffin? Why, you're just a snot-nosed kid."

Adam looked down his long nose at him and lifted his swollen upper lip as if smelling something unpleasant.

Griffin straightened from his easy slouch as Adam approached to go out the door. "Maybe. But a kid can pull a trigger same as a ole man." He spoke in a conversational tone, but only a very stupid man would have failed to understand the warning.

"I've chewed up younguns like you and spit them out. You're a nothing and will always be a nothing." Adam went to shoulder his way past.

A gun leaped into Griffin's hand and he pressed the muzzled into Adam's belly. "It wouldn't take nothin' a'tall to blow yore guts out. I'd do it, but it'd be too quick 'n too easy. I want ya to hang 'round, ole man, 'n eat my shit."

"You're . . . crazy. I don't even know you." Shaken by the gun barrel that pressed painfully, Adam stuttered.

"That redheaded bastard you sent to hang me knows me. Tell him I'm alookin' for him."

Adam went out the door without looking back. He climbed into the landau and snarled at Jacob, "Get goin'."

"Where we goin', suh? Ta the ranch?"

"No, you fool. To the house on A Street. I'm not leaving town yet."

Jacob put the team in motion and turned off the main street toward the small frame house Adam had purchased to use while he was in town. The black servant knew he was in for a bad time. The master was in a temper. That Mister Cooper must have busted him up good. Jacob's thick lips split into a grin. Lordy, but it would have been fine to have seen it happen!

Adam sank back against the soft leather seat and anger took control of his mind. By God, this is the end of it. That bastard could rot in hell as far as he was concerned. He'd humiliated himself long enough trying to lift that by-blow up by his bootstraps and make him somebody. Parnell couldn't be a son of his, even if he did look like him. He's a throwback, is what he is. That goddamn Sylvia was from bad blood and Cooper had inherited it. The sonofabitch would never get a dime of Clayhill money or a foot of Clayhill land. He'd see to that. He'd leave it all to Della first, even if she was a whore.

Adam straightened his hat and dabbed at his bleeding mouth with his handkerchief. He had some thinking to do. Goddamn that Dunbar. If he'd done what he was told to do none of this would have happened. He hoped the nester killed him, then he'd see that he was hanged for murder. By God! It might be a way out.

"Turn down toward the stock pens, you black sonofabitch, and be quick about it."

Dunbar and a crew of men were waiting besides pens several feet deep with fresh manure. The stench, the flies, the constant bawling of cattle was so offensive that Adam gestured to move away. The men mounted and followed the landau a few hundred feet upwind.

"Howdy, Mr. Clayhill." Dunbar edged his horse close to the carriage when it stopped.

"That gawddamn nester's in town. I'm givin' you another chance, Dunbar. Either do something about him or flag your ass out of the territory."

"Well . . . ah . . . whatta ya want done, Mr. Clayhill?"

"What do you think I want done, you fool? What I told you to do in the first place." Adam's eyes roamed over the faces of the men that flanked him. "If you can't do the job, I'll find someone who . . . wants a nice fat bonus. Did you find that horse herd?"

"No, sir. But we will—"

"You'd better. And, Dunbar, forget what I told you about Cooper Parnell. Do you understand?"

"You mean 'bout layin' off him 'n not—"

"Exactly."

Dunbar grinned and tobacco juice ran from the side of his

mouth. "I know what ya mean, Mr. Clayhill. Ya ain't got nothin' to worry 'bout . . . now."

Adam nodded and poked Jacob in the back with his boot. The whip cracked over the back of the team and the landau pulled away.

Fisher, one of the men who had been with Dunbar at the cabin on the Blue, edged his horse close to Dunbar's. "Why didn't ya tell him the army bought that herd and ya didn't even get to lay a eyeball on the gent what sold 'em?"

"Ya ain't got no brains, Fisher. That's why I'm ramroddin' this outfit and you ain't. Ya don't give a bastard like Clayhill bad news till ya can give him good news first. He's pissed at Parnell, 'n if I read him right, he's sayin' get rid a his bastard along with the nester."

"Ya reckon it was Parnell that busted his mouth?"

"Nobody else'd dare."

"Haw, haw, haw! I'd a liked to seen it. Ya didn't tell him you'd hired on new men, neither, Dunbar. Ya'd—"

"Shut yore gawdamn mouth, Fisher. Ya 'n Peters 'n Barclay go on back to the ranch. Me 'n Brice 'n Hollis can take care this little matter for Mr. Clayhill."

"That's fine with me. I ain't awantin' to tangle assholes with Cooper Parnell." Fisher waved to the two men Dunbar named and they rode off down the track.

Brice Fulton slouched in the saddle, his eyes following the expensive landau as it pulled out of sight behind the buildings. So that was Adam Clayhill, the big muckity-muck Dunbar worked for. Dunbar was a big, stupid ass, and it hadn't been any trouble at all to find out he'd been sent to hang a nester and that he'd run onto him with Lorna and Bonnie and the gent called Parnell that had brought Lorna back to Light's Mountain. He'd paid that black-haired bitch back for using the whip on him, and he'd pay back more if he caught her. Dunbar said Bonnie had the smallpox. Shit! She'd had the kid. If she was still living, the nester and Parnell knew where she was. By God! She was his, as sorry a slut as she was, she was his; and nothing left him until he was ready to run it off.

"The ole man's payin' a bonus. Is that why ya run the rest off?" Hollis asked.

"Why split somethin' six ways when it can be split three? 'Less yo're thinkin' ya'll need help with a skinny kid 'n Parnell. He's the one to watch."

"I can take 'im," Hollis said and adjusted his gun holster on his hip.

"It won't be easy like it was shootin' down that gal's pa, or shootin' that Tyrrell kid in the back 'cause you was scared he'd tell," Dunbar said. "We need to figger out a plan 'cause we cain't just go in an' open up on 'im."

"Why not?"

"Why not? This ain't the backwoods, Hollis. This is town. There ain't no law here, but folks don't hold with shootin' down a man less'n he's shootin' back."

"We'll wait till they leave town."

Brice fingered the scars on his cheeks where Lorna had cut him with the whip and hatred boiled within him. He wasn't through with Lorna Douglas, not until she was naked and bleeding and begging.

They walked their horses along the back of the stores that fronted the main street. Dunbar knew of a cantina where they could stay out of sight and wait. For a dollar and the promise of a bottle he could hire a down-and-out drifter to keep watch and let him know when Parnell and the nester rode out.

A cowboy, half-walking, half-running, rounded the corner of a building, and Dunbar pulled rein.

"George? What the hell ya doin' in town? Gawdammit, I told ya to get out to the west range last night."

"'N I'm agoin'! First I'm agoin' to beat the ass off a feisty little split-tail."

"Yo're agoin' now, gawdammit!"

"Don't crowd me, Dunbar. I said I'm agoin'. But first I'm catchin' up with a black-haired bitch in britches and I'm usin' her whip on her butt, then I'm agoin' to plow the hell outta her."

"Hold up," Brice said, moving his horse in between the cowboy and Dunbar. "What kind a horse is she ridin'?"

"She headed north outta town on a big gray. Gawdamn bitch whipped my hat off with a bullwhip and cut me with a knife—"

The butt of Brice's rifle smashed into the cowboy's face with such force Dunbar could hear the bones crack. George dropped like a sack of grain and lay still.

"What the hell'd ya do that for?"

"'Cause I ain't wantin' him followin'. It's Lorna Douglas he's talkin' 'bout. We'll head off that bitch 'n we'll have us some bait. If'n Parnell's sweet on her like Hollis thinks he is, he'll come. 'N we'll have us some fun while we're waitin' for him. If'n anybody's plowin' the hell outta that bitch it won't be a two-bit blowhard, it'll be me."

"Wait a minute," Hollis protested. "You got a woman. Lorna's mine. I done told ya—"

"Shut yore mouth." Brice's rifle barrel arched over to point at Hollis.

Brice's words hung in the vast hollow of silence. Dunbar watched uneasily. He needed both of these men until the job was done. Then they could kill each other. In fact, he hoped they would; it would save him from having to do it.

"We got to catch up with her afore there's any plowin' done. Jist don't forget, our job's to get Parnell 'n the nester. *That's* what the ole man's payin' for." He led off and after a few paces, he heard the horses fall in behind him.

Cooper and Griffin completed their business at the Land Office and Griffin proudly pocketed the deed to the land.

"Kick me, Cooper, 'n wake me up," Griffin said while they stood on the board porch and looked up and down the street. "I'm still not believin' I got me a ranch 'n money to stock it 'n all."

"Hell, no, I'll not kick you. You might wake up and shoot me." Cooper's stomach was knotted and his heart thumped painfully from his run-in with Adam Clayhill. God, he thought, would he ever get to the place where he could see that old bastard and not want to puke? Aloud he said, "You're awake, Griff. Come on, I want to find out if anyone in town's seen Lorna. She might not have come here. She could've gone to Winona."

"Hey, Griff!" The voice came from across the street. A tall man lifted his hand, waited for a wagon to pass, then came through the dust stirred by the rolling wheels.

"Kain!" Griff stepped out into the street and gripped his friend's hand. "Mrs. Parnell said you'd be here. I was sure hopin' I hadn't missed ya. It's good t'see ya, Kain."

"It's good to see you, too, Griff. When you rode off that night to lead Clayhill's men off I expected you back in a couple of hours. It's been more than a month."

"A lot has happened, Kain. I almost got to the Pearly Gates that night and would've if Cooper here hadn't a stepped in. It's goin' to take some tellin'. First off, did ya take yore cut from the horse money? If'n ya did, ya got a hell of a price."

"I did get a hell of a price. What I left with Mrs. Parnell is yours."

"I want ya to meet Cooper Parnell. He saved my bacon a couple a times, like ya've done, Kain. I'm athinkin' I must a done somethin' right sometime, or I'd not met up with friends like you all.

"Cooper, this is Kain DeBolt, the friend I told ya 'bout."

Cooper judged men by the look in their eyes, the set of their shoulders, the firmness of their handshake. Even if Griff hadn't sung Kain's praises for days, he'd have liked him.

"Are you sure this is the one, Griff? I don't see wings or a halo around his head."

"What 'round his head?"

Both men laughed. "I'm glad to know you, Parnell."

"Same here."

"Ya'll not believe all I've got t'tell ya, Kain." Griff couldn't keep the smile off his face.

"I'll believe it. You've been telling me tall tales for a year or more."

"I don't think he could make up a taller tale than he'll be telling," Cooper said. "I'll leave him to it while I see McCloud at the mercantile."

At the end of the block Cooper glanced back to see that Griff and Kain had moved over next to a building and were deep in conversation. He spared a second to wonder about the man who had befriended Griff. He certainly wasn't what he'd expected, but then, he thought, he'd never expected a woman would be able to tear him up as Lorna had done. He turned into McCloud's store.

"Howdy, Cooper. Be with you in a minute," McCloud called from the counter. "Mrs. Colson, a churn's a churn. Some of the ladies like the crock churn, others swear by the barrel churn. I even sell the small glass Daisy churns, even though they hold about a gallon of milk."

"Well, I don't know . . ."

Cooper strolled the crowded aisles while he waited. Damn woman! Why didn't she make up her mind? McCloud was right. A churn's a damn churn! Finally McCloud was carrying the heavy crock churn out to the wagon hitched in front of the store. He came back in and motioned Cooper to the back of the store.

"Sorry about that, Cooper. Some women—"

"I'm looking for someone. Have you seen a woman in britches riding a big gray horse?"

"I knew you were agoin' to ask. She was in here 'n bought a hat. She was a pretty little thing. My, but she was a pretty little thing. She hadn't been to town but a few times, she said. The little gal carried a bullwhip 'n a rifle 'n she looked like she could use both of them."

"That's her. Where did she go?"

"I don't know. She went to Mable's to eat. I watched her go in. A few hours later her horse was gone, so guess she rode out."

"How did you know I was looking for her?"

"She asked if I knew you. She also wanted to know where she could find Red Dunbar, that sonofabitch who works for Clayhill."

Cooper groaned. "I was afraid of that. Thanks, McCloud. I'll go talk to Mable." He turned at the door. "If she comes back in here, hog tie her till I get back."

"I'm thinkin' it'd be a job."

Cooper didn't answer. His bootheels beat a rapid tattoo on the boardwalk. He was so deep in thought he would have walked past Griff and Kain if Griff hadn't hollered at him.

"Cooper. Has she been here?"

"She's been here. She was in the store and bought a hat. McCloud said she went to Mable's to eat."

Kain's questioning eyes went from one man to the other.

"I ain't got to that part a the tale, Kain. Ya know the woman that held Dunbar off with a knife till Cooper got there? She come to town to find the men who burned down her house 'n killed her pa. She's 'bout this high." He held his hand up to his eyes. "'N she's black-haired 'n got blue eyes, not really blue, but purty as a picture. She'd be ridin' a big gray stallion that's meaner 'n a steer with a crooked horn. Have ya seen her?"

Kain's brows drew together in a puzzled frown. "An hour or so ago, a girl in britches flew into a teamster for beating his mule. A crowd gathered and watched her put the mule in a three horse hitch. God, don't tell me that's the woman you're looking for. She's a—"

"In britches?" Cooper asked. "That would be Lorna. Which way did she go?"

"Which way?" Kain echoed. "North."

"You talked to her?"

"Briefly. She flipped the hat off a hothead with her whip.

I sent him walking and took her to her horse in case he bothered her again. But she said..." Kain hesitated.

"Said what?"

"Said she was going to ... The House."

"The House? Good God! Do you mean Bessie's?"

"She said she'd tell Bessie I helped her. I took it from that that she was ... well acquainted with Bessie." Kain looked at Cooper's suddenly pale face and saw the agony he was feeling. "Maybe we're not talking about the same woman."

Cooper turned his back without answering and headed for the Land Office where he'd tied his horse.

"I'm agoin' with him, Kain. Will ya be here when I get back?"

"I'll come along with you out to The House. I've got to see if we're talking about the same woman. My horse is across the street."

Griff and Kain caught up with Cooper as he was leaving town. He didn't even acknowledge their presence. He was lost in thought. What in hell was Lorna doing at Bessie's? Did she have any idea what kind of place The House was? Had she decided to become a whore? Oh, Christ! She'd lost her mind! Seeing her father gunned down and her home destroyed had driven her out of her mind!

Chapter
Twenty-Three

Lorna's first instinct was to put her heels to Gray Wolf and get out of town as fast as possible. But her better judgment won over her desire to flee; a fast-running horse would attract attention. She guided the handsome, big stallion into a leisurely jog and made her way through the confusion of wagons, horses and buggies. Only when she was around the bend and out of sight of town did she let Gray Wolf run. With the wind in her face and her hair floating behind her like a black cloud, her spirits lifted, but only a little. It was wonderful to be free of the town, out in open space, away from the stench of slops, privies, and so many people.

Despite her bravado when she left Kain, Lorna was unsure and frightened. The first heat of anger and the desire for revenge had cooled and now she wondered if she had been wise to strike out on her own to mete out punishment to the men who had killed her father and destroyed her home without first devising a plan.

Her depression deepened and the memory of the times she'd spent with Cooper worked at her with rebellious persistence. Her dream had been to meet a man like Cooper. They would be friends and lovers and build a life together on the foundation Light and Maggie had left on Light's Mountain. Then, *bang*! All her dreams had vanished. All she had left were memories—Cooper's lips nuzzling her neck, his fingers seeking the warmth of her skin, the wild wanton desire that swept over her when she was with him. He no longer wanted her, she thought despairingly. By spurning his offer of marriage, stealing away in the early dawn, and setting his stock loose she had more than likely killed any feeling he'd had for her. She must face it—she was alone without family or friends.

Lorna allowed herself a moment of self-pity. Griffin and Bonnie had enough problems of their own without adding hers, and Volney was still recovering from his run-in with Brice. When this was over she would winter with Volney, then decide what she wanted to do. One thing was certain: she would never rebuild on Light's Mountain. That part of her life was over.

She pulled Gray Wolf up so as to not wear him out in case he had to run. She felt safer and more confident astride her horse. All her life she had ranged the length and breadth of Light's Mountain either on foot or horseback, watching, hearing, feeling and smelling all the moods and seasons of the timbered hills until she had become one with them. Asking nothing of anyone, she had been completely self-reliant, free of any obligation to anyone except herself. Her life had been good until now.

She followed the two-wheel road until it came close to a shallow, swiftly moving stream, pulled up and studied her back trail. Long ago Volney had taught her the way to survive was to watch her back and keep her rifle handy. She moved Gray Wolf down to the stream and dismounted. While he drank she filled her canteen and studied the area around her; gently sloping hills to the east, the road to the west. There was no sound but the twittering of birds, the singing of cicadas out in the sunlight and the gurgle of the swiftly running stream. She reasoned she was less than a mile from The House, according to Mable's instructions. Remembering the letter in her pocket she reached for it, unfolded the single, yellow sheet and began to read;

> Bessie, help this girl as a favor to me. She's fresh out of the mountains and has got it in her head to dress up flashy like. She's looking for Red Dunbar and three more who killed her pa. Talk sense to her 'n send her home. Guess you can tell she ain't no whore.
>
> Mable

Lorna looked at her reflection in the clear water. How could Bessie tell she wasn't a whore? Would she be willing to help her? Mable seemed to think so. She had forgotten to ask Mable about the girls at The House. She assumed Bessie ran a school for rich young ladies if they had dresses to spare. It would be hard to face them in ragged shirt, baggy britches and old blanket coat; but she had come this far, and there was no turning back.

Her one hope was that when she went back to town she would meet her enemies on a one to one basis. If that should happen she had no doubt of her ability to even the score. She had already decided to kill Hollis; she had known that from the moment she saw what he had done to her father. As far as Brice and Dunbar and Billy Tyrrell were concerned, she'd make that decision when she met them. The burden of what she must do lay heavily on her slim shoulders, and she slumped wearily. Maybe by this time tomorrow or the next day it would all be over, she could put this behind her and ride south again.

It was the middle of the afternoon. She'd had many new experiences already today. She couldn't afford to think about them now. She would file them away and think about them on her way back to pick up Volney. Climbing into the saddle, Lorna reined away from the stream. Gray Wolf scaled the bank and crossed the narrow shelf to the road. She attempted to turn him north and was brought out of her fanciful flight by Gray Wolf's odd behavior. He danced, tossed his head, and his ears twitched nervously. She looked to her back trail.

Two riders!

Instantly Loran recognized the lead horse as Brice Fulton's buckskin. Somewhere they had picked up her trail and were coming on fast. She wheeled Gray Wolf to send him north. She would pick the place to meet her enemies. Gray Wolf refused to respond, wheeled and turned. Lorna's eyes saw movement an instant before Hollis jumped his lathered horse off a small rise and onto the trail ahead of her. He was there to cut her off.

Damnation! They had caught her unprepared. There was no time to get her rifle out of the scabbard and get off a shot. She sent Gray Wolf back down the bank and across the creek. He went eagerly.

The big horse splashed through the water and was scrambling up the other side when a shot split the stillness. Gray Wolf faltered, and then regained his balance. Gamely he dug in and made it to the top of the bank. Just as Lorna was turning him into the trees she heard the shot and felt, simultaneously, the impact of the bullet that crashed through the big gray's head. He dropped from beneath her. Lorna jumped. She landed on her feet running. With her rifle in her hand, she plunged into the concealment of the thick brush that grew beneath the timber.

"Damn you, you filthy, rotten bastard! " she screamed. *Oh, Gray Wolf, they'd killed him!*

Wild with anger and grief, she pumped a bullet into the chamber of her rifle. She could hear a horse crashing through the brush and fired off a shot in that general direction before she scrambled upward through the tangle of red-leafed sumac to a pile of boulders. Behind that she knelt on one knee, waiting. *They'd killed Gray Wolf!* The slime! Filthy hogs! Bastards! Gray Wolf was worth ten of *them*!

There were no tears. There was no room for anything except the cold, deadly resolve to fight the men who had taken everything from her; her home, her father and now her beloved friend. That she was outnumbered three to one didn't occur to her. If she wanted to run, she could hide among the thick pines that grew so profusely on the side of the hill; grew so thick it was impossible for a horse to pass through them. On foot she was a match for any man. *But she was not running.* This was the showdown. It wasn't the time or the place she would have chosen, and she had to fight them all at one time, but so be it, if that was the way it had to be.

Suddenly Hollis came in sight, but a little way off. Without hesitation, she lifted her rifle and sighted. The bullet sent his hat flying. She chided herself for being so hasty and cocked the rifle for another shot, but he had bent low over the horse's neck and she couldn't bring herself to shoot the horse.

"Gawddamn ya to hell! Ya blasted bitch!" he shouted. He swung his horse quickly, scattering gravel along the creek bank. She could hear the horse plunging, and Hollis swearing as he tried to control it.

Minutes paced slowly by. Lorna held herself still, straining her ears, her eyes searching the rim of rocks and the edge of the timber along the creek bank. Nothing stirred, not even a bird. It was hot among the boulders. She removed her coat and placed it and her knife on the ground beside her.

She had been careless. She realized that. The stop beside the creek cost Gray Wolf his life and would possibly cost her hers, but what did it matter? She could justify her time on this earth if she ridded it of these varmints. She had lost everything in the world that was dear to her. All that was left was the opportunity to make the men responsible pay.

Patience. She could hear Volney's gravelly voice. Most things that were worthwhile took patience. Without it no man should go into the mountains. She had to wait and let them come to her.

Although her eyes and ears were alert, her thoughts wandered to Cooper. Would he know or care what happened to her? If Hollis and Brice killed her, they would make sure that no one would ever find her body. Would Cooper remember the good things that had happened between them, or the times she had screamed at him like a shrew, sneaked away from his ranch like a coward, and run off his stock? She realized she might die right here. She didn't want to die—

Something suddenly moved out there, but she held her fire. She couldn't afford to shoot at something she did not see clearly. She shifted her position, trying to see farther down the creek, watching for a chance to get at least one of her enemies.

"It ain't no use, Lorna." Hollis had moved to the north of where she thought he was. "Ya might as well come on out, give up. I ain't leavin' without ya."

She did not reply.

"We know where ya are. I don't want to see ya get hurt none. 'N ya will if'n we got to rush ya."

From down lower, among the maze of sumac, she saw sudden movement. She lifted the rifle but didn't fire. The movement stopped and she realized they'd been trying to sucker her into wasting a shot. Holding the rifle butt beneath her left arm, she picked up the knife.

Ten minutes went slowly by, and then she saw a dark form move from the shadow of the brush north of the sumac and start up the wash toward her. The minutes ticked by. Lorna hunkered down behind the boulder and waited. She held very still, listening. And then, somewhere, not a dozen feet away, she heard the faint breathing of another human being. She stood just as Hollis came out of the brush and into the open. When he saw her his face split in a triumphant grin.

"Ya little bitch! I'm agoin' to beat yore ass fer shootin' at me—"

The knife shot out of her hand with the speed of an arrow and landed exactly where she wanted it to land—the middle of the pocket on his shirt. Hollis gave a hoarse cry as he was flung backward, clutching at the hilt protruding from his chest. He looked stunned as he stood for an instant on spread legs before he fell heavily. He lay sprawled in the grass, shuddered violently, and then was still.

Lorna looked at his crumpled body coldly without a trace of regret for having killed him. It was as if she had killed a deadly snake that was coiled to strike. She was glad the man who had killed her father was dead. Her only wish was that she could get her knife back without having to expose herself.

There was silence again. Nothing moved. Lorna felt as if she were in a faraway place looking down on what was happening to her in this clearing. The sky above was an odd color, she was to remember later. It was a weird yellow, like nothing she'd seen. It was higher, vaster, and emptier than ever before. It seemed to her that the world was a great hollow bowl and she was in the center of it.

A heavy rustling among the sumac drew her attention and she watched it intently. The movement seemed to have no direction and she concentrated intensely on trying to figure out if it were an animal or a man disturbing the red-gold leaves.

There was not a breath of a sound to warn her. A rope, held by two hands, flipped over her head, looped around her neck and jerked her backward. She dropped the rifle and her hands clawed at the cord trapping the air in her lungs. She couldn't breathe. Panic beat up into her mind as she writhed and struggled. She kicked out helplessly. The blood swelled in her face, burning the skin, beating at her throat. In a suffocating red haze, she felt herself grow weaker and a darkness deeper than the night closed in. Her last vestige of reason was that she was going to die, and she hadn't told Cooper she was sorry about the horses!

Lorna was first conscious of her raw throat. She drew fresh, cold air in through her open mouth and whimpered at the pain as it passed through her windpipe. Gradually the haze lifted and she realized her arms were pulled up over her head and she was hanging by a rope looped over a branch well away from the trunk of the tree. She stiffened her bent knees and stood swaying. Sharp pricks on the bottoms of her feet brought her to full consciousness and she looked down. *She was naked!*

Wildly and frantically she pulled at the bonds holding her wrists and whipped the hair back from her face so she could see. A boot grated in the gravel. Lorna saw the boot and then another, and somebody laughed.

"Now ain't that funny? I allus thought she was a skinny bag a bones, but she ain't. Whooeee! Look at them titties 'n that black patch a hair. She's round 'n soft 'n got enuff meat on her to *last!*"

"I ain't likin' hangin' around here, Fulton. If'n it gets out what we done to her, they'll string us up sure as shootin'. Folks don't hold with botherin' women."

Sick with humiliation, Lorna's wavering gaze found Dunbar sitting on a boulder, his legs spread. He was tossing the knife he'd pulled from Hollis's chest into the ground between his boots. She glanced at the still body of the man she had killed. He had been rolled over onto his back and the pockets of his coat and britches were pulled inside out. His *friends* had lost no time stripping the valuables from his body.

"I said I'd have 'er naked 'n beggin'. Didn't I say that, Dunbar? I got 'er naked, 'n I ain't leavin' till I got her beggin'."

Brice walked around her and his fingers pinched her bottom and poked obscenely between the cheeks of her buttocks. She clamped her teeth together and stood as still as her frightened heart would allow.

"I'm agoin' to beat that little ass till it bleeds. Then I'm agoin' to screw'er into the ground." His rough fingers trailed through her pubic hair, across her stomach and up under her hair to pinch her nipple.

Lorna held her head erect and looked him in the eye. She'd die before she cowered before this swine or let him know how she burned with humiliation as his eyes and hands crawled over her nakedness! She vowed, at that moment, that she'd never give him the satisfaction of breaking her spirit. *Never!*

"Wal, do what yo're set to do 'n let's go. I thought we was agoin' to take 'er as bait—"

"*You* might a thought it, but *I* had another idea. 'Sides, there ain't agoin' to be enuff left for bait when I get through with 'er." Brice tangled his hand in Lorna's hair, jerked her head back and spit in her face. Her violet-blue eyes stared unwaveringly into his, and her straight, dark brows lifted slightly in a gesture of contempt as the spittle ran down her cheek. "Ya stuck-up bitch! Ya ain't on Light's Mountain, now, alordin' it over ever'body. Ya looked down your nose at me like ya was a queen 'n I was a dog. I'll have ya lickin' me like a bitch in heat, but first I'm agoin' to give ya a taste of the lash like ya done me when I come to ask ya a civil question 'bout my woman." His fingers worked at the scar on his face before going to the buckle at his waist. He jerked the thick leather belt loose from the loops in his britches and wound the end around his hand.

"Don't ya kill her, now," Dunbar cautioned. "That bitch owes me a few strokes with my rod for stickin' me with a knife 'n for keepin' me from hangin' that nester. The ole man chewed my ass good."

"I ain't carin' much if'n I kill 'er first or not," Brice said slowly. His eyes brightened with a fevered heat as they roamed her naked body, his mouth went slack, and his nostrils flared. "I screwed a dead Injun squaw once 'n got the biggest hard-on I ever got."

"Screwed a dead red ass?" Dunbar stopped tossing the knife to look at Brice with astonishment. "Why . . . that's not—that's not decent!"

"Who says what's *decent* 'n what ain't? If'n it feels good, it's decent. If'n ya ain't tried it, ya don't know what yo're missin'."

Brice walked slowly behind Lorna and she braced herself for the blow that was coming. It came sooner than she expected; a white-hot brand across her buttocks. She grunted under its searing bite. The next blow came on the heels of the first. She heard the sibilant rush of the strap as it came down across her back like a hot flame and clamped her jaws together so that not a sound escaped them. The breathy hiss of the strap sliced through the air again, and her entire back was enveloped in a sheet of agony. Brice moved around in front of her. Lorna saw the maniacal smile on his face through a blur of tears that filled her eyes despite her effort to hold them back.

"How do ya like it? Hurts, don't it?"

Saliva filled her mouth and she spat contemptuously.

Brice lifted the strap and brought it down across her abdomen. She clenched her teeth and almost strangled on the cry that knotted her throat. She closed her eyes to block out his face and the strap cut into her thighs, her sides and her breasts. The serpentine-fire engulfed her, but she refused to cry out.

She opened her eyes and saw the trees wavering, swaying and tipping dizzily. *She couldn't bear this!* Help! Oh God, please help! She tried to close her mind against the pain and think of something dear to her. She would think of Cooper. Darling, sweet, gentle Cooper, with hair like wheat-grass in the fall and eyes like the sky on a bright day.

The lash came down hard across her back and she bit into her lips to hold back the cry that demanded release. Somewhere in the darkness that began to float down and around her, a soft feminine voice said, Sing.

Lorna threw her head back and her eyes, clear and tearless, looked directly into those of her tormentor. She opened her mouth and her high, soprano voice, that had not deserted her, rang out strong and clear.

"Oh, don't you remember sweet Betsy from Pike,
Who crossed the big mountains with her lover, Ike,
With two yoke of cattle, a large yellow dog,
A tall Shanghai rooster and one spotted hog."

The strap hung from Brice's hand as he stared disbelieving at the small, defiant woman.

"Ya cowed 'er, all right."

The words from Dunbar and the nasty laugh that followed were like a bucket of cold water flung in Brice's face. His head jerked around to where Dunbar was sitting on the boulder.

"Shut yore gawddamn mouth, ya shithead! I ain't through yet." With that he brought the strap down across Lorna's shoulders with extra force.

A slight hesitation was her only reaction to the blow. As sweet as a bell, her clear voice rose in a great tumult of sound.

"Saying good-bye, Pike County, farewell
    for a—"

The strap landed across her breasts and the pain took her breath away. Separate fires of agony were kindled in every limb and it felt as if her arms were being twisted from their sockets. She heard one of the men laugh. She was almost at the end of her strength and so she prayed with a grim, terrible strength of will.

"Dear God, help me now. I will endure this if only you help me."

The strength came; she never knew its source, any more than she knew why she could sing while enduring such torture, but she accepted it gratefully. When she could breathe again her voice quivered slightly and then became stronger, more vibrant.

"One evening quite early they camped on
    the Platte;
'Twas near by the road on a green shady flat—"

"She's plumb crazy!" Lorna was dimly aware Dunbar had come to peer into her face. Her entire body was wrapped in a sheet of agony. His image danced before her eyes. "You done whipped her outta her mind."

"'N I ain't done—"

"I'm atellin' ya, we better go. We been here too long as
it is. There'll be some cowhands goin' to The House to get
their ashes hauled 'n they'll hear her caterwaulin'.'"

"She'll break. It won't be long till she's beggin'. When
she does, I'll quit. Beg, you bitch!" he yelled. "Beg, if you
want a inch a white hide left on your bones."

"Shee . . . it!" Dunbar went back to sit down. The bastard
was plumb crazy.

"Where Betsy, quite tired, lay down to repose,
While with wonder Ike gazed on his Pike County
    Rose."

The trees whirled ever slower and the raging flames on
her body sank to a warm and comforting glow. Lorna wasn't
aware now that she was singing or that other words were
coming from her lips.

"I'm dying. I love you, Cooper. We would've been like
Light and Maggie."

Dust lifted from the hooves of their horses. The autumn
sun warm upon their shoulders went unnoticed. The three
men rode silently, wrapped in private thoughts, each in his
own way concerned about the girl they wished to overtake.
Cooper's eyes wandered over the two-wheel track he had
taken many times during the last few years. He had come
this way when he came seeking help from Mary Gregg, the
former mistress of The House, when his mother was sick,
and he'd come this way to help his brother, Logan Horn, who
had been waylaid and beaten by Clayhill men much the same
as Arnie Henderson had been ambushed and beaten. These
thoughts passed fleetingly through his mind. There was no
room for reminiscing when his entire future happiness and
possibly Lorna's life were at stake.

Anxiety about her had driven him put Roscoe into a tiring
pace. After several miles he pulled up and walked him along-

side the road so he could study the hoof prints made only a short time before. He reined in and spoke for the first time to the men who rode with him.

"Gray Wolf's tracks are here, and the tracks of three other horses as well. Lorna rode in the middle of the road, the others side by side. She's not far ahead of them. Do you suppose they followed her out of town?"

"Them prints there is that roan Dunbar rides," Griff said and pointed to the ones he referred to. "I ain't ne'er goin' to forget that print. I seen it too many times."

"If it's Dunbar trailing Lorna, he's got Fulton and Johnson with him." Cooper's throat constricted and he swallowed audibly.

The tracks they followed were clear because the road hadn't been used since the night before. Cooper took one side of the road and Kain and Griff the other. They put their horses into a gallop and reached the place where the three horses following Lorna had pulled up.

"One peeled off and went up that rise," Griffin said.

"There's an upper trail up there."

"He's agoin' fast, Cooper. It's my guess he rode ahead to cut Miss Lorna off."

"The other two waited here long enough for one of them to finish a smoke," Kain said. "When they left, it was on the run."

Cooper jabbed at Roscoe's sides and sent the stallion pounding down the empty roadway. He reined in so sharply that his horse reared when he came to the place where Gray Wolf had come back up from the creek bank to the road and had balked, then whirled to go back to the creek. He bent low in the saddle to study the tracks. All was quiet. He could almost hear the pounding of his own frightened heart.

Then, from far away he heard a sound that shut off his breath for seconds while he listened. Lorna was singing!

There was anguish, desolation and pain in her voice.

"Long Ike and sweet Betsy attended a dance,
    Where Ike wore a pair of his Pike County pants.
Sweet Betsy was covered with—"

The song ended abruptly and all was quiet again.

Griff and Kain had gone toward the creek. They dismounted and motioned for Cooper. He followed Kain's pointed finger and saw the body of Lorna's big gray horse sprawled at the edge of the trees, its head lying in a pool of blood.

Fear such as he'd never felt before knifed through Cooper, leaving him weak. His breath left him in a grunting rush when Lorna's voice reached him again. It rose above the rippling of the water as it crossed smooth stones on its way to the river. Her voice was weak and it quivered, but she continued to sing in short gasps. Cooper began to run toward it. He splashed across the creek, went noiselessly through the sumac and up the slope, his boot heels digging into the sod. Now he could hear an odd, steadily repeated sound. *Plop! Plop!* It was followed by a break in Lorna's voice, and in a moment of horrible revelation he knew what it was. *It was the regular fall of a strap against bare skin.*

Rage, fear and desperation made Cooper move faster and more recklessly than he had ever moved in his life. But Griffin, lighter and more agile, reached the edge of the clearing seconds before Cooper did, and Kain a second or two later.

Lorna, her naked body covered with strap marks, her head sagging until her chin reached her chest, her hair straggling down over her face, hung from her bound wrists. From the description Moose had given him, Cooper knew instantly it was Brice Fulton who stood with the strap flung back ready to deliver another blow. Dunbar sat on a rock carelessly tossing a knife into the ground.

In the swift instant of reaction and action when he'd seen what was happening, Griffin was the first to move. With the speed of a cat he sprang into the clearing and fired at Brice. The bullet took away part of the hand that held the whip. Brice yelled and staggered back. Dunbar jumped up. Before he could draw his weapon, he was looking into the barrel of Kain's silver-handled gun.

"I ain't killin' ya yet, ya shit-eatin', belly-crawlin' bastard. I want ya to know why I'm adoin' it." Griffin's words were thrown at Brice in a voice that was cold and hard and strangely void of anger.

Cooper ran to Lorna, picked her up in his arms and held her tortured body against his chest, taking her weight off her arms, shielding her with his broad back. Her white, naked body was covered with fiery red strap marks from her neck to her knees, some of which were beaded with blood.

"Oh, darling! Oh, my sweet girl . . ." Cooper crooned to her and cradled her against his chest. He kissed her cheeks, her forehead, her closed eyes. "Sweetheart . . . I'll kill that bastard for this!" He held her tenderly, trying not to cause her more pain, and murmured love words against lips that were still trying to sing.

Griffin's gun spat and a bullet slammed into Brice's knee-cap. The big, burly man screamed like a panther and fell back against the trunk of a big oak, desperately trying to stay on his feet.

"I'm killin' ya for Volney Burbank. I'm killin' ya for what yo're doin' to Miss Lorna 'n I'm killin' ya for what ya done to Bonnie!" Brice threw his arm up over his eyes. Another bullet slammed into his hip bone. He screamed again and fell to the ground. Griffin's face was like a stone carving, his head thrust forward, his knees bent. "Ya treated Bonnie like dirt, ya sonofabitch! Before I kill ya, I want ya to know she's agoin' to have ever'thin' she wants from now on, 'n there ain't agoin' to be *nobody* alookin' down on her ever again."

The screams from Brice's throat were cut off when the

bullet from Griffin's gun tore a hole in the top of his head.

Dunbar, knowing he was about to die, looked wildly about. In a matter of seconds everything had changed. The tall, dark man who had been holding a gun on him calmly put it back into the holster and stood looking at him with his thumbs hooked in his belt, waiting, daring him to make a move. God, how he wished he'd never met that shithead from Light's Mountain. This cold-eyed stranger or that crazy, wet-eared kid was going to kill him. He didn't have a chance.

"He's mine, Kain. Back off!"

Dunbar's eyes shifted to Griffin and he knew, without a doubt, that he'd be the one. Goddamn that old Clayhill for sending him after that nester.

"Gimme a chance, fer God's sake! I was jist adoin' what the ole man tole me to do. He said to get rid a you. This mornin' he said Parnell, too. But I wasn't agoin' to do nothin' after I thought 'bout it. Hell—ya can't jist shoot a man down—"

"I just did. Fulton didn't deserve a chance. You don't deserve one either, but not fer what ya did to me, but fer lettin' him do *that* to Miss Lorna."

"I didn't have nothin' to do with *that*. He hated her worse 'n poison—he was crazy with it. Ole Clayhill hired us to get ya 'n Parnell. He said we'd get a big bonus. We wasn't agoin' to do nothin'. We was agoin' to just tell him we did 'n get the money. He's the one ya ort to get—"

"Ya lyin' sonofabitch! Ya burned Miss Lorna's house. Ya was there when they killed her pa."

"They made me go. I didn't do nothin'," Dunbar pleaded. "Johnson did."

"Draw, goddamn you! I'm agivin' ya a chance 'cause I tol' Cooper I would. Either way I'm agoin' to kill ya."

"I—I ain't no . . . gunfighter!"

Lorna, held in Cooper's arms, aroused. She opened eyes

that were unseeing, looked up at Cooper's face, and began to sing.

"Oh, don't you remember sweet Betsy—"

With a frantic eagerness to live, Dunbar grabbed for his gun. He had it halfway out of the holster when Griffin's bullet smashed into his forehead and flung his lifeless body back into the brush.

Without a second glance at the dead man, Kain swooped to pick up Lorna's coat and draped it over her nakedness. He reached up and cut the rope that held her arms to the branch above Cooper's head, then worked on the ropes at her wrist. When they fell away he could see that the circulation had been cut off from her hands. Her fingers were swollen and stiff. He massaged them gently. Lorna whimpered at the pain when the blood began to flow back into them. After a moment, she began to sing again.

"She's out of her mind!" Cooper said frantically.

"I think it's shock." Kain gently lifted her eyelid. "It could be that she's put herself in kind of a trance so she could bear the pain. Let's get her to Bessie's. She'll know what to do."

Chapter
Twenty-Four

It was almost midnight when Lorna woke.

Bessie had given her several drops of laudanum a few minutes after Cooper had carried her to the upstairs bedroom where he had insisted on taking care of her himself. He bathed her with cool soda water before he smeared salve on the places where the strap had broken her tender, white skin. Bessie stood quietly by. She realized that here was a man desperately in love with this woman with the beautiful black hair, clear white skin and slight figure. She couldn't help but feel a stab of envy when she saw how gently the big, rough hands touched her. She brought bandages and fresh water and made up a bed. Cooper allowed her to help him slip a nightdress over Lorna's head before he placed her on the clean sheets, covered her, and began his vigil beside the bed.

When Cooper was finally alone with Lorna, he found a brush on Bessie's dressing table, gently brushed her hair, and spread it, black as a crow's wing, over the pillow. With this done he sat down beside the bed, his eyes on her still face, and caressed the back of her hand with his fingertips.

The next few hours were the longest of his life. He relived seeing her hanging proud but helpless from her bound wrists. He heard again the sound of her singing. She had sung snatches of the song as he carried her past the dead horse that she loved, back across the creek to where Roscoe waited, and on the way to The House. Kain and Griffin had stripped her horse of saddle and bridle, brought them to The House, and returned with a wagon borrowed from Bessie to get the bodies of the three men.

Cooper watched her lovely face and remembered her dancing in the woods above the cabin on the Blue. He remembered her bravery; the way she'd held off Dunbar with her knife—waiting for him. He remembered the few lovely hours they'd spent alone in the dark on Light's Mountain. His body trembled as he thought of the precious way she had given herself to him. It was as if their being close, sharing the greatest pleasure God gave to human beings, was God's infinite plan. Making love with her must have been what God had in mind when he first created man and woman and devised a plan to populate the earth.

Loving her, he wanted to rage with savage destruction at the men who had done this dastardly thing to her. They had tortured her body, humiliated her, burned her home, killed her father and the horse she loved. But the ones responsible were dead. They'd already paid the supreme price. There was nothing else he could do to them.

"I'm . . . sorry . . ." Lorna whispered in anguish. Her head rolled back and forth on the pillow.

"What is it, sweet? Do you want a drink of water?" Startled out of his reverie, Cooper leaned down to stare at the deep frown on her face.

"Cooper." She said his name in a breathless whisper and stared at him with eyes out of focus.

"I'm here, sweetheart. I'm with you and nothing will hurt you again. I swear it," Cooper whispered, not knowing that tears filled his eyes and rolled down the stubble of beard on his cheeks.

Lorna's eyes cleared. She gripped his hand with surprising

strength. "Cooper? Where— Cooper! It's really you!" Her eyes went past him and then back to his worried face.

"It's really me. You're here at Bessie's. You've nothing to be afraid of. I'll not leave you . . . ever."

"Brice?"

"He's dead. So is Dunbar."

"I killed Hollis." She began to cry. Her mouth trembled and tears flooded her eyes. "I never, ever wanted to kill anybody. I just did it before I thought about it."

"He'd have killed you, sweetheart." Cooper wiped the tears from her eyes with a corner of the cover. "Don't think about it. You did what you had to do. It's over," he whispered huskily. "We'll go back to Light's Mountain and rebuild your house just the way Light and Maggie left it, and I'll live there with you forever if you want me to. Please, sweetheart, don't cry—"

"I can't help it."

"I love you, sweetheart. You've wiggled your way into every part of my heart." His voice shook with emotion. "I don't think I can live without you. I've always wanted you, right from the very first. But when I thought I'd lost you, I knew how terrible life would be without you. It doesn't matter where we are as long as I'm with you."

"I've been so wrong. It's you I want . . . only you—"

"Shh . . . don't cry, sweetheart—it tears me up." He kissed her, touching her lips gently.

"I don't . . . want to live on Light's Mountain." She astonished him now, as if she had caught his heart in her slender hands and drew it upward into his throat. "I want to be with you . . . as your wife. I want to live in the house my husband provides for me. It was wrong of me to want you to give up what you've worked so hard for and come to Light's Mountain. I deserved to be whipped—"

"No! Sweetheart—"

"I sneaked away . . . and let your horses out . . . I called you a pissant . . ."

His face was so close, their eyelashes were touching. He placed soft kisses on her eyes and sipped at the tears on her cheeks. He wanted so badly to hold her in his arms, but he was afraid he would hurt her.

"Don't think about it. We'll probably have more fights before our life is over. Think about tomorrow. I'm going to take you to the preacher in town and make you mine. That is, if you're able."

"Then we'll go home?"

"Then we'll go home."

"I don't ever want to be by myself again, Cooper. I was so scared coming to town. Cooper—" Her tears began to flow again. "They killed Gray Wolf."

"I know, darling. Don't cry. You'll not be alone . . . ever again. You'll have me and you'll have our babes when they come. You'll have a mother, too, if you want her. Ma will love you. She's always wanted a daughter to fuss over."

"I'll not know how to act." She lifted her hands and touched his face, his hair.

"Yes, you will. I'll be with you." He placed his head beside hers on the pillow. "There's a lot to tell you, but it can wait. I just want to kiss you and tell you that I'll spend the rest of my life taking care of you."

"Where are we? I've not ever been in such a pretty room, or in such a soft bed."

"You'll have as many pretty rooms as you want and the softest bed money can buy."

"But where are we?"

"We're at . . . Bessie's place."

"I was coming here. Mable said she'd sell me some clothes so I could dress up like a woman. Did her young ladies see me in those old britches?"

"Young ladies?"

"The ones in her school. Did they . . . laugh when they saw me?"

"Oh, sweet!" He placed tender kisses on her lips and spoke

against them. "I'd have killed anyone if they'd laughed at you. I'll tell you about this place in the morning."

"Can you get in here with me?" Her eyelids drooped. "I'm so tired."

"I'll sit her beside. I might hurt you."

"Please." She yawned helplessly and spoke against the hard line of his jaw. "You won't hurt me."

"All right. Lie still."

Cooper blew out the lamp, shed his clothes quickly and slipped into bed beside her. She turned on her side and tugged at his arm until he lifted it so she could get closer. She snuggled her head on his shoulder, placed her arm around his neck, and sighed contentedly.

"This is grand, Cooper, my love. We can sleep like this every night after we're wed," she whispered sleepily.

"Every night for the rest of our lives."

"Oh, Cooper, that's such a short time..."

Kain drove the wagon that took the bodies of the three dead men back to town and Griffin rode alongside leading Kain's horse. Griffin's mind was still crowded with thoughts from the happenings of the day before and from the things Kain had told him during the long talk they'd had while waiting to see if Lorna would be all right.

Last night, they had both declined the invitations of the girls who made their living at Bessie's.

"Thank ya kindly, ma'am," Griffin had stammered when Minnie had came up behind him and whispered the invitation in his ear. "But I got me a woman who's awaitin' fer me."

"Lucky woman," Minnie said and turned her attention to Kain. "How about you, good lookin'?"

"I already asked him." A buxom blonde smiled at Kain and ran her fingertips along the edge of his jaw. "I got me a raincheck."

Kain and Griffin had talked briefly with Cooper before they left Bessie's that morning. He and Lorna were staying at Bessie's for a few days and were going to visit the preacher in town before going home. Both men congratulated him and shook his hand.

"Tell Ma I'm bringing home a bride," Cooper said with a wide grin.

"I'll tell 'er," Griffin promised. "I'll be gettin' one of my own soon as I can get Bonnie to town."

Now, as they approached town, Griffin began to feel the dissatisfaction that always swept over him when in a crowd. He ignored the stares of the townspeople as they passed, for word had spread that a wagon was coming in with three dead men in the back of it. Kain turned down A Street and continued on to a neat frame house with a new privy behind. Adam Clayhill's landau was parked in a shed and two horses were in an attached enclosure.

Kain pulled the team to a halt, wound the reins around the brake and jumped down.

"Back off, Griff," he said when Griff started to dismount. "This is my show."

"I'll help ya with the bodies—"

"Stay mounted. I'll do it."

One by one, Kain carried the bodies of the dead men to the door of the house and dropped them. They lay, stiff and awkward, sprawled on top of each other, arms and legs jutting out. As he dumped the last one, the door flew open and Adam Clayhill stood glaring, his hands on his hips.

"What the hell are you doing?"

"Bringing back your trash."

"What do you mean? Get those gawddamn bodies off my doorstep. Who in the hell are you, anyway?"

"To answer your first question, this trash being the trash you hired to get *rid* of Griffin." He tilted his head to the mounted man. "And Cooper Parnell. This is the same red-headed bastard you hired to hang Griff and steal the horses we spent six months breaking. As you can see he bungled the job. You should pick your men more carefully, especially when you have murder in mind."

"What the hell is it to you?" Adam hunched his shoulders forward and peered more closely at the tall, dark man with the black brim of his hat shading his face. He felt sharp amber eyes stabbing into him and realized that this was a dangerous man. Fear touched him, but only slightly.

"Griffin and Cooper Parnell are friends of mine. If you want to live another few hours, weeks, months, or years, my advice is to steer clear of them."

"Are you a gunfighter they hired?" Adam sneered.

"Call it that if you want, but no money exchanged hands. Of course, that wouldn't make sense to a bastard like you."

"I don't know you." For an endless moment Adam stared, his senses shocked by the contempt in the stranger's eyes. Then he said hesitantly, "Do I?"

"No. You don't know me at all. You ... never did even try to know me."

"Never did try? What the hell are you talkin' about?"

"I'm talking about a smooth talking sonofabitch who went East to get a socially prominent wife of means in order to enhance his standing in the community. The woman he brought back was my mother, Etta DeBolt."

"Kain?" Adam would have stepped out into the yard if not for the dead bodies at his feet.

"Kain DeBolt. A boy grows into a man in fifteen years. I was just a kid, but I knew how rotten you were. I couldn't convince my mother, so she married you. I'm sure she died of disappointment and grief over being uprooted from family and friends and her failure to get the companionship she yearned for. You didn't care about her. You had control of the sizable fortune my father left her. There's just one thing you *don't* know. My father feared something such as this would happen, so he left my mother only a third of his fortune. The other two-thirds were put in a trust for me."

"But . . . why are you back? Why did you leave? I treated you like a son—"

"Bullshit!" The word exploded from Kain and it was the first time he'd raised his voice.

"So we didn't get along. I raised your sister—"

"You raised her to be a whore! I've been to Denver. I know what kind of place she runs. I pray to God that none of Mother's folks back East find out what she's become."

"That's not my fault. It's in her blood!"

Kain's knees bent slightly. "Say one more word, old man, and I'll kill you."

"I'm sorry," Adam said quickly. "I didn't mean that. Come in, Kain. Let's talk. I need a good man . . . one I can put in charge of my ranch. I've got no one to leave it to—"

Kain threw back his head and loosed a whoop of derision that echoed down the empty street. "By God! I've got to hand it to you, old man. You've got the gall of a government mule!" He sobered instantly and his eyes glittered dangerously. "I wouldn't piss on you if you were on fire." He spat the words contemptuously, turned his back and climbed back up onto the wagon seat. "If I hear you've set your hired killers on Griff, *or* Cooper, I'll be back—for you. I owe you plenty for what you did to my family. I'd kill you now and save myself a trip, but I think it'll be more interesting to wait and watch you hang yourself."

"Now, listen, Kain." Adam pushed one of the bodies over with his booted foot so he could step over the other two and get out into the yard. "I think we can work things out. You're obviously a businessman if you've handled money. It would be to your advantage to listen to what I've got to say."

Kain sailed the whip out over the backs of the horses and put the team in motion. He had to get away before he killed the sonofabitch. He wished for the hundredth time he'd never come back to Colorado Territory. His desire to see his sister, Della, had ended in a crushing disappointment when he found her running a brothel in Denver. He had stayed, wanting to lend a hand to Griff, a kid who'd had enough hard knocks to last a lifetime. Things had smoothed out for him now, and he was free to shake the dust of Colorado and head for California.

Adam stood in the yard and watched him leave. By God, there was a man. Why in the hell hadn't he seen it fifteen years ago? A stepson was as good as a son—better in fact. No one could blame him for the bad blood if he went wrong. Just as no one blamed him for Della. One thing was certain: He was going to find out more about Kain DeBolt. Goddamn! If he'd only known the kid had money! He turned to go back in the house and almost stumbled over one of the dead men.

"Goddammit, Jacob!" he yelled. "Get your black ass out here and get rid of this trash!"

Two days later Cooper drove his bride home in a buggy he had rented from the livery. They had been married that morning. The girls at Bessie's had all vied for the honor of lending something to the bride for her to wear at her wedding, and she had accepted something from each of them. Lorna was shocked, then laughed heartily when Cooper told her Bessie's was not a school for young ladies but a brothel. The young ladies who worked there were very nice to her, but the way they eyed Cooper encouraged her to speed her recovery so they could leave.

Cooper had told her about Volney, about the gold, which didn't seem to interest her at all, and about his and Griffin's trip to Light's Mountain. Once again he'd told her that he would live there with her if that was what she wanted, but she was adamantly against it. She'd outgrown that phase of her life, she said. She wanted to live in the place her husband provided for her, to be a helpmate to him. They would build a legend of their own.

"I'm going to try to be a good wife, but I can't promise that I'll not make you mad sometimes, Cooper," she said as they drove out of town.

"I wouldn't want you to make that promise, sweetheart, because I know you couldn't keep it." He tilted his head so he could look down into her eyes. His face was wreathed in smiles and his eyes shone with happiness.

She laughed, hugged his arm, and rested her cheek against it. Cooper smiled down at her. He'd never seen anyone who looked lovelier and his heart swelled with pleasure. She was wearing a sky blue dress with white lace at the neck and a tight bodice that showed the swell of her breasts. Minnie, one of Bessie's girls, had dressed her hair. It was swirled on top of her head and was pinned there with the gold hairpins he'd bought from Bessie. On a chain around her neck was a small gold locket—a gift from Kain. He had purchased it at McCloud's store and asked McCloud to give it to her when she and Cooper came to town to be married. He also left a short note, wishing them happiness and saying good-bye.

"Cooper—" They were in the quiet woods.

"Are you cold?"

"No. Do you think Kain will come back?"

"I don't know. It sure surprised the hell out of me to find out who he was. I'd heard there was a boy who left here."

"I liked him. I'm getting more friends all the time."

"Well, it's all right to *like* him," Cooper growled. "Just don't get to liking him too much."

"You're jealous! Does that mean you love me a lot?"

"What do you think?"

"I think you do. Cooper, I was thinking about that night in the barn. I wanted to mate with you, but you said you'd not do it until we were married because you didn't want to take the chance I'd get in the family way. You said that after we were wed you were going to drown in me. Are you still going to?" Her caressing fingers moved to the inside of his leg and stroked upward.

"Ah . . . darling!" He took a deep breath.

"I think you want to—now," she whispered devilishly and

spread her fingers in such a way he couldn't control the jolt
that shook him.

"Stop that! You little imp. We can't . . . not here!"

"When we get home? In your bed?"

"In my bed," he promised. "The minute we get home."

"I have to meet your mother first. I'm not scared anymore,
my love."

He bent to kiss her lips lingeringly, then slapped the reins
against the back of the horse to speed him along. Lorna had
never been so happy in all her life; such happiness was almost
unbearable in its intensity.

She began to sing.

"Down the stream of life together,
We are sailing side by side,
Hoping some bright day to anchor,
Safe beyond the surging tide.
Today our sky is cloudless,
But the night may clouds unfold;
Though clouds may gather 'round us.
Will you love me when I'm old?"

She ended the song and smiled trustingly up at Cooper,
her eyes soft with love.

"Yes, darling," he vowed. "I promise I'll love you till the
last breath leaves me, and even after that."

Epilogue

Spring came to the Rocky Mountains.

It was a warm day in May when Lorna and Cooper returned to Light's Mountain. They wanted to make the trip before it became unsafe for Lorna to ride because they expected the first of what they hoped would be many children before the summer ended.

They sat motionless on their horses and looked upon the cleared site that had once been Lorna's home. Only two tall rock chimneys and three walls of the rock smokehouse remained. The rest of the land had been cleared. Cooper moved his horse close to Lorna's and held out his hand. She slipped hers into it and gripped hard. When she turned to him she was smiling through her tears.

"It was a lovely place," she said simply.

They stopped at the small graveyard and pulled the weeds from around the headboards. Lorna spoke for the second time since she had come *home*.

"Papa loved Mama so much."

She mounted and took a trail to the top of the hill behind the homestead. Cooper followed at a distance. This was her private time—her homecoming.

Lorna stood on the bluff overlooking the valley and began

to sing. Her voice carried the length and breadth of the valley below. She sang of mountains and valleys and cool pools where the lilies grew. When she finished, she stood quietly. From far down the valley the call of a whipperwill floated on the warm spring breeze. Lorna mimicked the call. Soon an old Indian on a spotted pony rode into the clearing. A red feather was tied to each of the gray braids that lay on his chest. He dismounted and stood looking at her with his arms folded proudly across his chest.

"It's been a long time since I've seen my father, White Bull."

"Yes. Word had come of what happened here and to our friend. My heart is sad that I was not here."

"Your duty is to your people. The men who did this paid with their lives."

"It is good that you no longer need the protection of White Bull. You have the Wasicun, your husband."

"Yes."

"The old days are gone, Singing Woman. It pleases me that you have made a choice."

"Yes," Lorna said again. "I want you to know my husband. He is a man of honor."

"I know of Cooper Parnell and his brother Logan Horn. My people are made welcome on his land. You will be safe with the Wasicun. My heart is glad, and our friend's spirit can rest in peace."

The old Indian looked at her silently for a long moment, then he mounted his pony and rode away without a backward glance.

Lorna watched him leave and for only a moment felt a twinge of homesickness for the days of her childhood on Light's Mountain. Then she saw Cooper riding toward her. She ran to meet him. He scooped her up in one arm and placed her sideways across his thighs, whistled for her horse to follow, and guided Roscoe back down the trail.

From the safe circle of her husband's arms, Lorna looked back over her shoulder and called, "Good-bye, Maggie. I'm going home."

Author's Note

The town of Junction City is the fictitious name for Loveland, Colorado, a beautiful city just east of the Rocky Mountains, as I imagine it would have been had it existed at the time of this story.

All the persons in this book are fictitious with the exception of such historical figures as Colonel J. M. Chivington, a former Methodist minister. As commander of the Military District of Colorado he was responsible for the deaths of five hundred Indians, mostly women, children and old people in a deed known as the Sand Creek Massacre. However, the people in my story could have lived in the territory in the early 1870's, where the harsh realities of life made some behave in ways less than human toward their fellow man and strengthened others to build the great state of Colorado.

At the present time I am working on the third story of the trilogy. It will deal with Kain DeBolt, Adam Clayhill's stepson.

Dorothy Garlock